"Stunning. Heart-wrenching. Breathless. Not since *Gone with the Wind* have I read an epic novel that has stolen my heart, my breath, my sleep to such a jolting degree. *Love's Reckoning* marks Laura Frantz not only as a shining star in Christian fiction today but as a shooting star who soars skyward to the glittering heights of Rivers and Higgs."

—Julie Lessman, award-winning author of the Daughters of Boston and Winds of Change series

Praise for Laura Frantz

"You'll disappear into another place and time and be both encouraged and enriched for having taken the journey."

—Jane Kirkpatrick, bestselling author of *All Together in One Place* and *A Flickering Light*

"Laura Frantz portrays the wild beauty of frontier life, along with its dangers and hardships, in vivid detail."

—Ann H. Gabhart, author of *The Blessed*

"Frantz paints a vivid picture of the tough life out in the wild, and yet her characters demonstrate that it was possible to have a wonderful life."

—*RT Book Reviews* for *The Colonel's Lady*

Books by Laura Frantz

the
Ballantyne
LEGACY 1

Love's
RECKONING

A NOVEL

LAURA FRANTZ

Revell

a division of Baker Publishing Group
Grand Rapids, Michigan

© 2012 by Laura Frantz

Published by Revell
a division of Baker Publishing Group
P.O. Box 6287, Grand Rapids, MI 49516-6287
www.revellbooks.com

Printed in the United States of America

Library of Congress Cataloging-in-Publication Data
Frantz, Laura.
    Love's reckoning : a novel / Laura Frantz.
        p.   cm. — (The Ballantyne legacy, book 1)
    ISBN 978-0-8007-2041-4 (pbk.)
    1. Families—Pennsylvania—Fiction. I. Title.
PS3606.R4226L68 2012
813'.6—dc23   2012011939

Scripture quotations are from the King James Version of the Bible.

This book is a work of fiction. Names, characters, places, and incidents are the product of the author's imagination or are used fictitiously. Any resemblance to actual events, locales, or persons, living or dead, is coincidental.

The internet addresses, email addresses, and phone numbers in this book are accurate at the time of publication. They are provided as a resource. Baker Publishing Group does not endorse them or vouch for their content or permanence.

Published in association with Books & Such Literary Agency, 52 Mission Circle, Suite 122, PMB 170, Santa Rosa, CA 95409-7953.

12   13   14   15   16   17   18   7   6   5   4   3   2   1

To Randy, my Silas

The Lord's my shepherd, I'll not want,
He makes me down to lie
In pastures green: He leadeth me
the quiet waters by.

My soul He doth restore again;
and me to walk doth make
Within the paths of righteousness,
Ev'n for His own name's sake.

Yea, though I walk in death's dark vale,
yet will I fear none ill:
For Thou art with me; and thy rod
and staff me comfort still.

My table thou hast furnished
in presence of my foes;
My head Thou dost with oil annoint,
and my cup overflows.

Goodness and mercy all my life
shall surely follow me:
And in God's house for evermore
my dwelling-place shall be.

23RD PSALM OF DAVID IN METRE,
CHURCH OF SCOTLAND HYMNARY

1

He that would the daughter win
must with the mother first begin.
ENGLISH PROVERB

YORK COUNTY, PENNSYLVANIA
DECEMBER 1784

'Twas time for his daughters to wed, Papa said.

But he had a curious way of bringing wedded bliss about, sending all the way to Philadelphia for a suitor. Eden Lee felt the dread of it clear to her toes. The ticking of the tall case clock turned the quiet, candlelit room more tense. Was it her imagination, or was her father about to do something rash? For days she'd sensed something was coming, something that would turn their predictable, unhappy world upside down—and now this unexpected letter from the city . . .

Liege Lee stood by the hearth, his firm-jawed face darkening as he looked down at the paper in his hand. Beside him, Louise Lee piped a rare request.

"Liege, please, we have so little news from the East. Read it aloud."

Eden smiled a bit tremulously at her mother's quiet plea, her gaze falling from her father's sternness to the soft contours of her sister's face as she sat mending by candlelight. Yet her attention kept returning to the post, her own sewing forgotten, as his gravelly voice resounded to the room's cold corners.

"The trade guild promised me another apprentice several months ago. At last we have a letter." He unfolded the crumpled paper, spectacles perched on the end of his narrow, pockmarked nose. "This man is a Scot, trained in his home country before being bound to an American master in Philadelphia. Since the war's end he's been at a forge manned with a dozen apprentices in the heart of the city. His master has died, and he's seeking a position in the West to finish his training. He comes well recommended." Clearing his throat, he returned to the paper in hand. "The man writes, 'I am unsure if this post will reach its destination. Likely the package I am sending will not. My hope is that one or the other of us will arrive safe and sound by December's end.'"

There was a stilted pause, then a gasp. "December's end!" The linen slipped from Mama's work-worn hands into her lap. "Any day now? But I thought he wasn't coming till spring!"

"Aye, any day," Papa growled, turning to take his daughters in.

He lingered longest on Elspeth, Eden noticed, and with good reason. But her great roundness was buried beneath her sewing, and she didn't so much as lift an eyebrow at Papa's stern scrutiny. Any day now Elspeth's child would be born.

But which would come first? The apprentice or the babe?

This was what worried her father, Eden knew. He had plans for her wayward sister that couldn't be breached by the early arrival of the stranger.

"You both know what this man's coming means?" he thundered across the small parlor. The stern words made Eden's insides curl. She looked up, waiting for Elspeth to do the same, but her sister was simply ignoring her father, as she was prone to do when she disliked his dictums.

"Elspeth Ann!"

She finally snapped to attention, light and shadow playing across her lovely face, and met her father's eyes.

"You both know what this means, aye? You and Eden?"

"Yes, Papa," Elspeth murmured dutifully.

Eden's needle stilled and she simply nodded, grieved, barely detecting the telling sympathy in Mama's eyes at their predicament.

"The plan is this," he went on. "If the apprentice comes before the babe, the jig is up and he's to wed Eden. If he comes after the babe is born, he's yours, Elspeth. You know how things stand with an apprentice."

Mama nodded, her wistful expression revealing she knew of such matters firsthand. Years before, Papa was apprenticed to her father, a master gunsmith, and she'd been part and parcel of the contract. Though rumored that she loved another, tradition held sway. 'Twas a time-honored practice that apprentices marry into their master's family, as if some ironclad rule passed down from King George himself. Though times were changing and the war had been won, Papa was holding on to the past with both fists.

Studying his craggy face in the low glare of lamplight as he pondered the letter, Eden bit her lip. She suspected Papa's scheming had less to do with marrying them off than tying the man down for more mercenary purposes. Though every eligible suitor in the entire county trooped into their blacksmith shop to beg, barter, or pay coin for the ironwork turned out, none had yet passed muster—or could abide the thought of her father as father-in-law. How like Papa to forge a liaison with a complete stranger, one who knew nothing of their affairs.

Oh, if she could but protest! Warm words festered on her tongue and raced round her head as she returned to her mending. *In all fairness, Father, this stranger you speak of is hardly a youth. He's at the tail end of his apprenticeship and shouldn't be coerced into keeping such a tradition. Besides, there's such a thing as love.*

But she couldn't be contrary. Her father's word was as unyielding as the metal he worked. Once, when she was five, she had spoken up—sassed him when she should have stayed silent—and had born a welt on her backside for a fortnight or better. Any backtalk had since been confined to her head.

"What's the man's name, Liege?" Mama asked, hands idle atop her lap.

"Ballantyne," he replied, perusing the accompanying package. "Silas Ballantyne."

Eden drank in every syllable, thinking it strong. Solid. Memorable. The last apprentice had been one George White, bland and utterly forgettable. Papa had disliked him from the first and nigh starved him, liberally applying the lash. He'd been but a boy. But this tradesman, from the sounds of it, was no mere lad. She'd not be sneaking him food like she had poor George, surely.

The rustle of paper and snap of string brought her head back up. The package this Scotsman had sent—cocooned in cloth and tied with twine—was slowly unwrapped. For long moments Papa looked at the metalwork as if struck speechless before holding the gift aloft. 'Twas a copper lantern, three sided, with a large hanging loop. From where she sat, Eden could see that the hinged lid bore a pierced scrolling pattern, every line elegantly worked. When her father lit the wick, they all watched in a sort of trance as the lantern's mirrored back reflected twice the light.

"Upon my soul, he's a city smith—and a master engraver!" Papa's eyes narrowed and nearly gleamed. "No doubt I could sell this for a pretty penny."

"'Tis a gift," Eden whispered, forgetting herself. "Gifts aren't for sa—"

A sudden jab to her ribs silenced her. "Gifts are kept solely by sentimental fools." Elspeth's hiss held characteristic sharpness. Lifting her chin, she looked at their father. "Think of it, Papa. Why not let it be a template? Think of the orders you'd gain! A fine Philadelphia lantern here in the wilds of York County."

Eden marveled that even pregnancy had failed to soften her sister's business sense. In the glare of lamplight, Eden's eyes traced the profile of Elspeth and their father and found them startlingly alike. Elspeth should have been a son. Papa had said so a hundred times or better. If she closed her eyes, she could almost imagine her sister in breeches and a linen shirt—and pregnant to boot . . .

"I'll wager this work would stop Jacob Strauss's boasting," Papa muttered. "The old German may be the best inventor in these parts, but I'll wager he's not seen the likes of this. Speaking of Strauss, has he settled accounts for that iron trim we made him?"

Elspeth lifted her shoulders in a slight shrug. "Best check the ledgers. I finished tallying them this morning."

"Check them? I cannot find them." His scowl deepened. "I've told you to return them to the parlor, yet you leave them continually in the smithy."

With a sullen gesture for her to follow, he left the room, Elspeth trailing. Eden glanced at Mama, now engrossed in sewing a baby garment as if nothing unusual had happened, no marital pronouncement had been made. Thomas played near the hearth with some wooden soldiers, making baby noises he'd yet to outgrow at age two. Sympathy softened her, and for a moment she forgot her own plight.

Oh, little brother, what is in store for you?

Weary, she set aside her sewing and crossed to the table where the lantern rested, its rich copper winking at her with a beguiling light. The same admiration that gave her father pause filled her as she took in its fine craftsmanship.

"So he's a Scotsman." Mama's eyes, gray as the doves that nested beneath their eaves, settled on her thoughtfully. "'Tis an interesting name he has. It sounds well with either Eden or Elspeth."

Warmth snuck up Eden's neck. *Eden . . . Ballantyne?* Hearing them paired so made her squirm, yet she couldn't deny that what little she knew about the man was pleasing. He owned a fine name, could pen a handsome letter, was generous with his talents. Not all apprentices were so blessed. Still, she whispered, "Perhaps he's big as a barn and missing all his teeth."

Mama gave a rare chuckle. "Perhaps he's handsome as a midsummer's day. He's certainly generous to send so fine a gift. 'Tis a wise man who wins your father over before the work begins."

But once the work began, would he stay on? Eden expelled a ragged breath. "Papa cannot seem to keep an apprentice."

"'Tis not your father's fault two lads have run off," she returned. "George White was not physically fit for the trade— so thin a strong wind would have pushed him over. As for Bartholomew Edwards, though big as a barn, he hadn't the smarts of a louse, your sister said."

"Papa does need an extra hand at the forge."

"Indeed, he does. York County is burgeoning and has but one able blacksmith." Mama's needle plied the flannel fabric with a sure hand as she recited the facts. "Your father is aging and the workload is heavy. Elspeth is almost one and twenty, you yourself are nineteen. 'Tis time—past time—one of you were betrothed."

Betrothed.

The very word sent a shiver through Eden. A man—*a husband*—was on his way, and she'd not yet felt a flutter of romance for any suitor . . . or the touch of a man's hand. "So the babe is to decide our fate."

Mama nodded. "You heard your father. If the babe arrives first, Silas Ballantyne is betrothed to Elspeth. If not, he's to be yours. There are worse things in the world than an arranged marriage, Daughter."

Looking up, Eden saw a shadow cross her mother's face, as if she'd caught herself in a lie. Had their present predicament sparked one too many painful memories? Gauzy bits of gossip gleaned over the years about her parents' beginnings swirled through Eden's head, tempting her to ask questions she'd not dared to before. But she simply said, "Does this man—Mr. Ballantyne—know there's to be a match?"

"That he's to wed one of you?" Mama lifted plump shoulders in a shrug. "Your father hasn't said, though the apprentice is likely aware of the tradition."

"I care not for such traditions."

"Eden Rose!" Mama blanched at this rare show of defiance. "Has Margaret Hunter been filling your head with rebellious notions—or Jemma Greathouse with the books she lends you?"

"No, Mama, I just don't care to be married. To anyone."

Mama looked at her like she had two heads. "Then what else would you aspire to?"

The probing question cut Eden to the quick, though she had a ready answer.

I aspire to something beyond the stifling confines of this house, far beyond Papa's fierce temper and Elspeth's contentious spirit, and the endless monotony of my days.

But she couldn't give it voice, not with Mama peering at her like she was privy to the inner workings of her heart and soul. No one must know her secret. *No one.* She'd best tread cautiously till the plan was in place. And pray the babe came before the apprentice.

☙

Standing by the meadow pond the next afternoon, Eden tried to look at everything through a stranger's eyes—through Silas Ballantyne's—but since she'd been born and bred here, that was hard to do. Now, in early winter, the place held few charms. The landscape was skeletal at best, full of shivering oaks and elms, low stone fences, and a ribbon of road in shades of gray.

Even the pond gracing the near meadow looked more puddle, swollen by rain, yet devoid of its blue brightness. 'Twas simply an uninspiring dove gray like all the rest, mirroring the dullness inside her. She longed for a little color. Her soul felt nigh starved for it. But she was no better, totally nondescript in butternut wool, worn leather shoes, and fraying bonnet.

Her gaze strayed to the little church on the hill, her imagination filling in what she couldn't see beyond the snowy rise— a muddy road, more meadows and fences, a few farms, then the tiny hamlet of Elkhannah with its gristmill, a school, and a scattering of timbered houses. The village of York, far larger and busier, was just beyond.

Though she'd just come from the neighboring estate, Hope Rising, she already felt the pull to return there. The rich taste of imported tea and raisin scones lingered on her tongue, compliments of its housekeeper, Margaret Hunter. Each Sabbath she and Margaret met regularly and saw to the needs of the tenants who lived on Hope Rising land. There were but twenty of them at last count, but someone always seemed in need of a basket or tonic, a pair of mittens or a kind word.

Eden glanced down the lane to the big house a final time, a great yearning skewing her insides. But it seemed Elspeth stood there watching, about to rebuke her for her gawking.

"You can find no fault with Hope Rising and no good at home," her sister had once said, a bite of bitterness in her tone.

Eden acknowledged the truth of it now. She'd always loved the very land the Greathouses owned, every hilly, timber-rich inch. Even in the depths of winter it never seemed to be lacking, nor steeped in mud as was their own home place. The glazed brick house topped with a gambrel roof glowed a rich red, warm as a fire's embers, as did every dependency surrounding it—smokehouse, icehouse, necessary, and summer kitchen—right down to the bricks in the garden walkway. Even the gate with its fancy scrolled ironwork seemed to smile in rich defiance at winter's bleakness.

Hope Rising was the only respite from what had always seemed a dreary life. Even with Master David and his cousins away, 'twas grand to her. Ever since she'd been small she was welcomed there, had imagined herself one of them. The cook had snuck her sweetmeats. The gardener showered her with flowers, tucking a peony or rose into the buttonhole of her simple homespun dress. The stable master, long dead now, let her ride a pony named Tomkin. And the elder Greathouse, a conundrum though he'd been with his rare smiles and rollicking temper, allowed his nephew and daughters to befriend her and Elspeth.

But it was not to last. Time and privilege had wedged its way between them. The three Greathouse girls had gone to finishing school and become proper Philadelphia belles while David went to England, enrolling at a fancy school called Eton. Eden and Elspeth remained behind to manage the wear and tear of ordinary life in York County.

Tucking the faded memories away, Eden focused on a redbird atop a shivering branch. She supposed she made a strange sight, standing forlornly by the pond. If the apprentice happened by, he'd think her fey—or a hopeless dreamer as Elspeth did. The thought spurred her down the tree-lined lane toward home, but as she went she was trailed by another, larger worry.

Just whose husband would Silas Ballantyne be?

Perhaps there was no need to fret. Perhaps he wouldn't arrive but become lost in the woods between here and Philadelphia. Or become the third apprentice to run off before his time. Such ponderings made her almost dizzy, like she'd been skating in endless circles on the pond for too long, just as she'd done in childhood.

When she was halfway across the icy meadow, snow began to fall, covering her worn cape with a lacy dusting. She felt a rush of wonder. Oh, let a snowfall dress the landscape like a bride! When the apprentice came, the only home she'd ever known would seem a magical place.

Not misery.

2

*Much may be made of a
Scotchman if he be caught young.*

SAMUEL JOHNSON

The winter landscape was like an old man—or a poor one
like himself, Silas Ballantyne decided. Full of sharp angles
and bony barren places, never quite comfortable or at rest.
But he was rich in spirit, he remembered, lest self-pity take
root. He had some tools. A violin. A vision. And he'd traveled
nearly fifty miles in two days, lacking but thirty more till he
reached York County. If he pushed harder he'd be there on
the morrow, but his gelding was acting a bit sore-footed, and
then the snow came, at first fragile as a dusting of flour and
then thick as goose feathers.

Squinting through the twilight glare he saw a light in the
distance—an answer to prayer. His stomach cramped at the
aroma of wood smoke and baking bread. What he'd give for
some bannocks and mutton stew. The memory of his Highland home sharpened and turned melancholy, so he thrust it
aside and grappled for a gracious thought. *The Lord giveth*

17

and the Lord taketh away, blessed be the name of the Lord.
Tonight the Almighty seemed a giving God, and Silas uttered
bethankit before seeing the colorful shingle flapping in the
swelling wind.

The Rising Sun Tavern. A far cry from the Man Full of
Trouble Tavern he'd frequented on Spruce Street in Philadelphia. There he'd downed seared ham with raisin sauce and
applejack each Sabbath, his one ample meal of the week. Here
he smelled roast sweet potatoes and goose and something else
he couldn't name—or afford. A handbill had been nailed to
the front door, which he perused tongue in cheek. Not all
taverns were what they claimed to be—nor were people, he
mused.

> Guests must be treated with kindness and cordiality, served
> wholesome food, and all beds, windows, crockery, and utensils
> to be kept in good order.

Tired and tempted, he tied Horatio to the hitch rail in
front and entered the large, smoke-filled public room to find
it bursting, the rattle of dice at gaming tables sounding like
dead men's bones. Shoulders slightly bent with the weight
of twin haversacks, rifle in hand, his first thought was to
stable his horse.

"How goes it, stranger?" A voice boomed from behind a
scarred counter, overriding the surrounding din.

"Well enough," Silas answered, turning that direction.
"I've a lame horse to see about."

With a nod and a whistle, the apron-clad man summoned
a servant and then bent to hear the lad whisper in his ear. He
straightened with a scowl. "The stable's nearly as full as the
inn this snowy eve. What else will ye be needing?"

"I've little coin left," Silas admitted. "Mayhap I'd best see
to my horse."

The shillings crossed the counter and disappeared into one of the man's many linen folds. He was enormous—big as a ship's sail, or so it seemed. Silas tried not to stare, stepping aside when the door behind him opened to admit a retinue.

A gentleman swept in ahead of three women, his beaver hat frosted with snow, the jewel-colored capes of the ladies the same. Beneath the wide brims of their bonnets, the feminine trio stared at Silas without a speck of primness as if he were a horse at auction. Heat crept beneath his collar and rose higher, encroaching on cold cheekbones. He shifted his rifle to the crook of his other arm, perusing the tavern floor with its alternating boards of white ash and black walnut, made bright by wooden and tin chandeliers.

"Ah, Mr. Greathouse!" The innkeeper tossed out a greeting and gave a little bow. "What brings you to the Rising Sun?"

"The weather and naught else," the young man answered moodily, knocking his hat against his knee. Snow spattered to the floorboards, glistening like discarded diamonds. "I'll wager we'll be snowed in here till New Year's and not make it to Philadelphia."

"You're abandoning Hope Rising then?"

"Just till the ice harvest. The place is deadly dull in winter, or so my cousins tell me." He slid his eyes in their direction, a rueful pinch to his mouth. "They crave the comforts of the city and all its distractions."

At this, the three women tittered and talked in whispers. Silas turned his back to them, overcome with the scent of lavender sachet and their powdered, feminine faces.

"I've one room left for your party, but it needs a good tidying first." The innkeeper summoned a harried serving girl. "Your cousins can wait in the ladies' parlor, and I'll have Effie serve them tea."

"Very well." Greathouse nodded his head at the women,

and they left the room, obviously familiar with the inn. He cast an appraising eye over the crowd, his ruddy features relaxing. "I'll have whatever they're having . . . if there's any left."

Chuckling, the innkeeper moved toward a far door Silas supposed was the kitchen. The supper smells were intensifying, and he was suddenly bone weary. Shifting his load, he waited for Greathouse to step away from the door and take the only remaining table before he made his way to the stable. The thought of a hay-strewn space, though cold, was far preferable to a flea-infested room where they slept six to a bed.

"So, man, have a seat." The gentleman—Greathouse—was looking at him, gesturing to a chair.

Surprise and suspicion riffled through Silas at the invitation. There were but two seats left in the room. He'd not insult the man by refusing. Besides, he had no wish to seek shelter in the stable just yet, though he did need to see to his horse. He disappeared for a time, then returned and lowered his belongings to the floor, taking the offered chair, eye on the huge stone hearth gracing the low-beamed room, its flames burnishing the paneled interior a pleasing russet.

"Are you traveling east or west?" Greathouse asked, hanging his cloak on a peg behind him.

"West," Silas answered, removing his battered hat.

"Oh? We're in need of an extra man at Hope Rising."

"Hope Rising?"

"Our family's estate—*my* estate." A look of bemusement lit his features. "Sometimes I forget my good fortune. My uncle passed last year, God rest him. Since he had but three daughters and no male heir, everything passed to me."

"You're not sorry about that, I suppose," Silas said wryly.

Greathouse chuckled. "His father, my grandfather, made his fortune as a privateer in the Seven Years' War." There was unmistakable pride in the words. "His first ship—a sloop— was called *Hope Rising*."

"I ken the name," Silas said quietly, a cold realization dawning. "I've seen the *Sally* and *Antelope* at anchor alongside it in Philadelphia." *Slavers, all*, he thought with a twist of disgust, appetite ebbing.

"Ah, yes, we've some business in Jamaica and the West Indies, and occasionally dock in Philadelphia. But I let my factor handle any unsavory matters." He averted narrowed eyes, clearly anxious to change the subject. "You're going west, did you say? You have the look of an able hand."

"I'm apprenticed in York County."

"Apprenticed?" Surprise lightened his features, and he raked a hand through unruly, straw-colored hair. "You wouldn't be bound for Liege Lee's, would you?"

"Aye," Silas answered as the innkeeper returned and set down a steaming trencher of more food than he'd seen in a fortnight.

"Two pints of ale and another plate," Greathouse ordered without pause. "I'm not a man who likes eating alone."

Taking a steadying breath, Silas wondered just what he wanted—and what he knew about Liege Lee.

Greathouse forked a piece of meat to his mouth and chewed thoughtfully, eyeing him with renewed interest. "How long before you're a master tradesman yourself?"

"A year or less."

"I could use a good blacksmith. My estate borders the Lees' should you, um, have need of employment in future."

The second plate was plunked down. Mindful that Greathouse was watching, Silas bowed his head anyway and uttered a silent prayer. The raucous laughter and rolling of dice all around him resounded far louder than his low amen.

"So you're a religious man. A Presbyterian, I'll wager."

His smile was thin and laced with warning. "You shall need a prayer or two before your time with the Lees is through."

Silas sat back in his chair, the man's insinuations wearing thin. But he lifted his own tankard in a sort of toast. "If they're such heathens, mayhap I'll convert them."

At this, Greathouse nearly spewed his ale in amusement. "That I would like to see, though their youngest daughter does have Quaker leanings."

"God is good at making silk purses out of sows' ears, aye?"

"She's no sow," Greathouse murmured around a mouthful of bread.

Smiling now, Silas took another sip of ale and pinned his gaze on the young man opposite, who was turning a shade shy of beet red.

Greathouse blundered, "I mean—well, our land borders the Lees' and—you see, we have occasion to meet."

"Who?"

"Me . . . and Miss Eden."

Miss Eden. The laird of Hope Rising was undeniably smitten. Warming to his easy manner, Silas decided to learn all he could. "So there's a daughter, then?"

"Yes, indeed, more than one." He wiped his mouth with a napkin, still looking like he'd been caught snitching something. "Though the eldest has been ill for some months and confined to the house."

Hearing it, Silas felt a clutch of concern. Two daughters too many. He wanted no distractions, no romantic entanglements. He simply had an apprenticeship to finish. And his future, unenviable as it was, lay far beyond York County.

"There's also a younger brother and the mistress of the house, Louise Lee. They've been there thirty years or better, since the time my uncle built Hope Rising." Greathouse studied him intently. "If you don't mind my saying so, you're a bit on the mature side for an apprentice."

"The war got in the way," Silas said simply. He looked to his plate, cutting off a bite of meat and wishing he could do the same with the conversation. He had no wish to recount his personal history. His main concern was the Lees and the situation he was walking into.

Greathouse leaned back in his chair. "The war, yes. I didn't serve myself, being the heir. My father and uncle forbade it and pressed someone else into service. You're from Philadelphia, then?"

"Nae, Scotland."

"I'd gathered that, given your speech. I see the outline of a fiddle in your baggage there. How long did you say you'll be with the Lees?"

"A year or less, unless . . ."

The sympathetic smile returned. "Unless you become the third apprentice to quit before his time?"

The third?

Silas set down his fork. Dread danced up and down his spine and nearly stole his appetite. He'd not been told this. The trade guild had simply given him a name and address. Liege Lee on Elkhannah Creek, York County, Pennsylvania. With the war won, he was fortunate to find a place, or so he'd thought. Like himself, nearly every apprentice in the colonies had collected a bounty and enlisted in the rebel army and was now seeking a position.

"I'll wager from the look of you that Liege Lee has met his match," Greathouse said with a smug smile. "And like I said, work awaits you at Hope Rising, should you need it in future."

Silas began the remaining thirty miles of his journey, fortified by a good meal and a sound if frigid night's sleep in the stable. 'Twas Tuesday morn, the last of December. Horatio, rested and well-fed, with no sign of lameness, gave him little trouble even in half a foot of snow. Yet he found himself wishing the journey was far longer, that something warm and sure and good awaited him at day's end.

As it was, the scanty facts learned at supper with David Greathouse left him at loose ends. Liege Lee sounded like a tyrant of a blacksmith with a wife. At least one bonny daughter. A young son. Two failed apprenticeships. The latter was common enough. Masters and apprentices did not always mix. Bound men ran off all the time. He'd considered it himself, but his convictions held him fast. He pondered it now, fighting anxiety.

Mayhap he'd best keep going and bypass the Lees altogether. His ambitions lured him westward to Fort Pitt, far beyond the boundaries of York. The lyrical names of the rivers there played in his mind like a melody. The Monongahela. The Allegheny. The Ohio. Indian words, all. But much as he wanted to, he couldn't push west till he'd fulfilled the terms of his contract. He'd have need of it in future.

The Lee farm, Greathouse told him, lay a league south of Elkhannah Creek. Silas measured his steps, taking note of his strange surroundings. He passed beneath a giant oak holding fast to a few stubborn leaves, majestic and stalwart in the newly fallen snow. All around him the countryside was rolling and open, so pastoral it reminded him of southern England. Gentle hills and meadows abounded, nothing as abrupt or raw as his Highland home. He'd expected more wilderness, a wild and rough beauty, and felt disappointment pool in his chest.

In time he passed an ornate gate with an *H* and an *R*

wrought in fancy iron, much as he'd worked in Philadelphia. Hope Rising? A long drive snaked past an abundance of linden trees, but he couldn't make out the house at road's end. David Greathouse was a man of means—a gentleman—thus his house would be the same.

His misperceptions shifted once again. He'd not thought to find signs of civilization—wealth—this far west, just modest farms at best. For a few moments he felt disoriented in the glare of blinding snow. He couldn't ask for directions or inquire how much farther he had to go, for no other steps marred the ground but his and Horatio's. A strong west wind was picking up, keening like women at a Scottish wake, and he looked uneasily in its direction.

His gaze snagged on an ice-encrusted pond just beyond a low stone fence. Greathouse land, he guessed. Surely the laird wouldn't begrudge him a swim. Though hardly the River Tay of his youth, nor the heat of summer, it would have to do. He reeked of horses and hay, hardly fit for company, even that of a tyrant blacksmith.

A good quarter of an hour later he was clean, though made of gooseflesh. A clean linen shirt, scratchy breeches, thick woolen stockings, and worn boots covered his frigid skin, and he was only too glad to slip into the confines of his frayed greatcoat again. His two days' growth of beard he could do little about, as he was lacking a razor. He'd lost both shaving kit and comb between here and Philadelphia when Horatio stumbled, spilling him into a ditch, but hurting little more than his pride.

On he walked, making note of every shrub and rock that raised its head above the snow, listening for the echoing cadence of a hammer striking iron. Heavy snowflakes began to dance down, and a biting wind made ice of his washed hair. Another quarter of a mile and he was soon in sight of a farm he knew was the Lees', given the distinguishing feature Greathouse had told him about—a bold, wrought-iron weathervane atop a large barn adjoining a blacksmith's shop, its stone chimney puffing smoke. The farmhouse was simple, if sprawling, and made of local limestone. All around it fallow fields lay like faded squares of an old, fraying quilt.

Would the Lees be expecting him? Had they received his letter? The lantern? 'Twas all too quiet below. Nary a dog barked. He felt a niggling worry for all that awaited based on David Greathouse's ominous words and his own Scottish good sense. And then his faith thrust him forward, checking his dread.

Father, to this place You've led me, and I thank You for safe travels. May Your purposes be accomplished here, whate'er they may be.

3

Let honesty be as the breath of thy soul.

BENJAMIN FRANKLIN

In the last remnants of daylight, Eden ran her hands over
the skeins of wool and flax she'd spun in the shadows of the
weaving room, caressing the distaff and ribbon that held the
fibers in place—a yellow ribbon proclaiming her unmarried
state. But her mind wasn't on her beloved Saxony wheel or
the hearth's fire that had flickered out an hour ago. She could
spin no matter what the hour if need be. Indeed, she had been
doing so since she was four.

This cold afternoon, every fiber of her being strained toward one thing and one thing only—a newborn's cry. Three
hours it had been, and no sounds other than the usual birth
noises of pain and weariness met Eden's ears. While her sister
labored in their parents' bedchamber below, she labored over
what she would say to the county busybodies.

Aye, 'twas an onerous birth, indeed.

The babe looks just like Papa, truly.

Nay, best wait a while to come calling.

She pondered the lies and excuses swirling through her head, grappling for facts. Likely Elspeth's labor would prove indecently short, as all things seemed to work in her favor. And the babe couldn't resemble Papa, as it wasn't his and Mama's. And no one should dare come calling till the Lees got their story straight. How were they to explain away the fact that they hadn't summoned the midwife when they'd always relied on her before? The snowy weather, Eden guessed, was a handy excuse—and they could always say the babe came early, hardly an exaggeration. And Mama, bless her, always had the bearing look about her.

Sighing, Eden struggled with this new complication, wishing for a different outcome, a chaste sister. How long would Elspeth keep weaving deceit and selfishness into the fabric of their lives? How long would Papa and Mama allow it? Unlike the fine fibers spun on her wheel, their lives seemed like tangled thread, knotted further by the coming of a babe who wouldn't know his or her true mother . . . or father. Eden took a breath and held it, back tense and eyes tearing, sending up a petition to a being she was unsure of.

Had the Almighty made this babe? Like He made the flowers in her beloved garden and the wind and weather? *If so, please let the child grow to be kind and good and giving, not like its mother.* Two wayward Lees were too many!

At her amen, the air was rent by a hiccup and a cry—so high and sharp it sent the fine hair on her neck tingling. She sensed it was a boy—hoped and prayed it was. A boy was less likely to take after Elspeth, would make a fine companion to young Thomas.

In moments, the door to the weaving room cracked open and Papa's voice filled the quiet space. "A son—just whose son, we know not. But 'tis as lusty a babe as has ever been born in York County."

Eden simply nodded, watching her father's sturdy shadow retreat, knowing he wanted to be at his forge among the sameness and predictability of the iron he worked, much like she sought solace in her spinning.

She hadn't asked how Elspeth fared and felt a twist of guilt. But she needn't wonder. Her older sister led a charmed life. Be it tallying ledgers or cavorting or begetting babies, Elspeth Lee came out as sleek and well-crafted as a fine Pennsylvania rifle.

◦◦◦

'Twas snowing harder, Eden noticed, and was shiveringly cold. Within minutes of Papa's announcement, she abandoned her spinning and went to the kitchen to check the spitted meat and baking bread before joining Mama and Elspeth in the bedchamber. Though she'd offered to be present at the birth, Mama had forbidden it. Her youngest daughter's virtue must be preserved, she insisted in a strained whisper. This seemed a bit odd given the fact Eden had witnessed a great deal of barnyard carousing and the birth of countless animals. But Mama held sway.

Since the York midwife was absent, Mama had had to manage everything herself, for not even the meddlesome Mistress Middy knew about Elspeth. All thought it was Mrs. Lee who was lying in. For months now Elspeth had been kept hidden out of fear someone would discern the truth. Bound by a lingering English law, a midwife was obliged to learn the father's identity for all unwed mothers. Her strategy was simple: she waited till the throes of labor to ask whom the father was. Oftentimes only then was the secret divulged, and the new parents later hauled to court and fined, chastised, and disgraced.

"Here, let me take him," Eden told her mother. "I've made a sugar treat."

29

With practiced hands she embraced the wailing, flailing bundle of flesh and brushed his open mouth with the treat that had always soothed Thomas. It pained her to see that even angry, he was every bit as handsome as Elspeth. She searched for some sign of his father in his livid countenance, names and faces of settlement men buzzing in her head like horseflies. David Hofstettler. Josiah Himer. Angus McEachon. Donal Shire. Wouldn't the father step forward in time, anxious to see his own son?

Frantic, the baby began sucking, but it was a short-lived reprieve. 'Twas his mother he wanted, her known scent and warmth, but Elspeth turned aside and slept, her comely form buried beneath a hill of blankets.

"She needs her rest." Mama's face held a telling anxiety, the tired lines of midcentury deepening. "Where is your father?"

"At the forge."

Their eyes met and held. Mama looked so worn it seemed *she* had given birth. "The babe is to be mine and your father's. Not a word is to be breathed otherwise."

"Yes, Mama." Why else had Elspeth pled illness and kept to the house so no one would know? The plan was nearly foolproof. Mama certainly looked the part—plump, full-bosomed, clad in shapeless wool or linen dresses. None would question the babe's origins.

"What will you call him?" Eden asked quietly.

"That I don't know. Your father hasn't decided."

So Elspeth wouldn't name her firstborn son. Eden felt a twist of grief. If this was her babe, she'd savor the sweetness of naming him, illegitimate or no. But Elspeth had never held with sentimental things, didn't care for children. Though perhaps, in time, she'd take to her own.

Whoever's son he was, this new one flailed in her arms and let out a war cry, sugar treat forgotten. Mayhap he was

Heinrich Grossvort's, as the man so loved the sound of his own voice. But Heinrich was so dark, and this child's hair was pale as bleached linen.

Watching, Mama sighed and pushed a graying curl behind her ear. "I'll swaddle and try to quiet him. Go below and ready the meat and bread. Thomas will be rousing and your father will want his flip."

Eden gave up her bundle, nearly wincing at his stubborn squall. Down the narrow hall she went, into the warm confines of a kitchen smelling of rosemary and thyme, so reminiscent of her garden. She felt nearly wrenched with longing to be lost in it. Truly, 'twas her garden she craved, just beyond the snow-covered door stone.

Dropping to her knees at the hearth, she took a bake kettle from the ashes and pretended the aroma of bread was a rose instead—the red damask rose she'd gotten from Hope Rising's gardener last spring. Lost in whimsy, she failed to hear the footfall or the knock.

"Begging your pardon, miss. Would this be Liege Lee's?"

The strange voice came from behind, so deep and rumbling it seemed to be underground. Eden felt a swift spasm of mortification. There was simply no getting up gracefully. Her backside, covered as it was by two petticoats and an indigo short dress, faced the stranger. With furious haste she pushed herself up by her palms and turned to meet him. A man filled the door frame, a shadowy giant.

Face aflame, she managed, "Would you be . . . ?"

"Silas Ballantyne."

Nay! Papa's new apprentice? On the day of the babe's birth!

His bearded face took on a swarthy hue. "I knocked on both front and back doors and had no answer." His tone was heavily Scots and a touch apologetic. "With all the noise . . ."

All the blood left her head and she had no answer. She'd gotten up too suddenly and the kitchen seemed to swirl.

"Eden, are you there?"

Her mother's high-pitched voice carried down the stair, and then she appeared, babe in arms. The nameless lad was screaming lustily with no thought to their fragile circumstances. There was no disguising a newborn's cry. All their carefully placed plans began to unravel fast as thread.

Mama's eyes grew wide as saucers, and her plump face paled at the sight of Silas Ballantyne. "I'll go get the master."

The kitchen's shadows seemed to deepen when the stranger shot a glance up the stairs as if he knew Elspeth was there—knew all their secrets—and had come to call them out. Or perhaps he was simply wondering where his lodging would be?

Quickly Eden took stock of him like Mama did her spice cupboard. Sturdy, wool-clad shoulders. Black boots and frayed breeches, and a greatcoat so shabby it seemed mere spiderwebbing in places. Hair as rich and multihued as the hard cider Papa kept locked in the shed, a damp amber-gold threaded with red. In their humble kitchen he cut an imposing figure. He stood, she guessed, more than six feet tall. She couldn't get a fix on his features, couldn't tell how pleasing or plain—

"Eden," he said quietly, in a voice so low it was nearly lost to her. "Like the garden."

Her head cleared. "The garden?"

"Aye, of Eden."

She tried to smile. "I—I'm sorry for my mother's haste. She's . . ."

"Busy with the babe," he finished for her.

"Aye, the babe." She turned toward the water barrel beside the kitchen door and plucked a pewter cup from a nail. "Born today. We've not even named him—" She bit her tongue all too late. *Oh my!*

He took the cup from her unsteady hand. "Today," he echoed, a touch of awe in his tone. "I'd heard you frontier women were hardy . . ."

While he took a long drink, she felt mired in a stew of subterfuge. Could he sense her panic, her deceit? She must speak of something else—anything. "You—you've come far without a companion."

"I had Horatio."

"Horatio?"

"My gelding."

She looked out the window in the fading light and saw a horse, its snow-capped nose at the pane.

"If this is the wilderness, there were no dangers along the way," he said. "No wild animals. No Indians."

Darting another look at him, she almost laughed despite herself. Did he think *this* the wilderness?

Silent as a savage himself, Liege Lee filled the doorway. "So, Silas Ballantyne, you've braved a snowstorm to get here." Voice gruff, he glanced at Eden. "Daughter, see to the man's horse."

The Scot turned and shifted his load, shaking her father's soot-stained hand. Eden began taking small steps backward, wondering if master and apprentice would take a liking to each other when such had never happened before. She could hear Mama down the hall but no more wailing. The babe was likely tucked in the worn cradle by the hearth. Supper awaited with the stranger.

❧

'Twas at supper that she noticed his thumbs. The candle-light seemed to call attention to their ends. At first she thought them injured. Had he burnt himself at the forge? 'Twas a dangerous work they did. Pity softened her, nearly made her

33

forget the babe in the cradle or little Thomas at her elbow making a mess of his beans. But it was the stranger's bowing of his head that most moved her. Was he . . . praying?

Silas Ballantyne seemed to marvel at their table. "I'd not thought," he said quietly, "to find such fare so far west."

Eden read deprivation and loneliness in the words while Mama smiled wearily and passed him more beef and bread. Glancing in Papa's direction, Eden waited for him to belt out the admonition that there was to be no talking at table. But to her dismay, and surely Mama's, he launched into a speech of all he possessed.

"I've got four hundred acres here along the Elkhannah, a fine wife, two young sons . . ."

There, he's gone and done it, Eden thought. *Claimed Elspeth's babe as his own.*

"A pair of marriageable daughters . . ."

Her bread turned to ashes in her mouth. She wanted to crawl beneath the trestle table.

He continued on, confident. Nay, boastful. "A fine harvest of wheat and flax, twenty head of cattle, countless chickens and an aggravation of goats, a bountiful garden, corn that surpasses eighteen inches an ear. Not all you've heard about this land is fabricated. The woods to the west of us really are alive with Indians. Settlers beyond the Alleghenies still fort up on occasion. Any questions?"

"Two daughters?" Silas asked, shooting a glance about the room.

Eden's fork stilled.

"Aye, two. One's ill and abed," Papa said.

Silas buttered a piece of bread, expression thoughtful. "Tell me about the forge."

The forge. Always the forge. Was he winning her father over already? Papa's grim expression beneath his shock of

34

graying hair told her he had not. Papa seemed tetchy, a bit on edge. Was he thinking of Elspeth? The babe beginning to stir in its cradle near the hearth?

"The forge." Papa forked a slab of beef onto his plate, voice rising as the infant's fussing intensified. "What about it?"

"How long you've been in business. How you come by your iron. What you turn out."

The crying could no longer be ignored. Eden got up, food forgotten, and fished the babe out of the cradle. Mama soon relieved her, her whisper low and urgent. "Make them both some flip. And mind your cap—it's all askew. You must put your best foot forward."

'Tis not my foot that needs to be minded but Elspeth's.

The Scottish apprentice now belonged to her sister, Eden realized with a little start. But Elspeth was abed. Disappearing into the kitchen, she measured out generous amounts of molasses, small beer and rum, and a dash of cream and egg. This she poured into two tankards, returning to the dining room, cap still askew, careful to keep her eyes off Silas Ballantyne.

4

*He speaketh not; and yet there lies
a conversation in his eyes.*

HENRY WADSWORTH LONGFELLOW

Silas watched the young woman at the hearth now that the room had emptied. Greathouse's words came rushing back and nearly made him groan.

She's no sow.

Nae, most decidedly not. Whatever Liege Lee's faults, he'd sired a lovely daughter. But it wasn't the snug lines of her wool dress that drew his eye, nor the worn lace kerchief dressing up her shoulders, nor the fact that her linen cap was a bit crooked.

A spitfire, he'd thought at first sight.

But as soon as she'd spoken, he'd detected a certain sweetness about her that altered his hasty opinion. And her smile . . . losh, bright as a sunrise, raising a dimple in her right cheek. But it was her voice that held him captive. He'd expected it to be high, girlish, simple. But when she spoke it was like a song. Soft and dulcet. Somewhat refined.

Leaning back in his chair, he crossed his arms and legs, waiting for the drink she made him. Into the flames went her poker before the tip turned his pewter mug sizzling. Though he'd been in the house an hour or better, his insides had hardly thawed.

When she handed him the mug, their fingers met and then their eyes, hers a startling indigo in the pale oval of her face. Shyly she turned back toward the fire, and he caught a flash of cherry red as she flipped the length of her hair over her shoulder. Bound with dark ribbon, it cascaded to her waist in lush spirals, thick as blackberry vine.

Eden, indeed.

The other daughter was ill, the master said. Just as well. If she'd been present and was half so bonny, he'd have been struck speechless.

When Liege returned, he took up his own mug, surprising Silas with his terse words. "We breakfast at first light. Eden will show you to your garret room. Tomorrow comes all too soon."

Silas looked from master to daughter, saw the pained expression that crossed her face then skittered away like mist, making him think he'd imagined it. But she merely lowered her head and nodded, expecting him to follow, he guessed.

Bidding Liege good night, he walked a respectable distance behind Eden, down a narrow hall past two closed doors, then up a small, winding stair to a second and third floor that nearly had his knees to his chin. Once, her taper nearly went out in a draft, but she cupped her hand around it and pressed on, finally pushing open a door at the very top of the stair.

The promised garret room.

It was small and prim, redolent of linseed oil and old wood. A narrow bed, a stove, a table, and a chair made it hospitable, and he was heartened to see a small window. Immediately he looked west, if only to look away from her. The snow made the land lantern-bright, the view unobstructed for miles.

He nodded his thanks, stepping around her, remembering he'd left his belongings below. Setting the candle on the table, she added a chunk of wood to the glowing Franklin stove before shutting it soundly. He'd seen such contraptions in Philadelphia but never one so small. Fit for a child, it barely came up to his shin, yet he felt its warmth from several feet away. *Bethankit*, he nearly uttered aloud. 'Twas a far cry from the unheated hovel he was used to.

With nary a look, she left him. He heard her soft footfall in the stairwell and wondered where she was off to. The babe was howling again with the keening pitch of a newborn, as if announcing Silas would get no sleep. Sitting in the too-small chair and finishing his flip, he contemplated whether or not to fetch his haversacks or wait till morning.

❧

Down the dark stairs Eden flew, berating herself for forgetting his belongings. The house below seemed empty of all but the babe's cries. Though he was tucked away in her parents' bedchamber behind closed doors, her ears—and nerves—felt shattered. To ground herself, she leaned into the parlor table where the Scot's rifle rested, her gaze falling to the smooth walnut stock bearing silver mounts, worked with a pattern of twisting acanthus leaves much like the copper lantern.

Had he fashioned this too?

This fine gun lacked a nameplate atop the barrel. Turning it over, she searched for a signature, finding it secreted beneath the side plate.

Silas Ballantyne, 1783.

A tiny ember of delight, of discovery, flickered in her heart. Those who labeled a gun so subtly often felt their craftsmanship was God-given and to display their name prominently was to take away from His work. Usually Papa made sport of such folk behind their backs when they brought their rifles for repair, but their humility had made a far different impression on Eden.

Perhaps . . . Her heart quickened. Perhaps this Scotsman was a believer, someone who could speak to her of God—more so than Margaret Hunter with her mysterious Quaker murmurings.

Listen to the Light, Eden. Quiet thy thoughts. Worship is deeper than words . . .

Hoisting the canvas haversacks and rifle and nearly gasping at their weight, she trudged back upstairs. The apprentice met her halfway, surprising her in the stairwell, relieving her of her burden and handing her his empty mug.

"If you grow cold . . . have need of another quilt—" she began.

"Nae," he said abruptly.

His terse tone surprised her. But he was weary, she reminded herself, in need of rest, with no understanding of her alarm. She glanced over his shoulder and into the garret, feeling a desperate need to rescue the private things she'd hidden there. She'd never dreamed Papa would want him upstairs and not in the room off the smithy reserved for apprentices. But the roof was leaking there and he'd had little time to repair it. Or might he have other motives? Like wanting him nearer Elspeth?

Whatever his motives, the garret had special significance for her. 'Twas Grandpa Gallatin's old room. All those stairs to its cramped rafters kept his old legs spry, he'd said. Her heart twisted further at the memory of Papa and Elspeth discovering her journal months before. Their shared laughter echoed long and loud even now. Made of scraps of rag linen sewn together by coarse thread, she'd been keeping count of her blessings within its pages, things that meant so much but they'd made sport of. Her spinning. The robin outside her window that sang her awake. Thomas's sloppy kisses. Margaret's tea and scones. Jemma's generosity . . .

It mattered little, she guessed, if this stranger found her makeshift book. Once Papa began his bullying, Silas Ballantyne would likely go the way of the other apprentices and she'd never see him again.

She began to retreat, a plea arising in her heart that he'd be too tired to notice his surroundings tonight. In the morning, once he'd gone to work, she'd sneak in and reclaim what was hers. Find a new hiding spot. Oh, but the garret room had been nearly perfect except for the occasional bat. Already her mind was whirling with other possibilities.

Lord, please help me find another hiding place.

Eden scarcely slept between the babe's ceaseless crying and the coming of Silas to her garret room. As dawn dredged the sky with golden light, she dressed hurriedly in the second-floor bedchamber she usually shared with Elspeth, only Elspeth was lying in below.

"Come, Eden, and help me with the babe," Mama whispered after breakfast when the men had gone to the smithy.

Entering her parents' bedchamber, she found Elspeth asleep atop the immense feather bolster, jarring her anew with their predicament. Had her parents slept in the trundle bed? Papa was not one for such concessions. The lines about Mama's eyes announced she'd not slept at all. Eden glanced at Thomas now rocking the low cradle so vigorously she feared the infant would be spilled onto the plank floor.

Kissing her brother, she slowed the cradle, and together they rocked the babe till his cries subsided.

"He's been fed," Mama said. "Now I must see to Elspeth."

Oh, Mama, hurry. I must go to the garret.

Flushing, she watched as her mother roused her sister and removed her nightgown, binding her bosom tightly with long strips of linen. To subdue her milk once it came in, Mama said. And it was well on its way from the look of her, Eden thought, lowering her eyes.

"Will you squeeze the very breath from me?" Elspeth protested sleepily, her hair spilling free of its braid and getting in the way. "You might as well lace me in my stays!"

Leaving the cradle, Eden took a brush from the washstand and crossed to the bed to subdue her sister's hair. With careful hands, she loosed the untidy plait, then brushed the length of it till it shone like yellow satin before twisting and pinning it into place.

Elspeth glared at them both, thunder knotting her brow. "How long must I lie abed?"

Mama's mouth set in a thin line. "A fortnight or better."

"I heard another voice at breakfast. Has the apprentice come?"

Nodding, Mama smoothed the bedcovers. "He's at the forge."

Elspeth's tired blue gaze turned sharp. "Well? What is he like?" At her mother's silence, she looked at Eden, who'd fallen into a tongue-tied perplexity.

"He's a man like all the rest," Mama finally said with a curtness brought on by a sleepless night.

With a sigh, Elspeth flopped back against the bank of pillows. "Must I lie here and wonder about my future husband?" When the babe began crying again, she turned her face away in dismay. "How am I to recover with such noise?"

Noise? Eden stared at her. *You should have thought of that before—*

Biting her lip, Eden scooped her nephew—nay, brother—out

41

of the cradle. While Mama took the chamber pot from the room, Eden paced up and down while little Thomas covered his ears. The day yawned long and she was already bone weary, fearful not even childbirth could dampen her sister's strong will.

From the tumbled bed, Elspeth sat up, wincing at the sudden movement. "Tell me, Sister, what does he look like?"

Exasperation fanned through Eden. She didn't want to dwell on Silas Ballantyne, nor the bewildering confusion she felt over their dilemma. The poor man had walked into a trap and she wanted no part of it.

"Come now, tell me. He is mine, is he not?" Expression coy, Elspeth softened her tone. "Papa has arranged it. I must know what my intended looks like."

Eden bounced the fussing babe. "He's . . . pleasing."

"Pleasing?" With a roll of her eyes, she leaned forward and extended both hands as if prepared to wrest the facts from her. "Is he short? Hawk-nosed? Portly? Plain?"

"He's . . . Scottish." Indeed, his brogue had stayed with her in the night, so honey-tongued he was. "His hair is the hue of hard cider. I—I don't remember the color of his eyes. He has to duck his head to pass through a door."

A slow, satisfied smile spread over Elspeth's face. Turning toward an icy window, Eden thought of all she couldn't say.

He has a fine rifle. His shoulders are broad. His manner is forthright. His knapsacks are heavy . . .

His thumbs are branded.

When she turned back around, Elspeth was on her feet, pulling on her petticoats. Though used to her sister's impulsiveness, this was too much. "Elspeth! What are you—"

"I cannot lie abed any longer." She stared back in triumph as if daring Eden to deny her.

"But you're weak, bleeding—"

"I'll not be on my feet long. Just long enough to meet this

man . . . *my* future husband." Her eyes shone with renewed purpose. "Besides, we must all play the part. I'm not the one confined to childbed. Mama is. Now help me manage my hooks."

Laying the newborn on the bed, Eden turned to her reluctantly, dismay riffling through her. The rich red calico had to be tugged into place, straining every seam—and with it Eden's every nerve. Elspeth hardly looked the invalid they pretended her to be. A practiced eye like that of Mistress Middy would ken the truth in a heartbeat. Eden prayed the Scot wouldn't be so discerning.

Lifting her chin like a general going into battle, Elspeth sucked in her breath. "I'll not be long. Tell Mama I'd like some toast and tea."

Eden watched her go like she had on so many occasions, to do as she pleased, without so much as a by-your-leave. Short of chaining her to the bedpost, who could restrain her? Perhaps Mama would intercept her in the hall.

Feeling drugged by sleeplessness, Eden tried to gather her wits as she soothed the babe. He was growing quieter, his eyelids heavy. Placing him in his cradle, she gave Thomas some yarn to play with, but he looked up at her with bleary blue eyes and rubbed his belly. Had Mama forgotten to feed him in all the confusion and fuss?

"I'll bring you some toast and gooseberry jam soon," she promised.

Nearly on tiptoe, she slipped from the room to the second floor and crossed the landing to the garret's winding stair. Up, up, up she climbed, anticipation making her breathless. The twenty-one steps had never seemed so far, and the delicious anticipation she'd always felt in escaping here in spare moments had been eclipsed by the apprentice's arrival. 'Twas no longer her room but his. Till he left or wed Elspeth and moved to another room—or another house—she'd not get it back.

43

She knocked before she entered, though she knew he was safely below in the smithy. The ring of a hammer was blessed confirmation—not Papa's angry cadence, but something more measured and sure. Pushing open the garret door, she found the beloved space nearly as tidy as she'd left it, but when she crossed to the desk, she opened the sole drawer to emptiness. Panic seized her. Her quill and ink and journal were missing. *Nay!* In its pages she'd strayed from her list of blessings and complained mightily about the prospect of marrying a stranger—an apprentice—upon a father's whim and a rusty tradition. Nay, not only marriage—she'd also recklessly penned the details of her plan. Her escape.

Dropping to her knees, she searched beneath the bed. Naught but a few dust motes that had escaped her broom. Dare she go through his belongings? Might he have put them in his haversacks? But the twin bags hung limply from a peg on one wall. Her restless gaze touched his gun and a fiddle sitting upright in a corner. A long horsehair bow lay in the windowsill.

The leather-bound books Jemma Greathouse had lent her were also missing. She'd hidden them behind the stove, which was now cold. What if Silas Ballantyne read her scribbling, her concerns about marrying a man she didn't know? Her hopes for the future? What if he'd given the journal and books to Papa? Sitting on the foot of the neatly made bed, she wrestled with her fears and groped for reason.

She could lie, say they weren't hers. But the mere thought was distasteful. Papa and Elspeth lied—indeed, 'twas like a second language. Her mother, while not outright untruthful, was frightfully evasive. Thomas, too young to form but a mouthful of words, had yet to show his true colors. Nay, she'd not lie. But she *must* find the tender outpourings of her heart and make a new hiding place.

The garret was now his.

5

There are charms made only for distant admiration.

SAMUEL JOHNSON

The smithy would be warm this snowy morn, thanks to the huge hearth that was the very heart of a blacksmith's work. Silas stood by the worn, blackened anvil and took stock of the place where he'd spend the bulk of his twenty-fifth year. Going to the woodpile, he fed the fire that had been banked the previous night, coaxing the embers to life. They flamed under his experienced hand, and he began arranging his tools by the low light. Accustomed to working from daylight to dusk, he'd been surprised when Liege Lee had been absent at breakfast.

"Mr. Lee is feeling the effects of the snow this day," Mrs. Lee had said as she served him eggs and bacon, thick slices of toasted bread, and gunpowder tea. "'Tis his gout, I'm afraid."

Silas listened without comment, marveling that she was on her feet so soon after a birth while her husband let a little gout keep him from his work. The night before Liege Lee had struck Silas as indomitable, surly, and immune to such frailties. Now, standing alone in the timbered smithy, he savored the stillness. For months he'd felt there wasn't a peaceful place in his soul.

Being sequestered in a large Philadelphia shop with a dozen or more men—many of whom would rather fight than work—had taken a toll. Before that had been Williamsburg and a British prison camp. But he'd not begin afresh by recalling this. Laying aside his hammer, he tried to do the same with the pain of his past. A frayed, leather-bound book was within easy reach, providing a blessed distraction. He glanced at the title, tongue in cheek.

A Present for an Apprentice.

He knew the contents well enough as it was considered holy writ among tradesmen, stressing a master's authority. He turned the battered tome facedown in silent protest, then took half an hour to familiarize himself with everything in the shop, wagering there'd be little business transacted on such a day. After filling a water bucket with snow—for he'd never find the well in such weather—he straightened and turned toward the creak of a door. The shadows were dispelling slowly, and he could barely make out the well-rounded form. That it was a woman there could be no doubt.

Eden Lee?

Nae, this woman was taller, fuller of figure. When she stepped into the hearth's light, all thoughts of Eden vanished. The elder daughter? The one who was dwiny—ill—and confined to the house? He shook off his surprise.

She was so unlike her younger sister he suspected they weren't truly related. Her flaxen hair was pinned and plaited, forming a sort of halo about her head. Bold eyes—a Scottish cornflower blue—assessed him much as her father had done the night before. She had a classic roses-and-cream, English-type beauty. The kind that made men wage duels and pen poetry and lose all good reason.

Her soft voice cut across the room. "Are you the apprentice?"

"Aye," he answered, clasping his hands behind his back and facing her.

"I'm Elspeth Lee." She hesitated, looking again at the door she'd just entered. "Since my father isn't here, I'll show you round myself."

There's no need, he nearly said, but she'd already turned away as if expecting him to follow. He bit his lip to keep any amusement from telling on his face. The image of the timorous Eden doing the same made a puzzling picture. Liege Lee had two daughters, but they were as different as night and day. This one might well be the spitfire he'd mistaken her sister for.

After a few minutes he forgot his reserve, impressed by the breadth of her knowledge as she spoke of ironwork that needed making, discussing details and design. Though he said little, she kept up a running conversation well enough without him.

"Since my father has but two small sons, it has been left to me as the eldest daughter to learn the trade. A blacksmith cannot operate alone, as you know. Papa has had apprentices—two runaways—but I help him as best I can and keep the ledgers. Would you like to see them?"

"Nae, I trust they're in good order."

She gave a curt nod, fingering some tongs absently, her features a bit strained. She was unwell, he remembered, mindful of her malady. Without warning, she sank down upon a near bench, her full skirts ballooning in a swell of red cloth, and looked entreatingly at him.

"Tell me of yourself, Silas Ballantyne."

He swallowed down a smile at her boldness and ran a hand over his bearded jaw, deciding to deal in generalities. "I've just come eighty miles from Philadelphia on a half-lame horse and ferried across the Susquehanna. Somewhere along the way I lost my razor. At five and twenty I'll wager I'm the oldest apprentice in America."

At this, she laughed, but the merry sound was snatched away as the door behind them opened and Liege limped in, incredulity etched across every hard line of his face.

"Your mother is looking for you, Daughter. She's in need of your help today, and quickly."

The dismissal was met with Elspeth's hasty retreat, and then Liege turned the full force of his gaze upon Silas. "Pray you never have such a daughter. That one should be in breeches, though she looks well enough in a skirt."

"She has a keen knowledge of the trade."

He gave a curt nod and reached for his battered leather apron. "And well she should, being at my side for fifteen years or better. The apprentices I've had can't hold a candle to her. We'll see if you fare any better."

⬿⬾

By midmorning, Eden felt as scattered as garden seed. Between helping her mother enforce Elspeth's lying-in and assuming all her chores, she was worn to a thread. But it was her missing journal that most wrenched her. She tried to push aside her flustered feelings as they worked together keeping the babe quiet while mending and making cheese and preparing noonday dinner.

"He's to be named Jon, after your grandfather," Mama said in low tones, settling in her rocking chair to nurse, though she could ill afford the time.

Hearing it brought about a tender pang. Grandpa Gallatin? Though six years had passed since he'd died, the void he'd left had never lessened. It was still felt here in the house and the smithy, where he'd worked with her father day in and day out. His patience had been the perfect antidote to Papa's grousing, always keeping him in check.

Stifling a sigh, she watched as Thomas tried to climb on Mama's lap, only to be shooed away with an agitated hand. "I'll not be tied down with the both of you. Go on now."

Sympathy tugged at Eden as Thomas puckered his round face in protest. Abandoning her task, she took his little hand and led him away. "You're big enough for your own cup now. Here's a pewter one with an *L* engraved on it." She poured him some cider and heated it with the poker as she'd done the flip the night before. Her reward was a tremulous smile. Though he spilled some taking it off the table, the cup finally made it to his open mouth.

Absently she watched him, schooling her thoughts, revisiting the morning's happenings. Elspeth was finally in bed again—in the room they shared—and Eden rued the loss of privacy. Oh, that she could fly to Hope Rising and find rest, peace! She'd not been there for a fortnight or better. Her soul chafed at the farmhouse's smallness as her mind roamed the mansion's many rooms, each holding myriad hiding places for her missing journal and books.

"Come, Eden, and finish the cheese," Mama said, bringing her back. "The men will be hungry this day with the weather so raw."

When she began serving noonday dinner, she felt so addled she nearly spilled the fried hominy in Silas's lap. He caught her wrist as the platter tipped sideways, steadying her, his gaze traveling from her trembling hand to her face. She imagined Elspeth's eyes narrowing as she mouthed "idiot" from across the table. But Elspeth's place yawned empty, and Eden felt stark relief.

Thankfully, Papa was at the other end, so immersed in his plate they might have done a jig and he'd not notice. She felt a faint hope they might converse as they had last night, but Papa's hospitality seemed short-lived. The rule of silence, forged in her childhood, was not to be violated twice. All that was heard was the clink of utensils and the whine and snap of the hearth's fire as if it begged for more wood, leaving her to wonder if Scotsmen liked a bit more merriment at their table.

Mama was missing, busy with Thomas and baby Jon, whom she could hear fretting mightily despite his being at the opposite end of the house with all the doors shut in between. When Eden went to fetch the apple cake from the kitchen, adding a generous dollop of cream atop it, she knew she must ask about her things—or burst. Soon Silas would return to work.

Serving her father first, she moved toward Silas, praying she'd not drop the dish. As she gave him some cake, he gestured to the empty chair beside him. Looking down, she felt a swelling relief. There, half hidden beneath the tablecloth hem, were her beloved things. Not once did Papa look up from his dish as she gathered them in her apron and returned to the kitchen.

Quickly she took inventory. All was as she'd left them— the borrowed books, the journal, and an unfamiliar volume of red leather underneath. *The Poetry of James Thomson.* Intrigued, she opened the flyleaf.

To Niel Ballantyne for services rendered, Sir John Murray, 1765.

A hundred questions sprang to mind, begging answers. Had he meant this for her? Her fingers touched one gilt-edged page after another, lips parting in surprise at the scrap of paper marking a particular poem. On it he'd written a note in a hand far finer than a man of his station should possess.

Eden, I did not mean to take your room, nor your books. Silas

Putting a hand to her trembling mouth, she tried to staunch her emotion. She was unaccustomed to such kindness. And she knew then he wouldn't mock her, nor read what wasn't his. Nay, he'd shared something of his own. Never having heard of the poet Thomson, she was intrigued. She couldn't wait to begin, but chores awaited. For now two lines would have to suffice:

Thine is the balmy breath of morn,
Just as the dew-bent rose is born . . .

Clutching the book to her heart, she sought a hideaway in the busy kitchen till her work was done. Since Elspeth would soon be up and about—indeed, had shocked them all by going to the smithy at dawn and ruining her best slippers in the snow—the kitchen was not safe. Nearly on tiptoe, Eden traded the warm room for the cold hall, peeked into her parents' bedchamber, and found Mama nursing Jon by the hearth.

The summer parlor, then. 'Twas her favorite room by far. Full of cast-offs from Hope Rising, it had a pretense of grandeur and nearly made her forget she was a prisoner of the farmhouse. The plaster walls were covered with copper-red paint, and the overall impression was charming, if a bit discordant. In winter the room was closed off, as the family preferred the smaller parlor with its mammoth hearth adjoining the dining room.

Closing the door, Eden shivered. The icy floorboards seemed to penetrate the soles of her shoes. Everything smelled of dust, disuse, and beeswax. Pondering the furnishings, she chose a seldom-used secretary, its heavy lines forbidding. Surely no one would bother looking here. She hid her things and then left hurriedly, making her way to the weaving room, when a sudden hiss stopped her cold.

"Eden Rose!"

The strident voice couldn't be ignored. Pushing open the

bedchamber door, she opened her mouth to answer, but Elspeth galloped right over her. "What were you doing in the summer parlor?"

Panic engulfed her. "Putting something away—"

Elspeth placed a cautionary finger to her lips. "Come in and shut the door. I don't want anyone to hear us."

Eden did as she bid, albeit reluctantly. Smoothing her apron, she sat down on the edge of the bed, wondering about the high flush on her sister's face.

"Why didn't you tell me he was so handsome—or so amusing?"

The apprentice? Eden made her face appropriately blank. "I hadn't . . . noticed." This was only partly true. She'd noticed far too much—but none of the things Elspeth did.

Rolling her eyes, Elspeth resumed her usual exasperation. "How are you to catch a husband with your head in the clouds?"

"'Tis not my husband we're discussing, but yours," Eden reminded her.

"Yes, you'd best remember that." A smile thawed Elspeth's coldness, and her blue eyes sparked. "I suppose he'll suffice, though I've never cared much for Scotsmen. You know those MacMasters and Gows with their drunken antics over the hill. They're so . . . unpredictable. Like a greased pig on market day. One never knows which way they'll go next."

Like you, Eden thought but didn't say. *Perhaps you've met your match.*

"How are you feeling?" she said instead, tucking in an unkempt bed corner.

Leaning back against the bank of pillows, Elspeth sighed and fingered her braid. "I'm hungry and bored. You must light a lamp, bring me my sewing. Mama wants me to rest, but I need to finish those pillowslips for my dower chest."

Eden's eyes drifted to the twin trunks fashioned by their

grandfather's hand on either side of the small hearth. Elspeth's bore her initials, its smooth walnut lines pleasing in their simplicity. Eden's was embellished with leaves and flowers much like the ones on Silas Ballantyne's fine rifle. And while Elspeth's was but half full, her own was burgeoning. Some days she could barely close the lid without rearranging half the contents.

"Would you like something to eat?" she asked, hoping to change the current of conversation. "Mama and I made chicken pie and apple cake."

"I'm surprised there's any left. How is the Scot's appetite?"

"He has fine manners," Eden admitted.

Unlike many of the men who'd sat at their table, he'd not wiped his mouth on his sleeve or licked his fingers or belched at meal's end, nor asked for a second serving, though he'd eaten more bread. Wheat was scarce in Scotland, he'd said.

"We'll see how he fares with Papa at the forge." Elspeth looked toward her dower chest absently. "Best not be hunting up the parson just yet."

Eden nearly sighed aloud in relief, seizing on the chance to distract her from any further probing about the parlor. "The parson's been quite busy. Two of the Greathouse tenants wed last week, though Wealthy Heinz and John Masters eloped, or so Margaret Hunter told me."

"Eloped?" Elspeth wrinkled her nose. "How dull! No wedding dress nor cake nor gifts."

"'Tis romantic, I think."

"You would. I plan to be married in the summer parlor. In your yellow silk."

Hearing it, Eden felt a sinking dismay. 'Twas her favorite dress—a cast-off from Jemma Greathouse, who'd grown too stout to wear it. Elspeth had had a fit when Jemma sent it round in the carriage from Hope Rising right before Christmas. The memory bruised Eden still.

"'Tis a snub!" Elspeth had stormed through angry tears. "They're always gifting you, inviting you to the house!"

"But 'tis too small for you. Look how narrow the bodice and sleeves are." Eden had pointed out the obvious, feeling the heat of Elspeth's anger and fearing the consequences.

Since childhood Eden had often found her treasured things cut up or soiled with ink. To avoid this, she had often given over the coveted item. But this gown, which she'd hoped might be saved for Philadelphia . . .

"I'll soon fit into the dress, once I leave this bed." Elspeth's eyes, now cold as creek ice, brooked no argument. "Just bring round some toast and tea, no cake. And don't forget my sewing."

Eden returned to the kitchen, her mind on more than the yellow silk. She felt weighted with the vision of her sister standing in the parlor at some hazy date in future, holding hands with Silas Ballantyne. Elspeth was altogether too eager to wed. To appease Papa and Mama, perhaps, who were weary of her waywardness?

Whatever the reason, fidelity was not her sister's strong suit. She liked to dally, never settling on one suitor for long. So many men came to do business with their father. Elspeth flirted with them all, or so it seemed, only to sneak out with someone at night. Eden hadn't an inkling who the babe's father might be. Though in time, once the boy grew long-limbed and strong of feature, wouldn't his parentage be plain? And the truth be told?

However wayward, Elspeth liked her secrets and was good at keeping them. It seemed a very small thing that Eden had her secrets as well. Just a journal and some borrowed books, a plan for the future. But Elspeth . . . Eden felt caught in a sticky web of deceit. Her sister was the spider and Silas Ballantyne was the poor, unsuspecting insect that had wandered into her and Papa's path.

6

Fear not for the future, weep not for the past.

PERCY BYSSHE SHELLEY

"Play for us, Silas!"

The childish voices were like a song, carrying musically over moor and heather as tendrils of fog lay like white ribbons in the lowlands. Adjusting his plaid, Silas turned, finding a veritable troupe trailing him.

"D'ye think the sheep would listen to such music?" He snagged the smallest child about the waist with his crook, smiling as she squealed with delight. "I've not brought my fiddle this day, lassie."

The sheep had long since scattered, and he was tempted to shoo the noisy bairns home, then remembered they had no crofts to return to. The October air was chill, and some of them lacked shoes, their thin, shivering limbs drawing his notice and sharpening his concern.

"Go on wi' ye now," he growled, eyes damp.

"Our maithers sent us oot while they pack the carts," the

55

eldest boy said. "They dinna want us underfoot. The laird says we're to be gone by noon or else."

Aye, noon. Silas knew the decree well enough, though his own family was exempt.

"I dinna want to be gone to the coast!" the smallest girl wailed. "Faither doesna like to fish. And Maither cries and cries . . ."

"Ye know what they've said if we dinna obey—they'll burn us oot like they did the tenants o' Sutherland," another said.

"Look!" one boy cried, stabbing a dirty finger at the sky. "It's begun!"

Silas let his crook fall from his fingers and felt a ripple of fear at the ominous words. The children were running now, toward the blaze, toward certain danger—

With a hoarse cry he shot up like a loosened spring, limbs bound in a tangle of bedding, eyes wide open and heart slamming in his chest. The dream receded, that black day dwindling down to ashes in the firestorm of his thoughts. His gaze landed on the violin beneath the west window, the bow resting along the sill, reminding him of where he was—abed in the garret room, not digging for charred corpses in a blackened hovel.

He was here, in Pennsylvania, the Franklin stove leaking smoke, the backlog he'd added to the fire at midnight the true culprit. Opening the iron door, he scattered the glowing remains and added more wood, lighting a candle before shutting it soundly.

What he'd give for a little peat. A croft. His own thin bolster with its woven plaid. The sweet sound of music beneath smoky rafters. The familiar slant of sunlight through a narrow window. Sitting on the unfamiliar bed, he tried to calm his muddled thoughts and stem the tide of memory. His father had been aging. His mother was ill. The duke had promised they could remain. But in the end the laird had not kept his promises.

By fleeing Scotland and coming to the American frontier, he hoped the past would loosen its leaden grip. Though he bore other, visible wounds like the stripes across his back and his branded thumbs, none retained so vile an ache as the memories. They clung to him like the chill of the River Tay, as hard to dislodge as the Scots blood that flowed through him. His beloved mother had been wrong.

Not all wounds of the heart healed.

His restless gaze swung to the far wall, where the lone candle burnished his fiddle a deep russet. How was it that a man could switch countries and dwellings and clothes, but habits were harder to alter and heredity always held sway? Since boyhood, he'd not been content to look at the instrument's fine lines without feeling the need to bring it to life with his bow. His father had been the same. Unlike here, there'd been more music in their home than silence. Playing was an act of worship, his father said. And so their humble cottage had been more kirk. Even in the assembly rooms of Edinburgh and Aberdeen and the more familiar ballroom of the duke of Atholl, there'd been a reverence in the most strenuous reels and jigs. Those who listened to his father play went away changed. And then they came back again.

Picking up the instrument, he felt a sudden solace. That he was his father's son there could be no doubt. In Scotland's southern Highlands, he was not so much Silas as Niel Ballantyne's son. In musical circles it had been much the same, even without a fiddle in hand. But here in America he could be whom he pleased. He could even change his name. And he need never take up a fiddle again.

If he set it down once and for all, might it not stay the memories?

Still, a hundred strathspeys and slow airs filled his head and heart, each bringing its own echo of the past. Was it any wonder, after such a dream, he felt like playing a lament instead? Picking up his bow, he began to play so low and slow it couldn't possibly be heard. Or so he hoped. Liege Lee didn't seem like a man much given to music.

⤜⤛

For once Eden was still abed as dawn warmed the windowpane. Drawing on her dressing gown, Elspeth looked down at her sister, lingering on the tangle of hair spread upon the pillow—a sheen of queer, crimson gold. In winter it darkened to ruby; in summer it seemed sunlight itself. Why she insisted on wearing it down as she'd done her whole childhood mystified Elspeth. It made her look like a girl, not a young woman of nearly twenty. But that was all well and good, she mused, if the Scot had a wandering eye.

Opening the door, she nearly winced at its squeaking. Sliding through a crack was no longer a simple matter. The babe had turned her into her ample mother, a fact she hated. She could hardly look at her son or hear his cries without feeling stouter. Now that her milk had come in, her bosom felt like a boulder even bound in the loosest stays. The mere brush of fabric against her skin sent every nerve shivering. She needed to be abed, but curiosity called her forth. She simply must know why Eden had been poking about the summer parlor.

The neglected room felt encased in ice this morning. Evidences of Hope Rising were everywhere, stinging her afresh. When old Greathouse had died the year before, the mansion's rooms had been emptied and fine Philadelphia furniture brought in. The heir, David, was as frivolous as his uncle had been frugal. All of York had benefitted, though there had been more than one brawl over a London-made clock

58

or piece of French crystal. Rather than hold an auction as any sensible man would do, David and his foolish female cousins had given most everything away. Though Eden was awed by their benevolence, Elspeth felt only contempt, as did their father. Secretly he'd turned around and sold some of the items they'd received.

Wanting to escape the room as soon as possible, Elspeth began opening drawers and compartments for she knew not what. Her airy-headed sister was always reading and scribbling in spare moments. Likely she fancied herself a female poet. Time spent at Hope Rising was no doubt giving her lofty notions. Or was there more?

Her searching hands stilled. Could Eden be smitten with David Greathouse? Or David with her?

A river of envy seemed to flood her soul. Though the Greathouses were far above their humble station, it would be just like David to cast conviction aside much as he had Hope Rising's furniture and marry beneath him. As heir, he could do as he pleased, surely.

Slamming shut a drawer, Elspeth remembered the Greathouses were in Philadelphia till spring. With so many city belles for David to choose from, Eden's charms would fade away or be forgotten. Or so she hoped. Slightly mollified, she left the summer parlor. What did it truly matter? Her own future seemed equally sunny with the coming of Silas Ballantyne.

⟲⟳

Was the man trying to be obstinate, or was he simply testing him? Silas wondered. Standing with the anvil between them, Liege and Silas had been double-striking a particularly challenging piece of iron but couldn't get into the needed rhythm to finish it. Each blow of the master's hammer was slightly off-center, thus throwing Silas out of sync. His impatience spiked with every miss. Mayhap the old man's gout was plaguing him.

Liege Lee's very presence was plaguing Silas.

Though snow still blanketed the landscape, the forge's fire was an inferno, turning the situation more tense. The linen shirt Silas wore, mended so many times it was threadbare, clung to him in places. Sweat slicked his brow and trickled down his back, making him want to scratch his new beard. Liege was only slightly less damp, perspiration catching in his graying whiskers and shining off his creased forehead, his stocking cap lopsided.

'Twas his third day of service. Mayhap it was time to test the master. Extending a steady hand, he reached for Liege's hammer as it hung limply by his side and saw a flash of anger contort his face. But Liege stood by silently as Silas worked with both tools, finally beating the piece into submission.

"Egads, man!"

Silas waited for further condemnation or praise, but Liege said no more. Handing him the finished work to inspect, Silas moved on to the next need, a particularly challenging copper latch for a well-to-do tradesman. Despite his attention to his task, Silas was aware of endless silhouettes darkening the smithy door. Though the weather was frigid, men still came. To have something made or mended. To talk trade or politics or simply warm themselves by the fire while they waited.

The morning passed in a whirl of work, each project requiring a different tool and skill, and always a careful eye. Before Silas had finished forging a link on a broken chain, Elspeth appeared, summoning them for dinner. Though he turned his back to her and removed his leather apron, he felt her eyes on him. Unlike Eden, who kept to the house, she always seemed to be hovering.

"When she's well, she'll assist us," Liege had announced that morning when Elspeth brought him the ledgers.

When she's well . . .

Though pale, she looked robust, Silas thought. Hardly the invalid he'd envisioned when Greathouse had first spoken of her. He refrained from saying the smithy was no place for a woman. Injuries—burns—were easily gotten. And the male attention she was sure to garner was not a thing to be trifled with, surely.

Bending over his work, Silas had asked quietly, "What is your daughter's malady?"

Silence.

Though he didn't look at Liege, he sensed the man's surprise and confusion. Apprentices did not question their masters, and Silas expected a swift reminder. But instead of uttering a rebuke, Liege mumbled about his gout.

Silas thought of it now as he followed Elspeth down a rock path overhung with what looked to be an unfinished arbor. Rose canes, pruned severely, stood layered in old snow on both sides. She walked slowly, he noticed, and he felt a spasm of guilt. Mayhap she *was* ill. His suspicions, easily aroused due to his own misfortunes, were likely out of place here. *Judge not lest ye be judged.* He'd best take things at face value till he knew the moods and rhythms of this strange household.

Stopping to wash in a corner of the kitchen, he noticed Eden taking bread from a beehive oven to the right of the hearth. She worked quietly and efficiently, never looking up—basketing the bread, stirring the soup, layering meat and cheese on a platter—all with a bandaged hand. Concern riffled through him. Though he'd been here but a few days, it was long enough to know she was the girl of all work. But with a mother newly delivered and an ill sister, why would it be any different?

Thomas played quietly by an open cupboard, studying Silas with somber eyes as he passed through the kitchen, while the bairn slept in his cradle near the hearth. Mrs. Lee and Elspeth were already seated in the dining room. He took his place at one end of the table, waiting for Liege to occupy the other, and tried to quell his discontent. At least he had warm lodgings here—and more food than he'd ever dreamed of.

Fixing a thankful eye on the pewter and redware in front of him, he heard the kitchen door squeak open. Eden came in, ladling broth into bowls and placing all else on the table. When she sat to the left of him, she bowed her head briefly and he felt a sting of surprise. Other than this, there was no grace said at the Lee table. The practice—or lack of it—was so strange the meal always seemed to be wanting, as if missing seasoning or salt.

How did a girl—a young woman—like Eden warm to Christ in a cold household?

"She has Quaker leanings," Greathouse had said.

How had that happened? Silas wondered.

His eyes roamed the mustard-colored walls, the simple furnishings, and the gaping rock fireplace. Without Liege, the room was missing its usual tension, and he found himself wishing the master would stay away and they could enjoy one meal in peace. But Elspeth was to his right, and peace, he was finding, had little to do with her presence.

"So, Mr. Ballantyne, what do your people partake of in Scotland?"

Her pert question hung in the air, shattering the rule of silence. Silas shot a glance at Mrs. Lee, who was frowning at her eldest daughter. Eyes down, Eden began to spoon her soup with her bandaged hand as if nothing had been said.

"Since Papa isn't here, I'm not going to pretend he is."

Elspeth looked pointedly in her mother's direction, rebellion in her gaze, before glancing at the empty doorway, her voice dropping a notch. "Besides, I know so little about Scotland. 'Tis a shame I've been no further than the outskirts of York County, not even to Philadelphia."

Swallowing some cider, Silas kept his tone low. "We Scots eat a great many things, like neeps and tatties, but prefer Cabbie claw and haggis."

"Ha-haggis?" Elspeth echoed, taking up her spoon.

"Sheep's pluck—heart, liver, lungs."

At this, Elspeth nearly choked on her soup. Eden's mild expression turned amused. Beside her, Mrs. Lee looked slightly aghast, as well she should, Silas thought.

"Well!" Elspeth recovered her composure. "'Tis glad I am we're in America, then."

He nearly smiled. "You have no Scots in your family line?"

Mrs. Lee brushed her lips with a napkin. "My people, the Gallatins, are from France—gunsmiths, all. The Lees—weavers and blacksmiths—hail from middle England."

"Well to the south of the barbarous Highlands," he muttered, taking some bread.

Mrs. Lee cast a skittish glance at him as if attempting to steer the conversation in a safer direction. "May I ask your father's occupation?"

"Fiddler," he said.

Her eyebrows rose ever so slightly. *Fiddler . . . drunkard . . . no-good vagabond.* Silas well knew what she was thinking.

"To the duke of Atholl," he added quietly.

There was a surprised pause, spoons suspended in midair.

"My, you have noble associations." Elspeth fixed her blue gaze on him. "How is it that you came to be here, among us common folk?"

How, indeed. The question seemed edged in glass. He

avoided her probing and reached for the butter. "'Tis a long story best told away from table."

Though he sensed Mrs. Lee's relief, he knew Elspeth's curiosity was kindled. He saw it in her eyes, sensed she would be on his heels till every detail was spilled. For now she was looking at his hands—his branded thumbs—and he suspected she might ask about them outright.

"Are you ever homesick for Scotland?" Eden was at his elbow, leaning toward him ever so slightly, her voice so soft he thought only he had heard. Till now she'd never said more than a mouthful of words to him, and he found her voice like all the rest of her—winsome and amiable and maddeningly hesitant. But before he could answer, Elspeth trounced on her question like a cat upon cream.

"Good heavens, Eden. If Mr. Ballantyne longed for home, would he be here?" Elspeth all but rolled her eyes as she reached for the butter. "I think not."

Silas leaned back in his chair. "Aye, betimes I miss Scotlain." He addressed Eden as quietly as she'd addressed him, aware that Elspeth strained to catch their every word. "But the longer I am here, the less I think of home."

Elspeth wedged her way into the conversation once again. "How long have you been in the colon—I mean, these United States?"

"Since '75—the eve of the Revolution." Even as he said it, he could hardly believe the war was won. Or that he could return to his homeland if he wanted, though there was little to return to. As it was, his overriding passion to go west reduced that desire to ashes. Even now his eyes drifted past Eden's russet head to the west window and the bleak, snow-laden landscape beyond.

Elspeth's strident voice drew him back to the table. "Do you find this part of Pennsylvania to your liking?"

"I hardly know it," he returned.

"Oh, 'tis quite fine once the weather warms," she said. "Papa will no doubt need your help with the plowing and planting come spring—"

The words were snatched away when Liege appeared, giving them all a sound drubbing in a glance. "What is this? You not only sup without me but talk furiously at table?" Taking hold of his chair, he jerked it backwards and sat down heavily, favoring his gout-ridden leg.

Eden leapt up to pour him some cider while Silas looked askance at his plate, falling into a sore silence with the rest of them. The master's mood shifted like a compass point, he was learning, unsettling everyone around him. So different from his father's table, where an abundance of talk and laughter made up for the meager fare.

His appetite gone, Silas excused himself and returned to the smithy, trying to summon thanks for such a tenuous situation. 'Twas just as well he'd not fallen into the lap of a warm, loving family or an exemplary master. He might be tempted to stay. As it was, his every instinct warned him to flee. Which he would do, Lord willing, come autumn and the fulfillment of his contract.

If he could last that long.

7

To speak kindly does not hurt the tongue.

ENGLISH PROVERB

'Twas First Day, as Margaret Hunter called the Sabbath, the most favored day by far. Papa wouldn't let Eden go to church, but he had fewer qualms about her going to Hope Rising, though he complained mightily when she did. This January morn, the snow was spitting again and Eden debated whether to walk or ride Sparrow, her mare. 'Twas important she return the books Jemma Greathouse had lent her and check on the tenants.

All morning she'd flown through her necessary chores, thankfully kept to a minimum on this day of rest. As she hurried down the lane, conspicuous as a cardinal in the felted wool cape Jemma had given her, she tossed a look back at the garret, thinking she heard the twang of a fiddle. Her imagination, surely. Silas wouldn't play with Papa and the new babe in the house. He'd been reading but an hour before when she'd trudged up to the garret with a bundle of wood.

He'd met her on the landing, book in hand, surprising her

just as he had when he'd forgotten his haversack. This time he took the wood, a rebuke in his jade eyes. "From now on I'll fetch my own wood."

"But—"

"I ken where the woodpile is."

"Papa—"

"I'll deal with your father. Besides, I'm handier than you with an ax."

Heat rushed to her face, and she looked down at her hurt hand. The cut from the ax was not deep but had bled profusely and was still tender. Slipping it behind her back, she tried not to wince as he watched her. Light from the open garret door spilled down and dispelled the early morning dimness, highlighting the handsome, lean lines of his bearded face. She read impatience there . . . and something else. A distinct wariness.

"Good Sabbath, Miss Lee."

The words were clipped, like the closing of a door. She sensed he wanted to be rid of her, that the wood was but a ruse. She took a step back, disappointment quenching the small hope in her heart that they might be friends. She wasn't even sure he was what she hoped him to be—a believer—though he bowed his head at meals, same as she.

"I'm s-sorry," she stammered, "to trouble you."

With that she began backing down the steps. It took an eternity to reach bottom—would he not shut the door on her humiliation? Being rebuffed was not new. Papa and Elspeth were masters at it. Why would this be any different? Yet somehow, without her consent, Silas Ballantyne mattered. And when he did shut the door—soundly—her eyes filled with tears.

⌒⌒

Silas began crossing out the days on the crude calendar he'd made in his journal. Meticulous by nature, he made note of the hours he kept, the iron he worked, even the vagaries of weather.

14 January, Friday—Snow. Thirteen and a half hours labor. Wagon and carriage hardware for York.

15 January, Saturday—Weather clear and cold. Twelve and a quarter hours labor. Seven wagon rims. Two cranes. One lock.

16 January, Sabbath—Fasted. Prayed. Spent the forenoon reading Scripture.

Rebuffed Eden Lee.

He hadn't penned the last three words—there was no need. The hurt in her eyes was engraved in his head and heart more indelibly than ink. He'd merely meant to save her a task or two by refusing the wood. Nae, that was a lie—he'd meant to erect a wall. He wanted nothing from the Lees but a fulfilled contract, an end to a too-long apprenticeship. Best establish the boundaries from the first. Still, he regretted his rudeness—and the haunting feeling that Eden Lee was in need of an ally and 'twas Elspeth he should be chary of instead.

The next day, as if to make up for his behavior, he began to split all the wood for the household, making sure she never lacked. 'Twas quite a turnaround. Since his arrival the month before, he'd hardly looked up from his work and paid so little attention to his surroundings he nearly failed to make note of the weather. He came when called for meals, spoke only when spoken to, and spent Sabbaths alone in his room. Yet the time dragged on. His temper grew as jagged as the blade that lined his boot. He felt lifeless, joyless, weary. Who'd have thought it was his beard that would make him go begging?

❧

'Twas Eden's habit to split and stack wood following the noonday meal, just as it was her task to feed the house fires.

When her ax and wedge went missing, she felt a flicker of alarm, only to find Silas in the woodshed behind the kitchen, his breath pluming in the raw cold, his chopping meting out a steady rhythm. Though she hovered between thanking him and avoiding him, the latter won out. She tarried beneath an eave, waiting for his return to the forge, but he showed no signs of stopping. Would he stack the wood to the very rafters? Needing to return to the kitchen, she gave him nary a glance to and from the well till he stepped directly in her path.

"I need no wood from you," he said, eyes grave. "But I do need your help with a razor."

"A razor?" she said, surprised. "There are razors enough in York."

"Aye," he said, looking contrite. "But I've no time to go there."

"I thought . . ." She hesitated, trying to picture him without the heavy shadow across his cheeks and chin. "I thought you always wore it so."

"Nae, I lost my shaving kit coming here."

"And you want me to go to York?"

"Mayhap. I've coin enough." His eyes sharpened as he studied her. "Surely there's some task you can attend to there. You look in need of a brush, some hairpins yourself."

She nearly squirmed at his blunt assessment. Putting a hand to her wayward mane, she touched a loose spiral as it fell to her waist. Somehow, in the midst of milking and tending the animals that morning, she'd lost her hair ribbon. She began to back up, forgetting her wood, feeling hot as the fire she would soon stoke.

Amusement rode his features. "I've ne'er seen a lass so aflocht."

Aflocht? Her brow furrowed. Flustered? Excited? Harried?

That was certainly how she felt in his presence. "I'm going to fetch you a razor," she whispered. "But first I must tend to my hair."

His solemn mouth quirked in a half-smile. He *was* teasing, then. She felt a swelling relief.

"Mind your wood," he told her gruffly, settling a load of oak in her arms before returning to the smithy.

She watched him go, fascination gnawing a hole inside her. One moment he was friendly, the next aloof. There were two Silas Ballantynes, and she never knew which she'd encounter—though she knew which she liked best.

Now, pondering their exchange of days before, she mulled his request for a razor. Likely he thought she'd forgotten. She wanted to help, but she'd not go to York. She hadn't been to the village in two years or better. Papa was unpopular there, and Elspeth's antics gave rise to gossip. Eden had witnessed the cold stares of the shopkeepers, felt the snubs of village women despite her best efforts to be friendly. Nay, she'd not go to York, not even for Silas, though she did feel she owed him for minding her wood.

Drawing back her hood, she let a few swirling snowflakes light on her hair and face as she walked. The gate to Hope Rising was but half a mile. No wagon or horse had passed this way for some time to turn the snow to slush and mud. All was pure. Sabbath-holy. With most of the tenants hunkered down for the winter and the Greathouses in the city, the grand old house was lonesome indeed.

She could smell the tea cakes Margaret Hunter made, their spicy scent swept along by the breath of the wind. Cinnamon. Nutmeg. A pinch of allspice. Her stomach cramped in anticipation. She was running now despite the snow-slick lane, free of her burdens for an hour, perhaps two. Margaret's beloved quarters were by the kitchen garden and consisted of a little brick cottage with a gabled roof, much like Hope Rising, only in miniature.

When small, she and David and the Greathouse girls had had a heyday here. The surrounding woods, the ivy-drenched dovecote, the icehouse, chill and echoing, had been their playground. Mama had brought cheese and honey to Hope Rising then, taking tea with Margaret Hunter, for they were the best of friends. Strangely, Elspeth was missing from these memories. She'd been helping Papa in the smithy, Eden guessed. She rarely came then, or now.

As she knocked on the familiar door, Eden recalled her awe at the great house as a child. Over time it had shrunk in size and become what it was—a small, English-style manor, somewhat fading in its grandeur. How many years had she stood here like this, waiting for Margaret to answer? Not many more, if she had her way. Mere weeks, perhaps, till she'd see Philadelphia.

"Lord be praised! I didn't think to see thee this Sabbath, Eden. Not with all the doings at thy place." Squinting from the snow's glare, spectacles perched primly on her nose, Margaret Hunter opened the door wide, gray silken skirts rustling. Eden's eye was drawn to the chatelaine attached to her bodice, its delicate silver chains dangling with various keys, tiny scissors, and a pocket watch. Margaret was pragmatic, if nothing else.

"I smelled thy cakes clear down the lane," Eden teased. "A blizzard couldn't have kept me away."

"Come in," Margaret said with a flurry of her hand. "Shed thy boots and we'll take our tea by the fire. I want to hear about the new babe. Thee certainly have a busy household of late."

Eden nodded, her high mood plummeting at the mention of little Jon. "The babe is named after Grandfather Gallatin. He's a wee, sweet thing."

"Whom does he favor? Thy mother or thy father?"

Neither.

Avoiding Margaret's eyes, she kept her tone light. "His hair is fair, if he has hair at all, and his eyes are blue."

"All babies have blue eyes, seems to me, though I had none of my own. And his lungs—are they strong?"

Eden withheld a yawn. "He sleeps all day and howls all night. I'm afraid none of us, including the apprentice, are getting much sleep." Though he'd never complained, she'd noticed the weary lines in Silas's face and feared what they meant. He needed all his wits to face her father in the smithy. Sending up a silent prayer on his behalf, she peeled off her cape and sat in her usual chair, spreading her skirts about her so her damp hem would dry.

"He's new to the world yet," Margaret said. "Likely he'll adjust to life outside the womb in time."

As she poured tea, Eden swept the plaster walls in a glance, eyeing the new window coverings she'd not noticed last time. The red checks dressed up the small parlor and gave it a summery feel, far preferable to the black window dressing that signified Margaret's extended mourning. She'd been widowed two years.

"So thy apprentice has come."

At her wording, Eden nearly winced. She looked down at her steaming tea, forgetting to take cream and sugar. "His name is Silas Ballantyne—and he's Elspeth's, not mine."

Now what had made her say that? she wondered. And why was there a note of lament in her voice?

Kind, amber eyes regarded her thoughtfully. "So thy father is going to hold with tradition and arrange the marriage? Between thy sister and this Silas?"

"Papa is very determined." Eden reached for a tea cake still warm in the basket. "Elspeth is aware of the situation. I fear the apprentice is not. He's been here but a month. There's been no courting as of yet. Elspeth is recuperating."

"Ah yes, the besetting illness." Sitting back in her chair, Margaret looked more somber than Eden had ever seen her. "And what if the apprentice favors thee and not thy sister?"

"I . . ." She hadn't considered this. Why would he? Elspeth was the comely one, the clever one. "Well, Elspeth is the eldest . . ."

And Elspeth always gets her way.

"Do thee favor anyone, dear Eden?"

"Me?" Suddenly the fire seemed too warm. The tea burnt her tongue. "Nay," she sputtered and nearly choked, the tea cake finally going down. "I simply feel sorry for apprentices bound by tradition."

Margaret nodded thoughtfully. "Where does this young man hail from?"

"Scotland." She struggled beneath Margaret's gaze, afraid she'd given the wrong impression. Did Margaret think she was smitten? Coveting Silas as her own? Best pick her words carefully. "He's been in America since before the war. But he rarely speaks of it. He's simply a poor tradesman." *Though he has a fine fiddle . . . a gun . . . some leather-bound books.* Bending low, Eden searched in her basket as if groping for safer ground. "I'm anxious to learn how the tenants are faring. And I've brought you some cheese curds and a little something I made."

As Margaret exclaimed over the offerings, Eden arranged her sewing discreetly on her lap. Usually she brought hand-work—a bit of embroidery or lace to bestow on Margaret or leave for one of the tenants, some sachet from the rose petals and lavender harvested from her garden. Something feminine—not this.

"What are thee working on today?" Margaret's brows peaked in curiosity. "A man's shirt?"

73

"Yes," Eden confessed. "Papa owes the apprentice a set of clothes per his contract. I lack but one sleeve." Truly, Silas was in dire need of a new shirt—and a shave. His entreaty by the woodpile returned to her, made the heat climb to her cheeks again as she bespoke her strange request. "Might you have a . . . razor?"

Margaret looked up from her steaming cup, surprise enlivening her plain features. "Is that in thy contract too?"

"Nay." Eden gave her a sheepish half-smile. "But Silas is sorely in need of such."

"Well then, I seem to remember that my Miles had a shaving kit."

"Please, I didn't mean—"

"Now, Eden, what need of a razor has he in heaven?" At this, she disappeared into a bedchamber, returning with far more than Eden had hoped for. "The blade stands a good sharpening, but all seems to be in order."

The Sheffield steel kit was encased in leather and bore a brush, a straight razor, and a small mirror. Gratitude suffused every part of her. "Bethankit," she uttered without forethought.

"Bethankit?" Margaret adjusted her spectacles, a slow smile dawning. "What means thee?"

"I—I think it means thank you but I'm not sure." Slipping the shaving kit into her basket, Eden resumed sewing, the needle's point grazing her palm and making her grimace. "'Tis something the apprentice says at meals. He says little, actually, so 'tis easily remembered."

Taking a sip of tea, Margaret watched her ply tiny, even stitches. "This Scotsman, despite being a man of few words, seems to have made quite an impression."

Eden feared it was a lasting one. "He's different than any man I've met. Granted, I've not met many . . ." She was rambling now, trying to put into words the impossible. Quiet Margaret, given to confidences, had a quality that drew Eden out, made her confess things she dared not give voice to anywhere else. Things that Elspeth would laugh at and Mama had no time for. "I think," she ventured, exposing the hope in her heart, "that he may be a believer."

"A believer?" Across from her, Margaret poured more tea—rich oolong, banished during the war, and only recently returned to York. "Thee must bring Silas to Hope Rising some Sabbath. I'd like to meet him."

The pleasure Eden felt at the invitation lasted but a second. Could she? Without throwing the whole household into a spin? He was Elspeth's intended, not hers. All would look askance at the invitation, even Silas himself. She was never quite sure of him. He ignored her most times, rebuked her for bringing him wood, loaned her books, then waylaid her and begged a razor . . .

Examining the banded collar, she tied off a length of thread, wondering if Margaret was lonely and seeking company, thus the invitation. But loneliness, she knew, was an elusive notion. Wasn't she more lonesome in the midst of her busy household than anywhere else on earth?

"'Tis quiet here without the Greathouses," Eden murmured, hoping to change the current of conversation.

Margaret moved the lamp closer. "David will be back soon for the ice harvest, and then 'twill be spring. He and Dennis Hastings, the new overseer, are expecting a large flock of sheep. Now that the war's won, the English cannot restrict wool as they once did. Then there's all the plowing and planting to see about. I'll be airing out the house shortly and making ready for the girls' return."

The news buoyed Eden's spirits. She missed the Greathouses when they were away, especially Jemma, though it was Beatrice, the eldest sister, who'd taken part in Eden's scheme. Not even Margaret knew what they were planning. Eden felt a sudden qualm, but now was hardly the time to be confiding anything. Best wait till the plan was firmly in place. Margaret would be pleased, if surprised, to learn her destination involved the Society of Friends.

For an hour or better they talked in low tones, sipping their tea and sewing. Intent on finishing the shirt, her back to the window, Eden was unaware that it was snowing harder, the sky darkening like dusk instead of noon. The pealing of distant church bells made her finish her stitching with haste.

"Thank you for the tea—and company," she said. "Perhaps the weather will clear next First Day and we can visit the tenants."

With that, she fairly flew down the cold lane, the snow obscuring her view of the meadow and pond. Turning, she took a last hungry look, but her gaze caught on the small, stone church atop the hill. It overlooked Hope Rising like a sentinel, a beacon. Here dissenters gathered to worship as they wished, without the Church of England's interference.

She knew little about them but wanted to join them— wanted to sing their songs and hymns and have her soul stirred by their preaching. Listening to the bells each Sabbath was poor recompense. Even now her heart twisted with longing as she heard the echo of their music and imagined how the church might look crowded with worshipers.

As the last bell sounded, Eden turned down the humble lane toward home, trying to shrug aside the sadness that descended each and every Sabbath as she did so, preparing herself for whatever upheaval awaited inside.

Thank You, Lord, that Hope Rising is a rest for me, and You've provided both shaving kit and shirt.

She reminded him of a sith—a fairy—Silas thought, not so much in looks but in manner. Nae, he didn't believe in such, but he'd been so long steeped in Scots lore he knew the signs. In her scarlet cape, with her hair spilling down and touched by snow, he stood spellbound near the garret window as she came down the winding lane. With a basket on her arm, she seemed to dance rather than walk. The music of the kirk bells sounding in the distance only lent enchantment to the scene.

Sitting down on the bed lest she look up and see his gawking, he ran a hand over his beard and rebuked himself for feeling elf-shot. Watching her, wondering where she'd been and if she'd remembered his razor, he fought the tight feeling in his chest, almost believing he'd succumbed to the sickness thought to be caused by fairies. It didn't help that she hadn't minded her hair like he'd prompted. With it unpinned, every tress a silken tangle, she all but begged to be paid attention to.

He could hear the careful closing of the front door, sense her soft tread on the landing. The house was suddenly still. Even the babe had stopped crying. With every step she took, his pulse seemed to climb along with her. And then he heard . . . nothing. Was she trying to tiptoe? Avoid him? The thought turned him sick inside. He'd seen how she sidestepped everyone in the household as if avoiding a blow. And he'd been as guilty, wanting a wall between himself and all the Lees, brusque with her as he could be.

He pulled open the garret door. She hovered five steps down, cheeks crimson from the cold, her unbound hair glistening with melted snow. Between them lay a leather case and a bundle of linen on a smooth step. He reached for it just as she did and felt the warmth of her fingers graze his hand.

"I—" she began.

"You—" he said in tandem.

"Remembered," they finished together.

Holding the leather case in one hand, he unfurled the linen with the other, surprise riffling through him. Made in the prevailing style, the shirt was full cut, with a banded collar and dropped shoulders. He could see that the work was well done, the cloth fine. Spun on her own wheel, no doubt.

"The shaving kit is from Hope Rising. I made you the shirt, but I hurried so." Her tone, her expression, were sweetly apologetic. "The stitching is not very fine."

"Not fine?" His tone begged to differ. "I need nothing fancy."

She looked down at her empty hands, to the cut that bore a rosy scar. "Papa was to give you a suit of clothes per the terms of your contract. I've not enough cloth to make a weskit or breeches. Not yet."

"I need little, ye ken. Just a roof o'er my head and enough food to stem the gnaw of hunger."

She brightened, reminding him of a child eager to please. "I could knit you a hat, some stockings. Our winters are very cold—"

"Nae." As soon as he said it, he felt a tug of regret. Her lovely face grew pinched. Gentling his tone, he added, "You can ill afford more work."

Her chin lifted. "'Tis my way to do such things. If it's not your shirt I'll be sewing or your stockings I'll be knitting, 'twill be someone else's."

The softly spoken words put him in his place. "I'm in your debt." He shifted in the doorway, suddenly at sea. "D'ye have need of anything? I could make you a ladle, some tongs for the kitchen. A cowbell or two."

"Might you have another book?"

"How goes the Thomson?" he asked, remembering the poems he'd lent her.

She smiled, the dimple in her cheek deepening. "Fareweel,

ye bughts, an' all your ewes, / An' fields whare bloomin' heather grows."

Her Scots was so charmingly mangled he couldn't check a grin. "Here's another you might like." He stepped back into his room and produced a worn copy of brown leather. "I've but three more, other than the Buik."

"The Buik?" she echoed, taking the offering.

"The Bible."

Something so poignant passed over her face at his answer, he found himself nearly holding his breath. She asked quietly, "Might I have that instead?"

He hesitated. "You have no family Bible?"

The answer was in her eyes before it reached her lips. "Nay, no Bible . . . no Buik."

He'd suspected the Lees had no Holy Writ, just as they said no prayers. And he sensed he'd erred in his asking, as she was turning the color of her red cape. "Mine is in Erse—Gaelic—or I'd give it to you straightaway."

Her eyes filled with tears. His gut twisted. That she was thirsty for heavenly things, there could be no doubt. He'd oft felt the same so understood her need. Yet he had needs of his own. And he needed to distance himself, starting now . . .

"Might you . . . read it to me?" she queried.

Heat climbed up his neck. "'Tis a big book."

She looked away and he saw her disappointment.

"Aye, I will," he said. "But when—where?"

When she glanced up at him again, her face held a rare resolve. "Here in the stairwell. I don't know when. Soon. For now I must see to noonday dinner."

With that, she started down the steps. He watched her go, wanting to change his mind, call her back. The weight of what he'd just committed to, simple as it seemed, nearly made him groan. 'Twould be easier to simply attend kirk, he reasoned, thinking of the stone church atop the hill. He could see it now in the distance, had watched a few faithful congregants emerge despite the sullen weather a half hour before.

He wanted no complications, no romantic entanglements. If Elspeth had asked him, he would have questioned her motives. There was a slyness about her, a cunning, that was entirely absent in Eden. Aye, Eden was cut of a different cloth. With Eden, her hunger was for the Word, not him. Not time spent with him. And she was willing to risk her father's ire—for ire it would surely be—to get the spiritual sustenance she craved. Who was Silas to deny her?

A snatch of a Gaelic Psalm wended its way through his tangled thoughts.

> My God with His lovingkindness shall come to meet
> me at every corner.

Even in a stairwell.

8

Books, like friends, should be few and well-chosen.

SAMUEL JOHNSON

In her bedchamber, Elspeth struggled with the pair of front-lacing stays Mama had made her, allowing for her added girth. Swiping at a tear with a cold hand, she cinched herself tighter than common sense allowed, ending with a knot at waist level. Her full bosom seemed to shudder with the effort, and the bone points sharpened and pricked her skin. But naught was as painful as the thought of Eden's slim yet full-bosomed figure. So girlishly fetching. So unsullied. Envy rose up and snatched away what little sweetness she'd felt upon awakening.

"Coveting always makes one poor," Mama said. But this did little to assuage Elspeth's hurt. She supposed she'd have to starve herself to regain the fine figure the babe had ruined, while Eden, uncaring and unkempt with her hair and person, drew the eye of one too many men. Expelling a sigh, she eased Eden's best dress on, waiting for the sound of straining seams.

Betimes she wished she'd not dallied with fire as she'd done.

81

If anyone discovered who had sired Jon, what a ruckus would be raised! She'd thought to use the child to her advantage but didn't know how it could be done. If the facts became known, Mama's perpetual melancholy would deepen and Papa's shaky reputation would be a shambles. Likely Eden would never marry, and Thomas and Jon would be cast in disrepute as well. She doubted Jon's father would own up to the transgression even if she did.

She turned to look in the mirror a final time as Mama's voice climbed the stairwell, calling her to breakfast. Time to put her plan in place. Oh, how she hoped Silas would be at table. After a near-fatal misstep with little Jon, she hoped to make a better way and must tread carefully.

⌒⌒

Despite her father's insistence that the Sabbath was no different than any other day, Eden strove to honor its significance, if only subtly. "Honor the Sabbath and keep it holy," said the embroidered plaque hanging in one of the tenants' cottages. She had pondered it during a number of Sabbath visits, and it seemed engraved upon her heart and now guided her hands as she set out Staffordshire plates and utensils atop the blue-and-white-checked tablecloth.

The simple act set her aglow with quiet joy. If it felt pleasing to her, was it honoring to God? Did He care about such simple things? She crossed to the corner cupboard and took two bayberry tapers from a candle box. Even with the snow's brilliance, the windows were narrow and the room was winter-dark. As she set the tapers in pewter holders, she sensed she wasn't alone. Behind her, Elspeth stood in the dining room doorway, on her feet again after a morning spent in bed. And she had on . . . the yellow silk. Immediately all the light left Eden's soul.

"Why are you taking such pains at table?" Elspeth asked,

disdain marring her features. "Bayberry candles? 'Tis not Christmastide! Papa will have a fit!"

Why are you taking such pains with your appearance? Eden wondered. But she simply said, "I thought . . . perhaps . . ."

"You aren't smitten with the apprentice, are you? Thinking he might find you more attractive by candlelight?"

What? The mere suggestion pinched her with panic. Eden darted a look toward the doorway, fearing someone might hear. "I merely meant to brighten the room."

Elspeth took the tapers from her, voice chilly. "Mama needs you in the kitchen."

Sensing a confrontation brewing, Eden left the dining room. Though dismayed by Elspeth's wearing her dress, she was more embarrassed. The lovely silk was hopelessly out of place. 'Twas fit for a dance—a day in Philadelphia—not a simple Sabbath dinner. But Elspeth had ever liked making a spectacle of herself. There was little doubt left in Eden's mind that her sister was fully recovered, found Silas to her liking, and was now in outright pursuit.

"Come, Eden, and slice the bread." Mama barely looked up as she stirred butter into a mound of turnips. "We're a bit tardy. You know your father likes his meals on time."

Eden surveyed all that Elspeth had left—potatoes unmashed, beets unseasoned, gravy in need of thickening—as her mother took a roast from the turnstile spit.

"Your sister tires so easily—and I don't want her dress spoiled," Mama continued. "Carry everything to the table and then I'll call your father."

Biting her lip and slicing the bread so hastily she nearly reinjured her hand, Eden tried to make peace with her mother's comment. So the dress was now Elspeth's.

Care not for earthly things, but dwell on the heavenly.

The Quaker saying brought some solace, but her girlish

heart held on to the dress. Yet what need had she of such garb in Philadelphia? Soon she'd be clad in dove gray and white. Let Elspeth have her way. She, Eden Rose Lee, would rise above such things.

Gravy bowl in one hand and bread basket in the other, she backtracked to the dining room—and then wished she hadn't. Elspeth stood by the hearth with a much-changed Silas Ballantyne. He wore the linen shirt she'd made him and was shockingly clean-shaven. One look at him—at them—and she nearly dropped both gravy and bread. Elspeth was staring up at him so coyly, so fetching in her yellow silk, that Eden felt reduced to rags.

They'd been talking in low tones but ceased when she entered. Though Elspeth paid her scant attention, she saw Silas glance her way as she retreated to the kitchen. In and out of the dining room she went, hardly aware of setting the steaming dishes on the table. The aroma of noonday dinner turned a stomach already too full of Margaret's tea cakes nearly nauseous. 'Twas as if her sister had ground her heart beneath her heel.

Slowly she removed her apron and hung it from a peg by the hearth. "Mama, I'm not feeling well. I'd best lie down."

"Are you ill, Eden?" Mama studied her, pale eyes touched by concern.

"I don't know what I am," Eden answered as honestly as she dared.

Just heartsick. Over a foolish dress . . . and a clean-shaven man in a linen shirt.

"Well, be so good as to take a peek at Thomas and the babe on your way," she replied as Eden moved toward the door. "They're napping in our bedchamber, or should be."

Leaving out the door that led from the kitchen to the hall, Eden did as she bid. Little Jon, swaddled and snug in his cradle, slept while Thomas tossed fitfully atop his trundle bed. Thinking him cold, she covered him with a quilt before climbing the stairs to her and Elspeth's room, her spirits slowly lightening. Perhaps she should shun meals more often. By declining dinner she realized she'd moved straight to dessert—a coveted piece of privacy.

The thought quickened her steps and soon had her planted in the narrow window seat between their beds, Silas's book in hand. Though he'd slipped it to her in the stairwell a week ago, she'd only had time to peruse the title: *Travels and Adventures in Western Pennsylvania and the Indian Territories* by Alexander Henry. This time there were no mysterious words on the flyleaf to distract her or fill her head with romantic notions. She plunged into the dog-eared pages as if they could ease her raw feelings, alert to Elspeth's step. It came far sooner than expected.

Quickly Eden wedged the book between the feather bolster and rope springs of her narrow bed, then lay down and pretended to sleep. But the forceful shutting of the door signaled her sister's displeasure, and she opened an eye to see Elspeth tugging at the buttery silk, preparing to leave it in a careless puddle on the floor like she always did her things.

"Sister, we must talk." Clearly exasperated, she leaned over Eden. "And you simply must help me out of this dress!"

Getting up, Eden helped wrestle the too-snug silk off her, waiting for Elspeth to fill the silence. Eden sensed her frustration—and felt a bite of warning—before she'd uttered a single word.

"Is there something the matter with Silas Ballantyne's eyesight? Have you seen spectacles on his person?"

"No . . . why?" Eden ventured warily.

"He seems not to notice the things most men take notice of." Pursing her lips in contemplation, her fingers plucked at her new stays. "Have you noticed *that* particularity about him?"

"He does seem . . . different," Eden said carefully. "I cannot account for it."

"Perhaps . . ." Elspeth looked wildly about the room as if searching for answers. "Perhaps he has a sweetheart. Has he mentioned such to you?"

The question turned Eden queasy. A sweetheart? Not once had she considered this. "I've . . . hardly spoken with him." *Oh, Lord, forgive the lie!* "He's made no mention of such."

"There must be someone else. I want you to find out."

"Me? But—"

"You know how important this is to Papa, to have a second man at the forge. Business would double and we'd all benefit—have finer things." Elspeth paused and took a breath. "Besides, 'tis time for me to marry. Past time. Silas is to my liking and I've told Papa so. I want you to find out why he seems so reluctant—if he loves another."

Eden sat down on the edge of her bed, taken aback. Though used to her sister's edicts, this was too much. "How can I do such a thing?"

Elspeth's sky-blue eyes hardened as they took Eden in. "I don't give a cat's meow how you do it—just do it! Look through his belongings, ask him outright."

"What?"

"He might have a letter—some private papers—in his room. You'll think of something—but you *must* find out."

So Elspeth was demanding she trespass? Search the garret? Eden quailed at the thought. "'Tis Papa's place to delve into such matters."

"I've already spoken with Papa. He doesn't want to seem too forceful. He believes things should develop naturally between us."

Naturally? Through their scheming? And when had their father shied away from forcefulness? A sliver of insight pierced

Eden's disgust. She stared at her sister without focus, a new thought dawning.

Papa is unsure of Silas.

He'd run roughshod over his former apprentices, yet since Silas's coming he'd been far more restrained. True, Silas had been with them only briefly, but Papa's harshness and irascibility had been muted in that time. Perhaps this was simply due to his gout. This last attack had been particularly painful, responding to no remedies and requiring more spirits than usual. Sometimes the more Papa drank, the mellower he became. Lately he seemed almost . . . bearable.

"What is going on in that red head of yours?" Elspeth demanded, studying her with renewed suspicion.

"I'm simply tired," Eden replied truthfully, yet even as she spoke she was pulling herself to her feet and smoothing the counterpane, thinking of Mama alone in the kitchen. Below, the babe had resumed his crying, but Elspeth seemed not to notice—or care—and was already curling up on her own bed.

Swallowing down a rebuke, Eden turned and hurried downstairs, finding Thomas wailing louder than Jon. Gathering up both of them, she sank onto the rag rug before the bedchamber hearth and tried to shush them. Remembering the tea cake in her pocket, she fished it out for Thomas, who immediately crammed the crumbling remains into his mouth. He was simply hungry, she guessed, as was Jon.

Nestling Jon nearer, she drank in his flawless features. Oh, but he was a beautiful child—pale and plump, his alert blue eyes catching at her heart. Well-fed he was, if not wanted. To think that she, Eden Lee, might soon be in a place surrounded by such foundlings . . .

The thought wrung her heart. Babies left on doorsteps or in dark alleys. Unwanted. Unloved. Without father or mother. The stories the Greathouse sisters told her about the foundling hospital haunted, invading her dreams at night and shadowing her by day.

Oh, Lord, hasten me to Philadelphia.

⁂

Lying on his bed in the inky darkness at the end of another long week, Silas willed his thoughts to stay quiet. But they were as unsettled as dust devils, stirred into a tempest by a great many things. Elspeth's flirting. Liege's gruffness. A forge that needed ten men, not two. A household in silent turmoil for reasons he couldn't account for . . .

Eden's absence.

"Where is she?" Liege had demanded prior to noonday dinner, staring at her empty chair as if he could conjure her up and place her there.

"She's out visiting," Mrs. Lee murmured, taking a seat.

"I suppose she's consorting with that Quaker widow again." Liege glared at Mrs. Lee, countenance livid. "Let me guess, the Greathouses are gone and she's taken it upon herself to go comforting the tenants in their stead."

"She had a basket to deliver to Widow Baker. Some buns for the McAfee children—"

"Baskets and buns, indeed." Elspeth looked up from arranging her napkin in her lap, a smug smile twisting her lips. "She's been skulking about so lately, I suspect she has a lover out there somewh—"

"Elspeth Ann!"

It was the first time Silas had ever heard Mrs. Lee speak above a whisper. The table stilled, all eyes fixed on Elspeth, who didn't so much as flinch or blush, though she did lower her voice a tad. "'Tis the truth, Mama. Best keep an eye on Eden. These mercy missions of hers are occurring far too often. I wouldn't be surprised if she does have a suitor among Hope Rising's tenants."

Silas swallowed down a retort in Eden's defense. At the far end of the table, Liege said nothing and simply surveyed the overflowing dishes before yanking his chair out to sit down. An awkward moment passed as Silas waited for the prayer that wouldn't be uttered. The master was simply letting the rule of silence descend before reaching for the nearest serving dish.

Now, turning toward the flickering Franklin stove, Silas shifted on the feather tick, eyes closing then roaming the beams overhead restlessly. Though he'd once thought Eden meek, his opinion of her was altering. In her own quiet way she was defiant, risking her father's ire in an effort to be of service, with little sympathy from the rest of the household, just accusations and insinuations . . .

Losh! He might have been lying atop a bed of nails he was so aflocht.

Below he heard the gentle opening and closing of a door. Pushing himself up on his elbows, he waited. Would she come to him now? In the stairwell? Wanting to read Scripture with him? Extricating himself from the blankets, he swung his feet to the frigid floor and grabbed his breeches. The wool felt rough to his calloused hand, reminding him he needed a new pair. But the shirt she'd made him was downy soft and held her unmistakable fragrance—a subtle smirr of lavender. It set his senses afire for all the wrong reasons.

The garret door opened without protest—he'd oiled the hinges to ensure it would. But the stairwell was black as iron and held no hint of a welcoming candle. He expelled his breath, yet his chest clenched harder. Elspeth's words at table returned and nearly made him groan.

She's been skulking about so lately, I suspect she has a lover out there somewhere.

Did she? Nae.

But Elspeth, with her flindriken ways? Aye.

9

Ask no questions and hear no lies.

ENGLISH PROVERB

"Come now, daughters! 'Tis nearly time for the weaver and there's much to be done!" Mama's voice rang out with unusual vigor, her arms full of skeins of thread spun on Eden's beloved wheel, her careworn face alive with the anticipation of a skillfully wrought coverlet or tablecloth. Of all the chores and tasks they tended to, none was as welcome as the weaver's coming, at least to Louise Lee.

The previous autumn Eden had finished dyeing the hanks of wool that would be woven, hanging them from the garret rafters to dry. The dyeing shed behind the barn still reeked of indigo and butternut, but within a fortnight the laborious task was done, her hands and apron no longer stained.

'Twas February, Eden recalled with a little start, the month that signaled winter's end. Once the weaver arrived, they'd hear naught but the loud clacking of the loom, a giant beast of wood and rope that erupted endlessly when Mr. Lackey was in residence. Except Mr. Lackey, old and infirm, wasn't coming, but was sending his son, Isaac, in his stead.

Eden saw the light in Elspeth's eyes when Mama announced the news and told them to make ready, and her stomach gave a little flip of alarm. Her sister was bored—restless—and had recovered her feistiness. Eden feared it as she did her father's wrath. Though Elspeth was smitten with Silas, might she use the weaver to force Silas's hand? Stir up a bit of jealousy? She'd done such things before, pitting poor George White against one of the York men . . .

"The forge is quite busy today, and your father has no time for the animals." Mama studied both her daughters as if weighing her options. "'Twould be best if you, Eden, minded the barn while Elspeth prepares the weaving room."

It was a task Elspeth often usurped, knowing how Eden loved to make ready. Hiding her disappointment, Eden turned away but didn't miss the smirk on Elspeth's face. Though Mama was still giving her sister light duties, Eden didn't mind. She found solace in the barn and the earthiness of every crevice and corner—the welcome nickering of the horses, the lowing of the cows, the silly antics of the half-wild cats. Let Elspeth gloat all she liked. Soon Eden would be leaving for a greater work, a more meaningful existence.

She went out the back door, shivering in the cold despite her cape and heaviest wool dress. The heavy snow of more than a month ago—the one that had ushered Silas into their lives—had melted, making a muddy mess of the normally neat farmyard. To reach the barn she had to pass by the smithy. Its front door was open wide, and several unfamiliar horses were hitched to the railing just beyond. Busy, indeed.

"Eden!" Papa's voice rang out amidst the incessant hammering inside, hardly audible above the din that had cost him much of his hearing by middle age.

She came closer till she stood in the doorway, eyes adjusting to the smoky light within. Papa was near the bellows with several York merchants while Silas stood at the forge, heating an iron bar. Seizing it with his tongs, he swung the glowing rectangle across the chisel before cutting it neatly in half with two hammer blows. Eden flinched and felt her mouth go slack. She'd witnessed such countless times, but never had Papa made such short work of it. Yet he was, she reminded herself, aging and gout-ridden, whereas Silas was hale, hearty . . .

And so handsome it hurt.

Seemingly unaware of her, he began to hammer the hot iron into the necessary shape, his attention fixed on his task, the forge's fire turning his hair damp at the temples. He wore an old linen shirt, not the new one she'd made him, and a leather apron hugged his waist. The look of his worn wool breeches and scuffed boots tugged at her, a reminder that all his worldly possessions had fit into two small, if heavy, haversacks. Every lean, muscular line of him drew her notice, but it was the smudge of coal dust on his cheek that rent her heart. It turned him boyish. A bit vulnerable. More a victim of Papa's scheming.

Truly, Silas looked strangely out of place in their humble shop. Just why this was so Eden didn't know, yet across the hay-strewn space she sensed he didn't want to be here, that while his hands bent iron, his heart and soul were far away. And she felt a desperate need to know where his thoughts took him, for she'd so often felt the same, confined to this stifling place.

Papa, still in conversation with the men, reached out and pulled the iron ring of the bellows that fed the flames. The great brick fire pit glowed a deep burnt orange, so intense she felt its heat clear to the door. When small, she'd been terrified of the bellows. Big as an ox and fashioned from its hide, the bellows expelled air like some hungry, half-crazed beast. She fancied she felt the breath of it even now and shied from the exploding sparks.

92

Casting a glance her way, Papa raised his voice. "Daughter, bring Half-Penny in to shoe. Silas will meet you in the back."

Hiding her surprise, she nodded, wishing she could run back to the house and mind her hair. She'd not even brushed it this morning, just bundled it like a shock of wheat and tied it with a blue ribbon. A riot of tangles it was, spilling to the small of her back, red as the forge's fire. Since Silas had rebuked her, she'd been more mindful of how she looked. But today, busy as he was, he'd likely not notice.

Into the barn she went, past the plow that was Papa's pride, breathing in the scent of the hay stacked nearly to the rafters. Conscious of her task, she hurried toward the far stall, humming a little tune to calm her nerves. Horatio and Sparrow eyed her sleepily when she passed. She stopped at a barrel and filled a nosebag with oats. Half-Penny snorted when she slipped a bridle over his head, as if he knew what she had in mind.

"You're to have some new shoes," she announced, looking down at her own mud-spattered boots and thinking of the dainty calamanco slippers Jemma had been wearing when she last saw her. Rather, *trying* to think of shoes, anything other than the man awaiting her back at the smithy. Leading Half-Penny out of the barn, she glanced up and saw Elspeth watching from the weaving room window. Her stern countenance reminded her of her unwelcome mission.

There must be someone else. I want you to find out.

Turning away, Eden rounded the smithy's rear wall and sank ankle-deep in mud, her short skirt hem dragging and darkening to a murky brown. At least Elspeth couldn't see her now.

"Eden." With a nod of his head, Silas greeted her, wiping the sweat from his brow with a rolled-up shirt sleeve. His forearms, even in winter, seemed tan, so well-sculpted and thickly corded she became distracted and forgot to return a greeting. The hands that took hold of the bridle seemed to belong to someone far older, not a man of thirty or less. And then there were his thumbs . . . Sorrow wet her eyes, made her bite her lip to ground herself.

Why must everything pierce her heart?

With nary a glance at her, he moved the big horse into position, running a hand down its sleek, copper-colored back before he took a long look at its hooves. This was Elspeth's moment, Eden remembered. She had only to ask one bold question on her sister's behalf. 'Twas far easier to speak to a bent head than stare straight into his keen eyes, truly. Why then did she feel afraid?

"Silas." She leaned nearer. "Do you . . ." She swallowed hard and felt she might choke. All her practiced words took flight. She couldn't . . . wouldn't . . . But she must.

"Why . . . are your thumbs branded?"

"Why?" His head came up, stark amusement in his eyes. "Wheest, Eden! What about, 'Good morning, Silas,' or 'I'd be pleased if you would shoe my horse,' but 'Why are your thumbs branded?'"

Warmth shot through her—overwhelming, mortifying. She wanted to sink lower than the matted hay beneath her feet. Half-Penny was forgotten now as they faced each other. Asking about a sweetheart would have been far better!

Stricken, she watched him walk away. His broad back was to her now, his capable hands heating and reshaping the right size shoes at the forge. He returned and held Half-Penny's foreleg in place between his knees, fastening the hot shoe to the hoof wall before driving in the nails. Eden wrinkled her nose at the smoke, but the gelding's tail twitched nonchalantly. 'Twas a painless procedure, but one she'd never liked. All she could think of was her own tender feet.

"You—you don't have to answer." Her whisper held abject apology.

He seemed not to hear, lost in his work. When he finally

spoke, his voice was low. "Soon after I came to Philadelphia, I joined the American Army as a courier and was taken captive by the British. An officer ordered me to clean his boots." He let go of the hoof and looked down at his thumbs. "I refused."

She stared at him blankly.

His gaze met hers. "'Tis a punishment the Crown metes out to common criminals, especially Scots. After six months they decided I was more use to them unshackled and set me to mending their muskets." He paused, jaw hardening. "But lest you feel too sorry for me, my brothers fared far worse. Ewan died at the Battle of Stone Ferry. Roland was felled by fever before any hard fighting began."

Pity nicked her. "What of your father and mother?"

"Not here . . . heaven."

Alone, then. "I'm so . . . sorry."

Sorry I asked. Sorry about your grievous losses. Sorry you are here in a situation more prison than apprenticeship.

"So, Eden . . ." As he secured the second shoe, he asked through the hammering and the smoke, "Why were you not at Sabbath dinner?"

Why, indeed. A bold question for a question, she guessed. There was no pretending she hadn't heard. His voice held a cadence as firm as the tool he wielded so well. Only she couldn't tell him she'd gotten a stomachache from one too many tea cakes. Or that the handsome sight of him that day had put fire to her heels and she'd fled . . .

"I was out visiting Hope Rising's tenants. Margaret, the housekeeper, likes me to accompany her. We visit those in need—the sick and grieving. I gave no thought to the hour, to dinner, and took cold."

"I saw you out walking. I thought you'd gone to kirk."

"Kirk?"

"Church."

"I've never been to church," she confessed.

He looked up again, the light of disbelief in his eyes. "No kirk?"

"Papa forbids it." Her voice fell to a whisper. "He's a former Friend, you see. But he was read out of Meeting long ago. For dancing."

"Your father was a Quaker?"

She reached out a hand, her palm brushing the rough wood of the stall as if to ground herself. Never had she spoken so freely with a man—except for David. Nor did she spill family secrets, though this particular tidbit had ceased being the gossip of York County long ago. "You're familiar with the Friends?"

"Aye, I rubbed shoulders with them oft enough in Philadelphia."

Had he? Was he also familiar with the foundling hospital, then? Excitement flared inside her then sputtered. Philadelphia was such a large city, and the hospital, Bea had told her, was on the very outskirts, far from the domain of tradesmen in town. Besides, what interest would a blacksmith have with abandoned babies?

"So your father forbids you from going to Meeting?" His voice pursued her, brought her back to the smoke of the stall and his green eyes. "To the church on the hill?"

She glanced over her shoulder anxiously. "Papa's no fonder of Presbyterians than the Friends."

Setting his tools aside, he looked down at her. "D'ye want to go, Eden?"

She felt a tremor of alarm. What did her wants have to do with it? Papa's word was law. She could only imagine the ruckus that would be raised if she traipsed up the hill. Still, Silas's steady gaze lured her. His invitation was so beguiling, so quietly and enticingly stated, she entertained the notion. Briefly.

He took up his hammer again. "I'm going to attend next Sabbath, should you want to go with me."

With that, he left Half-Penny to her and returned to the forge.

10

Wanton kittens make sober cats.
EIGHTEENTH-CENTURY PROVERB

Elspeth crossed to the rear window of the weaving room, where Eden's spinning wheel stood idle. Hanks of dyed yarn hung from the rafters above her head, awaiting the loom, but she took no notice of anything but Eden returning Half-Penny to the stable. A feeling of satisfaction set in. It had taken little coaxing to convince Papa her sister needed a few minutes alone with Silas. All he had to do was provide an opportunity under the guise of work. Yet watching Eden cross the muddy barnyard, knowing she was timid as a titmouse, Elspeth felt suddenly vexed. Had she even asked Silas the burning question?

She heard Silas at work again, knew it was him by the very tenor of his hammering. Papa's had a less vigorous manner of striking, as if forty years of blacksmithing had worn him down to a rusty nail. Not Silas. His hammering was sure as a church bell, pealing out of the smithy like steady music on a summer day. She hoped he wouldn't grow deaf as a doorpost

97

in time. But if he did, she thought consolingly, he had other charms aplenty.

"Elspeth Ann, have you even begun to work?"

Mama stood in the doorway, a wrinkle marring her brow. The babe was in arm and she was bouncing to quiet him, every shake making her plump figure quiver.

"I've begun," Elspeth said, turning away from the window. "But I'm feeling a bit peckish."

"Why don't you sit and spin what's left of the flax, then? I'll have Eden bring up the wool when she's done in the barn, though I've a mind to call her in now to manage the babe. He's been fed but won't stop his fussing."

Elspeth came closer and looked down at the red-faced, squirming infant and tried to keep her distaste from her face. If he was sweet-tempered, she might take to him more readily. But the truth was she'd never been fond of children, not even Thomas, so she wasn't surprised when her own son left her cold.

"I think the only thing Eden's not afraid of is a screaming baby," she said, taking a step back.

Mama bounced harder. "She's always had a way with children and animals, like you have a head for business."

"I'll fetch her from the barn," Elspeth offered, as anxious to see how her sister had fared with Silas as to be free of Jon's fussing.

She waited till Mama went below before preening at the looking glass in her room. A few brushstrokes of her hair, a pinch to her cheeks, a broach pinned to her bodice, and she was nearly done. Poking about on Eden's side of the dresser led to her coveted orange water beneath several layers of petticoats. She wrinkled her nose. More of Jemma's cast-offs. Holding up the slim glass vial, she applied the scent liberally. Like the yellow silk dress, the cologne was rich, enticing. Far more her scent than Eden's.

Her simple day gown would suffice. Made of heavy corded linen, the horizontal blue stripes were the hue of her eyes and enhanced every nuance of her full figure. Turning before the looking glass, she nearly forgot her mission. Silas might be immune to her charms thus far, but the weaver's son had collapsed like a spent sack of wool at her attentions last winter.

"You *didn't?*" Elspeth tried to school her ire, but Eden was proving so exasperatingly dense—and she was so irate herself—that her tone had turned blistering.

Eden looked up from the hay she was shoveling into a feeding trough, pausing long enough to lean on her pitchfork. "Silas is not a man to be asked such questions."

"Oh? I beg to differ." Looking over her shoulder to make sure no one was lurking, she hissed, "If you don't ask him, I'll tell Papa you're up to no good at Hope Rising, that your so-called Sabbath outings are naught but a ruse to dally with a man."

The threat found purchase. She saw the hurt in Eden's eyes, sensed her dismay, felt a twist of guilt that she'd already planted a seed of suspicion.

Eden's voice shook with suppressed emotion. "You know I help Margaret see to the tenants—"

"So you say. Papa hates your association with that Quaker woman, your handouts. He only allows it to curry favor with the Greathouses." Folding her arms, she continued in low tones, "How many times must you be told? Papa and Mama want to see me wed. A partner is needed at the forge. At last we have someone who suits Papa—and myself. Not only can Silas fashion anything out of iron in half the time, he's a skilled gunsmith and engraver besides . . ." Her voice trailed off as the barn door creaked in the wind.

Eden resumed her haying, clearly downcast but far from obliging. Irritation rising, Elspeth moved to stand between her and her work. "You simply must play your part. I'll give you till week's end to ask Silas your question." She turned on her heel, remembering the babe at the last. Swinging back around, she planted her hands on her hips. "You'd best finish up here. Mama needs help with little Jon. He won't settle."

Eden resumed her work, expression now placid as the meadow's pond.

"Till week's end," Elspeth hissed again, satisfied when her words brought about the wince she wanted.

<hr />

The scent of oranges, so exotic it reminded Silas of tales he'd heard of the Caribbean, wrapped round him like a woman's arms. Distracted from the metal inlay he was working on a gun plate, he leaned into the trestle table and set his tools aside. Behind him, Elspeth stood, perusing ledgers and occasionally marking something with a quill and ink.

Near the bellows, Liege was talking with several customers, mostly farmers and tradesmen. Silas was beginning to learn their stout frames and bearded faces. Most were German with dense-sounding names. Brunner. Kaufmann. Hofstettler. Schmidt. These men formed the backbone of York County. And lately they'd come trooping into the smithy to watch him work, ordering iron that was both costly and complicated, as if trying to test his skill.

"Silas."

He turned at the honeyed tone, wariness clutching him. The scent of oranges grew stronger. The forge's fire felt overwarm. Elspeth was looking up at him in that beguiling way she had, and he felt the pull of it clear to his bones.

"How much trim did you finish for the dower house Mr. Becker is building?"

Without effort he recited, "Twenty-six hinges and latches, a dozen shutter bolts, four tongs, six andirons, two pokers, one hundred fifty-six nails." He well knew the total—the man had been so exacting he'd had to check his work repeatedly as he'd loaded the order into the wagon.

"I wonder why I keep accounts, your memory is so fine," she said with a little smile, dipping her quill into an inkwell.

Aware Liege was watching, Silas removed his leather apron without comment and hung it from a nail, then passed to the water bucket and took a long drink. He had to deliver some iron to Elkhannah after the midday meal and was only too glad to leave the stifling confines of the forge and get a bracing breath of air. Still, he wished he could go by horseback and not wagon. Horatio was in desperate need of a run. Though Eden and Liege took prime care of all the animals, his gelding was becoming barn sour and was loath to leave his stall.

"Daughter, bring me the ledgers."

Silas felt Elspeth follow his every move before doing her father's bidding, even sensed her disappointment as he turned away. She wanted him to tarry—had been baiting him to talk for half an hour or better—but he left the smithy without a word and passed through the half-finished arbor, pausing to gather a load of firewood.

Pushing open the kitchen door, he found a scene he was all too familiar with—the babe squalling in his cradle, Thomas strewing blocks and toy soldiers wherever he toddled, an apron-clad Eden at the hearth, face flushed the hue of her hair. Though the door banged shut in his wake, she didn't so much as glance up at him.

Dumping the wood into a box by the door, he stepped round her and fed the fire a few chunks of oak. Her head was bent as she stirred a fragrant skillet of fried apples, and he spied a wisp of hay in the long ringlets that fell like fire to her waist. He plucked it free without her knowing and tossed it into the hearth. As his hand fell away, he was besieged by a startling thought.

That this was their kitchen and Eden was . . . his.

Warmth suffused his face. So distracted, he failed to see Thomas toddle to the table and pull a colander off its edge, spilling dried beans in every direction.

Wheest! Harnessing his temper, he scooped the lad up with one arm and set him in an empty copper cauldron before picking up the crying bairn and draping him across his shoulder. The swift action brought immediate quiet, capturing Eden's attention as she took bread from the oven. Seeing Thomas in the huge kettle, wide eyes peering over the brim, she began to laugh. The music of it spilled like sunlight into the dreary kitchen, reaching to the room's cold corners. Silas stood transfixed, struck by the irrepressible warmth and charm enlivening her features, so different than the staid lass he thought he knew.

Placing the bread on the table, she moved toward him, arms outstretched. His breath seemed to stick in his throat. But she wasn't reaching for him but the babe, still mysteriously quiet. She planted a kiss on his wee nose, her gaze lightening, and looked toward the dining room door. "I'm sorry 'tis so noisy. Mama is busy with the weaver—they're dressing the loom."

So there was to be another mouth to feed, he mused. And more work for her. She smoothed Jon's silken head, her touch sure and gentle.

"You have need of a kitchen girl," he said, looking down at her.

"I *am* the kitchen girl," she replied, as if to make light of his complaint.

Behind them Thomas had found the kettle's wooden paddle and had begun a dirge that would raise the dead.

Her smile held an apology. "Do you miss Philadelphia?"

He gave a slight shrug. "The hammering of a dozen men or a bairn's crying are all the same to me."

"What's it like? Philadelphia, I mean." The faraway look in her eyes confirmed his suspicions that she'd never been there but wanted to go. Desperately.

"Busy. Beautiful in parts. Not so beautiful in others."

"Did you see much of the city?"

He measured his response, not wanting to disappoint her. "My hours were long. Sometimes I had leave to attend the Franklin Institute for lyceum lectures."

Surprise lit her features. "Lectures for apprentices?"

"Aye, in science and machinery, for those who wanted them. There was even an apprenticeship library. The boardinghouse I lived in was not far from it."

"The Greathouses have told me about Bartram's Gardens and Solomon's Book Shoppe." When he said nothing, she continued quietly. "The Greathouses are our neighbors—at Hope Rising."

"Aye, I met them on the way here," he said above Thomas's pounding. "At the Rising Sun Tavern."

"Master David and his cousins?"

"Aye," he replied, recalling the sisters' close perusal of him. "Greathouse had pity on a poor apprentice and bought me supper."

"That sounds like him." Shifting Jon to her other shoulder, her smile faded into something that resembled . . . longing. At least to his keen eye.

He spoke of you, he almost said, then cast the thought aside. What wouldn't dislodge as readily was Greathouse's stumbling and flushing when he spoke of her. The recollection gave way to a startling thought. The heir to Hope Rising . . . and a blacksmith's daughter? In Scotland the idea would be heidie—scandalous. Here in York County he was less sure.

His musings ended when Elspeth entered the kitchen, arms full of ledgers, expression sullen. As if realizing they stood quite close, Eden stepped away from him, features tightening. Without provocation, the babe resumed his crying and Thomas his pounding, and everything returned to chaos.

All seemed to pour into the kitchen at once—Mrs. Lee with the weaver, Liege with two York men, and Elspeth in the center, dark as a thundercloud.

Despite their crowded table, not a word was uttered. With Silas and Papa at each end and she, Elspeth, and Mama on one side facing the three male guests, Eden didn't dare lift her eyes from her plate. Isaac Lackey, directly across from her, seemed possessed of the same appetite as before, when he'd come with his weaver father, his weskit buttons near bursting. To her right sat Silas. Though nary a look was exchanged, his presence steadied her, helped stave off her dread of the coming confrontation with Elspeth.

Twice in one morning she'd missed the opportunity to broach Elspeth's question.

Do you have a sweetheart?

Soon, at meal's end, Elspeth would corner her and Eden knew she'd pay the price.

When they were but girls, Elspeth had simply pinched Eden to show her displeasure, waiting till her mouth was full of peas or porridge before inflicting secret pain beneath the table. Sometimes in a fit of retaliatory fury Eden had kicked her back. But somehow, over the years, repeated pinching and verbal lashings had worn her down and she responded with no more than tearful silence. Elspeth's latest threat still echoed in her ears.

I'll tell Papa you're up to no good at Hope Rising, that your so-called Sabbath outings are naught but a ruse to dally with a man.

The heavy silence, the clink of utensils, the enthusiastic chewing and swallowing of the weaver, fueled Eden's hopes that her life in Philadelphia would be far different. At least she'd not be a kitchen girl. Her life would consist of babies and feedings and changing clouts, of notations on charts and consultations with hospital staff, or so Bea had told her. *If* they accepted her. If they didn't hold her father's transgressions against her. Or her own lack of spiritual training.

When the meal ended, Silas and her father and their guests returned to the smithy. Mama and Elspeth went upstairs with the weaver, leaving Eden to clear the table and mind the children. She nearly sighed aloud with relief. Elspeth's wrath was averted, if only for the time being.

⚬⚬

"Daughter, I must speak with you."

The stern summons in the quiet of the kitchen seemed more like a death sentence. Papa stood in the doorway, having just come in from the smithy.

Had she left something undone in the barn? The kitchen?

A fortnight before, she'd forgotten to bolt the smokehouse door and he'd given her a lashing—just a few flicks of a horsewhip on the backs of her legs, but they'd yet to heal. Trepidation ticked inside her as she set her ash bucket aside and followed him down the hall into the cold summer parlor. He'd been drinking—heavily—for his gait was more a shuffle and the stench of spirits wafted back to her in his wake.

A candelabra burned on a table, but the room was a ghostly

black. Dusk had fallen two hours before, snuffing what little remained of winter daylight. Eden looked longingly at a window and the secretary that hid her journal. Since secreting it there she'd not had a chance to return, carrying Silas's book with her instead. The little tome on western exploits and Indians had fit neatly into her pocket and kept her well occupied in spare moments.

Taking a wing chair, Papa motioned for her to retrieve his pipe on the mantel. Her fingers shook as she kindled it by candlelight, as there was no fire. Long, excruciating moments passed as he drew on the stem, smoke pluming, while she sat latching and unlatching her fingers in her lap in miserable anticipation. Flip made him mellow; rum surly. She couldn't tell which he'd had and nearly flinched when he studied her with bleary eyes.

"Daughter, you grieve me nearly as much as your sister. What have you to say for yourself?"

Rum, she decided. *In abundance.*

"Sometimes I think the Lord has given me two troublesome daughters to repay me for forsaking my Quaker roots."

'Twas a complaint she'd often heard and was all too weary of. But the sting of it never lessened. He wanted sons. Grandsons. Not an illegitimate child who cried incessantly and reminded them all of their failings. She and Elspeth had erred on that count too. They'd not given him proper sons-in-law nor the heirs he'd harped upon since they'd come of age.

"These two years past, while your sister has gone cavorting about the county with whatever man she fancies at all hours of the night, you have looked the other way and done little to stay her."

Her head came up. Was he blaming her for Elspeth's waywardness? She'd told Mama—warned her—countless times. *Mama, Elspeth is missing from her bed . . . I don't know*

*where she's gone or with whom . . . She's just left . . . and left
again.* But Mama, with tears in her eyes and silence on her
lips, hadn't told him. And she, Eden, was to blame?

"Papa, I—"

"You said nothing to your mother or myself, nor rebuked
your sister. Now that she's given birth to whose child we
know not, your behavior is again more hindrance than help."
Though his words were a bit slurred, they were strung together by the heat of his anger and forceful as ever. As every
syllable swelled, full of censure, she feared he could be heard
clear to the parlor where Silas and Isaac played chess and
Mama and Elspeth sewed.

"Finally, at long last, Elspeth has taken a liking to a worthy
man and seems willing to settle down. Most importantly, York
County has taken a liking to the work Ballantyne turns out. In
truth, the path to my door has never been more trammeled."
He drew hard on his pipe. "You must play your part to keep
him here, to help bring about your sister's happiness. Your
mother's health and peace of mind depend on it as well."

This she knew to be true. She'd read the sadness, the despair, in Mama's eyes all too often. It grieved her nearly beyond bearing. "I—I understand—"

He leaned forward. "Speak up, Daughter! Don't sit there
cowering like a mouse!"

"I understand." She swallowed hard, hating her timidity,
knowing it vexed him even more. "I know what is needed."

"I trust you do, but let me spell it out lest there be a misun-
derstanding." He cleared his throat, graying eyebrows slanting
down like the frown that sullied his mouth. "Act as matchmaker between your sister and Silas. Arrange occasions for
them to be together. Absent yourself from their company."

She looked down at her lap again, certain Elspeth was
behind this summons.

"Circumstances are in our favor. David Greathouse has just returned to Hope Rising and has sent word round that he needs help with the ice harvest. There's to be skating, a dance. All well and good for courtship and marriage. The sooner your sister is wed and settled, the better." His tone lost some of its heat, and a thick cloud of smoke obscured his features. "And after Elspeth is settled, Daughter, I have plans for you."

11

I can make a lord, but only God Almighty can make a gentleman.

JAMES VI OF SCOTLAND

Lying abed, listening to the weaver's loud snoring across the hall, Eden tried counting sheep—anything—to keep her worries at bay, but the darkness seemed to magnify her fears and return them to her tenfold. Images of ice harvesting in years gone by, of dances at Hope Rising, of skating on the meadow pond, failed to lift her spirits. Papa's words in the parlor the night before set her teeth on edge. Her mission was unbearably clear. She was expected to play the part of matchmaker. And then Papa had plans for her.

Except she had her own plans.

When, she wondered for the hundredth time, would Bea return with word from the foundling hospital? With the Greathouses as founders and benefactors, securing a position there seemed uncomplicated, or so she'd thought. 'Twas her leaving home, if she ever did, that was sticky as syrup.

Turning over, she felt the bulge that was Silas's book beneath her pillow. She'd finished it but half an hour ago, right before an icy draft had stolen the candlelight. Papa wouldn't allow a second taper to be lit, just as he wouldn't let them add a backlog to their bedchamber fire no matter how frigid. Her lips felt numb from the cold, bringing back the brutal winter of '77, when the cider froze in the cellar and Margaret's fine china cups cracked the moment hot tea touched them.

Remembering, trying to count her blessings, she lay shivering in her heaviest wool dress, wondering how Silas fared in the garret above. Fast asleep he'd likely be, she guessed, warmed by the coveted Franklin stove. 'Twas a perfect time to return his borrowed book. She'd simply lay it on the top step for him to find at first light.

The moon cast a golden crescent on the plank floor, lighting her way to the door. Holding the book close to her racing heart, she wondered why she felt so jittery. Aflocht, Silas had called it. Taking a deep breath, she paused to make sure Elspeth was still sleeping—and nearly forgot her mission.

In repose, her sister looked almost angelic. With her honey-eyed hair loose about her face, the spark and intensity that marked her countenance by day was softened by night. Seeing her thus, Eden almost believed change was possible, that Elspeth might one day be different. Motherhood had made her even more beautiful, lending a pleasing roundness in all the right places. Once again Eden couldn't push down her own dissatisfaction with herself in light of Elspeth's loveliness. And she knew that despite any matchmaking efforts on her behalf, Silas would succumb to her sister's physical charms in time, just like so many other York County men had.

∞

She was stepping lightly, Silas thought. Though he sensed it was Eden, he feared it was Elspeth. The day was coming when he'd have to put her in her place, and he preferred to do it in the privacy of a stairwell, not before her kin.

Still dressed despite the midnight hour, he'd been reading within the warm circle of light made by the Franklin stove, ears attuned to the settling of the household. Another time he might have missed the slight noise on the stairs, but not tonight.

Standing in his stocking feet, he opened the garret door. Firelight eclipsed the darkness, falling across Eden's upturned face a few steps down. Their eyes locked and he saw her surprise. Putting a finger to her lips, she gestured to the book atop the highest step. Indecision gripped him. Should he simply let her go without a word? Or bid her stay?

Stay, came the insistent echo as if from outside himself.

Though the light was poor, he saw that she'd been crying. Her indigo eyes were red-rimmed and so troubled he knew her father was to blame. When Liege had called her from the parlor, Silas's concentration had promptly dissolved and he'd lost the game of chess he'd been winning moments before. 'Twas all he could do to not grab Liege by the throat and give him a memorable thrashing.

"I didn't want to wake you," she whispered. "Your book . . ."

"I was not sleeping." He picked the volume up. "What did you make of it? Henry's adventures, I mean."

"I didn't want it to end. I could see the mountains and rivers so clearly." Her thoughtful expression clouded. "But it made me wonder why anyone would want to go west into the wilderness. Colonel Johnston says it is a desolate country, uninhabited by anything but wild Indians, bears, and rattlesnakes."

He felt a strange disappointment. "Colonel Johnston?"

"He lives in Elkhannah and served in the French and Indian War."

"Did he say nothing about the beauty of the place? And

all the land for the taking?" Stubbornness turned him blunt.
"Which would you believe, Eden?"

"Colonel Johnston, of course," she whispered solemnly,
"because he's been there."

He nodded absently, sensing she had no wish to discuss
such matters but had come seeking something else entirely.
The Buik. He stepped back inside his room and retrieved his
Bible, then handed it to Eden. Surprise skittered across her
face, and she sank down atop the steps in a swirl of wool
skirts, caressing the worn cover as if lost in holy wonder. He
thought of the many times he'd tossed the tome carelessly
into his saddlebags and felt a sliver of guilt. Had she never
held a Bible, God's living Word?

"Go ahead," he urged. "Open it."

She did this ever so carefully, while he brought out a candle
and sat on the step above her, watching her slender fingers
move over the unfamiliar text. "I . . . I hardly know where
to begin."

"You're in the Psalms. 'Tis a good place to be." He thumbed
a few pages forward. "D'ye want me to read it to you, Eden?"

She simply nodded yes, eyes on the page. Looking over
her shoulder, he kept his voice low, the reading short, but his
Scots was so thick he wondered if she heard it properly. "The
Lord's my shepherd, I'll not want. He makes me down to lie
in pastures green: He leadeth me the quiet waters by . . ."

When he'd finished, she said in a whisper, "Read it again.
Please. In your Gaelic."

Surprised, he obliged, quoting it from memory, and she
looked away, her profile so lovely he felt his senses spin. His
mind was no longer on Scripture but the gentle curve of her
cheek . . . the profusion of lashes that lay like gold fringe
upon high cheekbones . . . the elegant slant of her nose. His
gut gave a wrench of warning.

He returned to the garret and brought out quill and paper, crowding the twenty-third Psalm onto a scrap of rag linen. "Take it to heart," he said quietly, "then you'll have no need of a Gaelic Bible—or sneaking about in a stairwell."

Nodding, she took the paper and folded it till it was no bigger than an acorn. Tucking it in her bodice, she got up and started down the steps before turning back, a new light in her eyes.

"Bethankit, Silas Ballantyne."

On the Sabbath, just as he'd promised, Silas went to church. Before he rode away on Horatio, he paused beneath Eden's bedchamber window, an unclouded invitation in his eyes. What, she wondered, was it like to do as one pleased? Go where one wanted without asking, without fear of reprisal? She followed him up the hill with her eyes if not her feet, an intense longing building in her breast. Ever since he'd asked her—nay, challenged her to go with him that day in the smithy—the image of them sitting side by side in the little church had haunted, taunting her timidity.

Years before, she'd peeked in a narrow window when no one was about. There were benches, a crude pulpit, a stove. All was clean and spare, like a field gleaned after harvest. She felt a plummeting disappointment. What had she expected? Stained glass and angels' wings?

As soon as Silas left, Papa began thundering about rebellious Presbyterians and stubborn Scotsmen and the sins of the Anglican Church. Elspeth, coming in with her sewing basket, slammed the bedchamber door shut with her shoe. Seeing Eden at the window, she crossed over to stand beside her, their father's shouting undiminished below.

"You'd think Silas was a Quaker the way Papa carries on

113

so! I'll take a rebel Presbyterian any day." Elspeth's vexed expression grew amused as she looked beyond the cold windowpane. "Notice Papa saved his ranting till Silas was well out of earshot."

Yes, Eden thought with a small surge of triumph. *Papa is unsure of Silas.*

Together they watched him clear the meadow fence at a near gallop and traverse the pasture with its sinkholes and stones. *How like him*, Eden thought, *to choose a different way*. She would have taken the sure route—the road.

"My, but he cuts a fine figure on that horse of his." Dropping her sewing basket into a chair, Elspeth gave a mock curtsy, chin lifting in determination. "I believe I might have need of church. The day is fair if cold. May I borrow your bonnet?"

Eden simply stared at her. Was she daft? Somehow Elspeth's asking was far more disconcerting than her habit of simply taking what she wanted. Without waiting for an answer, Elspeth flung open the clothespress and helped herself to the said bonnet, and a cloak too.

"You shall be late," Eden warned, thinking of the long walk up the hill. "People will stare—talk."

"Exactly." Elspeth smiled her brightest smile. "'Tis time I show my face again after so long indoors. People mustn't think I'm an invalid. And I shall have a ride home on Silas's horse."

Amazement washed through Eden. "But Papa—"

"But Papa what?" Elspeth paused from tying the chin ribbons of her bonnet. "You're not worried about his forbidding us to attend church, are you? I'm merely doing a little matchmaking, something you seem quite incapable of. You might at least look happy for me. I'm finally settling down like Papa wants. He'll have the son-in-law he wants—the smithy he wants. Grandsons."

Though Elspeth always seemed to choose her words carefully to inflict the most hurt, none yet had the force of these. How flippantly she spoke of bearing Silas a son! Grandsons! And she'd now pretend to have an interest in church to achieve her ends? Eden felt she'd been jabbed with a hot poker. Or was it more dismay that Elspeth had the nerve to attend church when she didn't?

Eden watched her go without a word, watched her hurry across the frosted grass to climb the hill. Sinking to the window seat, Eden took from her bodice the scrap of Scripture that Silas had penned for her. The paper, warm from her skin, returned their staircase meeting to her in all its secret poignancy.

The Lord's my shepherd . . .

She'd already memorized the short Psalm and was hungry for more. Indeed, each word seemed woven into her soul the way the weaver wove his wares, taking the barest threads of her faith and making something beautiful and enduring as fine cloth deep inside her. Something that couldn't be taken away like Elspeth took her yellow silk and bonnet. These were her words—holy words. And they'd surely help her in her quest to reach Philadelphia.

As she traversed the lane to Hope Rising later that Sabbath morn to take tea with Margaret Hunter, her heart was sore over what was in store for Silas. But her soul was singing.

⸺❧⸻

Hoofbeats broke the winter stillness. Loud. Hurried. Purposeful. As Eden rounded the bend in the treed lane that brought her abreast of Hope Rising's gate, David Greathouse appeared on a black stallion. At the sight of her he reined in, dismounted, and gave a little bow. His breath and that of his winded horse plumed in the icy air like frozen white feathers. In a gesture that was charming and a bit bumbling, he removed his beaver hat from atop his head and nearly dropped it.

"Miss Eden, how goes the new year for you?"

"Well and good, Master David. And you?"

"Very well . . . at the moment."

He studied her till she felt heat touch her cheeks, and she in turn took him in beneath half-lowered lashes. He'd filled out a bit more since she'd last seen him, though perhaps she'd grown used to Silas's well-muscled leanness, which made the heir of Hope Rising seem stout. Her eyes fastened on his snowy cravat and the cape that bore the newness of the city, thinking how shabby she must look.

Giving his hat a twirl in his hands, he smiled. "I was just coming round to ask your apprentice if he'd perform at our party."

She felt a rush of pleasure. "The dance, you mean? After the ice harvest?"

"I hear he plays an exquisite fiddle."

Did he? Exquisite? How she loved the thought! Since his coming he'd not played a note, not that she'd heard. Her delight faded as she looked up the hill. "You'll not find him at home but at church."

"Ah, church . . . the place I should be." His expression grew rueful. "Since I've returned from Philadelphia I've been so preoccupied I've nearly forgotten what day it is. Will you ask him for me?"

She nodded, glad to see him, wanting to inquire about his cousins but feeling suddenly tongue-tied.

He flexed his gloved hands, then reached inside his pocket and withdrew a letter. "From Beatrice."

The unexpected sight unleashed a firestorm inside her. 'Twas her future, her pass to a new life. Or so she hoped.

Taking it from him with trembling hands, trying to keep her excitement from showing, she smiled her thanks. Just how much did David know of her plans? Though Bea was his cousin, she was notoriously closed-mouthed.

His brow raised in question. "Have I missed much being away? How fares your family?"

She tucked the letter into her basket, eyes drifting to a bird preening on an icy branch. "Papa and Mama are well. There's a new babe at the farm." She swallowed hard, anxiety crowding in. Having known her for so long, did he suspect she was hiding something? "The apprentice seems to be charming the whole county with his work."

"So I've heard. And young Thomas? Your sister?"

"Thomas is fine, thank you. As for Elspeth, she's well—well enough to go to church."

Surprise lightened his eyes, followed by amused understanding. "With Silas Ballantyne, I suppose." He chuckled and returned his hat to his head. "Where are you going?"

"To Margaret's for tea."

"Would you like me to escort you?"

She nearly laughed. *For fifty feet?* "'Tis kind of you, but I'm nearly there. And my basket isn't heavy."

"May I have the first dance then?"

She met his eyes, finding them so different from Silas's. David's were mild, like his manners, and so gray they seemed without color. "You've asked me that since we were very young," she said, feeling their old kinship return, "when Master Gilbert came to Hope Rising to give us dancing lessons."

He reddened, eyes on his boots, and raked a hand through his sandy hair till it stood on end, reminding her of the boy he used to be. "Yes, but we're no longer so young and the dancing master is no more, and I'm thinking you may have other admirers."

"None," she said softly, though Papa's ominous words held the hint of a coming match. Remembering it now seemed to snatch all the sunlight from her soul. Could her old friend see that too? "Good day, Master David. And yes," she added, turning and tossing a shy smile over her shoulder, "you may have the first dance."

12

Two is company, but three is none.
EIGHTEENTH-CENTURY PROVERB

Two hours later in the glare of midafternoon, amidst church bells pealing, Eden returned down the lane, straight into the path of Silas on horseback. Elspeth sat behind him, arms wrapped firmly around his waist. The sight jarred Eden from her pleasant reverie and left her as overcast as the sky above. While Silas and her sister had just spent the morning together, in the place she longed to be, she'd been at Hope Rising, nearly forgetting Elspeth's glee. Truly, Elspeth had never looked so triumphant. A numbing hurt took hold that had everything to do with Beatrice's disappointing letter and nothing to do with the sight of them together. Or so she told herself.

She hoped they'd merely nod and go on their way, but nay . . . Silas came to a stop in the middle of the lane. Holding the reins loosely, he looked down at her, wearing a bemused expression she'd not seen before. Was he wondering why she'd not accompanied him instead of Elspeth? Thinking her reluctance was refusal? Disinterest? Fear of her father?

She kept her eyes on his greatcoat, the shirt she'd made him peeking out beneath. Despite his modest dress, she was always struck by his person, his presence, and today he loomed large. And Elspeth . . . There was no denying she was positively regal in back of him. No doubt she'd turned every head in the church with her colorful cape and feathered bonnet.

Horatio pawed the ground as if impatient with their dallying. No one said a word.

Awkwardness rent the air, so thick that Eden finally blurted, "Master David has asked that you play your fiddle at Hope Rising."

Silas shifted in the saddle. "Why would he?"

"'Tis a tradition to hold a dance after the ice harvest," she explained, thinking he'd be pleased. "Musicians are always in demand."

He continued to regard her warily. Had Papa not told him help was needed? Why, the event was the talk of the entire county, anticipated for months. Still, she read no pleasure in his expression.

"I've not heard of any ice harvest," he replied, raising the fire in her cheeks.

After David's courtly manner, she found Silas abrupt, even gruff. Had she erred in asking, somehow offending him, and in so doing pleased Elspeth? A satisfied smile pulled at her sister's mouth as she gazed down from her queen-like perch.

"Come, Silas," Elspeth urged. "I'll tell you all about it later. My sister seems determined to turn us to ice with her chatter."

"So be it." With that, he slid from Horatio's back, reins dangling, and reached for Eden.

Her eyes went wide as his hands spanned her waist beneath the soft circle of her shawl. He lifted her off the ground, her basket tilting precariously, and set her in the warm saddle he'd just vacated before slapping the gelding's backside. Horatio

shot forward in the direction of the farm, Elspeth clutching
Eden's middle without a look back.

∾

Silas snatched up the paper that fluttered to the ground in
Eden's wake lest it get soiled. A letter? He had no wish to read
it, but the monogrammed post lay wide open and seemed to
demand he do so. Across the bottom was a sprawling signature that bespoke elegance, ease. The author was no mystery.
After spending the morning with Elspeth, he now knew the
name of every man, woman, and child in York County. Beatrice was a Greathouse, Eden's friend . . . and Elspeth's enemy.
The few words penned therein left him a bit upended, and
the timorous Eden he thought he knew grew hazy.

*Dearest Eden, The position you seek is
delayed till spring.*

He folded the paper and slipped it in his coat pocket, surprise sifting through him. For a few minutes he stood still, the
winter wind biting him, and turned up his coat collar as he
tried to make sense of the cryptic message. Was Eden leaving
York County? Or simply seeking work within its confines,
mayhap at Hope Rising? He felt a stinging disappointment,
followed by a return to reason. What did it matter? Let Eden
have her position, her plan.

He had his own.

∾

Come Monday the weaving was but half done. Having
been with them a fortnight, eating numerous meals at their
table, sleeping in the summer parlor, and playing countless
rounds of chess with Silas in the weary evening hours, Isaac

121

Lackey had turned out but a few rugs and coverlets. The paltry offerings were now spread over the dining room table for their perusal—a few napkins and towels, twin sheets, a rug, and other smaller items—making Eden wonder what else Isaac had been doing.

She watched as Mama ran her hands over a tablecloth of vivid red and green, her practiced eye finding a flaw or two. "He lacks the skill of his father. But weavers are so hard to come by and we are in such dire need of woolens, I'll not complain."

Even as she said the words, the loom upstairs had gone silent—again. Eden felt a keen dismay. But Mama seemed not to notice. Her face resumed its placid lines, her expression benign. She simply turned to her pattern book, pointing out two designs.

"Go show Mr. Lackey these, Eden. I simply must have two more rugs worked in this way."

Nodding, Eden set down the pewter she'd been polishing and wiped her hands on her apron, trying to master her dislike of the lazy Isaac. The profound quiet boded ill, but thankfully, before her foot touched the first step, the loom's clacking resumed. She imagined him throwing the shuttle back and forth across the stretched wool, Elspeth assisting, neither of them pleased with her unexpected appearance.

When she reached the landing, her heart seemed to grind to a halt. The door to the weaving room was closed, though Mama insisted it always be open.

The pattern book grew damp in her hands. Again the loom stilled. Breath held to the point of bursting, Eden pushed open the door. Isaac sat on his bench, but his hands were no longer on his work. They were on Elspeth, who was kissing him.

The pattern book fell from Eden's hands. Elspeth swirled around on the bench, her face a stew of surprise and indignation. Isaac simply looked smug, taking up the shuttle again as if nothing untoward had happened.

A startling question cut through Eden's mortification. Might Isaac be Jon's father? The timing was certainly right. He'd last been here the previous winter . . .

Scooping up the book, Eden opened the door wide, voice trembling at their brazenness. "Mr. Lackey . . ."

Thoughts of Silas crowded out what little remained of her composure. What would he say to this? Her sister was so fickle—so unfaithful. The shame that should have been Elspeth's suffused Eden from tip to toe. "Mama needs two more rugs worked in this pattern," she whispered, handing Isaac the book. Hearing the babe crying below, she turned and fled.

❦

Silas spread the tobacco-colored map upon his desk—Eden's desk—in the garret room. The light slanting through the sole window highlighted every geographical feature that lay beyond the Allegheny Mountains to the west. Simply looking at the topography set his soul on fire. 'Twas a holy passion he had to push west—to move beyond the boundaries of who he was and what he'd been born to—to who he felt called to be.

Or was it a less holy, burning ambition instead?

He'd logged less than two months in York County, and already his soul chafed at his tenure. Yet if the Lord deemed it necessary for him to tarry here, he would. His sprawling indenture had an end, and he knew the date like his own name day.

Eighteen October, 1785.

He riffled through his haversack and brought out a second map far different from the first. This one he'd nearly memorized. In the far left corner was the outpost of Fort Pitt, situated on an oft-disputed, arrowhead-shaped tip of land known as the gateway to the West. He'd heard of the raw breed of men there, of disease and lawlessness and Indian unrest, yet the more he learned, the more he saw beyond the danger and violence to what it would one day be. In the matter of trade, this new land was ripe for exploitation and settlement. Settlers were now plotting out the makings of a village, a Scottish stronghold. For years Quakers had pushed the intrepid Scots toward the borders to fend off the Indians on the Pennsylvania frontier. Pittsburgh was the result.

His longing to have been among the first wave of immigrants was fierce. Posts near the Forks of the Ohio and beyond were now well established, and men were getting rich through the Indian trade. Now there were rumors of a different sort of wealth—of coal and other natural resources buried deep in the western hills, there for the taking. One day the territory would surely be filled with the smoke and soot of Edinburgh. Pittsburgh even boasted of becoming a second Philadelphia.

Leaning back in his chair, he ran a hand through his unkempt hair and sighed. All that stood between him and his future was a precarious apprenticeship, the Allegheny Mountains, and two hundred miles of unfamiliar wilderness. Rolling up the maps, he returned them to his haversack along with Beatrice Greathouse's letter to Eden. If she came to him in the stairwell again, he'd return it to her.

Though he tried to dismiss it, the letter's terse words tore at him. Did she seek a position at Hope Rising? Were her parents aware of her scheme? Nae, reason told him. The plan was in place to escape this contentious place.

Hers—and his own.

CXD

It was nearly nine o'clock when Eden made her way to the barn, rags and liniment in one hand, lantern in the other. She needn't have bothered with a light, the moon was so luminous. Stopping by the smokehouse, she set the lantern atop a barrel. Curing hams dangled overhead from thick rafters, and the pungent tang of saltpeter, pepper, and sugar was nearly smothering. As she snitched bacon from a barrel, she felt as duplicitous as Elspeth.

Her breathing quickened at the muted strains of a fiddle. Was Silas in the barn? Keeping a wary eye on the barn's cracks, seeking his tall outline, she prayed he was at the far end and she could slip in and out unnoticed. They hadn't spoken since yesterday when she'd met him and Elspeth in the lane. She'd not thought to find him here now. His lovely music nearly made her forget her mission. But for the injured dog awaiting her, she'd have turned back.

She'd placed the pup behind the haymow in one far corner, well out of harm's way. For a moment she felt a flash of exasperation at having so tender a heart. "Let the dog die," Papa had said when she'd found the gangly pup shivering and bleeding in the pasture a week before, the victim of a wolf or worse. But its queer eyes—one brown, one gray—had seemed pleading, a test of her newfound faith.

The Quaker saying she'd stitched on a sampler and hidden in her dower chest propelled her forward. *I expect to pass through this world but once. Therefore any good work, kindness, or service I can render to any person or animal, let me do it now, for I will not pass this way again.* Though not Scripture, it seemed an echo of the same.

The barn door opened with a groan, but the fiddle music masked it. Silas was down with the horses, well away from the dog's piteous moans, yet each time the fiddle trilled higher, the pup would raise its head and howl. Eden clapped a hand over her mouth in amusement and dropped to her knees in the hay. The pup paused long enough to lick her hand, tail thumping wildly, before resuming his lament.

"There's naught wrong with your wagging," she said in hushed tones, relinquishing the bacon, "or your howling."

Unwrapping his foreleg, she applied the liniment to the deep gash, the herbal scent supplanting the strong smell of hay. Working by the low glow of lantern light, she realized too late the fiddling had ceased. Only the usual barn sounds surrounded her—a pigeon's nesting, a rooster's crowing, the creaking of old rafters in the wind.

Slowly she turned. Silas leaned against the stall, bow and fiddle in hand.

"You needn't stop your fiddling," she said, getting up as gracefully as she could. "I like a fine jig."

"So your father lets you dance."

She nodded. Strangely, he did, though it had been the ruination of him. "I've never heard such playing as yours."

He grinned, his teeth a flash of white in the dimness. "Screechy and scratchity, you mean."

"On the contrary." Awe edged her voice. "One would think you were fiddler to the duke and not your father."

"Aye," he murmured. "On occasion."

"Might you be . . ." She bit her lip, remembering their confrontation in the lane. "Practicing? For Hope Rising?"

He gave a terse nod, and she had the distinct feeling he was no more pleased with the mention than he had been at first. Disappointment sank like a stone inside her. She'd wanted him to have something to look forward to—to break the monotony of his days. There was so little joy in their lives, and so much work. She'd hoped they might share a dance. The admission brought a queer stitch to her stomach as a deeper realization dawned. Might his playing bring back memories of Scotland—all he'd lost?

He looked at her and then his fiddle. "I ken little of what you colonials dance to—the music, the steps."

Was this the trouble then? Moved by the stark vulnerability in his eyes, she blurted, "I could show you."

But even as she offered she felt a paralyzing shyness. He was studying her in that earnest way he had, as if daring her to do so. She wouldn't go to church, his intensity seemed to say. Would she dance then?

She gathered up the rags and liniment and prepared to leave, but he caught her wrist as she turned away. "Nae, Eden. Stay."

His tender insistence, the touch of his fingers, was like a lure. He set his fiddle and bow down and took the things from her hands.

"'Tis mostly simple country dances," she began, but the whispered words died in her throat.

"Such as . . . ?" His tall shadow touched hers.

"'Sir Roger de Coverly' is but one." Her voice was barely a whisper. She felt the chill of the barn. His warm gaze.

Slowly he took up his fiddle and struck a familiar tune. She would stay, the starting note seemed to say. As she stepped into the walkway between the stalls, alarm shot through her. What if Papa, Elspeth, found them thus?

Back to him, hands on her hips, she summoned all her courage and began to step lightly, eyes shut, following the intricate pattern of a beloved country dance. The music wafted to the barn rafters, surrounding her, wooing her, nearly making her giddy.

That lassie o' yours, m' lady, has a good ear.

The words returned to her from a far-off place, spoken by the dancing master at Hope Rising years before. She'd been but nine. Now she was nearly twenty. Back then she hadn't cared that her mother beamed at the compliment. Now it gave her confidence.

"Sir Roger de Coverly" faded and the Glasgow reel began. Her steps were sure, his timing flawless. And his playing—oh, 'twas heaven's own! She felt she had wings! When the music ended she slowed to a dizzy spin, eyes still closed, and felt his hand in hers, his other warm about her waist, as together they matched their steps over the hay-strewn space.

"You need no music, Eden. You need only me—and I you."

She thought she must be dreaming. Is that what he said to her at the last, his breath warm against her ear? Simply thinking it sent little shimmies of pleasure coursing through her. No man had ever spoken to her in such a way.

A dream, truly.

The house was tucked into bed, but Elspeth was awake, waiting. She sat up as Eden entered their bedchamber, eyes shining in the gloom, her arms folded across her chest. All Eden could think of was finding her with the weaver but a few hours before.

"Where have you been? 'Tis late." Elspeth's tone, ever accusing, was a wounding whisper. "I was about to fetch Father."

"I was with Silas in the barn," Eden answered, with a confidence born of near elation.

And Elspeth said . . . nothing.

No threats. No tears. No tantrums.

13

Distance lends enchantment to the view.

ENGLISH PROVERB

Five days later the weaver left. 'Twas the Sabbath, and Elspeth went to church with Silas again. How diminutive she looked beside the strapping Scot, the pointed contrast drawing Eden to the bedchamber window. Silas was, she lamented, deliciously long of leg and wide of shoulder, as handsome from the backside as the front, just as Elspeth said. Eden watched them go, wishing it was raining torrents or on the verge of a blizzard so they'd be confined to the house. But the morning was clear, the church bells tolling beneath an endless blue sky.

Church was suddenly acceptable—permissible—for Elspeth, all in the name of courtship. "Absent yourself from their company," Papa had said. "Arrange occasions for them to be together." Well, that she would do, if reluctantly.

Thankfully, mending by the fire with Mama ate up the long morning, and then Eden was free. Free of the farmhouse, if not the memory of Silas and Elspeth. Since Margaret Hunter was ill with a cold and unable to take tea, a crock of soup had to suffice, which Eden delivered to her door. Then she hurried back down the lane, skates in hand, oddly expectant.

On the frozen meadow pond was David Greathouse—and a young woman. A sweetheart? Eden's heart quickened. Nay, just Jemma, the two of them breaking the Sabbath in plain view of those who kept it on the hill. Jemma waved and skated her way, steel skates shining beneath bell-shaped skirts. Sitting on a low stump, Eden worked to attach her own worn blades to her boots, binding them with leather laces. Despite their decrepit condition, they felt wonderfully familiar, easing the soreness she felt over Silas and Elspeth just a bit.

"I've come home!" Jemma called, her breath curling in the icy air. Bedecked in a snug pelisse and muff lined with swans' down, she was crowned with an enormous bonnet, the conglomeration of flowers and fur adding height to her small stature. "Bea and Anne are staying at the townhouse in Philadelphia. But I didn't dare miss the ice harvest, so I'm back in York."

Eden stood on wobbly legs. "No one said a word about your coming."

"I begged Margaret not to. I wanted to surprise you." She helped Eden onto the ice and sighed in satisfaction. "Solid as a brick. Perfect for harvesting, if it doesn't rain. Remember last year?" She made such a face Eden gave a rueful smile.

"All I remember is skating on water. Everything was slush and mud and misery."

"This time I'm praying for snow. Wouldn't that be romantic? We could bring out the colonial cutter and sleigh about." Jemma began to skate away from her, circling and doing a little twirl, swans' down glistening in the winter light. Of the three sisters, Jemma was the youngest and most animated, making merry wherever she went, her laughter as infectious as influenza. Eden felt her spirits rise as she skated after her, aware that David was coming toward them, hands behind his back, features obscured by his tall hat.

He bowed when he reached her, giving her such a wink upon straightening that she paid scant attention to the church bells announcing an end to the service on the hill. Clasping her mittened hands, he tugged her toward the center of the pond where the ice was smoother. Perfect, he said, for dancing.

"I cannot wait for the ball," he told her. "We must practice here while we can." His gray eyes were alight in a way reminiscent of their childhood, warm and inviting and slightly mischievous. At times she felt they were still eight years old. Betimes she wished they were.

"I'm not as sure-footed as you," Eden reminded him, listing to one side.

"You shame me in the ballroom. At least let me have my way on the ice." His gloved hand held hers fast. "Have you asked Ballantyne if he'll play for us?"

"Yes," she answered breathlessly. "He will." Though she'd kept to the house since their shared barn dance, certain songs seemed to carry on the still night air, tempting her to join him again. Silas's playing took her breath away—his instrument seemed a living thing. *His fiddle is on fire*, she thought. She wanted to say so yet didn't want to rob them of the joy of that discovery.

They clasped hands, circling and spinning to the imaginary reel in their heads, forgetting about such mundane matters as harvesting ice. The pond's surface was slick in places and she nearly fell, but David was always near, steadying her, saving her from embarrassment. Time seemed to stand still, broken only by the persistent ring of church bells.

"Ah . . . we have an audience." Jemma gave a cordial wave toward the south end of the pond, but the downward turn of her mouth revealed her true feelings. Eden's own high spirits seemed to skitter to a stop.

'Twas Elspeth and Silas, without Horatio, as they'd walked to church this morning. Eden noted the triumphant tilt of Elspeth's head and the possessive way she had hold of his arm, as if branding him as hers. She'd best get used to it, Eden scolded herself. Once they wedded, were living and loving beneath their very roof . . .

The punishing thought was followed by a plaintive prayer. *Lord, please hasten me to Philadelphia.*

Excusing himself, David left her and Jemma standing in a tight knot while he skated toward Elspeth and Silas at the edge of the ice.

"So she's captured another heart, even if she had to go to church to do it." Jemma tucked a loose russet curl into the side of her bonnet and forced a smile. "We'd best skate over and greet them lest she accuse us of snobbery or worse."

Eden wished the ice would open up and swallow her. She was becoming increasingly uncomfortable around her sister and Silas, and her resulting discomfort showed in stupid ways—a dropped dish, a misplaced word, a forgotten task. Likely she'd now fall and lie sprawled on the pond for all to see.

David was carrying on a lively conversation with Silas about the coming harvest, speaking of such things as ice plows and tonnage, wagons and cleats for horses. Even from afar, the deep timbre of Silas's tone enticed her. She'd grown all too fond of his rich Scots speech. 'Twas like music to her as much as his fiddle—a haunting refrain wherever she went, if one could be smitten simply by the music of a voice . . . or a violin.

Eden skated slowly toward them, focusing on the copse of pine on the hill, her skates, Jemma's composed smile. Her legs were wobbly now, her ankles sore from being so long off the ice. Jemma gave her arm a reassuring squeeze, as if sensing how the sight of Elspeth shook her.

Sliding to a stop, Eden stole a look at Silas. In the cold his handsome features were ruddy, his eyes an enlivened green. And his hair . . . had he cut it? No longer was it tailed and tied back with black ribbon. Its shorn ends splayed over the collar of his shirt and curled a bit. Like a gentleman's. Like David's. She made herself look away, felt the release of Jemma's fingers on her arm before becoming aware of another reality. Elspeth was looking straight at her, violence in her blue eyes.

"I'd best go," Eden whispered, wondering if her jellied legs would hold her. The dull blades of her skates made hard work of the ice as she returned to the far side of the pond where her boots rested, Jemma in her wake.

"You must spend the night at Hope Rising before the ball," Jemma insisted. "We'll help each other make ready. Margaret will be too busy to play lady's maid, and Colette stayed behind with Bea and Anne in Philadelphia. Besides, I've just the gown for you." Her voice dropped to a conspiratorial whisper. "My only concern is what Elspeth will be wearing."

Eden stepped off the ice. "Your yellow silk."

"Oh, will she now?" Her inquisitive eyes seemed to smolder. "When I sent the dress over, it was for you, if I remember." When Eden remained silent, she gave a slight shrug. "Well, we'll make sure neither my gown nor yours is in that color. Yellow is passé for a winter ball, anyway."

Eden warmed to the vibrancy in her voice, her generosity, and noticed she was looking back at David, who still stood talking with Silas.

Jemma said quietly, "He watched you skate away."

"What?"

"The Scottish apprentice was watching you," Jemma whispered.

Eden's hands stilled on her skates. "Watching for me to take a tumble, you mean."

"No, Eden. Watching like a man who cannot watch enough."

Their eyes met and held. Jemma was all seriousness now, concern clouding her fair features. "Take care, dear friend, with Elspeth."

Shivering, weighted by the warning, Eden began to walk across the brittle meadow toward home, skates dangling at her sides, words of leave-taking lodged in her throat. Jemma knew Elspeth's true colors. Her warning was well-founded— and was one Eden would heed.

"Till Friday," Jemma called after her. "The ice harvest begins at first light. The ball is on Saturday. Pray for snow!"

Six days. What, Eden wondered, would happen between now and then?

CO&∞O

Tar and feathers!

Elspeth chafed as the clock struck eight. Boredom had long since set in, fraying the edges of her composure as she sat and sewed linens for her dower chest.

Sedately. Industriously. Prettily.

There were just the four of them in the parlor—she, Silas, Eden, and Jon. Mama, most obliging, had gone to her bed-chamber with Thomas half an hour before while Papa's gout had him soaking his leg in a steaming tub in the kitchen. She could smell his pungent pipe smoke seeping beneath the closed door, mingling with the medicinal herbs from Eden's garden.

For half an hour or better she'd been trying to get Eden to go upstairs, but her sister was making a fool of herself with the babe before the snapping fire, cooing over him with whispers and kisses as if he were her own. The sight turned

Elspeth's already sour stomach. For once Jon wasn't fussing. Dressed in a loose-fitting gown that had been Thomas's, his downy head was covered with a lace-edged cap. He was beginning to be all rolls and dimples and would now smile at no one but Eden. 'Twas naught but stray dogs and needy tenants and fussing babies with her.

Jamming her needle into the soft cloth, Elspeth finished embroidering her initials with scarlet thread, itching to stitch Silas's as well. They were sitting in a triangle of sorts—Silas at one end of the cavernous hearth and Eden at the other while Elspeth occupied the Windsor chair at the heart of the room, Silas's lantern at her side. That way she could keep her eye on them, make sure nothing was afoot. Though there'd been no wayward glances or shared words, deep down she felt something was amiss, and it aggravated her so much she felt she'd fallen into a briar patch.

The Scot, she mused grudgingly, was the most challenging man she'd ever met. He seemed to live mostly inside his head, like Eden. Undistracted by normal pursuits, saying but little, rarely smiling, he put her in mind of a magistrate or preacher. He was never idle. Even now, after thirteen hours spent at the forge, he was whittling a toy for Thomas, a mound of shavings at his feet. Later he'd practice for the frolic at Hope Rising. She sometimes wondered if he slept. The garret was often lit far into the night, shining a square pattern upon the ground outside her bedchamber window.

A thin smile curled her lips, and she bent nearer her sewing lest they notice.

Perhaps that light was but an invitation.

❧

Eden tucked a sleeping Jon into his cradle after swaddling him, leaving her parents' bedchamber for her own. Both

Mama and Thomas were abed and she tiptoed past, though her thoughts remained in the winter parlor where Silas and Elspeth lingered. 'Twas improper for them to be unchaperoned, but her parents, wanting to hasten a match, cast all conventions aside. Nor should she pay it any mind, she told herself, fastening her thoughts on Philadelphia.

Shivering, she sought refuge in the window seat of her room, where she could see the distant lights of Hope Rising through the threadbare trees. David had ordered a dozen three-sided lanterns from Silas and was putting them to good use. Now, at nine o'clock, the place was lit like a bonfire. The sight solaced her, reminded her that the ice harvest was but three days away. She'd been given permission to go earlier when Jemma sent a note round unexpectedly.

"So Miss Greathouse is home and seeks your company?" Papa had tossed the summons into the forge's fire, gray brows nearly touching in contemplation. "Will Master David be there?"

She had nodded absently and looked about the smithy, wondering where Silas and Elspeth were, waiting for Papa's grudging approval—or another tirade.

"Go then. Be of service." He waved a hand in dismissal as if she was naught but a pesky fly. "But don't return home without something to show for it."

She nearly winced at his blunt wording. He meant a suitor, surely. Though most every unmarried or widowed man in the county would likely come to both harvest and ball, none had appealed to her yet. His cryptic words of a fortnight before returned and sent another chill through her.

After Elspeth is settled, Daughter, I have plans for you.

She prayed drinking had muddled his mind to make him utter such and he'd since forgotten the matter in the swell of sobriety. Thinking of her uncertain future, she rued the loss of Bea's letter. Had she dropped it in the lane? Here at home? Dismay trickled through her. No one must know about Philadelphia. Not till the plan was in place and she'd gathered enough courage to go.

Blowing out the candle, she lay down, fully dressed, wishing she had nerve enough to disobey Papa's dictum of letting the fire die at night. This very morning she'd awakened to ice in the wash pitcher atop the washstand, a boon for the coming harvest but for little else. At least Silas was snug in the garret room. Somehow the simple thought of him deriving some comfort in this cold house gave her some comfort in return.

She could hear Elspeth's purposeful footfall on the stair, and in minutes her sister was in bed, her soft snores assuring Eden she was indeed asleep. What had she and Silas talked about after she'd left the parlor, if indeed they had talked? Was he becoming smitten? She tucked the hurtful thought away. Down the hall the clock struck ten. She lay still, waiting for the muted sound of Silas's violin, the Scripture he'd penned scrolling through her thoughts.

The Lord's my shepherd, I'll not want . . .

Her hungry heart craved a shepherd. She wanted to know why, if the Lord led her, she was often left wanting. In want of more Scripture. More solitude. A different sister. A position in Philadelphia. A fire in the hearth to stop her shivering. An end to all the turmoil within and without.

Pushing back the covers, she was but halfway to the door when a noise sounded above her head. Shutting her eyes, she leaned into the door frame, fisting the wool gloves she'd made him. The music was slow and low, more a lament, so far removed from anything he'd ever played that she went completely still. *His fiddle weeps*, she thought, yet it wooed her with its sweetness, warm as a lover's touch.

For long minutes she just listened, summoning the courage

to open the door and ascend the garret stair in the dark. Hell, Papa said, was full of fiddlers. If so, Eden mused, surely heaven had its share. Thankfully Papa, deaf as he was getting, couldn't hear the music. Mama wouldn't complain if she did. Elspeth showed more irritation than interest in his playing, though Thomas often cocked his head and clapped his little hands.

She climbed upward, the music masking her movements. As she placed his gloves on the step, the playing ceased and the door opened. Light spilled down the steps like water on a hillside, illuminating the narrow stairwell.

"I heard your playing," she whispered.

"Am I keeping you awake?" Concern skimmed his features. "My fiddle does not like this cold, else I'd be in the barn."

Her throat constricted. How could she explain that she didn't want him to stop . . . ever? She simply gestured to the gloves. He leaned down and gathered them up, a bit solemn, as if wondering why she bothered looking after him. He stepped back inside the garret and held something out to her. "Careful you don't cut yourself."

Her eyes widened. "Skates?"

"I saw you stumble on the pond. These should give you no trouble."

Warmth rushed to her cheeks—and Jemma's flattering words melted to nothingness in her mind. *The Scottish apprentice was watching you . . . watching like a man who cannot watch enough.* Jemma had been wrong. He'd merely had pity on her because of her miserable skates.

She turned the shiny blades over in her hands, disappointment softened by wonder. These were no ordinary skates. Like everything else he made, they bore his unmistakable mark. The front blades were curved upward in the shape of a swan's head, graceful and shiny and smooth, so lovely they made her heart ache. He'd made them at the forge, right beneath her father's watchful gaze, in spite of his penny-pinching and thundering.

"A kindness for a kindness," he said, fisting his gloves.

Nay, she thought. This was more than a kindness. 'Twas daring—and a rebuke that Papa hadn't seen to it himself. "Thank you."

She studied him, drawn to the way the light framed his sturdy shoulders and gilded his hair. Flustered, she tried to summon the real reason she sought him out. Scripture. This alone propelled her to leave her pride at the foot of the stairs and come begging under the guise of giving him gloves. For a moment she felt as deceitful as Papa and Elspeth.

"I ken you need more than skates," he uttered.

She flushed at his insight, hoping the way her heart was hopping about her chest stayed hidden. "Yes."

Soundlessly, he brought out the Buik and sat down beside her, placing a candle on the step above. A stray draft wreaked havoc with the flame barely illuminating the Gaelic print. She marveled at his surety as he turned toward the back of the thick tome straightaway. Here was a man who knew where he wanted to go, even on the printed page. She lingered on his hands, clean yet creased faintly with coal dust. No longer did she see the scars, the branding. She saw only capability and purpose and strength.

"The book of John," he said quietly but with conviction. "'Tis the Lord of the universe's love letter to you."

She'd never before heard a preacher but was sure he sounded like one. The richness of his English and Gaelic sent shivers running down her arms, much like his music did. Twice she interrupted him, questions clamoring. He answered her carefully, even gently, and she felt undone by his tenderness.

"Would you write something down?" she whispered. "To take to heart?"

Shivering, she ached to follow as he returned to the garret, wanting to curl up on the rag rug by the Franklin stove. But she had to be content with a meager look at the room that had once been her hideaway. On the opposite wall was a map rife with black markings, some books and papers beneath. Curious, she stood to get a closer look, unmindful of the candle flame licking her dress hem. The sour smell of scorched wool wrenched her back to the stairwell as a cry of alarm crept up her throat.

Next she knew he was beside her, snuffing out the candle and her smoldering hem with his bare hands. She watched, taut with terror. More than one house had burned down in York County from such carelessness. And in the depths of winter, with nowhere to go . . .

"Are you hurt?" When he stood, his mouth—his warm breath—brushed her ear.

The gentle question circled in her head but made no sense. *He* was the one who'd just been burned! Stricken, she clasped his hands between hers out of habit, nearly bringing them to her lips. Like she did Thomas when he burned himself at the hearth, in a flurry of sympathy, as if she could kiss away his hurt. Above her thundering heart she could hear the click of a door below, loud as a musket in the quiet house. She let go of his hands.

Oh, Lord, please, not Elspeth!

Silently, Silas drew the door to the garret shut, blocking the light. His hands cupped her shoulders, anchoring her to the step, steadying her in the inky blackness. He faced her, his bristled chin grazing the top of her head. Comforting. Reassuring. A bit light-headed, she leaned into him, felt the soft linen of the shirt she'd made, senses aswirl with his nearness and strength. For a few exquisite seconds she couldn't think, couldn't breathe.

No other sound came. When he stepped back, cold air rushed between them. Without a word, he cracked open the garret door so that the candle within lit her way to her bedchamber below. The paper on which he'd written the Scripture was tucked in her hand. She couldn't wait till morning to read it. 'Twas precious to her as a love letter. A *billet-doux*, Jemma called it, practicing her French.

'Twas Christ's love letter to her.

14

Eat to please thyself, but dress to please others.

BENJAMIN FRANKLIN

For once Eden didn't want to go to Hope Rising. A medley of excuses tethered her to home. She had mending undone. Jon was especially fussy. Thomas had taken a fever. Elspeth was working in the smithy longer hours, leaving the running of the household to their overburdened mother. All morning she dragged about as if lead lined her shoes. Strangely, it was Mama who sent her packing.

Looking up from her dough tray, Mama cast a weary glance at the clock and simply said, "Be gone, Daughter. You're needed elsewhere this day."

And so off Eden went down the lane the eve of the ice harvest, pondering her reluctance, wondering what mischief Elspeth would concoct in her absence.

Father, protect Silas, please.

The sky was a pearl gray, low clouds weighted with snow, and a north wind licked the edges of her scarlet cape and

142

tried to usurp her bonnet. Steadying it with her hand, she was glad to find shelter among the linden trees—but they seemed colder than she, limbs bare and quaking, as they lined the long drive to the stately house.

Bypassing the handsome front door with its bold brass knocker fashioned by Papa's own hand, she sought the servants' entrance on the west side. There Margaret Hunter greeted her, looking like the Quaker she was in a prim wool dress, her salt-and-pepper hair captured in a severe knot beneath a cambric cap.

"Margaret, have you recovered?" Eden asked as she was ushered into the cozy keeping room in back of the immense kitchen.

"I can be nothing else on the eve of the harvest," she returned with a slight smile, pressing a handkerchief to a nose still reddened with cold. "David and the tenants are working themselves to the bone gathering tools and outfitting sleds and the like. They're planning on taking three tons of ice this year."

Three tons? Twice what they'd harvested in years past. Eden removed her bonnet, thinking of the coming work, praying it would prove successful.

"Shed thy cloak and I'll take thee to Jemma. She's all a-dither trying to decide which gown to wear to tomorrow's ball. First 'twas the painted silk, then the brocade, and now the velvet and lace. Likely when she sees thee she'll change her mind yet again."

Eden smiled. "'Tis half the pleasure, isn't it? Wondering what to wear?"

"Well, wondering must give way to deciding—and Jemma's having none of that." Margaret looked exasperated. "She has one too many new gowns when a single one would suffice!"

The snap of Margaret's heels atop the polished floor of the foyer seemed to announce their coming. Jemma leaned over the banister above, stripped to her petticoats and stays, pocket hoops astride her hips, a gloriously expectant smile upon her face. It wasn't Eden she addressed but Hope Rising's housekeeper, whose countenance held an uncommon sternness.

"Now, Margaret, don't look at me that way. Not even David is about to see me so. This old house echoes with emptiness."

"There are workmen coming to hang the crystal lusters," Margaret rebuked her, pausing at the foot of the staircase. "I would hate for them to utter abroad that they'd seen thee undressed."

Jemma simply laughed as Eden began the long climb upward, the freestanding staircase circling an elegant papered wall made bright with peacocks and green foliage. Unchanged since her childhood, every echoing room and fixture still left Eden slightly openmouthed with wonder. She supposed it wasn't grand as Philadelphia mansions went, but never having seen one, she had no such template in her mind.

"So what will it be, Jemma?" Eden asked, a bit awed at the disarray of the sumptuous room. "The silk, brocade, or velvet?"

"Nary a one!" With a flutter of her hand, Jemma motioned her in and all but slammed the door. "I'm so glad you've come. I miss having Bea and Anne here to cluck over me. But Margaret! Bah! Would that she was still sick and abed!"

"Then who would warm all that cider for the workers tomorrow?" Eden chided gently. "Or greet guests as they come to dance?"

Jemma's smile resurfaced. "Did you peek into the ballroom?"

"I've only seen the outside, not the inside."

"'Tis big as the ice pond! And so new it smells of paint. Don't stand too near the walls, mind you, lest you smear your dress."

"*Your* dress, you mean." Eden perched on the edge of a tapestry chaise and drank in the luxury that was Jemma's room. Pale peach paint. Delicate Chippendale furniture with its scroll and shell design. Large windows that overlooked Hope Rising's perennial garden and dovecote. Everything smelled of lavender water and powder. Was it any wonder after being in this elegant, peaceful bower, the mere thought of returning home made her melancholy?

Jemma threw open an immense wardrobe and stood, hands on hips, tapping her foot impatiently. Gowns of every hue and fabric were draped across chair backs and tables about the room. A stool displayed hair ornaments, a dressing table glittered with jewelry. Hat boxes were stacked about a bureau, tempting Eden to look inside.

"Tell me, Eden Rose, what color takes your fancy? And what shall we do with your hair?"

Ever mindful of Silas's rebuke, she felt her hand fly to her head self-consciously. "You decide which gown. As for my hair . . ." There was resignation in her voice as she fingered her wayward mane. Freshly washed, it hung in damp strands to her hips. "I shall wear it up, for the first time ever."

Jemma nodded approvingly. "We hardly need the curling tongs, just some pearl-tipped combs." She selected a jade gown with a deep rose petticoat. "How about this?"

Dismay sat squarely in Eden's stomach. The bold colors, the plunging bodice, the richness was all wrong. Elspeth would say she was putting on airs.

Casting her a knowing look, Jemma dropped the dress onto the floor and continued digging. "Don't fret—I've no wish to dress you like a doll. You prefer a simpler look, I know." Rummaging further, head buried in costly fabrics, she let out a little cry. "Voilà!"

With a triumphant smile, she pulled out a cloud of lilac silk. The bodice was adorned with silver flowers and leaves, the neckline ruched with a darker lilac ribbon, the quilted petticoat snow-white. Elegant and utterly feminine. Before she'd even touched the lustrous fabric, Eden had fallen in love.

"Yes," she whispered in confirmation and awe.

"You must try it on, though we'll be hard-pressed to fit your full bosom into so narrow a bodice. But with Margaret's help and my French stays . . ."

Eden's hands went to the hooks of her dress as Jemma began examining the gown's petticoat. "I only wore it once— to a boring tea at the Biddles' townhouse—as it pinched my waist so. You can have it for keeps." She paused, wicked humor in her eyes. "Speaking of waists, your sister's is none too small. I suppose all that time playing invalid over the winter has added a stone or two. I'm surprised she can squeeze into your yellow silk."

Eden kept her eyes on her own fumbling fingers. Did Jemma suspect little Jon's origins? Not once had Eden even hinted of their shameful secret. As she bent over to step out of her dress, the scrap of Scripture she'd hidden fluttered from her chemise to the floor. Startled, she reached out to retrieve it, but Jemma was faster, plucking the paper from the rich carpet.

"Eden, are you keeping secrets from me?" Her brows arched in question. "I've been wondering if you have a suitor."

"I—nay," Eden replied, reaching for the lilac silk. "Go ahead, read it if you must."

A rustle of paper preceded Jemma's rapt perusal. "For God so loved the world, that He gave His only begotten Son." Her delight faded. "Why, 'tis Scripture, not a love note! Who penned this? The hand is unfamiliar."

"Silas Ballantyne."

"The Scots apprentice?" Jemma's expression changed from surprised to disbelieving. "So he's a lettered man—and religious, even outside of church?"

"He seems so. And I—well, I simply want to learn the Bible . . ."

"The Bible?" Jemma's stare was blank. "I could lend you one from our library."

"Papa won't allow it," Eden said, gently pulling at a stray thread. "He burned our family Bible when he was read out of Quaker Meeting. Besides, I couldn't possibly hide such a big book—"

"Come now, Eden." Jemma's eyes were unusually canny. "I think this has more to do with your apprentice than your father."

Eden's hands stilled on the lush silk. "Please don't call him my apprentice. He's Elspeth's. Papa is desirous of a match. Everyone knows he needs a partner at the forge—"

"Then why is this Silas slipping you Scripture? And why are you keeping it close to your heart?"

Why, indeed? How could she explain her longing? Or confess Silas had almost made a game of it? Lately he left notes for her in all sorts of places . . .

In her egg basket. *Create in me a clean heart, O God.*

On her spinning wheel. *I can do all things through Christ which strengtheneth me.*

The toe of her work boot. *And ye shall know the truth, and the truth shall make you free.*

At the bottom of her mending. *Blessed are the peacemakers.*

Delighted, she'd memorized each one before secreting them in her journal, where she'd added Silas to her list of blessings.

Sadly, Jemma had little interest in spiritual matters. Not even Margaret's influence over the years had penetrated her worldly shell.

The dress forgotten, Eden sank down on the loveseat again. Though fearful of causing her friend undue hurt, she found it far easier to speak of Philadelphia and her hopes, however foolish, than Silas.

"So Bea is trying to arrange a place for you in the city?"

Jemma looked utterly deflated. "And neither of you have told me."

"I was going to tell you—eventually—but the plan may not happen. If Papa gets wind of it . . ."

"I know, I know." Sympathy creased Jemma's brow, and she passed the scrap of Scripture back to Eden. "You're unhappy at home. Elspeth is a constant thorn. Your father is no better—'tis been so for years. But you still haven't told me what learning Scripture has to do with all this."

Eden felt new fears welling and worked to keep her voice even. She'd have need of such poise in future. "The hospital board expects their staff to be well versed in spiritual matters. I am not."

"But you were educated in our very schoolroom. Mr. Seldridge taught us the Bible. Granted, not a great deal of it."

"I remember very little. 'Twas long ago. If the hospital finds out my father forsook his Quaker roots, that I've never once been to Meeting, to church—"

"Yes, of course. I understand." Though Jemma's voice stayed calm, her eyes registered unmistakable alarm. "But you're playing with fire in regards to your father—and Elspeth. Does the apprentice know of your plans?"

Eden plucked at a worn seam on her petticoat. "Nay."

"Nay?" Jemma threw up her hands. "Oh, Eden! Sometimes you are so maddeningly simple! What if Silas Ballantyne misconstrues your interest in Scripture for interest in him?"

Eden lifted her head, a new worry dawning. "What?"

With a roll of her eyes, Jemma expelled an audible breath. "I do believe you're the only girl I know whose head would be swimming more from Scripture than a handsome Scots tradesman!" She chuckled, her vexed expression softening somewhat. "Don't look so perplexed. Perhaps he sees you for the simpleton you are. 'Blessed are the pure in heart,' and all that. Though I must admit I wouldn't blame you for being smitten."

Eden took her tirade to heart, wishing she had but a kernel of Jemma's worldly wisdom. "Do you find him . . . handsome?"

"Do I?" A satisfied smile curved her lips. "I'll simply say this. When I first set eyes on Mr. Ballantyne at the Rising Sun Tavern, I was taken aback by his fine looks. And then I looked at Bea, who was staring, and saw Anne staring too. If you put him in a cravat and frock coat and breeches, every belle in Philadelphia would be fighting over him, not to mention the ones here in York. But alas, Elspeth has her claws in him, so he's met his doom."

Doom.

It was a word Eden disliked but found frightfully fitting. Sighing, she returned the Scripture to her bodice, trying to push Silas to the farthest corners of her mind.

She must get to Philadelphia posthaste.

A rogue wind sent the smithy doors banging, and Silas set lead weights against them to hold them open. They'd been loading wagon after wagon with ironwork all afternoon, and Eden's pup was gamboling about their feet with comical abandon. Twice Liege had shouted at the mongrel, which went slinking away only to return, tongue wagging, begging for company. He'd taken a strong liking to Silas, who'd made peace with his howling in the barn on the eves he spent fiddling. Now the pup was hopelessly underfoot and too slippery to tie up.

"Blast the cur!" Liege bellowed, wiping his brow with a scrap of linen. "Where's Eden gone to?" His disgruntled gaze swept the smithy before pinning Elspeth. "Where's your sister?"

"At Hope Rising, playing lady's maid to Jemma Great-house, likely. You gave your permission, Father." She looked up from the ledgers, quill in midair. "The ice harvest begins on the morrow, remember, then there's the ball."

"Which means you'll be shirking your work and attending also, no doubt." Liege tossed some tongs onto a table with a clatter. "I expect Silas to return you both home afterward. No later than midnight."

"Midnight? But the festivities go on till dawn."

"The dancing, you mean?" He shot her a disgusted look before taking in Silas. "I'll not have my apprentice fiddling himself to pieces, not even for a Greathouse. There's been no offer of payment, I suppose."

"Nor should there be." Silas faced him, hammer in hand. "I'll not play for hire."

"Nay? Then what will you play for?"

"The man asked me as a favor—"

Liege tossed up a fist as if deflecting his words. "Playing twelve hours without ceasing is no favor. 'Tis slavery." His scowl deepened. "The going rate for a frolic is two and six-pence to five shillings. I'll send word round that I expect—"

"You'll do no such sending round." Silas's rebuttal re-sounded to the far corners. "Our contract here is from dawn till dusk, excepting the Sabbath. No more, no less. If I want to fiddle myself to pieces, the call is mine to make."

Liege stared at him, visage reddening. No doubt he didn't care for a set-down in front of his daughter—or anyone else—but Silas held firm.

"Then I'll charge for your time on the ice," Liege replied, stalking out of the smithy as fast as his gout would allow.

Silas could hear another wagon approaching just beyond the smithy door. Lately business had doubled, but he felt no pleasure that it might be due to his work. He wiped his brow on his sleeve, the forge's fire burning his backside. As he positioned another piece of iron trim atop the anvil, Elspeth was at his elbow, the citrus scent of her overwhelming.

"I'm sorry about Papa, Silas. His leg is ailing him, which always spikes his temper." She handed him a cup of water, her gaze wandering to the door. "Why not take a rest? 'Tis been a long day. I'll see to the next need."

He took a drink, guessing the time, as he had no watch. He'd been waiting for Eden to call them in to supper, then realized anew she was missing—gone to Hope Rising. Her pleasure at being summoned there washed over him in a punishing wave. Never had he seen her so speeritie—so delighted—as when the Greathouses were mentioned. Weary as he was, he had no wish to recollect it now. Nor her dancing down the lane like Hope Rising was her home.

Picking up a stone, Elspeth hurled it at Eden's dog before he could stop her. It yelped and ran away. "Silas, are you listening?"

"Nae."

"Well, at least you're honest about it." Placing a hand on his arm, Elspeth returned his attention to her flushed face. Her eyes were hugely blue, reminding him of wild hyacinths . . . his Highland home. "Do musicians take leave of their instruments and dance?"

"Why d'ye ask?"

"Will you dance with me—at the ball?" Her expression for just a moment held a touching vulnerability. He'd seen the same in Eden—often. As if she was unsure of him, as if she expected only harshness from him, as she did her father.

"A dance, aye," he told her, returning to his work.

Her hand fell away and he sensed her disappointment. A dance he would give her, but nothing more.

15

*A winter's night, a woman's
mind, and a laird's purpose often
change.*

SCOTTISH PROVERB

Toward evening it began to snow. Standing by a damask-clad window, Eden felt a startling delight as the realization sifted through her. She'd prayed for snow. God had answered. Did He truly care about so small a matter as ice? The harvest would be a great success if the weather held.

She could hear David's voice ringing enthusiastically down the hall and turned in time to see him come through the drawing room door, shrugging off a greatcoat salted with flakes. He tossed it over a chair, then removed his hat and deposited it on a table, his fair features pinched with cold—and etched with surprise.

"Eden . . . what are you doing here?"

She gave a little shrug, unsure of her welcome. "I can disappear if you like." In the firelight, she detected a flicker of unease on his part, followed by a show of good manners.

"Don't you dare. I was expecting Jemma, is all."

"She's with Margaret seeing about supper."

"Ah, yes. We've a new cook." His expression grew grim. "You're brave to stay on."

She smiled, wanting to reach out and smooth his rumpled hair like she used to in the schoolroom, trying to master his impossible cowlick. "Jemma tells me she's good at making soup."

"Yes, and little else." He came to stand beside her at the window, pushing the drapes aside to better see into the twilight. The meadow lay before them, surprising her with its white beauty, the snow falling so fiercely it obscured the frozen pond. The scene was beautiful—even a touch romantic—with the crackling fire casting a golden glow about the room.

He looked down at her. "I'll take you to see the ballroom once supper is over. It's a bit grand for York, but so well done even miserly Uncle Eben, God rest him, would approve. The lusters are finally hung. Never mind that everything still smells of paint. 'Tis the price you pay for building in winter."

"I'm sure 'tis beautiful. Much better than the third-floor ballroom."

"Much bigger." His eyes glinted with anticipation. "And we'll have no mishaps, I'll wager, with guests on the stairs. You probably recall the brawl last year?"

She blushed at the mere mention. Surely he remembered how she'd hidden in the broom closet, a timid mouse. The rabble of York, as Papa called them, had had too much hard cider and not enough work. The failed harvest had turned some of them mean, one of the reasons Bea and Anne had excused themselves this year. Even Jemma had been badly frightened, fearing they might tear the place to pieces.

"This time I've hired help to keep order—some of the miller's sons."

A wise choice, Eden thought, as they were all burly as millstones. His arm brushed hers as he loosened his cravat. Face warming at this familiarity, she wished Jemma would appear. Lately she felt a bit odd alone with David, as if their old camaraderie was slipping away and turning them in a new direction. 'Twas in a word, a look, a too-long silence . . .

"Eden," he began. "I—"

A sudden commotion from behind made them pause. "Oh, there you are, David! Why didn't you tell me you'd come in? Cook's been waiting dinner." Jemma's bright smile negated her scolding. "Have you been here with Eden all along?"

He ran a hand through his disheveled hair, his tone rueful. "For a few minutes, anyway."

"You must be ravenous after working in this weather all day long."

Eden turned toward the table set for three before the ornate hearth, leaving them to their banter. The familiar French Sevres crystal and china were a blessed distraction, winking at her, making her wish she had on something other than a worn wool gown with a scorched hem.

She lifted her eyes to the stern, somewhat disapproving countenance of Eben Greathouse, eternally set in oils in a large gilt frame above the marble mantel. How was it that she, a blacksmith's daughter, was at the table of the heir to half of York County? The question seemed to take her by the shoulders and shake her, demanding she give answers when none were needed before.

Pleasure faded to wonder, then confusion. She swallowed past the sudden catch in her throat. She was here because Jemma was like a sister, because the Greathouses were kind and generous neighbors, because long ago her mother used to deliver cheese and honey to Hope Rising . . .

A chill danced up and down her spine.

Could there be more?

Light from the garret fell in a perfect square to the snowy ground below, ornate as a piece of Brussels lace. Elspeth studied it from the window seat of her bedchamber, far longer than she usually contemplated anything, indecision taunting her.

Should she or shouldn't she?

'Twas nearly midnight. She couldn't imagine what kept Silas awake. David had sent word that every available man was needed at Hope Rising by first light. As it was, Silas would get little sleep. Papa had been working him hard of late, so much so that she'd rebuked him again when Silas was out delivering ironwork in the wagon that very morning.

She remembered their confrontation now with renewed frustration, recalling how Papa's hands had trembled as he tried to hammer out a slab of hot metal that would have taken Silas half a minute. He'd been drinking again. His gout drove him to it, she knew. She wondered if spirits worsened his condition, as the doctor had recently suggested. But before he could have elaborated, Papa had called him a quack and thrown both him and his Keyser's pills out the door, forbidding him to come back.

"Father."

He'd looked up, eyes bloodshot, impatience knitting his brow.

Oh, what terrible timing on her part! But she had to seize the moment lest she lose it altogether. She threaded her fingers together and said firmly if quietly, "You're working too hard. You're working Silas too hard."

"Am I now?" The downward slant of his mouth twisted

into a fiercer frown. "He doesn't complain to my hearing—nor should you."

"He's likely too tired to do so." Fighting down her impatience, she worked to keep her voice even. "He's too tired to do much of anything—including any courting."

"Oh, so it's courting, is it? And bedamn the work?"

She set her shoulders at his icy tone. "He's not only slaving here from dawn till dusk but often misses supper to play at weddings and wakes all over the county."

"So? He's getting paid for his trouble."

Aye, and none of it was going into Papa's pocket. *That* was the real trouble. She quashed her growing fear that some pert miss might tempt Silas elsewhere and simply said, "Father, listen to reason. You are hampering the plan—*your plan*—before it comes to pass. The overdoing can come later, once we're wed. Give him time—"

"Give him time? You've been by his side nearly night and day since his coming here. If he's not taken with you now, he likely never will be."

Humiliation lashed her and she struck out at him with vehemence. "Because he's too tired! That's why! Between you and David Greathouse pressing him for all sorts of projects, he doesn't have an idle minute. I'm simply asking you to ease up a bit, leave Silas alone at the forge with me more often. Why don't *you* make deliveries in the wagon instead of sending him all over the county? It might rest your leg and accomplish more good in the end." She glanced about the smithy in frustration, certain a bit more privacy would achieve her ends.

I've not met a man I can't charm, many of whom darken the door of this forge, including Jon's father.

She pondered it now as she studied the square of light upon the snow, trying to plan her next move. There was something about Silas that made her tread lightly as no other man had. She couldn't put her finger on it no matter how hard she tried, and she hated that it rendered her powerless. Regardless of her dress or cologne or sashaying about, Silas hardly looked at her. She might as well don breeches and boots!

She went to the bedchamber door and opened it slowly, listening to the household settling. With Eden at Hope Rising, she had the run of the second floor. The garret stair she knew like her own name, even in the dark. Below, Jon began wailing again—a strangely welcome sound that masked any creaking she made on her climb. She was halfway to the garret when his crying ceased.

Uncertainty pulsed through her. She hovered, eyes on the light beckoning beneath Silas's door. And then, before she drew her next breath, he'd snuffed it out. The click of a lock and the taut stretching of bed rope assured her he'd lain down. She felt a stinging defeat, as if he'd heard her after all and avoided her coming.

❧

Snow was still falling. Eden awoke in the night, Jemma slumbering beside her, and slipped through the bed curtains, a brilliant backlog in the hearth lighting her way to a window. Perhaps too much snow was as bad as rain, she mused groggily. How would they clear such a load from the ice? Curling up on the window seat, she tried to see beyond the frosted pane but soon fell asleep.

At daybreak, the shouts of men beyond the window shook her awake. She'd dozed against a bank of cushions, hardly in need of a blanket, for Jemma's room was far warmer than her own. Dawn touched the sky—a gentle palette of pink and cream. The snow lay on the land and pond nearly a foot deep, with little sign of abating.

Through the blur of whiteness, she dismissed the men one by one, mostly Hope Rising's tenants and its overseer, till she came to Silas. Easily distinguished by his height, he was surrounded by a dozen or more men huddled in heavy coats that would soon be shed when the cutting began. For now they were shoveling snow off the pond, creating a creamy drift around the edge. Horse-drawn sleds awaited, ready to bear their loads to the two icehouses behind the main house and summer kitchen.

Donning worn boots and cardinal cape in the keeping room below, Eden ventured out to help Margaret, who'd left a plain trail, pushing a small cart just ahead of her. 'Twas a long trek across the meadow, where a huge kettle of cider hung over a fire, its leaping flames melting the surrounding snow.

Margaret greeted her with a warm if weary smile, adding spices to the kettle. "Our prayers for wintry weather have been answered this day." As Eden stuck out her tongue to taste the flakes from behind a gloved hand, Margaret chuckled. "Thee are as excited about the snow as a little girl. Have thee brought thy skates?"

In answer, Eden held up the ones Silas had made her, anxious to be on the ice, and smiled at Margaret's appreciation.

David was at the pond's center, marking a pattern across the glistening surface to show where the work should begin. Silas was coming toward him with a long crosscut saw, expression stoic. Her gaze swung like a pendulum between the two men.

Silas wasn't as steady on his feet as David, at least on the ice, though his skates glinted new like her own, fashioned for the work to come. He'd had little time for skating as a lad in Scotland, he'd said, with blacksmithing and sheepherding to be done, and an abundance of music to be made at the duke's beck and call.

It seemed every man had a different tool—saws, axes, sledgehammers, and the all-important pikes to pull the ice blocks free and load them onto the sleds. 'Twas bruising work, requiring a great deal of strength. Though there were a few graying heads, she saw mostly young men, the pride of York County, many who'd helped with the harvest since they were small.

Donning her skates, she kept to the outskirts of the pond, watching Silas as he stood with the saw, his dark profile in stark relief against the brilliant backdrop of white. She lingered on him as she would never do at home, for he was seemingly unaware of her, intent on the matter at hand. With so many men in her line of sight, she might have been looking at any one of them or simply watching the work. No one would know.

His shorn hair curled against his coat collar, and she marveled anew that he'd cut it. Melting snowflakes gave it the sheen of rich Chinese silk. The shadow of his beard turned him a bit roguish, heightening the intensity of his eyes, straight nose, and unsmiling mouth. All so very pleasing. No wonder Elspeth was smitten.

Beside him, David seemed a bit too short. A bear in his bearskin coat. There seemed an edge to both men today, a tension barely reined in. She sensed a multitude of emotions at play beneath their handsome exteriors and wondered the cause. David's mood, she'd learned long ago, could alter as quick as mercury, and like many a Scotsman, Silas no doubt had a temper. That he'd not lost it with her father seemed a miracle.

The morning passed with few mishaps, the first sled lined with sawdust and loaded with huge blocks of ice. Eden stood with Margaret, passing out cups of hot cider to the laborers as women and children began to gather—to flirt or skate or watch the work—along the edges of the pond. Though she saw no sign of Elspeth, she braced herself for her coming.

"Eden."

The voice, a bit hoarse with cold, raked the edges of her composure. Silas stood behind her, awaiting a steaming cup, which she delivered with an unsteady hand.

Margaret's amber gaze took him in. "Is this thy apprentice, Eden?"

The wording brought about a near-crushing embarrassment. "Y-yes, this is Silas Ballantyne." She fastened her eyes on his greatcoat, finding refuge but forgetting introductions.

"Welcome, friend Silas." Margaret's tone was as cordial and deferential as if greeting General Washington himself. "I'm Margaret Hunter, Hope Rising's housekeeper."

He gave a slight nod. "Eden has made mention of you."

"Eden is like a daughter to me. Faithful. Industrious. Kind. I don't know what I'd do without her."

At such high praise, Eden turned away, hoping to dispense more cider, but Silas was the last in line.

Margaret seemed determined to stay him. "And how do thee find York County?"

He hesitated—a bit too long, Eden feared. He didn't like it here, she sensed, but was reluctant to say so. "'Tis not Scotland, nor Philadelphia," he said. "But it has its charms."

His eyes met Eden's, and she saw a spark of amusement there. A sly warmth. And then it vanished so quickly she thought she'd imagined it.

"I'd thought to see Elspeth," Margaret said, looking about. "She's tardy this day."

"She's busy," Silas replied, "preparing for the ball."

Eden detected wry humor in his words and felt a flicker of guilt that she'd fled to Hope Rising so readily. Their dear mother would get little assistance this day—and a mountain of tasks would await Eden once she went home on the Sabbath.

A sudden cry went up to return to the ice, and Silas finished his cider and thanked her, his gloved hands brushing her own. Flustered, she nearly dropped his empty cup as he walked away. Could Margaret see her high color? She felt nearly on fire with it and ached to remove her bonnet. The snow was shaking down with such abandon she could scarcely make out David at the heart of it all.

Margaret was studying her now, sipping her own cider. "Thy apprentice has fine manners, Eden."

Too fine for a tradesman, Eden thought. "I imagine he's picked up a few social graces being acquainted with the duke of Atholl."

"I've heard he plays a fine fiddle, like his father before him."

"Oh?"

"David has made inquiries."

Inquiries. In Philadelphia? The Greathouses had so many connections. Why should she be surprised?

"I must say I'm looking forward to the ball," Margaret told her, though she sighed when she said it. "I've always enjoyed a bit of entertainment . . . if all goes well."

With that, she moved toward the house to replenish the cider, her skirt hem trailing in the snow. Eden brushed off the brim of her own bonnet, wishing Jemma would join her, wanting Elspeth to stay away. There was no telling what the ball would bring with her sister in attendance. David had spoken of last year's near riot. Being a gentleman, he hadn't mentioned Elspeth's antics.

Oh my . . . Her face burned brighter in recollection.

16

*There, when the sounds of flute and
fiddle
Gave signal sweet in that old hall.*

WINTHROP MACKWORTH PRAED

Hope Rising's new ballroom was uncommonly elegant. David had told her its dimensions, a touch of pride in his tone. Ninety-two feet long, forty-two feet wide, and thirty-six feet high. Tall Palladian windows pulled the outdoors in, each pane sparkling with the light of a dozen crystal lusters. Eden felt entranced as she waited in one polished corner, half hidden by a potted palm from the greenhouse. Surely there was no finer ballroom in Philadelphia. Guests were beginning to gather in all manner of dress, from costly satins and brocades to more homely wools, depending on their station.

At Eden's side, behind the privacy of her lace-tipped fan, Jemma was providing a running social commentary of all who entered. "Ah, doesn't Miss Phoebe look grand in blue luster? I'd not thought to see her on the arm of Johnny so soon after being jilted. And look at Fanny Crockett there by the punch bowl! She has two suitors dangling, or so I'm told . . ."

Though Jemma had been away in the city, she didn't lack for local gossip. Eden was concerned only with Elspeth, but for the moment Silas was taking her attention. Gone were the shabby greatcoat and work clothes that marked him day in and day out. Someone—Margaret?—had supplied him a finely tailored shirt, among other things.

Eden took in all its gentlemanly lines, lingering on the creamy cravat tied in perfect symmetry about his neck and anchored at the back with a silver buckle. It flashed in the candlelight when he turned, drawing her eye. She couldn't see the rest of him for the surrounding musicians. Dismay burrowed deep inside her when she spied Elspeth lingering near the circular platform on which he stood, clutching a fan of her own.

For once, she failed to feel the sting of her sister wearing the yellow silk, perhaps because Jemma had spared no pains with Eden's appearance. All afternoon she'd been scented, groomed, and coiffed. Now, fully gowned, she flexed her fingers in the elaborate gloves Jemma had insisted on—snowy kid leather with a trio of mother-of-pearl buttons at the wrist. Infused with a rose-carnation fragrance, they were the rage among city belles.

Moments before, to her astonishment, someone had asked if she was one of Jemma's Philadelphia friends. She'd hardly recognized herself when she'd stood before the looking glass, nor could she blame Elspeth for staring at her from across the room. Even at a distance, she read blatant envy in her sister's eyes. Slipping behind the nearby potted palm brought little relief from her sister's ongoing scrutiny.

"Here's your fan," Jemma said, handing her one of painted silk. "You look . . . overcome, Eden. Are you too tightly laced?"

Truly, she was. Margaret had even broken a bodkin when binding her in Jemma's French stays. "I . . ." she began, extending the fan to cool her flushed face. "People are staring—"

"*Elspeth* is staring, you mean. Well, let her. It's her fault you're so lovely in lilac. She stole your yellow silk." Jemma's fan fluttered with unbridled enthusiasm. "David and I will lead the first dance, but he's told me you're to be his second. Which would you like? A reel? An allemande? Something a bit more sedate like the minuet?"

"'Tis been so long since I've danced, I'm unsure." The half truth nearly made her wince. She'd danced with Silas in the barn but a fortnight before . . .

Jemma snapped her fan shut, eyes on Elspeth. "I'll go ask Mr. Ballantyne which he prefers. 'Tis his music we'll be dancing to, after all."

Silas began tuning his instrument, occasionally looking up to keep apace of the growing crowd. Across the gleaming parquet floor, David Greathouse was stationed at the ballroom's double doors, greeting his tenants and other York folk while his cousin sliced through the throng in Silas's direction. Wearing sapphire silk, Jemma was hard to miss, and her arrival at the small stage upon which Silas stood was creating a stir. It served as a cue that the dancing would soon begin. Guests slowly began to clear the ballroom floor, though their excited chatter never lessened.

"Good evening, Mr. Ballantyne." Jemma's forthright manner had endeared her to Silas in the short time he'd known her. She smiled up at him and seemed to ease the social chasm that separated them. "My cousin and I would like to lead out with 'Sir Roger de Coverly.' Is that familiar to you?"

He felt a striking relief. "Aye," he answered. It was the tune most preferred by the Americans, much like a Scots reel, and he knew it well enough.

She toyed with her fan as it dangled from her wrist, her round face luminous in the light of the lusters. "David will partner with Eden Lee after that. Have you a second tune in mind?"

Turning, he conferred with the other musicians, a ragtag lot of York men in their modest best. "The minuet," he told her, "in three-quarter time."

"Very well," Jemma said, looking pleased. "After that you may play whatever you wish—or take requests."

She turned away, leaving him to draw his bow across each string, judging the sweetness of the tone. The black dress coat Margaret had lent him lay across the back of his chair, mayhap one of the master's own. It was too confining for fiddling, and though the room was cold, he'd soon grow warm in his shirtsleeves. A trickle of perspiration brought on by apprehension coursed down his back, reminding him he had no wish to be here among these people, as musician or tradesman or otherwise.

He watched Jemma walk past Elspeth with nary a nod as she stood to one side of the stage. Noticed, too, the tightening of Elspeth's features at the snub. Observing it, Silas felt a swell of sympathy for her. What, he wondered, made one daughter desirable and the other an outcast? That the residents of Hope Rising favored Eden was apparent. He didn't blame them. Her simplicity, her generous spirit, tugged at his own head and heart when he let it.

At the center of the ballroom, Greathouse was making a toast to the workers and to a successful ice harvest. Though they'd not gotten the coveted three tons, the icehouses were full and there was plenty of cold punch and the requisite syllabub to be had—a necessity for the long night ahead. 'Twas but eight o'clock. The laird wanted the dancing to go on till dawn. There'd be a few brief breaks spanning those hours and a light supper at midnight. Though a far cry from the duke of Atholl's assemblies, the gathering was impressive for York County. Americans had big ambitions, Silas mused. Now that the war was won, he guessed there was little to stop them.

Just below, Elspeth was looking at him, and he gave her a slight smile. He hadn't seen Eden but felt responsible for them both, as Liege had made it abundantly clear he was. Come the wee hours, he'd have to escort them home. A glance at a door opening to a balcony told him snow was still tumbling down. It would be a cold, bright walk and they'd need no lantern light.

Positioning his violin, he nodded at his fellow fiddlers and started the count before he struck the reel's opening chord. The rhythm was so infectious he could see a hundred heads nodding and feet tapping about the large room. Every strained muscle, every bit of weariness from the day-long harvest, began to recede as he played.

A great many couples joined David and Jemma for the long, rousing reel, their fancy dress a brilliant kaleidoscope of color. Though Silas was more intent on the music than the dancers, he looked up the precise moment Eden took the floor. A freshet of heat that had nothing to do with his exuberant fiddling shot through him.

Greathouse was gazing down at her, making her seem as small as a doll in a dress that was more flower than garment. Silk buttons held her skirts aloft for the dancing, revealing a richly quilted petticoat and kid slippers. Pearl combs were set like a crown atop her head, sweeping back her fiery hair in faultless curls rather than sending it plummeting unfashionably down her back. Out of drab wool, she was transformed. Not a blacksmith's daughter. Nor a girl-of-all-work. A rare beauty.

As he looked on, a stitch of concern lanced him. *Is that your intent, lass? To make the laird fall in love with you?*

His bow seemed unsteady. He forced himself to look away, to pay attention to the intricacies of the minuet and naught else. Pages of music were spread on the ornate mahogany stand before him—Corelli, Handel, Haydn, the Earl of Kelly—but he couldn't read a note. Her image seemed burned in his brain, and he doubted even Scots whiskey could dislodge it. 'Twas a relief to move on to the English country dances and quadrilles. When he looked up again, she was lost in the crowd, but he had little time to lament the fact. Out of the corner of his eye, he saw Elspeth leaving out a side door.

He finished the set and excused himself, exchanging his fiddle for his coat. It seemed an age before he'd navigated the crowd and gained the door Elspeth had just exited. The veranda outside was slick; he had to cross with care to where she was standing. Snowflakes lay on her hair and shoulders like a gossamer scarf, and her back was to the ballroom in rigid defiance.

He draped the coat over her shivering shoulders and worked to keep his tone even. "Why are you not dancing?"

"Why?" She looked up at him, tearstains frozen on her face. "Because no one asks."

"How can they when you're standing out here in the cold?"

"It doesn't matter if I'm here or there, not when Eden is the favored one."

There was a petulant tone to her words he didn't like, though he understood her hurt. "I ken what it's like to play second fiddle to someone. To be overlooked. Ignored."

"You?" Her expression was disbelieving.

"I'm naught but a poor apprentice who was but a poor fiddler's son before that."

"But your father was in the duke of Atholl's employ—"

"For a few shillings per engagement. Not enough to feed a family or keep his land, what little there was of it." He paused, feeling the weight of those lean years roll over him, wanting to move past them rather than resurrect them. "There will always be servants and masters, the favored and unfavored. Hold your head up and rise above it."

"'Tis hard to do with a sister who is always flaunting her favors." She faced him, the fire of jealousy in her eyes. "Did you see the dress she has on?"

Aye, to his everlasting regret. "'Tis not my concern, nor yours. Come back into the ballroom."

"But—"

"I have to return to playing."

She stiffened, tugging his coat closer about her shoulders. "You promised me a dance."

Impatience needled him. Och, but she was a handful and a half. "Aye, I did, but I'll not do so on a frozen porch and risk our necks."

Turning away, he went back into the ballroom. She followed none too meekly, though she did return his coat to the stage. Only ten o'clock. The night would be long indeed. Withholding a groan, he reached for his fiddle. At least where he was going there'd be none of this foolishness. He had to endure but a few more months of the Lees.

✌

Eden noted the moment Elspeth left the ballroom and felt keenly the instant Silas went after her. Jemma's chattering turned shrill in her ear, and the pastry she was eating became mush in her mouth. Without the force and skill of Silas's playing, his presence, the middling musicians seemed like wax figures upon the stage. She felt a glowing pride in his abilities and then pointed alarm when he disappeared.

Oh, Lord, let it not happen again. Please . . .

Fixing her eye on the door they'd both exited, she felt her heartbeat quicken. Had it been almost a year since Elspeth had coerced David into a secluded corner and disgraced herself? Everyone at Hope Rising knew she'd tried to seduce him, beginning with that bold kiss. A sickening trepidation crept over Eden at the memory. Would her sister now do the same with Silas? Murmuring she needed some air, she began pushing her way through the crowd toward the dreaded door. One man, then two, barred her way and begged her to dance.

"No, thank you . . . not right now, thank you."

Her voice held desperation. Long seconds ticked by in a sort of agony. Though she fixed her gaze on the nearest window, she could see little for the darkness outside. Suppose she found them in an embrace? The barest thought of it left her shaking. She was nearly to the door when it opened a bit forcefully. Silas entered, head down in a bid to be discreet, perhaps. Seconds later her sister followed, draped in fine broadcloth. The thought that Silas had set it about her sister's shoulders rubbed her raw.

"Would you care to dance, Miss Eden?"

She looked up into the flushed face of the gunsmith's son. Slowly they joined the press of dancers scuffing the newly laid floor as Silas took the stage and struck a cotillion. One partner . . . two . . . four. The evening passed in a sort of haze, leaving her thirsty and flushed, the distillation of sweat and spirits swirling like the couples all around her.

As the clock chimed eleven, Silas stood before her. He bent low over her hand in invitation and she curtsied, feeling a bit dazed as a Scots reel was struck. He'd claimed her in private. Would he now claim her publicly? *This* was no barn dance. She felt the heat of his hands through the silk of her gown as he clasped her waist.

The intensity of his gaze shook her, dark with passion and purpose and things unspoken. She couldn't look away . . . couldn't think. It might have been but the two of them, their pairing was so consuming, pushing everyone else to the far corners of the room. Her tumbled feelings left her breathless, and she could no longer shove aside a daunting realization.

Elspeth was not the only one smitten with a poor Scots apprentice.

∞

'Twas snowing again. The purity of the morning solaced Silas somewhat, seemed a balm for his brooding. Though Hope Rising's revelry had ended at four o'clock, he'd gotten little sleep. The hour he'd lain down he'd done naught but stare at the garret rafters, thoughts of Eden keeping him awake. At first light he'd traipsed through knee-deep snow to the barn, hoping to cool his thoughts as he readied the horses and sleigh to return to Hope Rising.

Greathouse had insisted he take the sisters home in his colonial cutter, though Silas suspected it was Eden he was most mindful of. The certainty had come to him slowly, crystallizing the moment the laird had led her onto the dance floor. Watching them, Silas was violently catapulted back to the past—to the eve of his sister's staining. 'Twas at a tenants' ball the duke's son had claimed Naomi Ballantyne for a dance. Too bonny by half—and utterly naïve—she'd succumbed to that reel with Jamie Murray. And far more.

His hands worked the leather harness with its bells and brass trim in rough bursts, belying his turmoil. The matching grays bumped about in their stalls as if sensing his disquiet. As he prepared to hitch them to the sleigh—so new that wax still adhered to the runners—he heard the whine of the barn door as it opened. Liege? No one had been astir when he'd passed through the house minutes before. 'Twas the Sabbath, after all.

He kept working—fastening, buckling, tightening—aware that he wasn't alone. But he hardly expected Eden to be the one watching. Not when she'd fallen asleep in the sleigh and he'd shaken her awake, thinking he'd have to carry her up the stairs.

"Silas?"

His efforts stilled. What, he wondered, did she call Greathouse when alone with him?

"What are you doing at this hour?" Her gentle question held a touching concern. Why, then, did it feel like salt upon a wound?

"Come now, Eden," he echoed tersely, not looking up, the harness frigid in his hands. "What does it look like?"

"You're returning the sleigh. That I can see." She came closer, surprising him. The force of his voice all but ordered her out of the barn.

Letting go of the leather trappings, he faced her. But it was Naomi he saw, so bonny and blithesome, her eyes a vivid lichen-green.

Her voice was soft. "You're upset."

His anger cooled in light of her tenderness. "I've no quarrel with you, Eden."

"Oh?" She stepped closer. "Then why is there such fire in your eyes . . . your voice?"

Once his sister had asked him the same. They'd stood a few paces apart in a sheep barn as he was choosing ewes from a pen of yearlings. Only he'd been but a bumbling boy and had no answer. But now . . .

"I'm not upset with you, Eden, but Greathouse."

"Master David?"

"Aye."

"Has he done you some harm?"

"Nae . . . though he may."

"Though he may?" Her tone, her expression, was rife with disbelief. David could do no wrong, she seemed to say, and he, Silas Ballantyne, could do no right. "What mean you?"

Taking a measured breath, he tried to push past emotion to sound reason, but the heat of his temper had the upper hand. "What d'ye know of life, Eden? Men?"

She flushed. "I—David is but a neighbor, a friend. He's . . ."

"He's a man. And I fear he'll take advantage of your charms."

"My . . . charms?" Confusion marred her features. "You must be imagining things—"

"Wheesht, Eden!" He ran a hand over his jaw, done with her naïveté. "I am not a blind man! I've seen the way he looks at you—"

"What?" She flushed a deeper rose. "David doesn't—couldn't—care for me—couldn't love me—"

"I said naught about love, ye ken." His Scots was so thick, so passionate, he doubted she got the gist of it. But the stricken look on her face assured him she did. Yet she was innocent of all this, he remembered. Untried. Untouched. Unlike Elspeth. She deserved some explanation for his outburst. He gentled his tone, glad for the duskiness of the barn. "At home—in Scotlain—I watched the duke's son make sport with my sister. I'll not stay silent and see the same happen with you and Hope Rising's heir."

Turning away, she stood with slumped shoulders. He could sense her shock, her working through all the shameful implications. Likely no man had ever spoken to her so bluntly. But what choice did he have? He resumed his work, only to be caught short by her quiet question.

"You have a sister?"

"*Had*, Eden." His chest grew heavy, his thoughts muddy. "She died in childbed, bearing Sir Jamie's son."

The silence lengthened and then she came nearer, her fingers touching the loose sleeve of the shirt she'd made him. "What was her name?"

Her name . . . The gentle question brought about a shattering ache. He'd not spoken it in years. "Naomi."

"'Tis beautiful."

"'Tis biblical. Like yours . . . mine." He met her eyes. He couldn't help it. There seemed to be an invisible cord that bound them, forged in the secrecy of the stairwell, keen and heartfelt. A tear spotted her cheek, sliding to her chin. He ached to brush it away, but the sudden mist in his own eyes caught him off guard. "I care for you like a sister, Eden. I do not want you hurt."

Her eyes shone in the shadows. She swallowed hard and let go of his sleeve. "I'm sorry for your loss, Silas. For all of them. 'Tis one too many."

She was remembering his family, Scotland, as he was, and his warning about Greathouse seemed to be lost in a cloud of melancholy. He'd learned not to dwell on the past. He'd not thought to mention it now.

"Take care, ye ken," he told her, returning them to the matter at hand. "If he should ever hurt you, lay a hand on you—"

"Silas, please." Alarm framed her lovely features. "Think no more of it."

She turned away, and he feared she wouldn't heed his warning. The allure of Hope Rising was too great. And her trust in David Greathouse was too deep. She was, like Naomi, so utterly and breathtakingly naïve. The thought of a man making free with her modesty, destroying her beauty and innocence in a swirl of lust, twisted his gut into a fierce knot.

God help her . . .

God help me.

17

That which is escaped now is pain to come.

SAMUEL JOHNSON

Though more than a month had passed since Silas had spoken so plainly to her in the barn, Eden's cheeks still burned at the memory. She avoided both him and David, her whole world upended by his strong words, before deciding his warning was simply clouded by the pain of his past. David was but a childhood friend. Not once had he behaved in anything but a gentlemanly fashion. Even lately, when she'd sensed something stirring beneath the surface of their long-standing friendship, his manner was as careful and deferential as Silas's own.

And Silas? She was like a sister to him. He'd simply spoken out of concern and affection. Still, this free speaking hurt her, as did the matter of Naomi and her babe. Their story haunted, trailing after her day and night. She felt a gnawing need to know what happened to Sir Jamie and Naomi's child but dared not ask. Only within the pages of her journal did she spill out her muddled feelings . . .

"Eden Rose, don't stand there staring!"

The vicious snap of Elspeth's voice returned her to the steamy kitchen and Jon's wailing and her own soapy hands.

"The babe is crying, and Mama has gone to York. Do something!"

Elspeth stood at the trestle table, punching down a mound of dough with both fists. Since she and Silas had returned from yesterday's Sabbath service, Elspeth had been in a high temper. Wary, Eden gave her wide berth. But now, with Mama missing, they'd been thrust together and it was Elspeth giving orders.

"Hurry and test the oven, then tend to Jon!"

Abandoning the dishes she'd been scrubbing, Eden went to the hearth, held her hand in the beehive oven, and counted to ten to test the heat before hurrying to her parents' bedchamber. When she leaned over Jon's cradle, he quieted, his plump face breaking into a sunny smile. Her heart twisted.

"Oh, wee one, you are such a sweet babe."

His tiny hand brushed her cheek as she lifted him and nuzzled his milk-scented neck, the linen of his swaddling smelling of dried lavender from her garden. Moving past Thomas asleep on the trundle bed, she glanced out the window. The March day held such spring-like warmth she was pulled to the front door. Closing it quietly, she walked through new grass toward the kitchen garden, gaze drifting across the zigzag fence of the pasture where the wheat and flax fields awaited seed. In years past Papa had traded planting and plowing for ironwork so that he could continue to man the smithy. This year he was relying on Silas instead.

Turning a corner, she was startled to find Silas standing at the edge of her herb bed, shovel in hand. The cold earth had been hand-turned and needed but half a day of stone picking to ready it for seed. 'Twas a task she'd always seen to till blisters spotted her palms. Had he done this for her? Gratitude welled inside her and she smiled her thanks. They'd not spoken in so long she felt suddenly tongue-tied.

Leaning on his shovel, he raked calloused fingers through his hair and glanced at Jon, answering her question before she'd even asked it. "The day is too fine to be confined to the forge."

Immediately she sensed something amiss. Had he and Papa had words? His features held a telling restlessness, and he was looking west again, as he so often did. It made her melancholy, as if he couldn't attend to the beauty at hand, and it was everywhere. All around them the land was slowly coming to life beneath the strengthening sun, its brightness dotted with wisps of clouds. Mares' tails, Grandpa Gallatin had called them, galloping across the delft-blue sky.

"I'll spend but one spring in this place," he said.

But one? Eden looked at him, her perplexity swelling. All the loose ends of late now came together at his words. Was this why Elspeth was so fractious? Had the matter of marriage been broached and shot down? Jon gave a little cry, and she shifted him in her arms, aware of his hunger but hesitant to feed him just yet.

"Are you leaving? Earlier than October?" The need to know raised a great lump in her throat. "Where are you going?"

His shovel struck dirt again. "I'll tell you where I'm going, Eden, if you'll tell me where you're going."

She took a step back, surprised by the keen light in his eyes, as if they shared some secret. Did he know about Philadelphia? She felt a whisper of alarm. How could he?

"I—I must see to Jon." With that, she spun away, hurrying to the house. As her hand touched the kitchen door, she was startled by the rasp of Papa's voice as he came out of the smithy.

"Silas! I must speak with you."

The gruff words bespoke a heated confrontation. She'd not heard such ire in her father's voice since he'd sparred with the last apprentice. Except George White had never stood up to the master. She sensed Silas had, and now Papa was defensive as a wounded bear.

Silas leaned the shovel against the wattle fence and began walking toward the smithy, his every step rife with resistance. Aye, something had indeed transpired. And it boded ill for them all. Her dread deepened when her father slammed the smithy's side door.

Lord, help him . . . protect him, please.

<hr>

"Nae." Raising his hammer, Silas resumed his work as calmly as if they were discussing the weather. "I came here to fulfill a contract, not take a wife."

Across from him Liege stood, hands on hips, face reddening. "Lay your hammer down, man, and speak reason. You well know 'tis tradition for an apprentice to marry into the master's family. 'Tis not a country custom. They do it oft enough in Philadelphia."

Silas gave the pike a heavy blow. "Tradition does not dictate my actions. 'Tis business between us, no more." He thrust the white-hot metal into the cooling trough, and a fierce sizzle filled the room.

Liege threw up his hands. "Is it a common Scots trait to be blind and unreasonable—and immune to a woman's charms?" His aggravated voice carried to the far rafters. "There are a great many men who'd gladly have my eldest daughter."

"Then why is she not wed?"

Liege swiped at his damp brow and stepped away from the forge's fire. "No one has suited her till now. 'Tis you she favors. Being sharp-minded, she knows what such a pairing means. This will all be yours—and Elspeth's. Business has tripled since your coming. I've scarce the ledgers to keep up. Soon you'll find yourself with enough coin to do as you please, go where you please. One day the Ballantyne name will be spoken of from here to Philadelphia."

Silas shook his head. "Men do not grow rich forging iron in small smithies."

"Who's to say we cannot?" Liege erupted with a sudden cackle, his mood shifting. "Your purse is only as big as your dream."

"I'll not wed your oldest daughter," Silas said again, "bonny though she may be."

"*May* be? You're a blind man! She *is* bonny! Are you betrothed, then? Intended for another?"

"Nae."

"Then why such caution?" Liege brought his hand to bear on the nearest table. "Speak, man! Speak!"

Silas fell silent, inspecting his work, refusing to answer. He could sense Liege's simmering was reaching a slow boil, and he prayed for patience, refusing to become embroiled in the scheme. But the master was not letting up this morning.

Liege circled the forge, his voice low and barbed. "You may sing a different tune when I terminate your contract."

"Then you shall have no apprentice or wedding," Silas replied, striking a clamorous blow to the pike as if to punctuate his words.

"Leave off your hammering and listen to me." Liege faced him, tearing off his apron. "If you'll not have Elspeth, how about Eden?"

The question was so mercenary, so coldly stated, Silas nearly flinched. His grip tightened on his hammer till his knuckles whitened. "So you do not care who I wed, just that I take one of them to wife?"

A loud banging on the smithy door spared him Liege's answer. Silas resumed his work, lost in a deluge of unwanted desires as the master turned away. Every hammer blow was a bit harder and high-toned. He bent the iron mercilessly, wishing he could do the same with his emotions. But it seemed Eden stood at his elbow, shadowing him, strengthening their tie.

When, he wondered moodily, had he lost his heart to her? The snowy day he'd seen her dancing down the lane? The night she'd snuck into the stairwell and brought him both razor and shirt? When Greathouse claimed her for a dance?

God forgive him, but he couldn't dislodge the memory of her in her purple gown, the small perfection of her waist, the lush lines of all the rest of her. Countless times in his dreams he'd pressed his mouth to hers, felt the silk of her skin against his work-worn fingers.

She *haunted* him.

He'd come here not wanting any entanglements, had meant to simply bide his time and go. But lately, despite his prayers and precautions, all his carefully constructed defenses had come crashing down. In the weeks since the ice harvest, he'd ached to hear her in the stairwell, but she hadn't come. He'd even entertained the foolish notion of wedding her and taking her west, the place she clearly had no desire to go. And now, Liege Lee had put temptation in his path and he found it nearly irresistible.

"I'll give you a month to make up your mind," Liege spat at him.

Silas turned round, the sledge slack in his hand, schooling his expression against the force of the ultimatum. The forge was empty now save the two of them. Liege had sent the farmer on his way.

"'Tis Elspeth or Eden," Liege said. "Or you'll be without a trade—and a roof o'er your head."

18

*But, oh! What mighty magician
can assuage a woman's envy?*
GEORGE GRANVILLE, LORD LANSDOWNE

Elspeth looked up from her sewing, eyes on Eden, who mended across the parlor, one foot absently rocking Jon's cradle. The tender sight set her teeth on edge but was less annoying without Silas there. She'd caught him looking at Eden on more than one occasion of late—or fancied he did. But tonight he'd absented himself and gone straight to the garret room after supper, thus sparing her any further suspicions.

"There's a fever going round," Mama lamented, watching Silas depart with a worried cast to her features. "His color is a bit high."

Threading her needle, Elspeth listened to his tread upon the stair. "Last night he came in well past midnight from playing at another frolic. 'Tis a wonder he can swing a hammer like he does."

Still, she sensed his absence was another matter entirely. Papa had forced the issue of marriage, and Silas had balked.

It could be nothing else. Though she'd sensed a confrontation coming, she'd feared Silas's response. She sensed his resistance in the stubborn set of his shoulders, the unyielding line of his jaw. The way he wouldn't look at her.

Papa, you might well have gambled and lost.

Never had she met a man who'd not given in to her. Therefore the fault couldn't be hers but his. Silas was as cold as stone. Granted, winning him had merely been a game at first. She'd simply wanted him to take notice, to look at her with the light of wanting in his eyes, and then it was she who'd succumbed. The long, hard-muscled length of him, the beguiling glint in his green eyes, the uncanny way he mastered every task, had turned him tempting as lemon tart to her hungry eyes.

Now, her gaze drifting to Eden, a shattering thought accosted her. Might he desire Eden instead? Lately the two of them seemed thrust together at every turn. She'd spied them at the edge of the garden, in the barn, by the woodpile. Having curried the Greathouses' favor, would Eden now steal Silas too?

Mama's voice sounded from a corner of the room. "Elspeth, let me examine your stitching."

Elspeth tried to smile and be obliging lest Mama sense her sour mood. But Mama rarely rebuked her. Even when she'd disgraced them all by bearing an illegitimate child, Mama had stayed silent. Elspeth glanced at the door, wishing Silas back, praying Papa would stay in the smithy with the ledgers. 'Twas just she, Mama, and Eden tonight. The children were abed.

Getting up, she took the pillowslip she'd been working on to her mother, who clucked in approval at the tedious embroidery. "Your dower chest is nearly full."

Aye, overflowing. Lately she'd snuck a few of Eden's linens

to add to her own. The embroidered *E* in scarlet thread was easily exchanged, and Eden, weak-willed as she was, wouldn't attempt to take them back even if she discovered the theft. Still, a sliver of guilt pricked her. Hadn't the last Sabbath sermon been clear enough?

Thou shalt not steal.

Well, lightning hadn't struck her for her sins thus far, and she'd done much worse.

◦◦◦

The next morning Papa summoned them to the winter parlor. Silas was at the forge—Eden could hear the reassuring ring of his hammer beyond thickly timbered walls. The sound steadied her a bit, though her porridge churned uneasily in her stomach. As Mama cleared the breakfast dishes away in the dining room, Papa stood by the fire, a black sternness on his narrow face. His gaze shifted from her to Elspeth as they stood before him shoulder to shoulder, heads down like two schoolgirls about to get a scolding.

Though Elspeth was rarely skittish, Eden sensed a telling nervousness about her sister that fueled her own angst. Had this meeting to do with Silas? Since they'd last spoken at the edge of the garden three days past and he'd been so troubled, Eden felt on tenterhooks. And now Papa's close perusal left her a bit breathless.

"Things have taken a turn with Silas," he said in low tones. "Be ready to wed by month's end."

Slowly Eden looked up. His hard eyes fastened on her and didn't let go. He spoke not to Elspeth, who wanted to wed . . . but *her*. A cold hand clutched her heart. She groped for words, but no sound came.

"Why do you address Eden, Papa? What is this 'month's end' you speak of?" Elspeth's tone turned a bit shrill, her chin quivering with suppressed emotion. "I beg to know what has happened with Silas—"

"Silence!" Papa clamped his pipe stem between discolored teeth, his words compressed but nonetheless forceful. "I've told Silas he's to wed one of you by month's end or he'll be turned out, his contract terminated."

"*One* of us?" Elspeth looked desperate, disbelieving. "You mean Eden, don't you? You're looking straight at her! Papa, how could you? I've told you for months now 'tis I who wish to wed him—" With a stamp of her foot, she burst into tears, turning Eden numb with embarrassment as she felt for a handkerchief.

"Keep a tame tongue in your head, Daughter! The choice is his to make, not mine. Circumstances have forced my hand. He seems intent on leaving York. I've proof." He reached into the folds of his shirt and withdrew a letter.

The sight left Eden sick. Silas had given her that letter and a few pence to mail it a fortnight ago. Had Papa intercepted the post? She looked closer. This paper lacked Silas's bold flourish and was *to* him, not *from* him. She watched in silent misery as Elspeth took the letter from his extended hand.

"'Tis from the factor of Fort Pitt. But why?" She opened it and scanned the contents, a smirk marring her tearstained features. "They have a position for him as blacksmith, and land as incentive? So he wants to go west into the wilderness? Likely he'll be scalped by the savages first!"

She thrust the letter at Eden, who took it reluctantly, bringing it behind her back with a trembling hand. Had they noticed? Nay. They were too busy talking—plotting—their combined voices buzzing like angry bees in her ears. Thankfully, Mama came and asked for help with Thomas and Jon. Eden went gladly toward the sound of their wailing, pocketing the letter, still reeling from Papa's pronouncement.

Had Silas stated his preference for her over Elspeth after Papa forced his hand? Was that why Papa's eyes had pinned her and led to Elspeth's storm of tears?

Oh, Silas, is it your wish to wed me? After saying I was naught but a sister?

Steps quickening, she burst through the door of her parents' bedchamber, a maelstrom of emotions seething inside her. Thomas quieted as she made a beeline for the cradle and took Jon to the trundle bed. There she lay down with them both, hugging them to her grease-spackled dress.

Her heart was thumping wildly—her head seemed split in two. Though she tried to keep her thoughts in check, they leapt out of bounds repeatedly, stirring her imaginings in wild ways. What if she was to lie down not with these wee ones but with a husband . . . Silas? What if it was his breath she felt warm against her cheek? His hands entwined in her tousled hair? His child she carried?

The possibilities pierced her and made slush of her insides. Such intimate thoughts, never before pondered, were both frightening and . . . pleasing. Squeezing her eyes shut, she felt hot tears trickle down her face onto the babes' heads. Jon quieted as she cried harder, while Thomas patted her cheek with a gentle hand. The intercepted letter to Silas lay crumpled in her pocket, a jumble of ink and misbegotten dreams.

∞

'Twas nearly midnight. Silas moved the twin tapers nearer till light gilded the dun-colored paper a rich gold. But he hardly needed the illumination. He'd studied the map of the disputed western lands of Pennsylvania till they seemed engraved upon his very soul. Blessed with a keen sense of direction, he knew if the map was flawed he'd still stay the course, even in the chilly thaw of spring, be it crossing swollen rivers or climbing greening ridges. He just hadn't planned to be on his way west so soon.

One month.

One month to wed or head into the wilderness. Leaning back in his chair till it groaned beneath his weight, he crossed his arms, eyes on the Franklin stove. Since Liege had given his ultimatum, Silas had prayed and pondered the proper course, refusing to give in to either anger or despair, knowing the Lord could handle Liege Lee if he couldn't. Till month's end he'd continue to do what he'd come here to do—work iron. And wait.

Fear ye not, stand still, and see the salvation of the Lord, which He will shew to you today . . . The Lord shall fight for you, and ye shall hold your peace.

The words from Exodus seemed to shore up his soul, his confidence, in unexpected, needful ways. On their heels, his mother's voice returned to him from a far-off place, bringing with it the memory of firelight and Scripture reading and doves cooing in the croft's farthest reaches.

Of all her children, he'd been the most gallus—rascally and full of mischief—and she'd oft reined him in with three words. "Hold thee still." The calm admonishment would serve him well once again if he could heed it. He expelled a ragged breath, wishing the Lord's will was as plain as the map spread before him.

Absorbed by dark thoughts, he all but missed the slight noise beyond the closed garret door. Eden. Was she coming up? Or going down? Her step was light, a mere whisper. For weeks she'd stayed clear of the stairwell, though he'd continued to plant Scripture in her path. They'd only come together at meals or by chance in the barn or garden. Without moving from his chair, he reached out a hand and pulled open the door.

She stood on the steps without speaking, paper in hand.
A letter? Aye, one addressed to him from Fort Pitt. He took
it, grappling not with the contents and all its implications
but with the sweetness of her presence.

"Papa took—stole—your letter." Her expression was mis-
erably apologetic.

"Aye, but I have it back again." He meant to calm her with
a word, still her shaking, but she looked up at him, making
him want to take her in his arms instead.

She leaned into the wall, her fingers plucking at her fraying braid. "'Tis not just the letter. 'Tis Papa's insistence—his
forcing you—" She faltered then met his eyes again. "To leave
here or wed."

The heat of anger pooled in his chest—not at the theft but
at the hurt Liege had caused her. Her chin quivered with emotion and he felt another wrench—for all the wrong reasons.

"So he told you?"

She nodded and looked away, and a great heaviness settled
in his chest. Was the thought of wedding him so painful, then?
Was this her way of telling him she wanted no part of it?

He tried to keep the ache he felt from telling on his face.
"The thought of leaving causes me no pain, Eden. I've had
many partings. God has all in hand." He spoke with a confidence he was far from feeling, and she nodded in turn,
dejection sketched across her every feature.

"When the time comes, I can outfit you for your journey—
with food, at least. You'll need a great deal of provisions for
so long a trek." There was stark wonder in her eyes. "Oh,
Silas . . . why? Why must you go so far?"

"Have you ne'er had a vision, Eden?"

She flushed and looked down at her hands, as if keeping
secrets. He remembered the letter she'd lost in the lane, recalled the cryptic words . . .

The position you seek is delayed till spring.

He'd nearly forgotten the letter, had misplaced it though he'd meant to return it to her. He retrieved the post from his haversack. "You dropped this coming home from Hope Rising. I should have returned it to you long ago."

She pocketed it and found her voice again, though she didn't meet his eyes. "Sometimes I have a vision to leave this place, but not to go west. The wilderness is for soldiers and Indians . . . trappers and traders."

"The West will not always be wilderness. Villages—future cities—are being settled as we speak. Tradesmen and artisans arc in short supply."

She was toying with her braid again, clearly uncomfortable with the conversation, as if she expected him to press her about her own plans. "But if you leave here you'll break your contract."

"I doubt the authorities at Fort Pitt care about such things, so long as I can do the work."

"But what of the land grant promised you? Four hundred acres or so, Papa says."

He ran a hand over his jaw and nearly sighed. Aye, Liege not only wanted a son-in-law, he wanted more land as well. Silas had long suspected it, but Eden was just realizing the unpleasant truth.

Alarm skittered across her face like storm clouds gathering. "Oh, Silas, why not just return to Philadelphia? 'Tis known to you—you can open a smithy there."

"Why?" Frustration tugged at him. "Because there were such great men before me, I saw no chance of being anything in that city. The Ballantyne name ends—or begins—with me."

She seemed to be trying to grasp it—the West, his ambitions, his need to leave—only to look away in confusion.

He longed to see the light of understanding in her eyes, her approval and affirmation instead.

Her voice trembled. "My father—his treatment of you—"

"Enough, Eden." He brought her chin up with the edge of his hand. "Not all his dealings are unsavory. He did promise me . . ."

You.

He bit the word back but saw she understood his meaning. He felt a bit aflocht himself as his fingers brushed her skin and fell away. No man had ever touched her, he wagered. Pure as lamb's wool, she was. He reached into his pocket, withdrew a scrap of paper, and passed her another Scripture he'd penned, bringing an end to their futile conversation.

Slowly she began backing down the stairs, clutching the paper he'd given her, quiet as a cat.

God, protect her, he prayed, *both now and when I'm gone.*

19

One sickly sheep infects the flock,
And poisons all the rest.

ISAAC WATTS

As the days crept toward Silas's departure, Eden tried to do her work but accomplished little. She burnt the bread. Curdled the milk. Spilled her sewing basket all over the floor, the fine Philadelphia needles from Jemma falling through the cracked floorboards into nothingness. Frantic for firm footing, she memorized the Scripture Silas had penned for her and turned her thoughts repeatedly to spring. Not his leaving. Not Elspeth's persistent flirting or Papa's conniving or Mama's melancholy.

Just outside the parlor's window, in the stillness of twilight, she could hear the birds' chorus and feel warmth in the wind. Joy gained the upper hand but for a moment as another worry ensnared her. Atop her lap Jon fretted, pulling at her bodice laces as if demanding she do something. He'd been peckish of late on account of his first tooth. Eden could feel its sharp point beneath his gum and rubbed a bit of clove oil there to ease him.

Heartsore, she rocked him, acutely aware of the man an arm's length away. Tonight Papa was in the kitchen nursing his gout, and Silas was the only solid shadow in the room. They'd all assumed their customary places, like actors in a stage play—she in the rocking chair by the cradle, Mama sitting opposite with Elspeth, sewing. Sometimes Elspeth played chess with Silas, rarely winning, her displeasure plain. Mostly Silas read or perused the *Pennsylvania Gazette*, their one frivolity. The weekly dung barge, Papa called it without apology.

Tonight the silence was broken by Silas's racking cough, so deep it made Eden wince. He'd taken a fever and cold of late, though his workload never lessened. Secretly she fretted he wouldn't be well upon leaving, that he might perish in the wilderness and none would know. She got up and made him some flip, rich with egg and cream and a few medicinal herbs. Their eyes met briefly as she handed him his mug.

She glanced down at Jon as she resumed her seat by the cradle. He gurgled a greeting and lifted fat fists in a bid for her to pick him up. Lately Elspeth made much of him in the evenings, though she'd never done so before. To try to give the impression she was good with children, Eden guessed. The deception set her further on edge. She was so weary of scheming, of secrets. She longed for peace. Green pastures and still waters, as Scripture promised. Surely the West held both.

She envied Silas his escape. No word had come for her from Philadelphia.

Would it ever?

∽

Silas continued to spend dawn to dusk at the forge, his cough slowly mending, his only respite the Sabbath. Elspeth seemed to thrive on these weekly outings, bedecked in finery he suspected was from Hope Rising, sitting raptly through the lengthy sermons, giving him no cause to wish it was Eden instead. And yet he found himself imagining amidst the peace of the little kirk that it was Eden who sat close beside him.

After silent Sabbath dinners, he saddled Horatio, lashed his fiddle alongside, and rode to the Golden Plough Tavern in York, the coin earned hidden at the bottom of his haversack. *God, forgive me for breaking the Sabbath*, became his echoing prayer. At least Liege, profane as he was, could not quarrel with him about that.

Though it had been three weeks since Liege had issued his ultimatum, no more had been said about wedding either daughter, but it weighed on Silas in both the busyness and the silences. With every swing of his hammer, it seemed he sent up a prayer for Eden's direction and protection along with his own. He'd posted a letter to Fort Pitt, wondering when or if he'd get a reply—or if Liege would try to intercept that too. If he left by month's end, he might well reach Fort Pitt before the oft-unreliable post.

'Twas a promising season to travel, if a bit mud-mired, far preferable than the snow that had brought him here. Spring was firmly fixed everywhere his gaze landed, and deep in his spirit he knew it was lambing time. He missed the sudden Highland storms, the earthy mustiness of the sheep pens, the fretful bleating and jockeying of the flock, the smell and feel of wool. Here there was just a wee smirr of rain and the gentle lowing of the cattle in the greening meadow. Despite the lush beauty all around him, something always seemed . . . lacking.

Would the West be any different—or was he himself at fault? Why could he not be content to live as a simple Scottish crofter or settle down with a daughter of a master smith? Always, always the vision pushed him forward. It was just as the midwife had predicted on the day of his birth—"This one will wander." To which his father had always answered, "Aye, but the Lord will go with him wherever he goes."

He expelled a deep breath and eyed Elspeth as she worked over the ledgers in a lantern-lit corner of the smithy. Clad in a comely linen dress, her pale hair tucked beneath a lace cap, she seemed never to leave the shop. He found her presence uncomfortable, the ledgers she kept a mystery. When she finally went to the kitchen and Liege was occupied in the barn, Silas stood at the desk where she worked, scanning the accounts line by line.

It was just as he'd suspected. They were charging double—sometimes triple—for their ironwork. When he'd first come, a ladle had been a few pence; now it had doubled in price. The andirons he made with nary a seam cost as much as a fine cabinet. The list was long and endless. Though much of their business was done by barter and not coin, careful accounts were kept of this too, and seemed to be heavily in Liege's favor. Anger snarled Silas's insides and made his frustration with his predicament burn bright. He could no more stop their unscrupulous dealings than change the course of the wind.

"Why are your figures so high?" he asked quietly when Elspeth returned.

She gave him a sidelong glance and capped her inkwell. "Papa said your work is worth every shilling. And no one complains." Snapping shut the ledger, she placed an appeasing hand on his bare arm. With his sleeves turned back to ease the smithy's heat, he felt the warmth of her fingers like the forge's fire.

An unmistakable longing shone in her eyes and she tilted her head, a tendril of gold framing her face. "'Tis almost the end of April, Silas."

"Aye," he said coolly.

"Papa is anxious to hear your decision . . . as am I." Her

fingers inched up his arm and toyed with the fraying patch on his sleeve. "I fear you're leaving. I usually don't speak of such things, but I beg you to consider. Mama is whispering of the wasting disease. Papa is unwell—'tis more than his gout that is troubling him. I fear he'll soon leave us to fend for ourselves—two helpless babes and three women. Don't you see your place here? This could all be yours—ours. What more could a man want?"

He stepped back and reached for an iron bar, but she blocked his way, catching him off guard. Next he knew she'd thrown herself in his arms the very moment Liege limped in. Pulling away, pulse ricocheting wildly, Silas reached for his sledge. Thankfully, Liege turned his attention to a sudden commotion outside as a stranger's voice sounded beyond the smithy door.

When he passed outside, Elspeth moved nearer again. "Silas, you must stay on—take a wife. 'Tis tradition." Tears turned her eyes a brilliant blue. "I know this trade nearly as well as you. We'd work together. If you wed me, all this will be yours—"

"You forget yourself." Though low, his voice held a stern rebuke. "'Tis the man who does the asking—or begging—if there's any to be done."

Her chin lifted. "I need no reminding—I'm simply offering you a sensible solution to Papa's proposal. Any man in York County would be glad for my hand, and yet you—a stubborn Scot—refuse me. Am I not comely enough? Not religious enough to your liking? Is there someone else? Right here under our own roof, perhaps? Are your sights set on Eden?"

He shot her a warning glance. "I've no wish to wed."

"You lie!" Fury painted her face an uncomely scarlet. "I've seen the way you look at her. Oh, don't glare at me and pretend you haven't! I've keen eyes in my head and know a man's ways. But you'd best wake up! You'll have no future with her by your side. Though she seems to be pious and good, she does wicked things—"

"Oh? And when does she find time to do these wicked things you speak of? Between spinning, tending livestock and bairns, gathering wood, and slaving in a hot kitchen?"

Fists at her sides, Elspeth looked over her shoulder to the open smithy doors. "I doubt she'd have you, anyway. My sister has her mind set on grander things."

At this, she caught up the ledgers and fled out the side door. The relief Silas felt was short-lived. Before he could raise his hammer, David Greathouse appeared, filling the main entrance of the smithy, eyes shifting from the forge's fire to Silas. A riding whip was clutched in one hand, and his clothes were fine, if mud-spattered. He looked, through no fault of his own, like the duke of Atholl's son. Solidly built and fair of feature, with thin, straw-colored hair, he lacked only Jamie Murray's insolent grin. Resistance rose up and turned Silas more tense.

God, forgive me for making ill-scrappit comparisons.

Laying aside his tools, he walked toward Hope Rising's laird. The man who'd done him no wrong. Who'd once bought him a meal. Who'd praised his fiddling. Whose only fault was his resemblance to Jamie Murray.

Silas thrust out a hand, which Greathouse shook with vigor. "Hello, Ballantyne. The forge is a tad warm today. I'm thinking you might be in need of a diversion—perhaps some greener pastures."

"I hear you've some sheep."

He gave a nod. "Word travels fast around York." Inclining his head toward the door, away from the forge's fire, he led Silas toward sunlight and fresh air, standing just beneath the crumbling eave.

194

"I've imported a small flock of Blackface based on your recommendation—around a hundred or so. Since I'm ignorant of the breed, I thought you might help."

"What d'ye want to know?"

"Their habits, preferences. Bloat and breeding and all the rest."

"You have pens, shelter?" Silas asked.

"Some, but I don't know if they're sufficient. What little I've learned is from books and sheep manuals. I was hoping you'd come to Hope Rising and take a look around . . . if the master allows."

If. That was the question. Silas's gaze trailed to Liege, who stood in the yard talking with a farmer. The master was less than obliging of late, and now with animosity simmering between them . . . "How about a good herd dog?"

"A dog? Nay."

"The shelties work well enough, but there's none better than a briard." Silas reached down to pet Eden's mongrel. "Get a young male if you can."

"I take it the duke of Atholl had that breed? How large was his flock?"

"Five thousand."

Greathouse looked chagrined. "I've a ways to go."

Silas gave a wry half-smile, his own mishaps firmly in mind. "'Tis better to start small and learn from your mistakes. Sheep are fickle creatures."

Liege's shadow fell over them just as Mrs. Lee called them to noonday dinner. The smell of fried apples and roast pork carried on a warm wind—an enticing invitation. Silas waited for Greathouse to leave, his eyes trailing to the fine thoroughbred hitched to the rail outside.

"I've come at an inconvenient time," Greathouse said, looking toward the house. "I'd hoped to speak to Eden."

195

Silas felt a rush of dismay, but Liege's dark countenance brightened as he limped their way. "Eden, you say? Stay on and speak to her after dinner, then. You've no dislike of simple fare, I'll wager, though I hear Hope Rising has a new cook."

"I'm afraid she quit her post after the ice harvest."

Liege chuckled, revealing tobacco-stained teeth. "Then you no doubt have an appetite."

Slapping David on the back in a gauche display of familiarity, Liege motioned him toward the house. Silas brought up the rear, surprise sifting through him. Would a laird sit at a tradesman's table? Though he and Greathouse had shared a meal at the Rising Sun, a tradesman's home was an altogether different matter. Social boundaries were rarely breached in Scotland, at least in daylight.

The image of Naomi flashed to mind. He felt a deep sinking in his spirit and heard Elspeth's taunt afresh. *My sister has her mind set on grander things.* He removed his leather apron, hung it from the nearest nail, and raked a hand through his hair, appetite gone.

Their arrival in the kitchen was creating quite a stir. At the sight of them coming through the doorway, Mrs. Lee nearly dropped a hot round of bread, the peel wobbling as she took it from the oven. Elspeth sang out a greeting as she stirred the gravy, expression smug. He dismissed them all, as it was Eden's reaction he sought. After tucking the babe in his cradle, she turned, and he caught the sudden splash of color across her cheeks as she took in the unexpected arrival.

"We've an honored guest today," Liege said a bit too loudly, leading them into the dining room. "Set an extra place."

Silas lingered at the washbasin, then turned to see Greathouse usurp his seat at the end of the table, Liege opposite at the far end. Elspeth was waiting, motioning for Silas to sit beside her in the place Thomas usually occupied, a hint of triumph on her face.

⌘

The meal Eden had found so palatable in the making now turned tasteless. With Silas across from her, David occupying Silas's place beside her, and Papa making conversation in an unusually brash way, she picked at the roast she'd seasoned and basted so carefully, the first bite sticking in her throat. For once she wished the rule of silence would descend.

All around her, masculine voices droned. They spoke of sheep. Spinning. Hope Rising's coming wheat crop. The rising price of goods brought about by war's end. She listened with interest as Silas spoke of water-powered spinning mills newly opened in Philadelphia and Boston for the manufacture of textiles. One day, he wagered, their simple Saxony and walking wheels would be a thing of the past. Eden couldn't conceive it. Machine-made cloth? She doubted it had the quality of what she fashioned by hand, each thread spun with pleasure and care.

After several uneasy minutes, her surprise at David's appearance eased somewhat, only to soar again at meal's end when Papa said, "Master David wants a word with you, Eden."

Startled, she lifted her eyes from her unfinished plate as Mama mumbled, "In the summer parlor, then."

The summer parlor? Eden froze. Why there and not here, with all present? She had no wish to be alone with David. 'Twas a touch scandalous, especially in light of Silas's warning. Across from her, Silas excused himself to return to the forge, his rich Scots lilt sounding a bit strained. Her own rise from her chair was less than graceful. In her disquiet, she dropped her napkin and nearly overturned her cider. Papa fixed her with a stern stare, allowing no exit.

Down the hall she went in David's wake. He seemed preoccupied, brow creased in contemplation, his mind clearly on the conversation at table. "He has a keen mind, Ballantyne."

"Yes," she acknowledged, not expecting this. But rarely had she seen him so interested as when Silas was talking trade in Philadelphia.

He entered the parlor and shut the door, and she stood awkwardly before him as he looked about the neglected room with its familiar furnishings. She realized then that he'd never been within the confines of their house, only the smithy. When she heard Jon crying, she felt a tug to go, but David took a seat on the settee, dashing her hopes. Unable to meet his eyes, she pretended to be preoccupied with a stubborn wrinkle on her skirt.

"Have you been unwell, Eden?"

Looking up, she met his colorless eyes. His simple question seemed cloaked with censure. "Unwell? Nay."

"We've not seen you at Hope Rising of late. Jemma is threatening to return to the city, and Margaret is missing your Sabbath teas."

"'Tis so busy now that spring is here." Truly, there weren't hours enough to do all her chores. She tried to push the weariness from her voice. "The new babe takes much of my time. With two little ones, Mama needs my help more than ever."

He seemed thoughtful but unsympathetic, forcing a stilted smile. Reaching into the confines of his coat, he withdrew a letter. "My oldest cousin seems fond of the post, especially where you're concerned. I sometimes suspect Bea has something up her sleeve."

Bea? Did the foundling hospital now have an opening? Her pulse picked up in rhythm, but when she reached for the letter, he brought it behind his back. His smile had slipped. A distinct coldness had crept in that chilled her like a winter's draft. He was unhappy with her. Because of her absence? Or the letter?

"Promise me you'll return to Hope Rising," he said.

"I . . . yes. I'll come visit next Sabbath. Please tell Margaret and Jemma for me."

At this, he released the letter, gesturing to the seat beside him. "I want to talk to you about the future."

The future? He meant Philadelphia, surely. Had Jemma or Bea told him? Weak-kneed, she sat beside him, wishing Mama would appear—or even Elspeth—and ease this very awkward moment.

"Silas has interested me in wool production and the possibility of manufacturing it here. You're a fine spinner, perhaps the finest in York. When I have a good fleece, I'd like to hire you to spin Hope Rising's wool." He paused as if weighing his words carefully, or perhaps weighing her reaction to them.

His words swept through her head, scattered as windblown leaves, a touch frightening in their newness. Nay, she'd not considered this. Philadelphia—the foundling hospital—was what she wanted . . .

"If the wool clip is large enough, I plan to employ some local women and have you oversee them. In the meantime I'll be looking into the machinery Ballantyne spoke of."

"'Tis . . . ambitious."

"Yes, but doable. I plan to import a larger flock in time. Shearing is still months away, but I need to be looking ahead." He was the David of old now, sharing his plans, including her. The frost between them had thawed. She clutched Bea's letter between her fingers, wishing he would go, but he leaned back and crossed his arms, studying her.

"I'd like to have you on the premises once the work begins. The empty cottage adjoining Margaret's should suffice."

What? The mere suggestion stole her breath.

He leaned forward, awaiting her answer. His probing gaze seemed to bore a hole in her. "Say you'll consider it."

Could he sense her reluctance, her confusion? She'd rarely said no to him, not even in childhood. He was ever amiable, if she was obliging. When provoked, his temper was nearly as thunderous as Elspeth's.

"Your father will give his approval, no doubt," he said.

Oh yes, Papa would leap at the offer. She groped for some vague answer, feeling dangerously close to a lie by agreeing to the plan. "You'll let me know when things are in place?"

"Yes, of course."

With that he got up and left, freeing her to tear open the post and devour the contents, his words still echoing in her ears.

> *Dear Eden,*
> *The foundlings increase in number but fail to thrive . . . So many babies and not enough wet nurses . . . The director has reviewed your application based on my recommendation and will place you in the next available opening . . . Your time is nearly at hand. When I send word, Jemma will accompany you to Philadelphia . . .*

Oh, Bea! She felt a wild, trembling excitement and then a profound dismay. She would have to tell Papa. Decline David. Risk their wrath. The futility—the foolishness—of it all now mocked her. Why didn't she feel her old joy at the prospect? Her plans, once so sound, seemed naught but sand.

She went to the towering secretary where her journal was

secreted and hid Bea's letter, gaze falling to the scrap of Scripture Silas had last given her. The holy words were in her heart and her head now, a strength and solace. God would guide her just as Silas had said. She would rest in that.

The Lord shall fight for you, and ye shall hold your peace.

20

Every path has its puddle.
SAMUEL JOHNSON

When she returned to the dining room, a tad upended and plucking at her apron, all but Silas awaited her, and he was uppermost in her thoughts. What would he think of her stepping into the parlor with Hope Rising's heir? Like they had some sort of understanding? Some tie?

"So, Daughter?" Papa demanded gruffly, pipe stem between his teeth. "Was there some business between you and Master David?"

She felt hemmed in by too many eyes. Elspeth's were the most daunting as she stood sullenly by the hearth, arms crossed and brow furrowed. Mama began clearing the table and cast Eden a sympathetic glance as she stuttered, "H-he—Master David—spoke of spinning and sheep."

"Well, what of it?"

She explained his plan carefully, avoiding his request that she live at Hope Rising, and felt Papa's impatience—and disappointment—mount with every word. "He said noth-

202

ing else?" he demanded, puffing so hard his features were obscured by curls of smoke.

She knew what he hoped to hear, and felt the warmth of it from her feet to her face. He wanted a different sort of proposal, ridiculous as it was, and felt she was somehow to blame for the lack. "He seeks Silas's help with the flock and training a herd dog."

His anticipation faded to irritation before rebounding. She could see his mind spinning, sorting, counting coin. "It might well prove lucrative once the flock is established and spinners are in place. Yet another reason for Silas to stay on. I can part with him half a day at a time and send him to Hope Rising. You, Eden, are to encourage Greathouse all you can. Do you understand?"

Tears stung her eyes. "But I—"

"Don't be daft, Daughter!" He knocked the ashes from his pipe against an andiron with such vehemence it broke. "This may well be your chance to make an agreeable match. 'Tis clear Greathouse is taken with you."

"T-taken with my spinning," she stammered, looking to her mother with a plea in her damp eyes.

Mama looked equally grieved. "Best not encourage her in that way, Liege. Master David is a gentleman, not a tradesman. Eden is but a—"

"Eden is but a what?" Papa's attention snapped to Mama. "A blacksmith's daughter? I beg to differ." The heat of his gaze bore down on her, and she shrank visibly. "And what's this drivel about a gentleman, *not* a tradesman? That never stopped you—a gunsmith's daughter! What have you to say about *that*?"

All eyes were on Mama now. Though Papa hadn't struck her as he sometimes did, she wilted beneath the force of his words, and Eden was left reeling as well.

Kicking the broken pipe past the dog irons into the fire, Papa turned and quit the room, leaving the women huddled in a sore circle.

Elspeth was the first to break the silence, though her voice was more demanding than soothing. "Mama, what did Papa mean by saying such?"

Confused, Eden looked at her mother. There was a lengthy pause followed by a heart-shattering realization. 'Twas just as she'd suspected. Mama had grave secrets of her own, begotten long ago, which still lingered.

With a sob, Mama covered her face with her hands and swept out of the room.

⌇

'Twas almost April's end. In mere days he would trade the garret for sodden ground . . . or stay and take a bride. The weight of Silas's dilemma was overwhelming at times, and then it rolled off his shoulders by dint of prayer. As it was, he was too busy to think of much beyond his labors, though he still worried endlessly about Eden, committing her continually to the Father's care, only to feel he was abandoning her himself. Should he not lay aside his vision instead? Stay and wed her, if she would have him, to ensure her own future?

In the mornings he worked the forge and, at Liege's insistence, spent afternoons at Hope Rising. Admittedly, the open air and flock of Blackface were preferable to the stifling smithy and a surly master. This afternoon, the sky had darkened nearly to indigo as the sun slanted west beyond a bank of brooding clouds, turning the ground a vivid green. Around Silas were a dozen bleating, wobbly-legged lambs and the briard pup gotten from Philadelphia. Young and eager to please, the shaggy dog mingled with the sheep and returned repeatedly to sniff Silas's welcoming hand.

Though the work reminded him of his Highland home, his surroundings muted the memory of hills and lochs, moss and heather. Hope Rising was graced with thick stands of oak and chestnut and ash, and lush meadows as far as he could see. His thoughts were as far reaching. How would it be to have such treasure handed down, passed from father to son, generation after generation? To do with as you wished, at least in your lifetime? Would the West give him such a legacy? Or was it simply a foolish dream?

A sharp whistle made him turn. David Greathouse came striding toward him, his frock coat flapping about his thighs, a lamb in his wake. Silas wasn't sure what sort of shepherd the laird of Hope Rising would make, but he had a fine flock, losing but three ewes out of a hundred, his twin rams untouched in transit.

"You'll need a good man—a dependable lad or two—to tend them when you go to Philadelphia," Silas told him, resuming their conversation of minutes before.

"Oh, I have no plans for Philadelphia, other than an occasional business matter," David replied, looking a bit winded, leaning into his walking stick. "In years past I was there for the social season, but 'tis time I settle down . . . think of matters near at hand."

Silas crossed his arms, feet widespread, fighting the tight feeling in his chest. Since Greathouse had met with Eden in the parlor five days before, he'd been plagued by fresh fears. Though he wasn't privy to what passed between them, she seemed more aflocht than usual, and he felt a new tenderness for her.

"My cousins and friends keep reminding me I should wed."

Silas felt the hair on the back of his neck tingle. He looked at the ewes grazing on a far hill, tone thoughtful. "'Tis time we speak of breeding, then."

"Breeding?" David seemed startled, a hint of red showing above his snowy cravat.

"Aye, breeding. Sheep."

"Ah, yes. We've yet to speak of that." He cleared his throat and glanced at his muddy boots. "I've read that one should choose breeding times carefully, depending on when one wants a crop of lambs."

"Aye," Silas said. "You've two horned, purebred Rambouillet tups. Quality stock. Just as you'd not think of dallying with a York lass but only a fine Philadelphia one, you need to pick your ewes with care. The same principle applies to sheep, ye ken."

David's ruddy color had risen to his cheekbones. He studied the copper head of his walking stick before glancing at Silas, grim amusement in his eyes. "Sound advice, Ballantyne. I'll not forget it."

"One more matter. Never turn your back on a ram."

"Oh? They're dangerous, then?"

"Deadly, betimes." Silas paused to let the words take hold. "And you'd do well to mark each tup with a harness during breeding season so you'll know the due date for each ewe."

David nodded. "A meticulous practice."

"'Twas the duke's own. You should have a fine flock with proper care. Now if you don't mind, I have a tavern frolic to attend."

"You're playing tonight? At the Golden Plough?" Interest sharpened his fair features. "Mind if I join you? I'm in need of an ale—perhaps a good game of draughts."

"Come along if you like," Silas said reluctantly, beginning a slow walk uphill.

They fell into step together, David's voice low and undeniably curious. "Are you just fiddling all these nights at the tavern? Or have you found a certain maid to your liking?"

Silas tried to keep his grin in check, the thought of Eden lifting his heavy mood. "Aye, one. But she won't be found in a tavern."

⚬⚬

'Twas the last of April. As if to lighten Eden's somber spirits, the day dawned bright, ushering in a lapis sky and summer-like warmth. Today Silas would announce his leaving. With that in mind, she went about her work, every strike of his hammer seeming to shatter her heart. Come morning she would hear it no more. Toward that end, for weeks she'd been ferreting jerky and cornmeal and dried fruit for his trek west.

To Elspeth's irritation and Eden's own dismay, they'd seen little of him lately but for meals, and when they did, he gave them naught but a glancing nod. 'Twas clear Silas had no wish to wed. The realization brought about a bruising hurt. But what did it matter? She had no wish to wed either. Philadelphia was her future. He'd made his feelings plain. She was naught but a sister to him. Like Naomi. Why, then, was her heart so sore? Because she'd been his for the taking and he'd refused her?

The alternative haunted her like a dark specter.

What if he chose Elspeth instead?

To stem the impossible thought, she took Jon to the garden midmorning and laid him down in a basket beneath a blooming redbud tree. Slipping off her shoes, she waded into sun-warmed soil and knelt to weed prim rows of peas, the rich scent of earth filling her senses and easing her hurt. Soon her herbs would hug the porch steps, flowers and vegetables growing in wild abundance amongst the buzz of bees. And just beyond, the beautiful willow that shaded the well like a green silk skirt . . . She must keep her mind fixed on her blessings, not her losses. *Not* Silas's leaving.

At Jon's first cry, Mama appeared to take him into the house and nurse him, weighting Eden with another worry. Since Papa had spoken so harshly to her the day David came, Mama had withdrawn and no amount of coaxing had returned her to normal. Eden had even caught the scent of wine on her breath. *Lord, no, not Mama.* Papa's imbibing was burden enough.

She looked up across the yard, beyond the garden's wattle fence, to see Silas come out of the smithy. Abandoning her task, she focused on his beloved form. Aye, beloved. The admission stung her, brought her to her feet. Not caring if Elspeth watched or that dirt clung to her hands and skirt, she abandoned her task and followed him.

He was affixing something to an elm's sturdy trunk near the woodshed, sending bark chips flying as his hammer drove in a nail. A birdhouse? Fashioned from wood and straw, it was mounted on a copper frame, a tiny gambrel roof protecting it from the elements. Practical. Charming. Heartfelt. She felt a shimmer of joy at such thoughtfulness.

Finished with his hammering, he said over his shoulder, "Something to remember me by."

The words brought her brief happiness to a sudden halt. *Oh, Silas, I need nothing to remember you by.*

He gave the nail a final blow. "I told your father I'm leaving. You probably heard his shouting."

Thankfully she hadn't, as she'd taken cheese to Hope Rising at dawn and Jemma had detained her. Nor had Elspeth mentioned it when she returned. Swallowing past the lump in her throat, Eden said, "I've some things for you—for the journey."

He nodded. "I leave at first light."

Overhead, lost in an array of budding branches, a bird chirped as if coming home. The sweetness of the song, the gentle beauty of the day, cut her afresh. Unable to look at him, she sought his handiwork instead. "The birdhouse . . . is it for wrens?"

He turned away without answering, passing out of sight. She heard the ring of the ax as he began chopping wood—a task that would return to her upon his leaving. Oh, but he'd lightened her load in myriad ways since his coming. How often she'd forgotten to thank him! Tracing his steps, she rounded the woodshed wall, swiping at a stray tear.

Seeing her, he paused. "Och, Eden, will you make me rethink my decision?"

Surprise skittered through her. "I've not come to do that, Silas—to make you change your mind. I only want to thank you."

His eyes held hers and wouldn't let go, warm as the forge's fire. She grew lost in them till her own eyes filled and nearly overflowed. It seemed he'd already left and taken her heart with him. She felt an overwhelming, aching emptiness . . .

He looked away. "Go into the house, Eden . . . please."

She took a step back and he resumed his chopping. He didn't stop, not even for noonday dinner. Not till dusk did his labors cease. A mountain of firewood awaited her in the woodshed, deftly cut and stacked to the rafters, a promise that she'd have need of no more till autumn.

◦◦◦

At supper, Silas's place had yawned empty. 'Twas a shame, Elspeth grumbled, that Mama's fine meal, her plum pies, went untouched. No one, not even Papa, had an appetite. He'd sated it with rum. Ever since Silas announced he was leaving, Papa had nursed one cup after another. The ring of his scornful words seemed to linger and poison the very air hours later.

"You're a fool, Silas Ballantyne! No man would shun such daughters—nor a trade! You're far more likely to make your fortune in Hope Rising's spinning operation than you are in the West. You'll soon find yourself lost in the wilderness or worse, daft as you are!"

As Elspeth pressed her ear to the smithy wall, her own anger simmered. *Silas must stay.* She'd not be content till he stood before Pastor McCheyne and made her his wife. Her dower chest was full. The yellow silk dress awaited. No man had seriously caught her fancy since his coming. She feared no one ever would. That she might be left wanting when she'd never been before pricked her like the sharpest thorn. It was time to take action. She rued that she'd waited, had let circumstances force her into a false propriety. Boldness had ever been her way, as surely as meekness was Eden's.

At least he hadn't chosen Eden. *That* couldn't be borne.

21

Change indeed is painful; yet ever needful.

Thomas Carlyle

Silas laid down his quill and looked out the garret window. Clouds were interspersed between scattered stars, blotting out the moon, dampening his hopes of a clear traveling day come dawn. Though he felt led to leave the Lees, he hadn't reckoned with the awful wrench of it. Across from him, his burgeoning haversacks waited, his fiddle case secured for travel. He'd leave his books behind, all but his Bible. The garret room would be Eden's again, to do with as she wished.

The Buik lay open, the taper's golden light illuminating Song of Solomon 2:14. The lovely words, without significance till now, seemed to lodge and splinter inside him. They reminded him endlessly of Eden.

Oh my dove, that art in the clefts of the rock, in the secret places of the stairs, let me see thy countenance, let me hear thy voice; for sweet is thy voice, and thy countenance is comely.

Stomach rumbling from fasting, palms blistered from a

feverish round of wood splitting, he was weary but couldn't sleep, every sense stretched taut. When he heard a noise on the stair, he shot to his feet, nearly snuffing out the taper adance on the scarred desktop.

An acute longing made him pull open the door a bit too forcefully. With the thought of his leaving, of never seeing her again, he nearly lost all reason. Who cared if the door creaked or someone heard? The sonsie sight of her in the soft candlelight was all that mattered.

She hovered two steps down, still clothed in a simple linen dress though it was midnight, her eyes red-rimmed. For a moment he stood stricken. Was he a fool to not declare his love for her, make her his? Wouldn't he regret not doing so the rest of his days?

"I've left some things for your journey in the hollow of the old oak in back of the barn."

Her voice was husky—from crying, he guessed. His own throat ached with the words he couldn't say. Tender words. Words of passion and promise. 'Twas now—or never.

"Eden . . ."

An unwelcome sound below skimmed the surface of his desire and turned him alert. There was the hasty click of a shutting door, a sudden footfall on the stair. Eden whirled on the step, tottering precariously, and his hand shot out and steadied her.

On the landing below stood Elspeth. Even in the dimness her ill will was palpable, her nightgowned figure stiff with rage. "Oh, Sister, wait till I tell Papa! You pretend to be so good, so pure—yet I find you sneaking about the garret doing shameful things! Have you just left his room? Has he—"

"Nae!" Silas's voice rolled down the stairway, firm and full of warning.

He moved to stand in front of Eden as Elspeth came swiftly

up the stairs. But in a heartbeat, Eden slipped past and faced her instead, holding out a hand as if to stop her shameful words. Elspeth grabbed at her sleeve, the candelabra in her hand wobbling wildly. Silas watched the tapers sway, panic soaring.

Her voice trilled higher. "You're naught but a tramp! What would Master David say to see you now, handing out your favors so freely?" Her free hand moved to Eden's throat, clenching tight, pushing her hard into the wall.

Clearly frantic, Eden jerked away and the candelabra fell, flaming brighter as it struck the step. Silas made for the light, a prayer on his lips.

Almighty God, not fire!

The skirt of Elspeth's gown caught the flame, but in her fury she was unaware of the danger. Both hands were about Eden's neck, and with a ferocious shove she sent her down the stairwell. The jarring thump of it struck Silas's every nerve. Pushing Elspeth aside, he all but jumped to the landing where Eden lay crumpled, a lump of linen and streaming hair. Sobbing, Elspeth moved past them into the largeness of the hall. He heard her voice and then Mrs. Lee's—hysterical, echoing. Elspeth was shouting wildly, loud enough to raise Liege, surely.

"'Tis Eden's doing—all of it! I found her on the stair—with Silas—"

"Your dress—'tis smoking . . ." Mrs. Lee's voice faded as she tended to the smoldering, blackened cloth.

Silas gathered Eden in his arms and moved toward the bedchamber. The room was strange to him—he'd never before seen it, only imagined how it might be. He didn't want to release Eden—didn't want Elspeth hovering. In moments she dared to come near, her expression as she stood at the foot of the narrow bed a tearful smirk, untouched by concern or apology.

Laying Eden down, he shouted over his shoulder, "Get her out of here!"

With a venomous glare, Elspeth fled. Mrs. Lee came closer, holding a candle higher, her lined face more grieved than Silas had ever seen. He touched Eden's cheek, the porcelain-pale skin already beginning to bruise.

"Eden . . ." The word was more prayer. "D'ye hear me?"

Her eyes fluttered open. "I'm . . . fine . . ."

"Nae, Eden . . ." She looked dazed, confused. His worry spiked. He'd once seen a man receive but a glancing blow to the temple and hemorrhage to death soon after. "Where d'ye hurt?"

"Just my head . . . where I struck the step." She swallowed hard and forged on. "Naught is broken. I'm just a little dizzy."

He knelt beside the bed, unmindful of Mrs. Lee, his anger dissipating a wee bit. His hands moved up and down her arms, over the soft silk of her collarbones and neck, checking for bumps and breaks, much as he had his sheep long ago. He couldn't examine the rest of her, so Mrs. Lee assumed the task while he moved into the dark hall. The sight of Elspeth lurking there curdled his stomach. She sidled up to him, a shameless specter in a clinging nightgown, and touched his arm.

He shook her off like a poisonous spider, the heat of his voice sending her back a step. "Take care, lass, or the ill you do will come back to you."

With that he climbed the garret stair and slammed the door.

❧

"She will mend, Silas. She has but a headache." Mrs. Lee spoke in low, placating tones, insisting he eat his breakfast, though the porridge grew cold in his bowl and the strong coffee failed to brace him.

He sat at the kitchen table, eyeing the rain-splashed window-

214

pane, haversacks and fiddle by the door. No one else had risen, though he heard rumbling upstairs. Thomas soon toddled in, bringing him toys as if to detain him, which Mrs. Lee eventually did.

"Mr. Lee is unwell this morning," she began, serving him more coffee. "He's asked that you stay long enough to load the ironwork when the cooper comes by."

"Aye," he replied, expecting Liege would try to stay him at the last.

The weather was against him anyway, the wind whistling mournfully as it wrapped round the house, punctuated by an occasional crack of thunder. Truly, he was in no hurry to leave Eden. He couldn't go till he saw her up and about, reassuring him that last night's episode was little more than a bad dream.

"Hopefully the weather will clear by noon," Mrs. Lee continued quietly, casting a wary eye toward the door as if fearing Liege hovered, "though we've had such a dry spring we're nearing a drought and are in need of a good soaking. You'd best eat if you can. You've a long trip ahead of you. Weeks—a month or more—till you reach wherever it is you're going."

She so rarely spoke in his presence that he was struck by the soothing sound of her voice—a more seasoned echo of Eden's, just as Elspeth's held the harsh tenor of her father's. He wondered how it was that Louise Lee had become the wife of such a hard man. 'Twas an arranged match, surely. Hints of comeliness still clung to her, though time and circumstances had not been especially kind.

As she moved about the kitchen, his predicament pressed down on him like a millstone. He was about to forsake York County forever. In time, the memories he'd made here, however bittersweet, would grow dim as tarnished copper. Eden would likely wed another, bear the children that might have been his, think no more about him. His chest rose and fell with an uneasy rhythm. He felt a crushing anxiety at the thought.

"'Tis plain to see she cares for you, Silas."

Surprise shot through him. He looked up from his untouched breakfast.

Mrs. Lee's countenance sagged with regret, the slope of her shoulders resigned. "I thought . . . hoped . . . you would take her with you." She came closer, and he saw tears shining in her eyes. "Once, when I was young like Eden, I turned my back on the one I loved and married a man of my father's choosing. 'Twas a terrible thing, never to be undone. Betimes there are no second chances."

"Eden never said she cares for me." But even as he spoke, he realized how foolish he sounded. Nae, she'd not wooed him with words but with deeds. A carefully stitched shirt and warm woolen mittens. An extra serving at supper. Stairwell meetings and lingering looks. Still, he said, "The wilderness is no place for a woman."

She set down a crock of honey, expression plaintive, full of a mother's hopes for her daughter. "The wilderness has little to do with one's heart. She cares for you, Silas, though you might see her as more child with her hair hanging down and her quiet ways. Beneath all that lies a strong woman—a brave woman. A gentlewoman."

She stressed the last word as if it had significance before turning her back to him and drawing a close to the conversation. His burden growing, he got up and poured his cold coffee into a slop pail and gave Thomas his porridge before retreating to the forge a final time.

22

*And then comes a mist and a
weeping rain, and life is never the
same again.*

GEORGE MACDONALD

Lightning rent the sky, followed by thunder loud as cannon
fire. Wincing, Eden prayed as she saddled Sparrow in the narrow stall. The little mare stood patiently beneath her unsteady
hands, though Eden knew she would turn skittish, perhaps
dangerously so, once they left the barn. The dismay she'd
felt at Silas's forgetfulness still lingered. Checking the old
oak after he'd ridden away, she'd gasped to see the supplies
she'd packed so carefully were untouched.

Time was against her, she knew. Silas was a far better
rider than she—unafraid of the elements—and had gained
an hour's time before she'd composed herself enough to leave
her room. Traces of tears still wet her cheeks, but it hardly
mattered. Though she wore a bonnet, the wind soon dashed
the rain in her face, washing it clean.

All she knew was his direction—west. He'd taken the road

over the hill with nary a look back. She'd watched him from her window, a frightful ache in her chest. Past the church and out of sight he'd ridden, though she knew his direction by heart. First he'd bypass Elkhannah before coming to the tavern on the outskirts of York, then ride on past the store and mill before spacious farms gave way to vast wilderness.

Her heart galloped harder than the mare's frantic hooves. Every inch of her, sore from falling down the garret stair, begged her to stop. Though midday, it was dusky dark, the mud already turning the hue and heft of molasses. A few miles more and she was flung into unfamiliar territory. The woods were closing in on her now, and the wide road had shrunk to a rocky ribbon.

No one knew where she was. She'd simply left without a by-your-leave for the first time in her submissive life. As the terrain grew more unfamiliar, she slowly realized her error. She should have stopped at the tavern to see if Silas was waiting out the storm. Highwaymen—thieves—frequented this road, small bands hiding in the woods to waylay travelers, no matter how poor. And she a lone woman . . .

Lord, be my shepherd. Take care of me, Your lamb.

The rain was soaking her cloak; it lay like a second skin over her linen dress, bulky and overwarm, so at odds with the icy finger trailing down her spine. Someone was following her—riding hard and fast, as much as the mud and weather would allow. She veered off the trail, the abrupt motion nearly spilling her from the saddle. Thunder rumbled, and she sensed Sparrow's panic before her frantic neighing began. Another boom and Sparrow bolted, straight into the path of a man. He turned his horse sideways and cut them off.

Silas!

The sudden stop unseated her from her horse, and she fell to the ground in an ungracious heap. But she didn't care. She was crying in sheer relief, thankful when he reached down and pulled her to her feet.

"Eden, are you hurt?" A wealth of emotion shook his voice. Surprise. Chagrin. Unchecked happiness. Taking hold of Sparrow's reins, he led them beneath a sheltering elm till a flash of lightning sent them scurrying toward a rock overhang that looked to be the start of a cave. There they stood, dripping wet and speechless.

This close, she could see shadows beneath his eyes, the scruffy beginnings of a beard, the firm set of his features beneath the brim of a new felt hat.

His chest heaved beneath his sodden greatcoat. "Why in heaven's name have you come?"

"Your supplies—" Her own chest rose and fell from her frenzied ride. "You left them."

The light faded from his eyes. "You came all this way through the storm—for that?"

"Why else would I come?"

He ran a hand over his bristled jaw and glanced at the surly sky. "Because you miss me, mayhap. Because you have something to tell me. Because you want to go west."

All shyness fell away and she looked hard at him in surprise. "With a man who thinks of me as a sister?"

"Och, Eden." A flash of exasperation rode his handsome features, and he came nearer, his eyes a soul-searching green. "A sister? Nae." His fingers skimmed her bruised chin. "You're more than that to me . . . far more."

"More?"

In answer he began slowly untying the chin ribbons of her bonnet, knotting the ends so that it dangled down her back. She waited expectantly—breathlessly—as he removed his own wet hat, setting it atop a lichen-edged rock jutting from the cave wall. Despite her cumbersome cloak, the touch of his hands on her shoulders sent a delicious shiver clear to her bones. He pulled her nearer, and she was enveloped in the heady scent of wet leather and her own soft soap. His mouth found hers at last, feather-light then firm.

Her first kiss.

She felt a breathless bewilderment that she didn't know what to do—where to put her hands, how to tilt her head. But he did. As he deepened each kiss, she nearly swayed. This was so . . . exquisite. So unexpected. Instinctively, her arms circled his neck as he held her tighter, nearly lifting her off the ground. She grew so weak with longing she gave a little cry when he released her.

Leaning back against the rock wall, crushing her bonnet, she felt naught like the Eden of old but some wild, untamed creature. He'd stirred to life every feeling she had and a few she never knew existed, and she had no wish to tuck such feelings away. She'd been brought to the brink of something new, something glorious, and felt suddenly and achingly unfinished.

She reached for him again. "Silas, please . . ."

He leaned into the ledge beside her, eyes dark with desire, his breathing a bit ragged. "Nae, Eden. I'll not love you here, but somewhere safe, sound—and rightly wed. As you deserve."

Was that what was missing, then? The Lord's blessing? Her eyes roamed his handsome features, seeing him in a new light. The self-contained Silas of old was gone, and in his place was a man who loved her—wanted her—and was about to leave her. Though she bit her lip till it nearly bled, anguished sobs tumbled out of her and she was back in his arms, not wanting his comfort so much as his kisses.

"I have your heart, and you have mine," he whispered. "'Tis enough, aye? For now?"

But she couldn't answer because it wasn't enough, not nearly enough. How could it be with a wilderness between them?

He held her, smoothing her damp hair back from her face, whispering things she'd never thought to hear. And then, in silent agony, she watched as he went back into the rain and rounded up their horses. They'd ride out into the storm because it was no longer safe for them to stay here alone and in each other's arms.

He helped her into the saddle, and she was conscious that there was no more thunder or lightning, just a warm, streaming rain. "I'll ride with you home and then be on my way again."

Numb, she tied her bonnet tighter and followed him out of the trees. They were riding fast, but her heart rebelled at every step. She was dully aware of the clean scent of rain giving way to something thick and hazy, but it wasn't till they crested the hill by the church that she realized its significance. The meadow and the pond were shrouded with smoke, the smell stinging her senses and filling her mouth when she opened it to breathe.

The barn, the smithy . . . on fire?

Frantic figures ran to and from the well like people possessed. Mama? Papa? Behind the barn's thick timbers, the cries of trapped animals rent her heart. With a little cry, she started down the hill, but Silas gave a rough tug to her bridle.

"Nae, Eden—go for help at Hope Rising!"

They parted, horses bolting in opposite directions. For the first time in her life, her heart pulled her toward home instead.

❧

By the time Silas rode in, the Lee barn was near collapse. Some brave soul had dashed inside and let the animals out, and he breathed a heartfelt bethankit, mindful of Eden. Cows, horses, goats, and pigs milled about in a sort of smoke-poisoned stupor, mired in mud, their distress adding to the confusion all around them. He dismounted, grabbed some empty burlap bags by the woodshed, and ran for the house.

Flames were licking the arbor connecting the kitchen to the smithy, and he smothered them, senses burning, the fabric blackening beneath his hands. Memories began to pelt him like hail, and he struggled to stay atop them. He was here . . . then Scotland . . . then back in York, his dire surroundings a reminder. Mrs. Lee and Elspeth were drawing water at the well while Liege made use of a rain barrel to replenish his bucket. His gout acted like a shackle, slowing him, hastening the fire eating away at the smithy wall nearest the barn. Though the rain was again drenching them, the barn's fire, stoked to an inferno by the haymow within, was beyond saving. At least the house, solid stone, would be spared.

"The forge!" Liege shouted.

Silas was doing all he could, though the smithy's rear wall was now a seething red, the corner posts charred to matchsticks. Smoke clogged his senses, and his muscles burned from heaving water. He was vaguely aware of a few neighbors—farmers—appearing in the smoke and heat, and then Mrs. Lee standing beside him.

"Where is she? My Eden?" Her soot-streaked face was wet from the rain, but he saw only her tears. "I thought you'd taken her with you. And then the fire started and I feared she was trapped in the barn."

"Trapped?"

"The doors were barred from the inside—Liege had to take an ax to break in and let the animals out. I thought—"

"I sent her to Hope Rising for help." The dark implications of what she said began to cloud his mind. He'd assumed—hoped—it was but a stray spark from the forge that had ignited the blaze. "Where are Thomas and Jon?"

"In the springhouse."

She moved away, disappearing through the smoke, as he worked to save a place he loathed and was well on his way to leaving but a few hours before. *Is this Your will then, Lord? Am I to stay?* His spirit rebelled, though he felt a staggering relief he'd not leave Eden.

Lord, help us through the next hours, whate'er they may bring.

⨯⨯⨯

Shadow-quiet, Eden paused outside the rear wall of the ash-laden smithy the next morning. She'd not meant to eavesdrop, but the sight before her begged pause. There was her father, seated, head bent, the burnt remains of his livelihood all around him. He made a pitiful sight, one she never thought she'd witness, and it tethered her to the spot.

Silas stood before him, straight-backed and solemn, his gaze never wavering. "I'll stay under one condition. The new contract will be per my terms."

Her father looked away, shoulders slumped. For a moment Eden feared Silas would temper his stance, and then, as if remembering all that was at stake, his resolve seemed to harden. "Nothing less."

Papa gave a curt nod, gray eyes flinty. "You know what they're saying round the county? That the fire is just punishment for my sins . . . for breaking the Sabbath and forsaking my Quaker roots."

Eden didn't doubt it. York was skilled at passing judgment. And who was to say that the Lord hadn't allowed it? She watched as Silas looked down at his boots lest Liege read the censure in his eyes.

"So you'll stay on—rebuild?" Papa asked.

"Aye," Silas responded, locking eyes with him again. "But I'll have it in writing first."

Eden could sense her father balk beneath his surface calm. But what choice did he have? Aging, gout-ridden, of poor temper and poorer reputation, he needed a younger man's strength and savvy to rise from the rubble.

"Very well, then." Limping to the desk, Papa fumbled for a piece of paper, quill, and ink, hands trembling as if palsied. "State your terms and be quick about it."

This was easily managed. Ever since she and Silas had returned yesterday and battled the fire, he'd prayerfully hammered out his conditions in his head, so he'd told her, expecting her father would press him to stay.

Paper back in hand, Papa read the contract aloud. "You agree to rebuild both barn and smithy and fulfill your tenure as apprentice to conclude no later than October of this year, so long as the following terms are met." He paused and scanned ahead, jaw tightening. "All overcharging in account books must be rectified." At this, he nearly growled. "You'll not be coerced into marriage, and you insist—what?—that Eden be allowed to attend church?" He shot Silas a withering look. "You'll be the gossip of the county squiring two daughters."

Silas shrugged. "One more matter. I've moved my belongings to the room in back of the smithy. I'll not take the garret."

Heaving a sigh, Papa dipped the quill into the ink pot and scrawled his name and the date.

"D'ye want a witness?" Silas asked him.

"Nay. I'll not shame myself twice," Papa muttered, passing him the paper.

Eden knew Silas had won a significant victory. Five months was ample time to rebuild the barn and smithy and finish his apprenticeship. The position at Fort Pitt would wait, or so they hoped. In the span of a tumultuous twenty-four hours, all had come clear. She felt a blessed relief.

At the sound of approaching hoofbeats she looked up, startled to find David dismounting just outside. He entered the smithy, eyes roving the blackened interior, clearly at a loss for words. Hidden in the shadows, Eden started to move away, then glanced back once more. David was asking something of Silas, some request or matter of business, as Papa looked on.

She paid no attention to the words, just the men themselves. 'Twas clear Silas was now in command. For a few, startling seconds the world as she knew it was turned on end, granting her a vision of what was to come. Men like her father and David would continue to exist, but in future they would be second to men like Silas. Her heart gave a thankful leap.

Oh, my love, you are meant for better things. Things far beyond the boundaries of York . . .

<hr />

Silas caught sight of Eden as she turned away and wondered if she'd been privy to all that had transpired. He felt such elation at the new contract in hand he was barely aware of David Greathouse's leaving, the thunder of his going a distant rumble.

"I've some lumber coming from York," Liege said, getting up from a stool. His dull eyes took in the charred south wall, sunlight fanning golden fingers of light through what was left of the smithy roof. "The hardware for Grossvort's dower house needs to be finished before we start rebuilding or he'll raise a ruckus. At least the anvil and bellows and our tools were spared, though I can hardly abide the stench of it."

For once they agreed. The smithy, ever oppressive, was now burdensome in a different way, the sour smell of wet ash and burnt wood overwhelming. Beyond the yawning front doors, the rubble of the barn still smoldered. The house, aside from minor damage, had been spared. As of yet no one was talking

225

about who was responsible, but from their haunted looks Silas knew they were wondering.

He moved a charred beam aside with the toe of his boot. "Who d'ye ken started the fire?"

"Who?" Liege shrugged bent shoulders and looked at the ground. "I have my share of naysayers, those who wish me ill. It could be anyone from a simple village lad making mischief to a business dealing gone sour." Turning away, he began a slow walk toward the house, pushing the smithy doors open wider and bringing an end to the speculation. "'Tis of little consequence now. What's done is done."

Silas begged to differ but stayed silent. He tied on his leather apron and set to work as best he could, completing the order Liege had requested before noon and composing what he would say to Eden when he next saw her. That morning she'd been at the paddock, brow furrowed in concentration as she proceeded to lead a curious assortment of tethered animals down the lane. Greathouse had offered Hope Rising's stables as shelter, and Liege had charged Eden with the task of caring for them there. Silas had watched, wishing he could go with her.

Midmorning she returned, stepping into the smithy's fiery confines, surprising him. She rarely ventured into his domain, but she was here now and had chosen her time carefully. Liege and Elspeth had gone into York to dicker over lumber, and Mrs. Lee was busy with the children inside. Laying aside his work, he faced her.

"You're going to stay on—till October." Her words were breathless—a bit disbelieving. The poignancy of her expression made his chest tighten. "And then . . . ?"

"You tell me, Eden."

She took a step nearer. "I overheard your terms. You've moved out of the garret. I'm to go to church."

"If you want to."

"If?" Her smile was like a sunrise. "I've wanted to go since I first heard the steeple bell sixteen years ago. But . . ."

"But?" he echoed.

But Elspeth. Elspeth wouldn't like it, they both knew. And that is why they must tread cautiously. He brushed the soft contour of her cheek with a sooty finger. "We'll proceed carefully. We want no trouble—no repeat of what happened on the stair."

She nodded, the ugly bruises she bore a telling reminder. "I understand. With all that has happened, we'll both be busy . . ."

Too busy for courting, her pensive expression seemed to say.

Tears lined her lashes, cutting him to the quick. She needed wooing—and wooing well. The Scripture he'd nearly given her his last night in the garret was tucked in his fiddle case, forgotten. Wiping his hands on his apron, he moved toward the back room. She waited while he retrieved it, her expression holding such an expectant eagerness he wished he had something more tangible. A handful of flowers . . . a string of pearls.

Tucking the paper in her hand, he bent and whispered the Scripture penned there in both Gaelic and English, his breath stirring the fiery tendrils near her ear. *Oh my dove* . . . She listened, head down, visibly moved. He cast a glance at the door, aching to run his fingers through her hair . . . to still her trembling mouth with his own . . . to make her his. As the unholy thoughts took hold, he pushed them away successfully one minute, only to take her in his arms the next. She came to him with a willingness that erased all his fears for their future, today and henceforth.

Lord help him, there was no going back, only forward. Once he'd tasted her sweetness, there would be no returning to staid glances and prim stairwell meetings.

23

*Love gilds the scene, and women
guide the plot.*

RICHARD BRINSLEY SHERIDAN

Eden left the privacy of the smithy the second her ears met
with the sound of the wagon signaling Papa and Elspeth's
return from York. She and Silas had been alone but a few,
fleeting minutes, and her heart was sore, sensing she'd have
naught but the memory to warm her for days . . . weeks.

"Back from Hope Rising so soon?" Her mother turned
from cleaning ashes from the hearth as she came into the
kitchen. "I feared Jemma would detain you."

"Not today," she said simply, tying on an apron and recalling her hurried morning.

The truth was she made her apologies to Jemma as soon
as the horses were stabled and the rest of the animals led to
pasture, as she had no wish to be away from Silas. Fortunately,
David had arranged for help, hiring a new stable hand to assist
her. But her thoughts were far from such mundane matters
this morning. She was as aflocht as she'd ever been in her

life, every raw emotion written on her flushed face, and the compassion in her mother's eyes confirmed it.

Touching her overwarm cheek, Mama whispered, "Oh, Daughter, take care."

The warning was woefully brief, but Eden understood completely. Her mother well knew her feelings. She felt a sliver of sorrow she hadn't confided in her before now. "Mama, I—"

Mama put a finger of warning to her lips. A sudden commotion gave them pause when Elspeth entered the kitchen, arms full of packages. Depositing them atop the kitchen table, she glanced at Eden, a strange glint in her eyes. "Since you're to go to church, Papa had me select some cloth for a new Sabbath dress."

Eden didn't know whether to grin or grimace. Her sister's preferences were not her own, and Papa's generosity was downright shocking. The silence grew stilted as Elspeth began yanking at paper and string, untying their purchases.

"I found a length of blue luster you might like—and one of rose brocade for me." With the dramatic flourish of a dressmaker, Elspeth draped the wares over her arm, including new garters and clocked stockings for them both.

The sight gave Eden pause. Something was afoot . . . but what? She touched the shimmering fabric, a bit disbelieving—and decidedly chary. "'Tis lovely—I couldn't have picked finer."

"I'm afraid we'll have to mind our dress hems. Papa wouldn't buy new shoes, and ours are so old they're shocking. But I did talk him into a length of lace. I daresay it's as fine as anything Jemma might find in Philadelphia." She held it aloft between gloved fingers, mouth twisted in a smile.

Eden saw that it was a type of fine, French bobbin lace, fragile as tulle and far more costly. What, she wondered, had come over Papa?

"It looks to be minionet," Mama marveled. "Perfect to trim a bonnet or handkerchief." She frowned at the sound of Jon's cry. "You'd best start sewing. Such fine gowns will take time to make."

Lost in the wonder of a new dress—and Papa allowing church—Eden was barely aware of Mama leaving the kitchen. She wanted to follow, to tend to Jon instead, but Elspeth's harsh hiss and frosty stare hemmed her in.

"I'm still trying to come to terms with you running off with Silas yesterday."

Eden's fingers stilled on the fabric. "I'd not thought to go with him." True enough. The prospect of heading west still unsettled her. "He'd simply forgotten his provisions."

Elspeth's probing gaze roamed her face as if searching for secrets—or noting the bruises, perhaps? In the upheaval of the fire, nothing had been said or done about the incident on the stair. Now Eden could scarcely lay down to sleep at night, certain of Elspeth's wrath at another vulnerable moment. Uncomfortable with her scrutiny, Eden went to the hearth and lifted the lid off a kettle to find stew simmering. She gave it a stir, wondering if her sister suspected all that bubbled beneath the surface of their own situation.

"I think you fancy yourself in love with him." Elspeth's tone turned mocking. "Why else would you go creeping up the stairwell at midnight?"

"Not all is as it seems, Sister."

Elspeth circled the table to stand beside her, heightening Eden's alarm. At least here in the kitchen there were no stairs to push her down—only the hot hearth. She took a step away from the leaping flames to stand by the relative safety of the beehive oven. But Elspeth's malice followed her, her voice a menacing whisper. "You have the heir to Hope Rising at your beck and call. Why would you want to dally with a simple blacksmith?"

Searching for a soft answer, she replied, "Silas may be a simple blacksmith, but he will not stay a simple blacksmith."

"Oh? And are you privy to his grand plans, then?" Elspeth rolled her eyes. "I know of none except a harebrained scheme to go west into the wilderness."

The slur stung, but Eden resisted any further defense of him. How could she put into words the growing certainty in her heart that Silas was destined for greater things? Things well beyond a forge's fire? But she could never share such thoughts with Elspeth—or anyone. "I lay no claim to any man's heart."

"So you say." Gathering up the rose fabric, Elspeth shook her head. "I don't understand how a simpleton like you can turn the heads of so many men. Just this morning in York the gunsmith's son spoke to Papa about you."

Eden faltered a moment before the name took hold. Giles Esh? She'd danced with him once at Hope Rising's ball and then forgotten.

"Somehow you've managed to hoodwink him as well."

The caustic words, though hurtful, seemed to roll off Eden like rainwater. Cocooned in the warmth of Silas's love, she felt a strength and contentment she'd never known. A sense of pity for her contentious sister stole over her. She met Elspeth's tear-filled eyes and felt a twist of surprise. Did her sister love Silas? Or was he simply desirable because he was unattainable? Would Elspeth, sharp as glass, ever win a man's heart? Or more importantly, know the love of God?

"We'd best begin work on our Sabbath dresses," Eden said, searching for some common ground, however fragile.

Elspeth pushed the lace her way, expression rigid. "You may have the minionet if you like. I daresay you're in need of such frippery far more than I. With three men vying for your attentions, you'll want to look your best."

She left the kitchen, but the overwhelming scent of citrus

lingered. Fingers listless on the fabric, Eden sorted through all that had been said, thoughts aswirl. Clearly Elspeth suspected something between her and Silas. He had urged caution, and she knew this was wise. What were a few months' discretion when they had the rest of their lives?

∽∾

Frequenting Hope Rising's stables in the days to come, Eden breathed in the familiar scent of stale hay and new milk. She walked cautiously past the stalls holding David's fine Virginia thoroughbreds, each looking at her with alert almond eyes, tails and ears twitching. She knew a few by name. Prince. Thunder. Lord Nelson. Atticus. Faced with their grand visages, she preferred her humble Sparrow—and the less temperamental Horatio.

She'd been here since first light this mid-May morning, milking the cows and feeding the pigs before turning Papa's horses out to pasture. She took special care of Silas's gelding, knowing he'd be pleased, giving the animal an extra nosebag of oats and a wizened apple. The sound of bleating in the near paddock filled her ears, and then the noise of the barn raising, of half a dozen thundering hammers and newly minted nails, sounded across the meadow.

Lately she dallied as she did her chores, hoping she and Silas would cross paths in the lane when he came to oversee the sheep. How he managed a barn raising, forge business, and Hope Rising was beyond her, but he seemed to accomplish all with relative ease. Papa, forever nursing his gout, had faded to the shadows. Since stating his terms a fortnight ago, Silas was more the master.

Warmed by the thought, she turned a bedimmed corner and started at a wet lick of her hand. "Sebastian!"

The briard, a great mass of shaggy hair and soulful eyes,

cocked his head as if to ask where Silas was. "Your shepherd is busy today," she said, stroking the heavy fur along his neck. "Lately I see as little of him as you, I'm afraid."

The lament was met with a throaty growl, and together they walked toward the open stable door. "You cannot follow me home, mind you." Gripping a milk pail by its handle, she stepped gingerly as the frothy contents sloshed about. "'Twould grieve me to tie you to the paddock again."

"No, we wouldn't want that."

Behind her, David's low voice slowed her steps. She turned back toward him, expecting—hoping—Sebastian would bound forward in welcome, but there was only the quiet thump of a tail in greeting. 'Twas just as she suspected. Sheepdogs bonded with the sheep—and shepherd. Sebastian knew that person to be Silas, not David.

The dog between them, David circled and took the milk pail from her. "I've told a groom to ready the pony cart. No sense hauling all that milk home by hand."

"The pony cart?" Surprise chased her solemnity away. "The old one of our childhood?"

"The very same. But I'm afraid there's no room for Sebastian."

"Once upon a time all five of us could fit, including the cat," she reminisced, the memory surprisingly plain. "You and Bea would fight over the reins."

"Oh?" Jemma's voice rang out from the other end of the stable. "I believe that was me, not Bea." Approaching them, she tugged on riding gloves, the slim handle of her whip tucked beneath her arm. "Don't you remember, Cousin?"

"I remember we'd go round and round the meadow, beating each other about the head with the whip," David replied, amusement warming his voice. "You sisters were all the same to me, though Eden tried to keep the peace."

"There was precious little of that," Jemma said with a flick of the whip in his direction.

He grinned and dodged the silver tip, intent on the cart, where he secured the milk with a leather strap. Eden lingered on Sebastian as he chased a butterfly around the carriage house, hoping he'd remain behind. She was anxious to be home, to be within the warm circle of Silas's affection, even if it was across a crowded table with only the barest look between them. When David hovered over her, she felt a breathless dismay.

"I'll escort Eden home. I want to ride over and see how the construction is coming."

"Oh? I thought I'd do the same," Jemma countered, walking toward her saddled mare.

Eden got into the cart, gaze falling to the chipped paint and rusted trim as David handed her the reins. "Why don't you both come?" she said, reluctant to be alone with either of them. Lately Jemma's probing left her undone, and David seemed to be forever underfoot.

"I'll follow later," he told them, turning away as if his hopes for a moment of privacy had been dashed.

With a wave, Jemma started out of the sunlit courtyard down the dusty lane, Eden following. The poor pony moved slowly, the gray growth along his nose and ears a reminder of his advanced age.

"Well, we might get there eventually," Jemma bemoaned from her perch in the saddle, "though both barn and smithy will likely be finished by then, poor beast." She maneuvered her mare nearer the cart. "My word, Eden! You look the same as you did ten years ago, sitting there in your simple dress with your unbound hair. Have you given any thought to wearing it up? You'll have to, you know, at the foundling hospital. I imagine you'll look very Quaker-like in their plain gowns and those little caps. It seems a good time to go to the city—what with the trouble at home."

When Eden said nothing, Jemma looked over her shoulder as if to make sure they were alone. "Is it true what they're saying? That the barn doors were locked from the inside?"

Eden nodded, gripping the reins so tightly her fingers hurt. She didn't want to dwell on Philadelphia or the fire, though the latter was the talk of the entire county. But Jemma wasn't easily dissuaded.

"Why not just set the fire without securing the doors?" she mused. "It seems like someone wanted to do the most damage they could, hurting the animals, destroying the haymow, obviously hoping the smithy would burn along with it."

"Papa is not well thought of," Eden confessed. The grudging admission made her realize anew how precious one's reputation was. He'd been building a wealth of enemies for years. "Any number of people might wish him ill."

"I'm thinking the trouble might not lie in York County but closer to home."

Eden sighed. "Elspeth, you mean."

"No . . . Silas."

"Silas? He would never do such a thing."

"No, of course not. But I do believe he's the cause of it all." Jemma's words, though calmly stated, stirred up a tempest inside Eden. "Think on it. Since his coming, he's turned your household upside down. People flock to the smithy to do business with him, shunning your father. Elspeth wishes to wed him. The tavern in York has doubled its patrons on account of his fiddling. He turns every head when he goes to church. No doubt he's added a few congregants there. David has even asked him to be overseer here at Hope Rising—"

"Overseer?"

"Yes, for an exorbitant sum that he's turned down. It seems he's intent on going west." She took a breath, eyes searching. "I wonder if you're not besotted with him as well."

Eden gripped the reins harder, hardly feeling the sudden jarring from a bump in the road. "Silas is not without his charms," she managed carefully, only to feel a telltale warmth when Jemma laughed.

"And might those charms account for your riding after him in the worst storm York County has seen for a decade or better?" Jemma's tone was gentle but insistent. "Everyone from the tavern patrons at the Golden Plough to the county magistrates saw you tearing after him. Come now, Eden. Look at me and tell me you don't fancy him."

The query begged answer, but Eden couldn't respond. Tears hovered on her lashes, and she brushed them away with the back of her hand, unwilling to lie. Her only refuge, she decided, was silence.

Jemma shifted in the saddle, a rueful slant to her mouth. "I think Elspeth believes you ran away with him that day . . . and she started the fire because of it."

Yes. The awfulness of it stole over Eden like a nightmare. Unbidden, her mother's words came rushing back, followed by Silas's. *Daughter, take care . . . We want no trouble—no repeat of what happened on the stair.* It was imperative their love, their future plans, stay secret. She'd not speak of it to anyone, even Jemma.

"As I was saying, should Bea summon you to Philadelphia, it seems a prudent time to go." With that, Jemma rode ahead of her into the chaos of the smithy yard.

The place was astir like a great hive, buzzing and bustling with the sweat-stained efforts of the local men Silas had recruited in the rebuilding effort. Guiding the pony cart toward the springhouse, Eden was aware of Elspeth standing by the

kitchen door, arms crossed, her features stiffening with dis-
approval as she took Jemma in.

❧

Elspeth retreated to the heavily leafed arbor where she'd
been perusing ledgers, a hot coal of resentment burning inside her at the sight of Jemma riding her fine horse into their
humble yard. Her anger cooled when she noted Papa ignoring
the youngest Greathouse, then flamed brighter when Silas
stopped his hammering to speak to her in that charming way
that enlivened his every feature. Though preoccupied, even
overburdened, he attended to his tasks with a quiet confidence
that belied his many demands—and she was furious to find
that it only made him more appealing.

She scanned through the columns of shillings, pounds, and
pence, many crossed out and adjusted at Silas's insistence.
This was one of the new contract terms, a point that caused
Papa the most difficulty. "I will not be a thief," Silas had stated
in his terse Scots speech, reversing years of accumulated greed
in just six succinct words. Such news had spread faster than
the fire, and they were now busier than before.

Laying her quill aside, she entered a kitchen crowded with
dinner smells—a robust stew, loaves of crusty bread birthed in
their oven, crocks of honey and butter, and an enormous bowl
of applesauce. She and Eden were confined to the kitchen,
for the dining room table was set for the workmen—one in
particular who'd caught Elspeth's eye, and who'd been eyeing
her in return that very morning.

For the moment her attention was diverted to the parlor, where women's voices cooed and crooned in irritating
rhythms. She didn't have to join them to know the object of
their interest. Jemma's voice eclipsed them all—and well it

should. 'Twas Jemma's own flesh and blood she fussed over, though she'd deny it if she knew.

The memory of David's brief liaison with her flashed to Elspeth's mind, along with the niggling certainty that he'd dallied with her when it was Eden he wanted.

Behind her, as if a bell had been rung, the men began coming in, Papa leading, Silas bringing up the rear. Mama was showing Jemma to the door, their chatter a rasp to Elspeth's ears. Tying on an apron, Elspeth prepared to serve, waiting till Papa was seated. He was talking of going to Philadelphia in the near future, surprising her and creating a hubbub at table. Having never been there, she listened hard before her attention swung to Silas.

He stood in the dining room doorway, his gaze riveted to Eden and the babe in the adjoining parlor. Her throat grew dry as envy tightened its grip, wrapping round her and snuffing any fine feeling. She couldn't deny what a fetching picture Eden made with Jon cradled in her arms, kissing and crooning over him till his fussing subsided. The babe might have been Eden's own she was so taken with him.

And Silas was so taken with her.

24

Let none but Him who rules the thunder put this man and woman asunder.

JONATHAN SWIFT

Within half an hour of Liege and Elspeth's leaving for Philadelphia, Eden blossomed like a rose transplanted from shade to sun, a fact that did not escape Silas's notice. At work by the sweltering forge, he smiled to himself as he caught sight of her through the open smithy doors. She fairly danced across the yard as she went from chore to chore, and his heart picked up in rhythm to think she might slip inside and warm him with her smile.

Liege's hastily arranged trip to the city seemed nothing short of providential. Obviously weary with watching the activity all around him, his gout ever worsening, he'd announced that he must procure new tools and other sundry items, though Silas suspected he went to seek medical attention. Elspeth had not wanted to accompany him, but she went quietly at his insistence, her back ramrod stiff as they rode east.

Silas watched summer's dust erupt beneath their wagon wheels, a prayer of thanksgiving on his lips. A fortnight or more they'd be away. A whole two weeks to woo his Eden. Properly. Passionately. Without fear of reprisal. To make up for the four weeks he'd just spent ignoring her, busy as he'd been with the rebuilding.

Finishing the ironwork in front of him, he passed outside to the garden, where an abundance of lavender grew along the wattle fence. Picking a fistful, he stood just inside the smithy door and was soon rewarded by her coming. She stepped inside the newly repaired shop, unaware of him behind her, and let out a small sigh, the sag of her shoulders expressing her disappointment at finding him gone.

Soundlessly he wrapped his arms around her, flowers at chin level so she had only to lower her face and inhale their fragrance. She did so—deeply—and then turned to him with a tentative smile, casting an anxious look about, as if expecting to find it all a dream and Liege or Elspeth watching them.

"No one is here," he reassured her, "but your mother and Thomas—" Hearing a baby's fervent cry, he smiled. "And Jon."

"Mama knows," she began. "About us."

"I thought it only fair to tell her."

"She won't breathe a word to anyone. Mama's good at keeping secrets. Oh, Silas, there are so many secrets . . ."

"Secrets?" Thoughts of David Greathouse and the letter from Bea crowded in, and he felt a sudden sinking in his chest. "None of your own, surely."

Her gaze held firm, and he found her eyes the same startling hue as the blooms in her hands. "I should have told you sooner about the babe . . . He's not Mama's. He's Elspeth's. We don't know who the father is. I—"

"Shush, Eden." He brushed her cheek with the back of his fingers. "I've suspected from the first."

"You have?" Her expression darkened. "But how?"

"A look, a word. I'm not a blind man, ye ken." He said no more. He wouldn't drag her through the mud of his personal observations, nor belabor her family's faults.

"Then you know Papa is troubled by more than gout—he's addicted to drink and has long been lying, cheating—"

"Aye, all of it." He placed a finger to her lips, surprised by the force of her confession. "But I'm only interested in you—us—our future."

Tears glinted in her eyes. "I want no secrets between us, Silas."

"No secrets," he echoed, his mouth near the gentle curve of her ear. "Then you should know I can hardly breathe for thinking of you. You're the most maddening lass I've ever known, and every day without you near is an agony to me." Taking her face between his hands, he moved to kiss her, but the sound of approaching horses gave him pause.

The regret in her face mirrored his feelings. "I'll be finishing my Sabbath dress tonight after supper. Bring your fiddle to the parlor—for Mama and me."

His disappointment deepened. "I've promised to play at the tavern. But I'll come in before—or after, if you're still awake."

She nodded, standing on tiptoe to brush her mouth to his. "The Sabbath is ours, Silas."

The Sabbath. A mere twelve hours hence. Her first Sunday in kirk. They hadn't gone to services since the fire, waiting for the swirl of gossip to subside, hoping they might go alone. The joy it brought him couldn't be measured. He found it hard to believe, steeped in his own Scots faith since childhood, that she'd never darkened the door of a church. He prayed it would seem to her a foretaste of heaven. Simply having her beside him would be a foretaste to him.

The small church, built of local limestone, was gray and crumbling, though sturdy tombstones sprouted like wild mushrooms in back of it, sprawling over the hill and beyond. They'd walked up the sunlit road well ahead of the tolling bell, and Eden seemed so overcome by it all she hardly said a word. But Silas was comfortable with their shared silence, and equally at ease when she peppered him with questions.

"How many people come of a Sunday?"

"Fifty or so, depending on the season," he answered. "Fewer in seedtime and harvest."

"Do I look . . . pleasing? Proper?" She stopped and turned toward him, her troubled expression her only flaw, the picnic basket on her arm swinging in consternation.

His gaze traveled the length of her. Clad in a new gown that mirrored her eyes, she showed her fine hand in every feminine pleat and tuck, right down to the fragile minionet lace adorning the bodice. He was as surprised as she about Liege's generosity in buying such goods. Today she had no need of Hope Rising's castoffs, truly.

"Something is amiss," she lamented softly, confidence ebbing. "I see it in your eyes."

"Nae, Eden." It was his turn to flush uncomfortably, the heat of his honesty rising to his face. "The only thing amiss is my thoughts. They're hardly Sabbath-holy."

Giving him a soft smile, she turned and increased her pace up the sun-drenched hill, the silk ribbons of her bonnet trailing to the small of her back.

Och, but she was a sore temptation even in a kirk yard.

He fixed his eye on a wooly clump of sheep grazing in a far meadow, wondering why the Greathouses had yet to attend church when signs of their beneficence were everywhere. The elaborately carved pulpit, the windows, even the collection boxes inside were Eben Greathouse's doing. Perhaps he'd been a religious man. His heir did not seem so. Though Hope Rising was but a stone's throw away, David Greathouse had yet to come up the hill. Silas's gut gave another wrench of warning.

Near the kirk but far from grace.

Within the building's austere confines, Eden followed Silas's lead, sitting beside him in a back pew after speaking with a dozen or so people in the churchyard, all expressing surprise at her coming—or more noticeably, Elspeth's absence.

"My sister has gone to Philadelphia with Papa," she said, which seemed to mystify rather than satisfy them. Beside her, Silas spoke quietly with the congregants about other matters, mostly sheep and the smithy, as if trying to lessen her discomfort.

Though she sensed their minds spinning with unasked questions, she was comfortable in the knowledge that appearing with Silas at church was well within the bounds of acceptable behavior. They'd give no quarter to salacious gossip. From all appearances they were simply the apprentice and the master's daughter intent on church. Yet even if these people entertained the blackest thoughts, nothing could dampen the near-holy awe Eden felt as her eyes roamed the hushed interior.

The smell of cold stone and warm candle wax filled her senses, as did the jingle of coins in the wooden collection box by the door. She felt a lingering embarrassment that she had nothing to give. Nothing but her heart. Her gaze kept returning to the stained-glass window behind the pulpit, drinking in every lovely shard—verdigris, crimson, ochre, ebony—all blending to form a picture of the Savior, the cross behind.

Beside her, Silas sat still, and she wondered what he

thought, if his time here made him yearn for the Scottish kirk of his boyhood. When the minister appeared, she felt a small start that she'd paid so little attention to the fact that he was a Scotsman. His lilt was less honeyed than Silas's, subdued by years spent in York County, perhaps. She simply knew him as Owen McCheyne, the widower farmer who lived north of Hope Rising, his white hair glinting like ice, his rugged features kind. He'd come often to their shop over the years, but Papa wanted little to do with him, and lately it was Silas who minded his business.

Though they'd been here but a few minutes, she was already loath to leave. The silence, the austere beauty of wooden pews and arched windows, lent a profound peace to the scene. Her troubled thoughts seemed to melt away as she listened to the solemn prayer intoned in Gaelic, followed by a Scripture reading. Silas took her hand as a Psalm was sung, their entwined fingers hidden beneath her voluminous skirts.

"Would the brethren care to give a testimony as to how Christ is precious to them?" one elder intoned from a far corner.

Eden watched as several men in surrounding pews stood up one by one to share how the Lord had made them alive in Christ. This was what her heart was hungry for—to hear firsthand the life-changing power of the Savior. Her Savior. Tears trickled down, dampening the lace of her bodice. She'd forgotten her handkerchief, so Silas took out the one she'd made him, a square of soft linen with *SB* marked in dark blue thread.

They were preparing to sit at the Lord's Table, McCheyne said. She watched transfixed as bread was broken and wine poured. And they were to . . . eat, drink? One by one the congregation went forward to receive something from the pastor's hand. Silas returned with a small lead token.

Seeing her confusion, he leaned nearer and whispered, "'Tis an old Scots custom called 'fencing the table.' The aim is to keep out those who shouldn't partake and keep in those who should."

"And am I . . . *out*?"

"Not if you speak with McCheyne after the service."

To show him she was spiritually sound? Her heart thumped harder. "But I can explain nothing . . . I only *feel*."

He nearly smiled. "I would worry if you felt nothing and could explain everything."

This only befuddled her further. As those around her celebrated this strange practice from which she was excluded, she mulled over what she would say. The service went another hour, then two, breaking for a meal in early afternoon. But it was the testimonies and Scripture reading that best fed her needy spirit, far more than the basket of food she'd brought. They sat together beneath an oak's leafy canopy, sharing their picnic and looking out on the lush valley and rolling hills to the west. To the wilderness. Their future.

"How long will it take us to reach Fort Pitt?" Her question was a quiet one. There were other people seated around them, too close for comfort.

His response was equally measured. "A month, if there are no mishaps."

Mishaps. The word turned her cold beneath the brilliant June sun. As if realizing his wording had gone awry, he said, "There will be none, Lord willing."

"Are there any churches in the wilderness?"

"Aye, the one I'll build you." His gaze held hers thoughtfully. "Christ's kingdom has no frontier, ye ken."

She warmed to the thought. "You have such plans. Ambitions."

"Are you only just realizing that?"

"I've known it since I first met you. You aren't made for York County, nor Philadelphia, but the West."

"And you, Eden? What are you made for?"

She gave him a tentative smile. "I'm made for you, Silas . . . I'm meant to be your bride."

The words, so heartfelt, had hurtled past a wealth of fear before reaching her lips. They seemed a binding promise here in the churchyard. With the sun caressing her skin and the promise of summer banishing winter's dark thoughts, she felt she had wings. She had only to look at the man beside her, savoring his nearness and the striking slant of his rugged features, to throw all caution to the wind.

"Not much longer now and we'll be one," he said in low tones, locking eyes with her. "Silas and Eden Ballantyne." The rich words were muffled by the ringing of the church bell, returning them to the service and a final sermon.

Afterward, when the pews emptied, she poured out her heart to the godly minister while Silas waited outside. When she joined him, she held a Bible, the worn leather cover obviously beloved, the contents the same.

"Pastor McCheyne gave me this." Her heart was so full she nearly couldn't speak. "'Twas his wife, Elizabeth's. They have no living children."

"Then you no longer have need of a poor apprentice penning you Scripture," he said, a teasing shine in his eye.

"I need you in other ways," she said, laying a hand along his cheek. "I will always have need of you, Silas."

25

Should I have learned to fiddle,
I should have done nothing else.
SAMUEL JOHNSON

Without Papa and Elspeth, the farmhouse had an entirely different feel. Time passed in a peaceful haze, full of whisperings and fervent kisses, twilight walks, and fiddle music far into the night. Even Mama seemed to bloom under Silas's oversight, talking and laughing more than Eden had ever seen, at last emerging from her melancholy shell. Though Mama had been denied her own happiness, her joy for them knew no bounds.

"Ah, you have Corelli, I see." Looking over the makeshift music stand in the summer parlor, Mama selected a song. "'Tis been years since I've heard his 'Adagio.'"

As Eden and her mother sewed by the light of the three-sided lantern, Silas wooed them with the sweetness of his tone. Sitting on a stool by an open window, he played with an uncommon life and spirit, and his slow airs left Eden breathless. The music seemed like candlelight—flaming, flickering,

247

trembling—each note hovering on the warm air. Unmindful of the sewing in her lap, she lingered on the easy gliding of his bow, his keen concentration, the elegant silhouette of the violin as it rested beneath his bristled jaw, knowing their newfound intimacy was not to last.

"So this was your father's fiddle?" Mama asked as he placed the instrument into her hands. "I see something just inside."

He nodded. "It reads 'Broken on the ice at Stairdam in 1764 and mended in Aberdeen.'"

Her eyes roamed the polished maple appreciatively. "Light as a feather and strong as an ox. Who is the maker?"

"Giuseppe Guarneri of Cremona—Italy. 'Twas a gift from the earl of Dalhousie."

Mama studied him, features softening. "You saved it from the fire—from burning in the clearances?"

He nodded, and Eden thought of all he'd told them these last few eves, things that still made her shudder. She sensed he didn't want to speak of the past, but Mama had gently drawn him out, and in doing so Eden began to measure her own blessings.

What were an ill-tempered father and sister in light of poverty, starvation, and loss? How would it feel to be forced from the Highland home you'd always known to a rocky coast, where conditions were so harsh that children had to be tethered to posts to keep them from being blown over the cliffs while their parents worked?

Though he spoke of it all dispassionately, she saw beneath his calm to the wounds beneath. The scars on his hands, she realized, were nothing like the scars on his soul. He'd come here to America, borne along on a tide of Scottish emigration, only to arrive in the colonies just as poor and hungry as before. How he—and his violin—had survived seemed a miracle.

His features assumed a rare pensiveness when he showed

them the Latin phrase burned into the wood beneath the strings. "It reads *Soli Deo Gloria*. To the glory of God alone."

"That is why the tone is so sweet," Eden said, taking up her sewing again. "'Tis heaven's music, truly."

He smiled and began playing a hymn. As she listened and mended, she tried to ignore the rising ache in her head, but squinting at the tiny stitches didn't help. A few minutes passed and she excused herself, taking an empty pitcher to fetch cider from the springhouse.

Beneath the light of a full moon, the skeleton of the barn loomed large, lacking all but roof and doors, reminding her that the livestock would need to be brought home from Hope Rising. She was glad, weary of meeting David every morning in the stables before he rode out to oversee his lands. Of late he seemed so fractious. He was concerned for her safety, he said, as was Jemma. The fire still worried them, unexplained as it was. She, however, barely thought of it, consumed as she was with Silas.

At the sound of a boot scraping the stone walk, she started. "'Tis only me, Eden."

Turning toward the warm voice, she extended a hand.

"There are wolves about. They've been harassing Greathouse's sheep. I don't want you out here alone." Setting the pitcher aside, Silas clasped her fingers in his own. "What's more, your father is coming down the lane."

She shut her eyes at the unwelcome words. How quickly time had flown! It had been but eleven days. She rested her head against his chest, heeding the creak of the wagon. How like Papa to press on in the moonlight rather than part with precious coin at a tavern. The groan of wagon wheels grew louder, shattering the calm in her spirit. She breathed in Silas's beloved scent, felt the bristle of his beard as she pressed her cheek to his.

"I love you, Eden. More than you know. More than life."

Yes. More than life. That was how she'd oft felt but couldn't put into words. "And I you."

He stepped away from her just as the wagon pulled into the yard. Unwilling to let go of him, she fastened her eyes on his broad shoulders as he walked toward his room at the back of the smithy. They couldn't risk being seen together. Their precious time alone had come to an end.

"Eden? Is that you?" Papa's voice was like the rasp of a saw. "Come help with the horses! Your sister is tired from the journey."

And so it had begun all over again.

❧

Elspeth was not too tired for a tirade. Indeed, the trip to and from Philadelphia seemed to have invigorated her temper. Eden felt nearly burnt from the heat of it. Wearing a new hat, an outrageous concoction of ostrich feathers and silk lilies fashioned by a city milliner, Elspeth stepped down from the wagon with the airs of Beatrice Greathouse alighting from a Philadelphia townhouse.

"I'll not leave home next time, I tell you. My very bones seem broken from such a ride! The so-called Forbes Road is a disgrace!" Pausing mid-rant in the yard, she turned and surveyed the nearly finished barn in the light of a full moon. "I thought Silas would be done by now. Papa was expecting it."

Her voice, strident enough to reach the back of the smithy where Silas boarded, was hardly necessary. He stood beneath the eave, arms crossed, with nary a greeting. Eden was struck by how forbidding he could be, a cold sternness marring his features.

Was he remembering their altercation on the stairs? Thinking of who'd sired Elspeth's child? Whatever it was, he gave no welcome. Catching sight of him, Elspeth averted her head and hurried into the house while Eden pushed down the overwhelming urge to throw herself into his arms, if only to shield herself from the hurtful things to come.

While Papa unhitched the team, she hayed and watered the lathered horses in a barn resounding with Papa's various complaints about the journey. The main thoroughfare to Philadelphia was in dire need of repair, he groused. A steep toll was exacted just outside the city, during which he'd felt fleeced. The tools he'd purchased were of inferior quality, the tavern fare worse. He hated the dirty air, the street urchins, the stench of Philadelphia.

Finally escaping to the house, Eden climbed the stairs to her bedchamber, where she fared no better. Elspeth stood before the clothespress, admiring her hat in the small oval mirror. She tilted her chin first this way then that, her eyes narrowing when she spied Eden. "I suppose we'll have to share my new bonnet, as Papa was in no mood to buy two."

Eden said nothing, amazed by how insensible Elspeth was to the fact she would never wear such an outlandish hat. She'd as soon parade about in her shift! Unhooking her work dress, Eden let it fall to the floor before untying her petticoat, aware that her sister's attention was now fixed on her.

"Why, Eden, you look quite pale. By now you're usually brown as an Indian from being in the garden." She held aloft a candelabra from a nearby table, suspicion narrowing her eyes as she focused on Eden's waist. "You aren't hiding something, are you? I remember how sick I was at first, hardly out of sight of the chamber pot. Let's see. Whose could it be? The gunsmith's son? Master David's? Silas's?"

Even hinting of such unspeakable, intimate things flooded Eden with a profound dismay. She looked away. "I've a headache, is all." Beneath the stark white hem of her linen shift poked her bare feet, an earthy green from grass stains. But she was too tired to fill the basin and wash them tonight.

"A headache? Is this to be a new malady of yours? You've never complained of such before."

A near-blinding pain in her right temple gave Eden pause. Till she'd fallen on the stairs more than a month ago, her head had rarely hurt. But now . . .

Leaving her clothes on the floor, she eased into bed, not bothering to brush and plait her hair. Mercifully, Elspeth snuffed the candles, undressing in the dark.

"I see you finished your Sabbath dress. It takes up half the clothespress." Her sour tone forewarned the gown would soon be hung elsewhere to make room for Elspeth's own. "So how did you find your first church service?"

Humbling. Inspiring. Miraculous. She bit her lip at Elspeth's caustic tone, glad she'd hidden the Bible Pastor Mc-Cheyne had given her in the garret. The past few mornings she'd been reading it aloud at breakfast, realizing that Mama seemed as Scripture-hungry as she. "The church is lovely. 'Tis a blessed way to spend the Lord's Day."

Though the darkness hid her, Eden sensed Elspeth grimace. "Blessed? 'Tis better to call it what it is—tedious. McCheyne should save his sermons for his sheep and spare us all any dullness in future."

The careless words sent a shiver through Eden. "Oh, Sister, best mind your tongue lest the Lord silence it someday." The caution was more breathless whisper than rebuke, but Elspeth pounced on it and spun toward her, a formidable shadow.

"Don't play holier-than-thou with me, Eden Rose. No doubt you're far more smitten with Silas than with an old sheepherder's sermons." She lay down, only to jump up again at the sound of a fiddle. Slamming shut the casement window, she collapsed atop the bed and wrestled with the covers. "I suppose you want to know all about Philadelphia."

Did she? Nay. Surprise gained the upper hand at the realization. Not once had she lamented the fact Elspeth had just gone to the city that once housed all her hopes and dreams. Silas's love for her had changed all that. Though she still had a heart for the foundlings, she felt the Lord calling her to a different task—that of wife and mother. Philadelphia no longer held the appeal it once did. She would go west, Silas leading. She had put her fears, her former plans, behind her for good.

26

Gardening is the purest human pleasure.

FRANCIS BACON

Eden dropped to her knees within the wattle fencing of her herb garden in the July twilight, unsure of what pained her more—her aching head or the gaping crater Sebastian had dug. Again. She supposed it didn't matter, as her leave-taking was creeping up as fast as the thyme along the far fence. Soon she'd be free from worries of mischievous sheepdogs and their fondness for digging, and ponder crossing mountains and rivers instead.

Taking up a trowel, she sighed. If she missed anything, it would be her garden, a place of pleasure and profitableness and peace. Though not as elaborate as Hope Rising's with its miniature box hedges and ornamental topiary, it was the work of her hands—and heart. And tending it meant more to her than ever after reading about her namesake in Scripture: "And the Lord God planted a garden eastward in Eden; and there he put the man whom he had formed . . . to dress it and to keep it."

She took in the feathery fennel and skin-softening mallow, gaze drifting to the purple spires of sweet rocket that grew more fragrant as the sun went down. Surely the West wasn't so wild she couldn't keep a garden. For now she needed a remedy for her aching head. Feverfew? Valerian? Skullcap? Margaret had advised her to take an infusion of lavender flowers—indeed, had made her drink three cups yesterday at tea.

Out of the corner of her eye, she saw the flick of a wagging tail. She sat back on her heels, her smile a trifle sad, a trifle wry. Sebastian had simply come looking for Silas again. She didn't blame him. Wasn't she always doing the same?

"Come along, Sebastian, and I'll return you home."

Making her excuses to Mama, she went down the lane, wanting to return before dusk overtook her completely. When she reached Hope Rising, she saw Margaret and Jemma sitting in the brick-walled garden, drinking tea, backs to her. 'Twas David who met her in the courtyard, a stable boy by his side. The lad ran to her and grabbed the rope round Sebastian's neck while he wagged his tail and looked back at Eden mournfully.

"Let me guess." David's expression was chagrined. "Sebastian has come calling . . . again."

"Yes," she said, a bit breathless from returning at a near run. "He seems to have a liking for my herbs."

He frowned and raked a hand through his hair. "I wish he had the same appetite for wolves."

"Jemma said you've lost two more ewes."

"Regrettably, but Ballantyne can't be everywhere at once. Nor can I. Besides, the sheep aren't what most concern me." His eyes swept her from head to toe. "Margaret tells me you're unwell."

She met his troubled gaze reluctantly. "Just a headache now and again."

"Headaches, is it? Any more trouble at home?"

She felt a tad cornered by his probing. Though Margaret was normally closed-mouthed, since the fire she'd been less so. "No more mischief, if that's what you mean."

"I hardly think such a fire mere mischief, Eden."

That she couldn't deny. But what could they do about it? "The barn and shop have been rebuilt, as you know. Now Papa has his hands full with the wheat harvest—"

"Have you given any thought to the spinning operation I told you about?"

"There's been little time." Impatience needled her as the sun sank like a scarlet ball on the horizon. She wanted to be away, repair the mess Sebastian had made . . .

He stepped closer. "You know that in future you can come to me, that Hope Rising is a safe haven. You could even move into the empty cottage now—"

"Nay!" The word erupted far too forcibly, and she rued the surprise in his eyes. "Please, David, I'm . . ." *Fine?* She teetered dangerously close to a lie. In truth, she wasn't well. She was missing Silas and becoming increasingly worried about Elspeth. And she couldn't dismiss the cold, hovering fear that something far more troubling than the fire loomed on the horizon. "You needn't worry about me . . . please."

Despite the lump rising in her throat, she forced a smile, if only to ease the furrow in his brow. She longed to tell him she would soon go west with Silas. 'Twas time David settled down as well. He was in need of a wife, Jemma said. Whoever he chose, she'd no doubt be a proper Philadelphia belle from one of the prominent families the Greathouses knew. Once they parted, Eden would likely never see Hope Rising again.

The realization made her melancholy, and she started to turn away lest he see the sorrow in her eyes. But he made a sudden move and caught her arm. "Wait, Eden. Promise me you'll come to Hope Rising if you need anything—anything at all."

Their eyes met, and she saw a wealth of childhood affection there. "I promise," she said, as much to appease him as to be on her way. Her head was throbbing now, steady as a drum, nearly making her dizzy, and the pressure of his hand hurt.

"Is Silas playing at the Golden Plough tonight?"

She nodded. "Nearly every night, it seems."

"Those York lasses like to see him come round." A knowing smile lightened his features as his hand fell away. "Some tarry outside the tavern and wait for him."

A little trill of alarm sounded inside her. "Do any . . . go in?"

"To hear him play?" He shrugged. "A few bold ones do, but he gives them nary a glance. His eye is on the West, though I can't fathom why. Fort Pitt is naught but a mud trough with dogs and pigs running amok through the streets, yet he pockets every bit of coin to that end."

She opened her mouth in his defense, then hesitated. Best stay silent lest David see into her heart. She tried to shoo away his disturbing words so they couldn't take root and cause her more worry. Let the York girls look and listen all they wanted. They weren't a part of the plan to go west. She was.

"I believe I'll ride over to the tavern for some draughts," he said, turning away.

Bidding him goodbye, she started toward home as if her heels had wings. Would that she could up and ride to the tavern and see Silas as easily. 'Twas weeks since they'd been alone. With Elspeth accompanying them to Sabbath services and the garden consuming all their energies at summer's peak, there was little time left for stolen kisses. If only she had a remedy for that as well. For now, valerian would do for the ache in her head, if not her heart.

The kitchen in the dog days of August had never been hotter. Eden wiped her perspiring brow with the hem of her apron, patience ebbing. Jon was wailing in the background, and a red welt glowered on her wrist after she'd tried to rescue the pot of beans Elspeth had spilled. They pooled on the worn floorboards in a brown mound, steaming and sticky.

Elspeth shot her an exasperated glance and began untying her apron. "You have no patience with me in the kitchen! No wonder I spill things! The smithy is far preferable to this—"

"Papa asked me to teach you." Taking a deep breath, Eden feigned patience. "How are you to feed a family, manage a household, without such skills?"

Elspeth snorted. "And how am I to learn? You throw into the pot a pinch of this and a pinch of that. How am I to follow?"

"Making cornbread is simple enough. One egg and a cup of buttermilk. One cup meal. A pinch of salt. A spoonful of bacon grease. Mix well."

Rolling her eyes, Elspeth planted her hands on her hips. "Little wonder you are so dull. There are far more interesting things afoot, but you take no notice."

"And what should I take notice of?"

"Papa is making plans. Something to do with the gunsmith's son."

Eden looked up from the mess on the floor, hope kindling. Was this why Papa wanted Elspeth in the kitchen? Was he about to pair her with Giles Esh? "Are you . . . partial to him?"

"Who? The gunsmith's son? Don't be ridiculous. Father tried to foist him on me first, and I refused him. It seems he prefers you anyway, daft as he is. My sights are still set on Silas Ballantyne, and don't you forget it."

Eden bit her tongue. *Then why are you running amok at*

night? 'Tis not Silas you're meeting with, surely. She turned away, thoughts aswirl. The troubling truth was that Elspeth could be dallying with any number of men who came to the smithy for business or who'd helped with the rebuilding. The thought filled her with a recurring dread. What if another babe was on the way?

From the corner cradle, Jon's cries grew more muffled as if his fussing had worn him out. As usual, her sister didn't give him so much as a glance. It hurt Eden, this shunning. At eight months, he was the plumpest, handsomest babe she'd ever seen. Though she tried to puzzle out his parentage, looking for a clue in his tiny features, his origins remained a mystery.

"I'll make the cornbread," Eden said in measured tones, taking up a whisk. "You fetch the cream and apple butter from the springhouse. We'll both clean up the mess."

"Oh my, Sister!" The smile Elspeth gave her was far from warm. "That's the bossiest I've ever seen you."

When the door opened unexpectedly, Eden bit her lip as Elspeth stood in front of the steaming beans, rearranging her full skirts as if to hide them. Silas and Papa were entering the kitchen for the noon meal, a merchant in their wake. There was a business matter brewing, one that involved Silas's three-sided lanterns adorning the expanding streets of nearby Lancaster.

Eden was acutely aware of Silas brushing past her on his way to the dining room, but she dared not look at him lest love and longing splay across her face. He was a master at hiding his own emotions, hardly giving her a glance. Not even Papa, sharp-eyed and sharper-tongued, suspected. Or so she hoped.

Today, with company present, table talk would be allowed. Eden began serving, beginning with their guest, then Papa, and lingering a bit by Silas at the last. Eyes downcast, she took in the broad sweep of his shoulders, the way his thick hair overlapped his banded collar and needed cutting. Her fingers itched to skim the shadow of his jaw . . . lay her head against the warm hollow of his shoulder. Her heart constricted. Elspeth sat across from them, eyeing Silas openly like she longed to do herself.

The bounty of their table gave the merchant pause. "'Tis Eden's doing," Papa was saying. "'Tis no secret she keeps the finest garden in the county." His bald-faced boasting, so at odds with his usual criticism, made her flush the color of the beets she served. "She's been putting by a wealth of goods for the winter. No doubt she'll make some man a fine wife."

"*Some* man?" The merchant's amused tone stopped her cold just shy of the kitchen door. "Word is . . ."

He had the grace to lower his voice, but Eden felt as if he'd shouted the words. She nearly dropped the gravy bowl as the drone of Papa's tone lowered in what she feared was affirmation. *The gunsmith's son.* It could be nothing else. She'd ignored Giles Esh's recent visits to Papa, thinking they were simply talking trade. Might they be arranging a match without her knowledge?

Heartsick, she cleaned up the spilled beans before rocking Jon to sleep by the open kitchen door, trying to court a reluctant breeze. The scraping of utensils on plates in the adjoining room set her teeth on edge. When she served a berry cobbler at meal's end, it seemed everyone was looking at her closely, as if Papa had just told them something momentous.

As she passed behind Silas's chair, he shot her a sidelong glance. "Eden, I have need of a good shirt."

'Twas Saturday—wash day—and he was to play at a wedding that evening. She nodded absently, though his request struck her as odd. He'd never asked her outright for such. She always left his clean clothes in a basket by his door.

She went into the side yard, where half a dozen shirts and breeches were draped over the garden fence. Darting a glance about, she brought one sun-warmed shirt to her face, breathing in the fragrance of linen and lye. But it was his scent she craved . . . his touch . . . the safety and security of his arms. Her heart turned over. Was he as lonesome for her as she was for him?

When she returned to the dining room, his chair sat empty. Papa and the merchant were deep in conversation while Mama and Elspeth cleared the table. Slipping out to the empty smithy, she found Silas's door ajar.

Oh, Lord . . . for a moment alone with him.

"Eden, come."

His tender tone was her undoing. Her heart gave a wild leap. Without a backward glance, she stepped into his room for the first time since he'd claimed it.

27

Gather the Rose of love, whilst yet is time.

Silas shut the door with a firm click, taking the shirt from Eden's hands. Pulling the garment over his head, he watched, bemused, as she turned her back on his bare chest, a faint tint to her cheeks. "You'll not be so modest once we wed, I'll wager."

She spun toward him, her fingers grazing his collar as she fumbled with a button. "Nor so clumsy. Only a few weeks more."

"Aye, Eden Ballantyne." His hand circled the back of her neck, her hair like silk beneath his calloused palm.

The sweetness of her rose up and turned him inside out as he bent and kissed her, his senses reeling dangerously as she kissed him back. He sensed her surprise and delight, her yearning for more. More than he could yet give her. Drawing back, he drank in the anticipation of what was to come. For now he had but a foretaste. There was only the two of them. The door was shut. No one and nothing else existed.

But the gunsmith's son.

Her expression clouded as he thought it, as if they'd already become one and she was thinking it too. He kept his voice low, mindful of Liege returning to the forge. "Eden, what is this about Giles Esh?"

Worry raced through her eyes. "I've heard naught of it till today. He danced with me at Hope Rising's ball. I—I've never encouraged him—"

"'Tis your father's doing." His voice softened in sympathy, though he felt a spike of alarm. She was just a pawn in a business deal; Liege hadn't even consulted her. "He wants another man at the forge once I leave. Being a gunsmith with some understanding of iron, Esh is the logical choice. And he is, by all accounts, smitten with you."

She simply looked at him in surprise. Losh, but she had no idea how tempting she was. Taking her hands, he turned them over and kissed them. "One day, Eden Lee, you'll have to fend off no man but me."

She was regarding him with such love and trust it rent his heart. A gentle and quiet spirit she had, more than any lass he'd ever met.

A new worry gnawed at him. Was he even worthy of her?

"There seem so many obstacles of late," she whispered. "David Greathouse keeps speaking of spinning, and now Giles Esh . . ."

He studied her thoughtfully. "I could tell your father my intentions."

"Nay, he'd simply use it against us—make things harder for us."

"He's given Esh permission to court you. Or so he said at table."

"Oh, Silas, what am I to do?"

He cupped her chin in gentle teasing. "You could simply

be a sonsie lass, hardly giving him a glance, pretending he's not even in the same county, like you do with me."

Dismay stole her smile away. "Doing so breaks my heart into little pieces."

"'Tis best for now," he said with a weary smile. "Till October." The thought filled him with a profound sense of wonder. She was nearly his.

Why, then, did he feel a nagging doubt that it was not to be?

Eden watched warily as Giles Esh approached her at the well. A good fifty feet from the kitchen door, the stone recess was surrounded by old apple trees recently laden with fruit. She knew why he sought her out, having received Papa's permission to court her. And their courting was to begin . . . now.

She surveyed him in the warm shade, trying to smile, trying to stay the judgmental thoughts that sluiced through her like the cider they'd just finished pressing. Through no fault of his own, Giles was so unlike Silas. Small. Thin. Pockmarked. Already losing his fair hair.

"Good day, Giles."

He removed his hat, turning the worn brim in his hands a bit awkwardly. "Good day, Miss Eden." The brilliant hue of his eyes, even in the shade, struck her hard. They were as blue as Jon's—and totally besotted. She lowered her bucket into the well, wanting to climb in after it.

He plucked an apple from a low branch and took a bite, chewing thoughtfully. "Your father's given permission for me to squire you to church come the Sabbath."

She worked hard to keep her dismay down. Elspeth had already intruded on this, her most favorite day. Would Giles too? She drew up the bucket so hastily she spilled half the water out.

"If you have need of church," she said quietly, "I would bid you come."

And so he did, sitting as close as he dared that next Sabbath while she pined for Silas further down the pew. Beside Giles, Elspeth managed to look bright-eyed despite her near-nightly jaunts, turning every head as she entered the austere little church in her outrageous ostrich feather hat. Eden eyed her buxom figure, fearing the worst.

As the opening Psalm was sung, she stole a look at her beloved, straight-backed and silent, eyes ahead. She missed their stairwell meetings, his fervent kisses. All summer their paths had hardly crossed. Sometimes he seemed to have forgotten all about her. And she was struck by the realization that his work, his ambitions, might well be the greatest rival for his affections. He was so driven. So fiercely determined.

As she'd read the Song of Solomon the night before in the garret when the household was asleep, her worn emotions had intensified and turned her breathless.

By night on my bed I sought him whom my soul loveth: I sought him, but I found him not.

❧

As the heat of August faded into a cooler September, dread and elation were Eden's constant companions. Soon she would be free of Papa's and Elspeth's fractious ways and Giles's unwanted attentions. The wilderness awaited, promising a sort of peace, yet as that day neared, new worries dawned. Mama seemed to have taken another melancholy turn, going about her chores teary-eyed and silent. Eden feared it was her own leaving that made her mournful, then remembered hearing Mama and Papa arguing more and more often behind closed doors.

She escaped to Hope Rising when she could, though it

no longer held the appeal it once did. Silas spent afternoons there, overseeing the breeding of the now-flourishing Blackface. Eden lingered at a fence, watching his tall figure in a far meadow as he moved among the flock, nearly forgetting Margaret was waiting. Steaming cups of hyson tea and rose petal sandwiches welcomed her, a far cry from the usual fare. Though Eden hadn't breathed a word of her departure, it seemed Margaret somehow suspected.

Margaret poured the rich brew into pristine cups, the hand-painted flowers and leaves adorning the china reminding Eden of her own fading garden. Absently, she wondered if any good tea could be had in the West. She doubted the porcelain pot she'd packed would make it over the mountains intact.

"Cream and sugar?" Margaret asked, ever polite.

"Both, please." Eden shifted in her chair, wondering how she'd manage with the babe. Jon sat on her lap, a chortling, cooing imp, his fists tightly fastened to his leading strings as he chewed them to soggy bits. At nine months, he was heavy as a tub of lard and twice as slippery, always trying to stand or crawl.

"I'll hold him for thee," Margaret offered, nearly groaning as she did so. "My, but he's a handful! How is his temper?"

"Sweeter now that he's supping on more than milk. Mama's trying to wean him as he tires her so."

Margaret tucked a ginger biscuit into one of Jon's dimpled hands. He turned it over, such a study of contemplation they both laughed. "He seems to be a deep thinker," Margaret mused with a chuckle. "At least where his stomach is concerned."

Eden took a sip of tea, trying unsuccessfully to hide a grimace. "Margaret, are you brewing something new?"

The question was followed by Margaret's knowing nod. "Thee are in need of some headache powders, Eden. I can see it in thy eyes."

Medicinal tea? "'Tis kind of you." She forced herself to take a second sip. "Now that the harvest is nearly over and the larder is full, I'm sure I'll mend."

Despite Eden's hopeful words, Margaret's expression indicated doubt. "I asked David to go to the apothecary on his recent trip to Philadelphia. He consulted Dr. Rush, who prescribed the powders."

Eden thanked her, eyes on Jon as he gnawed his biscuit. "Actually, my mind isn't on my own malady but someone else's." She took a breath. "I'm worried about Mama."

The sudden surprise in Margaret's countenance nearly stole her courage. She hadn't meant to be so blunt, but she felt an overwhelming need to know, to settle matters in her mind, before leaving home for good. "Since the fire, Mama hasn't been herself. Actually, before the fire, she and Papa had words about the past. I know you and Mama used to be friends. I remember her coming to Hope Rising when I was small. I thought . . . perhaps you'd know what the trouble was back then."

The silence stretched long and uncomfortable. "'Twas long ago, Eden. I scarcely recall it." Margaret looked down at Jon, her expression strained. "The Lord desires us to dwell on what is pure and lovely and of good report, does He not?"

"Yes," Eden echoed, dismayed. Within Margaret's carefully couched words was her answer. Whatever Mama had been a part of, 'twas not pure or lovely or of good report. Curiosity and confusion welled inside her, only whetting her need to know a hundredfold. Yet further questions seemed to stick in her throat.

Forcing a smile, Margaret gave a bounce to the babe on her knees. "Let's speak of other things—like the changes coming to thy household. Is it true the gunsmith's son is often there?"

Eden sipped the unpleasant tea, finding it far less galling

than this subject. "Papa wants someone to take Silas's place once he leaves."

She nodded. "David says he is bound for the West—Fort Pitt. York is not to his liking."

"He feels the Lord leading him into the wilderness," she said carefully, eyes averted. "I wish him well, wherever he goes."

The clock struck three, and Margaret waited till it finished chiming to say quietly, "I must admit I had once hoped . . . that thee and Silas . . ."

Eden set down her cup with a clatter. "I'd best be going. Jon is in need of a nap." She brushed ginger crumbs from his chin and hoisted him on her hip. He looked about with a satisfied smile, waving a wee hand and lightening the somber mood. "Please thank Master David for the headache powders."

She stepped out into the bright but fading glory of late summer, fearing she'd hurt Margaret by being so abrupt, wishing she'd not discussed Mama but had confided about Silas instead. The burden of secrets seemed heavy as lead. Elspeth wasn't the only one hiding things. Mama and even Margaret had secrets all their own.

◆◇◆

Three weeks. The time left in York County rode Silas like a burr. Giles Esh was coming round more often now, tarrying at the shop as if it was already his, garnering more attention from Elspeth, given that it was she who worked by his side. For that he was thankful. He couldn't ask Eden how she managed to elude Giles, nor could he inquire about the dark circles beneath her eyes and the telling leanness of her willowy form. A dozen pairs of eyes seemed to be on them all the time.

She's unwell, something whispered inside him, checking

his anticipation. What if she was unable to go west? He set the dire thought aside repeatedly, doggedly preparing for their departure. Though they'd only whispered about it in passing, the first leg of their journey would be marked with a wedding. Pastor McCheyne had joyfully agreed to marry them, waiving the usual banns. It was an old colonial custom, he'd said, in need of changing. They'd need only a license.

On their wedding night, they'd lodge at Ferry Tavern, the last civilized outpost Silas knew of before passing over the mountains. He had enough coin to keep them well fed every league of their journey, if not a roof over their heads. Fort Pitt was still a dream, but one now within his grasp. With Eden beside him, the great distance would fade to mere inches . . .

Shifting in his chair by the window, he breathed in the scent of hot cider and cinnamon, strong and sweet. It threaded through the winter parlor, the very essence of autumn. For a moment he was cast back to the unending orchards of Blair Castle with their gnarled, low-hanging branches bursting with aldermans and lemon queens and lass o'Bowries. A far cry from the American varieties Liege touted. Still, he'd made note of those apples in his journal, for his and Eden's orchard years hence. Newtown pippins and Roxbury russets and winesaps, to name but a few.

"Would you care for some cider, Silas?"

Mrs. Lee was at his elbow with a steaming mug. He took it, murmuring his thanks, aware of the scrape of Liege's cane across the plank floor as he made his way down the hall to bed. 'Twas only eight. Elspeth sat sewing across from Eden by the hearth. The bairns were asleep.

He checked the impulse to follow Liege and tell him he would be taking Eden with him. Best not do so till the very day. He was less troubled about Liege's response than Elspeth's. Their leaving was bound to turn explosive, as she was wranglesome as a keg of powder. He'd not provoke her till Eden was well beyond her vindictive reach. As it was, she lingered nearby every waking minute as if determined they not be left alone together, as if hoping she might somehow win his affection in the end. Even now she was staring at him openly, her voice low.

"Mama, I'm going upstairs. I'm feeling poorly."

Silas detected the falseness in her tone before she'd even risen from her chair. He didn't look at her. He swallowed some cider, his eyes on the low flames licking the kettle in the hearth's ashes. If she was ill, it likely had to do with running amok. Two nights prior he'd seen her slipping through the trees behind the barn to meet someone, somewhere. His heart had lurched. Her hair had been unbound much like Eden's, as if Elspeth meant to trick him into thinking it was she instead.

Nae, his Eden would not play him false.

Even now she was looking at him, sewing forgotten in her lap, a spark of hope in her expression, as if daring to think they might be left alone. He set his book aside and glanced at Mrs. Lee. Quietly, as if adhering to some prearranged plan, she withdrew out the same door Elspeth had passed through minutes before and shut it softly behind her.

For a moment neither he nor Eden moved, then he tugged the curtain closed, eyes returning to the door before resting on her. He ached to touch her, to breathe in her soft scent unhindered. No bairns. No overbearing father. No volatile sister. In mere days they would be left alone to experience the mystery . . . *and they shall be one flesh*. As he thought it, his heart seemed about to burst its banks. He reached into his pocket and withdrew a scrap of paper on which he'd penned a particular Scripture—a promise to carry them through the dwindling days.

I will betroth thee unto me forever.

"Silas . . ." Eden stood across the room, the candlelight calling out all the unforgettable details he loved—the clear depths of her blue eyes, the irrepressible warmth of her expression, every fire-threaded strand of her hair.

He left his chair and went to her, tucked the paper in her palm, and was rewarded with her soft smile. When his hands cupped her shoulders, he nearly shuddered from his need of her. "Soon I'll not have to bid you good night." His lips grazed the soft curve of her ear as he bent his head, half-forgetting to listen, to be alert. "You'll be by my side . . . forever."

"Forever," she whispered, "is hardly long enough."

Yet even as she said it, he knew how frightening it must be for her to leave the only home she'd ever known—and her mother, Thomas, and Jon. She'd not even been as far as Philadelphia.

She rested her head against his chest. "I'm almost ready. I've packed my things . . ."

"Am I to haul your dower chest o'er the Alleghenies, then?" he asked with a smile, not caring if he had to.

"Just one old saddlebag—and me—atop Sparrow." Tilting her head to one side, she looked up at him, tempting him to do more than simply rest his hands on her shoulders.

"Upon my soul, Eden." His throat tightened. He nearly couldn't speak. "You tie a man in knots . . ."

"Then kiss me and be done with it, Silas." She was all seriousness now, eyes dark with purpose. She placed her hands upon the broad level of his shoulders, surprising him. He kissed her then—or mayhap she kissed him. Their mingled desire nearly brought him to his knees. To counter it, he widened his stance and held her a bit less hungrily, his back to the door.

When the door flew open with the creak of a rusty hinge, he nearly cursed his folly. The telling surprise on Eden's face foretold the worst. His hands fell away as he turned toward the intrusion. Elspeth crossed the threshold, stiff and defiant, fists clenched at her sides. Silas held her gaze, rebuking her with a look for her rude entry, while Eden gathered up her sewing and left through the kitchen.

He expected Elspeth to speak, to poison the room with the spite contorting her fair features. A dozen retorts were on his tongue if she did. God forgive him, but the sight of her turned his stomach. When she spun on her heel to follow Eden up the stair—to berate her in private, no doubt—he started after her, only to be checked by a startling thought.

Love your enemies . . . Pray for those who persecute you.

Every ounce of his will rebelled at the unmistakable prompt. Nae, this command was simply too much.

⌾⌾

Eden braced herself for the onslaught of Elspeth's wrath, well aware she was on her heels as they climbed the stairs to their room. The silence was rife with withheld secrets, of smoldering passion and thwarted hopes. For a fleeting moment Eden felt a glimmer of compassion for her sister, and then it was smothered by fear. Elspeth was so volatile one never knew which way she'd strike—nor how deep. Before Silas's coming, any trouble had simply arisen over a coveted chore or dress, not a man. Not Silas Ballantyne.

The stakes were far too high.

Eden began to undress with trembling hands, trying to school her distress. All was now laid bare. She and Silas had been caught in each other's arms. Their love was secret no longer. *Lord have mercy!* What a tremendous ruckus Elspeth might raise!

Yet as the silence lengthened and turned less threatening, a slow realization dawned. Elspeth was afraid of Silas. And that fear, for once, kept her from lashing out.

Turning back the bedcovers, Eden slipped between cool linen sheets, hearing Elspeth do the same in the darkness. Truly, what were Elspeth's malicious words and venomous glances to her now? Once she left York County, she'd likely never see her sister again.

28

When nature gave us tears, she gave us leave to weep.

BENJAMIN FRANKLIN

Sixteen days. The old black saddlebag bearing a small padlock was buried in the barn loft, full of an assortment of needed things. Two handkerchiefs embroidered *EB*. Three pairs of worsted stockings with garters. An extra linen shift. Two petticoats. One dimity nightgown, never worn, with ribbon trim.

A wedding gown.

Eden's fingers had caressed the fabric, wonder bubbling up inside her. Made of chintz, it was the color of spring grass, the petticoat embroidered with tiny pink flowers and a winding vine. Buried in an ancient trunk, it had been smuggled to the barn and rolled into the saddlebag, terribly wrinkled but undeniably lovely.

"'Twould please me greatly to know that you'll be wed in the dress that brought me such happiness," Mama had told her in hushed tones. Hugging the lovely gown to her chest, Eden marveled that Mama had ever been young or carefree.

"I once wore it to a dance where I met the man I wanted to marry." Mama seemed on the verge of telling her more before fading to generalities. "One's first love is often the finest—the most enduring."

Yes. This was how she felt about Silas—and why it was a punishment to be apart. The last Scripture he'd penned returned to her with such poignancy it brought a pang tender as any wound. *I will betroth thee unto me forever.* She kept it close, tucked in her bodice, hidden and heartfelt.

Now, standing before the kitchen hearth, she tried to envision the home they would have. 'Twas the first time in days she'd had a spare, silent moment. Mama had gone to York with Papa. Thomas and Jon were asleep down the hall. Elspeth, she guessed, was working on the ledgers. A steady stream of business kept the smithy doors open even though the weather had turned cooler—mostly farmers in need of repairs of plows and tools after the harvest. The tentative ring of a hammer assured her it wasn't Silas at the forge but Giles.

A sudden simmering returned her to the stew that needed tending. It rimmed the kettle's edge in angry bubbles, a roiling brew of chicken and potatoes, onions and thyme. Behind her a door groaned open, and she turned to see a bleary-eyed Thomas, thumb in his mouth. Giving the stew a stir, she dropped down in a near chair and held out her arms to him. He responded with a sleepy smile she tried to commit to memory. Her throat tightened. When—*if*—she saw him again, he'd be more boy than baby. He climbed onto her lap, looking about in question.

"Mama will be back soon," she told him, reaching for the cup of cider he'd left unfinished at noonday dinner. He drank it down and took the biscuit she offered, ambling off to play in the corner where his toy soldiers waited.

She listened for Jon while she made porridge, sweetening it

with a smidgen of vanilla sugar, unable to check a smile. She well knew the way to the babe's heart. He'd balked at plain porridge, making Mama despair till Eden tried the coveted sweetener, using a small sugar hammer to dislodge a chunk or two. Together they'd laughed at his eagerness to eat.

She wished Silas would come in and replenish her wood, kissing her on the back of the neck as he'd once done when no one was about. Though Elspeth had caught them together in the parlor the week before, they'd been particularly circumspect since. And her sister hadn't said a word.

Eden looked up, her eyes trailing west. The sun was sliding toward the far horizon at midafternoon, orange and round as a pumpkin. Jon's porridge sat in a little pot in the coals, but no sound came from down the hall. She eyed the corner clock, and her hands stilled.

The Lord is nigh unto them that are of a broken heart.

'Twas the verse Pastor McCheyne had read at last Sabbath's service. Why would it return to her now? Checking the bread, she pushed the words aside, only to hear them echo again inside her. Thomas looked up as she moved toward the darkened hall. The door to her parents' bedchamber gave way beneath her hand, and she entered, eyes fastening on the cradle to the left of the hearth. Stout as he was getting, the babe had nearly outgrown it.

The low fire pushed back the shadows, and she dropped to her knees, laying a hand on the cradle's smooth side. "Jon?"

No flailing of arms in greeting or familiar chortle. Just . . . stillness. Surprised, she gathered him up, pressing her lips to his petal-soft cheek, avoiding his unblinking eyes. The cold weight of him when he'd been so warm and full of life but hours before . . .

"Jon? Jon! *Nay!*"

Pressing her mouth to his, she tried to give him breath—her

breath. But panic, black as night, pushed her to the edge of a great, breathless abyss. Shaking, she placed him back in the cradle only to pick him up again, dizzy with despair.

Silas . . . Silas would know what to do.

Somehow her trembling legs carried her to the smithy. Giles's back was to her—some farmers were taking his attention just beyond the open doors. Elspeth was nowhere in sight. Backtracking, Eden burst into Silas's room, Jon heavy in her arms, and found only emptiness. Haversacks and fiddle rested along one wall. Maps were spread open on a table anchored by lanterns. The bed's thin counterpane was smooth.

Gone . . . again.

Tears rose and overflowed, and great sobs burned her throat. Returning to her parents' room, she laid Jon lovingly in the cradle, tucking him in out of habit, her tears wetting his face. Unmindful of Thomas—of anything but the need to flee—she started down the linden lane at a near run, her heavy skirts weighting her all the way. Gold and crimson leaves crunched underfoot as she veered toward Margaret's cottage, only to knock without an answer. Winded, choking on her tears, she stumbled up the brick walk to the house, hoping to find Margaret. But there was no response.

Torn, she paused in the courtyard and looked toward home, her thoughts cloudy as the sky above. When the Greathouse coach came barreling round a corner, she stood in its path as if rooted to the ground and was nearly run over. Wheels and hooves drew to a sudden halt amidst a storm of dust, and David's tense face appeared through an open window.

"Eden, what is it?"

The concern lacing his voice only made her cry harder. Covering her face with her hands, her words came in tatters. "I—I'm here—to find Margaret."

"Margaret is with Jemma, who's unwell." Clearly craving privacy, he cast a glance at the coachman high on his perch. Flinging open the door, David motioned her in.

She backed up. "Nay—I—"

His face flashed impatience. "Come, Eden. We've no time for delay." With that he reached out and took hold of her arm, pulling her in and shutting the door soundly. Reluctant, she took the seat opposite, the scent of new leather and snuff embracing her.

"I'm on my way to Philadelphia for a physician," David said. "But first you must tell me why you're so upset." She swallowed hard, groping for speech as he fumbled for his handkerchief, supplying the words she couldn't. "There's been more trouble at home, I take it."

"'Tis Jon—I went to his cradle—I'd made him some porridge—he was sleeping overlong—" The image of him smiling and chewing on her bodice laces that very morning shredded her composure to ribbons. "H-he wouldn't wake . . ."

"What do you mean? Is he . . . gone?" When she began to cry harder, he went silent then said quietly, "Eden, I'm sorry. I know how attached you were to the babe."

With that he thumped on the upholstered ceiling with a tight fist. The coach began a slow roll forward, but Eden hardly noticed for her weeping. She was vaguely aware of the bergamot-laden handkerchief he pressed into her palm and the sudden shift as he left his seat to sit beside her. "When did this happen?"

"I—I just found him . . ."

"Was Jon ill, then? Did he have a fever like Jemma?"

She couldn't answer, shaken by the shock mirrored on his solemn face. He couldn't—wouldn't—suggest Elspeth might have hurt Jon . . .

"Were your parents at home? Your sister?"

"Mama and Papa had gone to York. I—I don't know about Elspeth."

He swore under his breath. "First the fire . . . and now this?"

She nodded. 'Twas hard to even speak, as her thoughts swung from home to Hope Rising and then back again.

Depositing his hat on the seat, David heaved a sigh. "Jemma took ill yesterday. Margaret fears it may be a virulent fever."

The dire words failed to penetrate Eden's grief. She sat, fisting the hanky, feeling her heart shatter over and over. First Jon . . . and now Jemma?

"This requires Dr. Rush's expertise. I don't trust these York physicians. They're fine for livestock, perhaps, not human beings." He studied her, eyes dark with concern. "You look in need of more headache powders."

She said nothing, craving fresh air. Turning her face to the window, she felt a start of alarm. They were well down the main road, moving at a brisk pace past low stone fences and unfamiliar meadows strewn with autumn leaves. She'd thought he was taking her home.

She opened her mouth to protest, but he waved aside her concerns. "You're in no condition to go back, Eden. Who's to say there won't be more trouble waiting? You shall be safer with me."

"But no one knows where I am." She made a sudden move toward the door handle, but he intervened, sliding the lock into place.

"I'll send word to your father at the inn ahead." Drawing the coach window closed, he returned her to her seat with a brusque look. "With Jemma so ill, you can't remain at Hope Rising. You'll stay with Bea and Anne at the town-house in Philadelphia till things settle down. I'm going to ask the county magistrate for an investigation into Jon's death. The fire I could do little about. I may fare better with the babe."

She shut her eyes as a fierce longing skewered her insides. It wasn't Philadelphia or more headache powders she needed, but Silas.

Her betrothed.

29

The world is a comedy to those that think, a tragedy to those that feel.

HORACE WALPOLE

Silas heard the chilling cry the moment he rounded the barn on Horatio. The sound sent the hair at the back of his neck bristling. Away an afternoon in York settling accounts, he'd expected to return to the sameness of forge and farmhouse, but the twilight eve held a strange tension. The keening cry came again—a woman's, not a bairn's—full of anguish and warning. Dismounting, he hobbled Horatio in front of the smithy, noting the doors were shut. The foreboding he felt doubled.

Merciful God . . . not Eden.

He strode into the kitchen, the burnt odor of a kettle left too long at the hearth overwhelming. In the winter parlor opposite, shadows danced on the firelit walls. Mrs. Lee paced before the hearth, Jon in her arms. One look told him more than he wanted to know. Across the room Liege stood silently with Giles, while Elspeth, pale as flax, sat woodenly in a chair, Thomas at her feet. His heart gave a lurch. The one who mattered most was missing.

"At last!" Liege said, his tone suggesting Silas was somehow to blame. "Have you seen Eden?"

"Not since breakfast," Silas returned uneasily. "What has happened?"

"She's missing," he said brashly. "And the babe's dead."

The bruising fact hardly needed stating. Mrs. Lee let out another strangled cry, and Silas looked away, throat tight, while the bairn's own mother remained dry-eyed across the room. He felt a searing anger when Thomas began to wail along with Mrs. Lee, and Elspeth did not so much as lift a finger in comfort.

Liege moved toward the hearth, pacing on the worn floorboards. "Mrs. Lee and I returned home to a kitchen full of smoke, Thomas untended, the babe dead in his cradle, Eden gone."

Silas looked toward Giles. "And you?"

Giles bristled. "I was at the forge—too busy to see to household matters. If Eden had come to me, I might have helped, but she did not."

"What of you?" Silas's gaze pinned Elspeth.

"Elspeth was with me in the smithy," Giles said. "We—"

"I did not ask you." Silas's eyes remained on Elspeth. "Did you see Eden?"

She met his gaze, shoulders lifting in a shrug. "I am not my sister's keeper. She was supposed to be tending things in the house while I was at the ledgers." The reply was so sullen, so sanctimonious, Silas was glad he was across the room lest he be tempted to strike her.

"So a child dies and everyone seems to be deaf and dumb?" His heated questions were met with silence. "None of you knows where she's gone—just that she's gone without a by-your-leave to anyone?"

He turned and left them, moving upstairs to the garret room, his tread heavy, his patience thin. Here the air was dusty and sweet, the narrow stairwell full of tender memories. The weaving room and Eden's bedchamber were bare as well, as were all the rooms save the parlor where they'd gathered.

Returning to the cool twilight, he searched the barn and all the outbuildings, every nook and cranny, before using the last bit of day to comb the surrounding woods. The fading light seemed to leach all the hope from his heart.

Lord, please . . . Eden.

Reluctantly he returned and looked toward the distant lights of Hope Rising. The possibility that she'd sought safe haven there doubled his angst.

⬥⬥⬥

Silas had never been inside the great house before. His work confined him to the dependencies and sheep pens. Standing on its front stoop, he made use of the huge brass knocker to summon a servant, unable to stop ill-scrappit comparisons from flooding his mind in the warm twilight. Hope Rising was little more than an outbuilding in light of Blair Castle's grandeur, yet it had a simple charm the duke's ancestral home lacked. The servant who answered was clad in plain woolens, not livery, his manner deferential.

"Good evening, Mr. Ballantyne."

"I've come looking for Eden Lee," he said brusquely, feeling time was against him.

He nodded. "Miss Lee isn't here, but I'll summon Margaret Hunter if you like."

Leading Silas to a room redolent of old books and beeswax, he excused himself, footsteps echoing down the candlelit foyer. The minutes unwound so torturously slow that Silas felt he'd been placed on a rack. His restless gaze landed on a portrait above the cold hearth. Though cast in shadows, the man's mien and hair color were nonetheless striking. Eben Greathouse? Privateer, slaver, benefactor?

"Silas." The quiet address was surprisingly straightforward. Friends shunned honorifics, he remembered, even a simple "mister." Margaret Hunter stood behind him. "I apologize for the delay. Jemma is ill."

Desperation turned him blunt. "I need to find Eden."

"Eden? I saw her from a window this afternoon. She was in the courtyard with David—he was on his way to Philadelphia. She got into the carriage." A frown marred her mouth. "I thought he'd return her home. She seemed upset, perhaps on account of Jemma."

"When was this?"

"A quarter past three. I well remember, as it was time for Jemma's medicine."

Hours ago. The facts left him hollow, a bit breathless. None of them made sense. "Why is the master going to Philadelphia?"

"To fetch a doctor. I fear Jemma may have a malignant fever." She raised a hand to graying hair that was usually faultless and tucked a stray strand beneath her cap. "May I ask if there's been trouble at the Lees'?"

"Aye." Silas still felt pummeled by disbelief. "The babe—Jon—is dead."

Shock lit her eyes. "From fever?"

"Nae." The denial gave way to a host of sordid things. He could sense her unasked questions, though he had no ready answers.

Brow furrowed, she moved to shut the door as if on the verge of some confidence. "Do thee know about the babe? His parentage, I mean?"

Silas simply looked at her, well aware of where she was leading.

"There's been talk that the babe is Elspeth's and . . ." She hesitated, tears glittering in her eyes. "David's."

He felt a sickening dismay. His Eden . . . with a rogue. The admission of Jon's origins cost Margaret dearly, Silas knew. A servant rarely betrayed a master, yet her Quaker convictions bound her to the truth no matter the consequences. He looked down, his worn boots decidedly out of place atop the lush carpet. He'd not considered this. Did Eden know? Likely not. She was so naïve, always thinking the best of others, especially those at Hope Rising.

"I fear David . . . and Eden . . ."

The coupling of their names made his blood run cold. "What about them?"

"David has long been besotted with Eden."

He held his breath, bracing for another bitter secret. *Lord, nae . . .*

Her gaze cleared. "But Eden is in love with thee."

His own eyes grew damp, reducing the grand room to a rich watercolor, though his voice held firm. "Aye, Eden is betrothed to me."

She nodded and looked toward a window. "There is another matter thee must know, Silas, though I'm loath to tell thee . . ."

ↀↀↀ

The lantern-lit stable was missing a groom, but Silas had no need of one. Hoisting a saddle from a near rack onto one shoulder, he made his way past countless stalls till he came to Atticus, Hope Rising's prize racehorse. The thoroughbred, recently brought from Virginia, whinnied in welcome. He ran a hand down the sleek, buff-colored back and thought of Horatio. Aging as he was, Horatio hadn't the stamina or speed of this stallion. And he needed both—desperately.

He swung himself into the costly, unfamiliar saddle, a prayer for Eden on his lips, all that he'd just learned making him breathless and afraid. Moving into the cool of early evening beneath a rising moon, he kept hoping Eden would simply step from the twilight into his arms.

God, grant me speed, safety, and wisdom.

⬳⬲

Exhausted, Eden dozed, lulled by the motion of the coach, only to come awake to lantern light outside her window. Such rocking made Jemma nauseous. But Jemma wasn't here, she remembered—she was at home and gravely ill. Other painful realities crowded in and jarred her awake. Jon was gone. She'd left Thomas alone. Shutting her eyes tight, she battled a bruising anguish.

When they rolled to a stop before a two-story tavern, she watched David alight and make arrangements for them to lodge. The pain of her predicament washed over her like an icy wave, and she surveyed the inn's shingle through tear-filled eyes. The Black Swan. Aside from spending an occasional night at Hope Rising, she'd never been beyond the confines of her feather bolster.

The sudden lilt of a fiddle carrying on the crisp autumn air twisted her heart—yet renewed her courage. Perhaps when David was preoccupied, turned his back for a few moments, she could get away. The overwhelming desire to return to Silas made her bold, yet David had assumed a hawk-like vigilance that was more unnerving at every turn.

"Come, Eden, supper awaits."

He helped her down, his hand on her elbow all the way up the pebble walk as the coachman sought the stables. Behind the front door, the tavern seemed to be bursting with a hundred strangers, all eyes inclined their way. They sought refuge at a corner table near the kitchen door, which opened and closed with a perpetual whine.

Pulled from her stupor for a few self-conscious moments, Eden realized what an odd pairing they made. David looked every inch the heir to Hope Rising in beaver hat and fine broadcloth, while she in her humble flowered muslin and wrinkled lace kerchief was naught but a tradesman's daughter.

"I've taken the liberty of ordering for you," he told her, "though I'm sure the fare isn't as palatable as your own."

She nodded but didn't know how she'd eat one bite. Grief had stolen her appetite and now filled her to the brim with a profound numbness. Even the aroma of freshly baked bread left her slightly sick. Her eyes drifted in the same direction as David's, through an archway to a second room clouded with tobacco smoke and reverberating with the rattle of dice. She'd heard of such places and could smell spirits, but her perusal ended when an enormous pewter plate was plunked down in front of her by a pink-cheeked serving girl.

She bowed her head briefly, then found David's eyes on her when she whispered "amen."

"How are you feeling?"

Touched by his concern, she tried to smile, eyes falling to the buttered beets and charred fowl before her. But she gave no answer.

"You're in need of some rum punch or flip to bring your color back." He took a sip from his own tankard. "It works wonders for whatever ails you. I recall returning from church in the winter months as a lad after crying in the meeting from the cold. Uncle would serve us flip to warm us."

He was making a valiant effort to distract her, she guessed, though she was in no mood for conversation. Still, she managed, "There was no church stove then?"

"No. Is there now?"

She nodded and picked up her fork, trying not to think of Silas or church or the Bible she so sorely needed hidden in the garret.

"Fortunately, there's a good hearth here," he said, buttering some bread. "I'm not sure about the rooms above stairs. You're welcome to sleep in my cloak."

The very thought returned a rush of color to her cheeks. He glanced toward a window, his mouth twisting in a wry line. "The weather has taken a turn. Some are forecasting snow. Can you imagine? Snow in October."

She bit down on a beet, so reminiscent of her own garden it brought about a crushing homesickness. Swallowing hard, she opened her mouth to beg him to take her back, then remembered Jemma. Poor Jemma, in dire need of a physician. Beset by new worries, she ate a few halfhearted mouthfuls, noticing his attention returning to the gaming room.

"The inn is overfull this chilly eve, I'm sorry to say, though the thought of sleeping six to a bed might well warm us." Finishing his meal, he asked for another tankard, looking askance at her nearly untouched plate. "I'll see you to your room so you can rest."

She followed him reluctantly after he set his cape about her shoulders, her hands clutching the fine fabric in her fists to keep it off the dirty floor. Doors were appearing on all sides of them, unfriendly in their austereness, but he showed a familiarity with their surroundings, leading her to a room at the top of the back stair.

He set a candlestick on a shelf just inside, and they surveyed the lodging together. A bed hardly big enough for two people was pushed against a far wall, a fireplace at its foot. A beleaguered table and chair rested atop a faded rag rug. Eden spied a chamber pot beneath a tottering washstand—and a tiny rat darting into a corner hole.

"'Twill do for one night," he said, looking down at her. "No doubt you'll find the Philadelphia townhouse more to your liking, though that's another forty miles or so."

"'Tis fine," she said awkwardly. "Think no more of it."

"I'm going below to play cards." He hesitated as if debating the wisdom of leaving her. "If you need me . . ."

At the shake of her head, he shut the door. She heard the jingle of keys followed by a click. Heart pounding, she rushed to the door and grabbed hold of the handle, her near elation snuffed when it held steadfast. He'd locked her in. But why? To protect her from other tavern patrons? Or did he mean to keep her . . . captive? The thought sent her scurrying to the sole window. But the drop from there was too high, the pitch of the roof too steep. She'd likely break her neck.

Shivering, she moved to the comfort of the hearth, cold hands outstretched to the feeble flames, seeking more than comfort. She was in desperate need of the Comforter.

Lord, be in this strange place . . . please.

Suddenly the high note of a fiddle pierced the air. She nearly flinched at its uneven tone, so unlike Silas's. A ribald ballad was struck, so loud she spun toward a dark corner, expecting to find the fiddler in her very room. But the merriment was directly below, seeping through worn floorboards, promising a sleepless night. Sinking down on the edge of the bed, she lifted the hem of her quilted petticoat, tore at a seam, and extracted a bit of wool to fill her ears. If only she could do the same to fill the hole in her heart . . .

The image of Jon's round face rose up, and she shut her eyes as if to block it, putting a hand to her mouth to keep from crying out. Coupled with her concern for Jemma, grief had her hovering on the brink of near hysteria in this strange place. The night loomed long.

Her hopes plummeted. She'd forgotten to make sure David had sent word of where she was. Silas would wonder.

Nay . . . Silas would be wild with worry.

30

I wish, I wish, I wish in vain
I wish I was a maid again.
TRADITIONAL FOLK SONG

His ill luck had returned. Haste and panic were poor traveling companions, and this trip he'd reaped the consequences
in spades. No coin. No canteen. No saddlebags. All he possessed was a keen sense of direction and a burning conviction
to keep going. Within five miles of his journey, Atticus had
cast a shoe, requiring him to stop and beg repair from a fellow blacksmith at a sleepy village. Foolishly he'd thought to
overtake Eden on the road or at some wayside tavern. Then
he recalled the Greathouse coach. Imported from London
before the war and painted a fashionable green, its German
steel springs and new wheels would fly over the rutted thoroughfare to Philadelphia as if winged.

Back in the saddle, he ignored the hunger gnawing his
gut, drinking his fill from a leaf-littered creek. The night was
cold, the moonlight fickle. His anxiety soared. Questions he
had no answer for pummeled his every step. He was sure of
but one thing: Eden's grief over Jon had made her flee. That

it had sent her into Greathouse's arms, if indeed it had, cut him to the quick.

One weary, uneventful mile gave way to the next. He felt the stinging bite of a snowflake on his bare neck, as if in warning. He was nearly out of hope . . . out of prayers. A light in the distance made him press on. A tavern?

Oh, merciful God, let it be so.

❧

The lone candle was nearly guttered but lit the room well enough to assure Eden that it was David who entered and no one else. Unable to sleep, she'd been sitting by the window, staring into the night, trying to wade through the darkness of sorrow to latch onto the Scripture hidden in her heart. Snow had begun shaking down, rendering the autumn air wintry. She started when he shut the door, unable to swipe the tears from her face before he saw them.

"Eden, you're shaking with cold. Why aren't you wearing my cape?"

It lay over a chair back—discarded in case Silas came. But she could hardly tell him that. He moved toward her and she stood, willing her trembling to end, squaring her shoulders in a show of strength. "I'm all right." But she wasn't. And she read the doubt in his eyes . . . and something else.

"Come now, Eden."

He settled the cape around her shoulders, his fingers fumbling at the fastening around her neck. A strand of her hair caught and she attempted to pull it free, but he intervened, wrapping the tendril around one ringed finger, his breath warming her cheek. She inhaled the unwelcome essence of brandy and rum and nearly recoiled but for the pressure of his thumbs as they rested along her throat. He began to make little circles on the bare skin there, raising goose bumps.

Startled, she stepped back, eyes on the candle as it sputtered on the shelf behind him. He came nearer, face shadowed, but she sensed his purpose—his misplaced passion. He wasn't the David she'd always known. He was someone else—a stranger—and the realization rocked her in new ways.

"By the devil, Eden, you're beautiful even in mourning." His hands were in her hair, his fingers loosening the ribbon that bound it. She felt a wild revulsion. No man had ever touched her so, not even Silas, whose touch was all she wanted.

Frantic, she pushed away from him. "Nay, David—please!"

She rushed for the door and pulled on the knob. It held fast beneath her hand despite her frantic tugging. Locked. Again. He was behind her now, turning her round like she was naught but a doll, clutching her shoulders with his large hands.

"Come, Eden, let me comfort you . . . and you comfort me. No one need know."

Comfort? What comfort did he speak of?

Her cry for help was more a strangled whisper. Though she pushed and begged and pleaded for him to stop, she was no match for his strength. Overcome by the stench of spirits, sweat, and pain, she nearly fainted. The cold room, the too-small bed, became her prison. And all her hopes for the future turned to ashes.

❧

"Aye, a gentleman in a fancy coach lodged here just last night," a stable hand said as he paused in his currying. "Had a woman with him, mayhap his mistress her dress was so plain. She was a beauty, though, with a head o' hair like fire . . ."

Silas fixed his gaze on the Black Swan's shingle creaking on its iron chain in a biting wind. "What time did they depart?"

The lad shot him a sheepish grin. "None too early on account o' the late night he had. A wee too much flip and faro kept him abed till nearly noon."

Silas didn't doubt it. Greathouse was one of the Golden Plough's best patrons. Masking his dismay, he returned Atticus to the rutted road, wishing his roiling emotions would fall numb like his hands and feet. The ache in his gut deepened, whether from hunger or anxiety he didn't know. Eden was ahead, as was Philadelphia, some thirty miles distant. The worst of his ordeal was over.

Or—he steeled himself against the taunting thought— 'twas just beginning.

⁂

Ribbons of light lay across the meadow beyond the dirty windowpane. Though Eden had lost all track of time, the sun's cold slant told her it was midafternoon. She tried to raise her head to look west, but the pain pulsing behind her temples was so severe she groaned. Still, she felt a desperate need to get her bearings. They'd traded the Black Swan for a less respectable inn a few hours before, when she'd grown too sick to continue in the coach. She felt anxious that they might never reach the city.

"Eden, must I fetch the doctor for you like Jemma?"

She felt David's cool hand on her forehead, brushing back the tangle of hair he'd undone in the night. His bloodshot eyes surveyed her with something akin to alarm.

Shuddering at his touch, she tried to sit up, reaching for the cup of cider he'd brought her as he went below for another drink. Every inch of her ached . . . from his rough handling? Or mayhap she was ill like Jemma? Fever seemed to burn her eyes . . . her very bones. Whatever it was, it was nothing like the ache in her soul.

Oh, Lord, have You forgotten me, Your lamb?

Slowly she made it to the door, hope kindling at finding it unlocked. Navigating the steep stairs was another matter. She felt strangely detached, her head and her feet at odds. Stumbling, she leaned into the wall and gripped the handrail, steadying herself with a deep breath.

The tavern smells she was coming to loathe were stirring all around her—unwashed bodies, overcooked meat, endless spirits. One shaky step . . . then two. Below, in the empty tavern foyer, the door groaned opened to admit a gust of wind—and a man.

Silas.

His green eyes were searching as he shut the door and glanced at the stairwell where she hovered. In the half light his face took on surprise, then stark relief. She could see the rise and fall of his chest beneath the linen shirt she'd made him. He'd ridden hard and fast—hatless and coatless—his exertion highlighting his anxious features.

Beneath the force of his gaze she turned away, stricken. The room spun a bit. She nearly lost her footing on the stairs. Shame spilled over her, filled every part of her. He couldn't see her like this. One look and he'd know everything.

⸎

When Silas saw her, relief made him even more light-headed, riding hard on the heels of his fatigue and hunger. "Eden." Saying her name was sweet to the taste, given he'd been tormented by the ludicrous worry he might never find her.

No one else was in the foyer, so it was only him she turned away from. *Him*, when she'd once looked at him with a love inexpressible, as if she couldn't have enough of him. He climbed the stairs slowly, sensing her anguish, fearing she might flee.

"Eden, look at me." The quiet plea set her shoulders shaking, and she dropped her face in her hands, tottering a bit on the step.

He eased a hand in back of her, palm flat against the rough wall to catch her if she fainted. The glorious length of her hair, usually bound so sedately if girlishly, hung in unruly, russet coils to her hips, flagrant as an autumn leaf. He ached to feel its silkiness, to find her ribbon and set it right. "Eden, I'm sorry . . . about Jon."

She looked up briefly, eyes red-rimmed, the shadows beneath them shocking. A knot of anguish expanded in his chest like a cable wound too tight. This was not his Eden. All the light had gone out of her. Something beyond the heartache over Jon weighted her and rendered her unable to meet his eyes. Gently he brushed her wet cheek with the back of his fingers.

"Silas, please . . ." She spoke to the floor, not him. "Don't . . . touch me."

His hand fell away. Dread lined his insides. "Eden, what has happened here?"

She hung her head. "You shouldn't have come."

"I'm here to take you home."

Fear flashed across her face. "Home?" Her voice held a frantic lilt. "I can't go back. I have no home—not with Jon gone—"

"You'll go with me." He placed a careful hand on her shoulder. "Like we've planned."

"Where?"

"West to Fort Pitt—straightaway."

"Nay!" she cried, backing up a step. Crossing her arms over her bodice simply drew attention to what she tried to hide. One of her laces, crisscrossed over an embroidered stomacher, was broken, dangling limply to her waist. She looked, he thought ruefully, unkempt as a tavern wench. "I—I cannot go with you—cannot wed you—"

His throat constricted. "We'll not speak of that now. You're weary—frightened and grieving." Taking a step up, he kept his voice low. "You've ne'er been so far from home."

Tears welled in her eyes, cutting him afresh, and then a swell of anger smothered any tender feeling. She was obviously ill and in need of comfort, mayhap a physician, while Greathouse likely lounged below amidst the din of the gaming room.

Though he was loath to leave her, he must. "Stay here, Eden."

Silas had no recollection of coming down the stairs or crossing the muddy foyer or striding into the smoky room where David Greathouse sat, dice cup in hand, pewter tankard at his elbow. Surrounded by a table of gaming men, Greathouse simply leaned back in his chair, gaze narrowing at Silas's approach. Five pairs of eyes fastened on him, clearly unhappy at the interruption.

"So, Ballantyne, what brings you to the Traveler's Rest?"

"You," Silas uttered, rounding the table. "Step outside."

"Outside? In this cold?" Greathouse reached for his tankard, steam curling around the rim. "I hardly think—"

"Aye—*now.*" With a sudden move Silas knocked the drink from Greathouse's hand, sending a frothy spray around the scarred table. Grim-faced, his companions shrank back, dice cups still.

Taking hold of his fine linen cravat, Silas yanked upward. Built like a bull, Greathouse was far from graceful in his exit, the chair sprawling backwards into the wall with a clatter.

Outside in the tavern yard, the two men faced each other,

their rapid breathing expelling in white plumes. Silas clenched his fists at his sides. 'Twas all he could do to keep from pulling his knife from his boot. "What is happening here?"

Greathouse's mouth formed a hard line. "We've been delayed. Eden is unwell. We traveled but ten miles today because she has a headache—"

"*She?*" His voice was thick with rage. "You traveled but ten miles because *you* lay abed till noon, too drunk to rise sooner."

Greathouse smoothed his cravat, surprise lining his features. "Aye, so I did. What concern is it of yours?"

"It became my concern the moment she stepped into your coach."

"*She* stepped, Ballantyne. I didn't coerce her."

"Nae? Margaret Hunter said otherwise. Eden was upset—in need of protection, direction. You took every advantage—"

Greathouse was walking away from him now, heading toward the stables at the rear of the tavern. Atticus was tied to a hitch rail there, a bit wild-eyed and lathered. Greathouse's tone turned incredulous as he rounded a corner. "What the devil are you doing with my horse?"

"Your *horse?*" Silas followed him, facing him across the stallion's sleek back. "We're talking about Eden, not an animal."

"Horse stealing is a crime, Ballantyne. I'll have you hanged—"

"Hanged?" Lunging at him, Silas grabbed for his collar over the curved lip of the saddle. "You've no time for it—I'll finish you off first."

Greathouse pulled free and backed away, nearly tripping in his haste. "You'll swing for murder, then."

"So be it. Then the world will be rid of vermin like you who debau—" The hateful word hung in Silas's throat. He couldn't spit it out his pain was so great. Stepping around Atticus, he shoved the laird of Hope Rising into the stable wall. But the satisfactory crack of skull against frozen timber was poor recompense. His anger demanded more—he wanted answers. He wanted Eden back, unhurt, the light of joy in her eyes . . .

Greathouse straightened, eyes narrowing into slits, a ruddy flush contorting his face. "You're simply jealous because she came to me first."

Had she? Silas felt a tug of alarm, then his anger flared at the man's smug expression. 'Twas Jamie Murray he saw, insolent and unremorseful, able to do as he pleased with nary a repercussion.

"Jealous?" he shouted. "Nae, just sick of a man who makes free with a lass while his infant son lies dead and his cousin may be dying."

Silas drew back a fist and punched him in the stomach. Groaning, Greathouse fell, then grabbed at Silas's legs, nearly catching him off balance. With a swift kick, Silas planted a boot square in his groin, rendering him speechless, all smugness gone. Minutes ticked by in a sort of haze, Silas consumed by rage and grief and pain. He knew better than to beat a man who was down, but injustice stirred like a demon inside him, spurring him on.

While Greathouse struggled to rally, Silas was hardly winded. Years of working iron was no match for a life of leisure or a recent spirit-sated night. Soon the master of Hope Rising was bloodied, bruised, and begging for mercy.

A small crowd was gathering despite the cold, and someone yelled "Lovers' quarrel" from an upstairs window. It was then Silas turned and saw that Eden had come outside. In the harsh afternoon light, he could discern purplish bruises on the slender stem of her neck and the skin above her embroidered bodice. Why this was so clawed at him, but he was too raw to see reason. He knew but one thing.

He wanted to kill David Greathouse.

❦

"Silas, *please*."

He turned toward Eden slowly, lower lip bleeding, chest heaving. His ragged dark locks hanging past the collar of his soiled shirt gave him a slightly rakish look. With a sudden move, he jerked Greathouse to his feet and thrust him toward the tavern, out of their sight. Casting a disgusted glance at the onlookers, Silas motioned her into the stable. There they stood speechless in the hay-strewn space, emotions running rampant. He drew a shirt sleeve across his bloody mouth, leaving a scarlet trail.

"I—I was afraid you'd kill him. I overheard you talking—shouting." Fear pulsed inside her, overriding her grief. All she knew was that she must end this, distract him, lest he learn what David had done. "Was Jon"—her voice caught on the name and broke—"David's son?" He gave a terse nod and she continued haltingly, "Is there more?"

"Aye, far more." Turning, he spat into the straw behind him. "You're said to be Eben Greathouse's daughter."

"Mr. Greathouse . . ."'Twas hard to utter the shameful words. "And Mama's?"

His eyes registered a shock nearly as great as her own. "Margaret Hunter said the trouble began years ago when Eben Greathouse wanted to wed Louise. He was growing wealthy and she was but a village girl, the daughter of a tradesman. His father was against the match, as was hers, and so she married Liege. But later, when Liege was away in Philadelphia . . ."

The words peppered Eden with the force of buckshot. She stared at him, trembling, mind reeling.

"There was a child . . . you."

She shook her head, disbelieving. "Surely Margaret's mistaken—"

"I saw his portrait yestreen. His hair is red as an autumn oak, like yours."

She well knew the portrait. Why hadn't she seen the likeness?

He went on quietly, eyes a stormy green. "Eben Greathouse attested to it on his deathbed in her very presence, though Margaret had long suspected. He'd always shown you special favor. He had a particularly bitter relationship with Liege."

She stared at him without focus as long-buried images from childhood flashed to mind, zealous as a spring flood. Eben Greathouse handing her mother down from a carriage . . . sending round gifts . . . making much of little Eden. *His daughter?* Putting a hand to her stomach, she felt bile burn the back of her throat. When she looked at Silas again, she thought she saw revulsion in his gaze and her humiliation soared.

"You no doubt heard everything." His tone was resigned, his face flinty. "Is it true, then, what Greathouse said? Did you go to him first?"

The accusation in his tone tore at her heart. As if she was somehow to blame. As if she was responsible for her family's many sins. "I—I tried to find you—I went to your room, the forge, but you weren't there." Tears choked her voice. "You were never there. 'Twas always the work—"

"Wheest! The work?" Disbelief blazed in his eyes. "And what—who—am I working for? You, nae? Our future? Answer me that, Eden!"

She pressed shaking fingertips to her forehead as pain seared her temples. *Our future.* That dream had dissolved in David's unrelenting arms, snatched away in the span of a single night. "Future? We have no future."

He stepped closer to catch her broken words. "I'll not listen to you, bewildered as you are. I'm taking you back to York—"

"Nay!" Her voice trilled higher, the image of Jon's cold body pressing in on her. "I'll not go back! You shouldn't have come. I beg you now—go away—"

"Enough, Eden." His voice, ragged with pain, was none-theless firm. "Say no more."

She began to sob as anguish twisted her insides, nearly bringing her to her knees. If not for his hands about her shoulders, she would have dropped to the hay at their feet.

"To Margaret's, then." He started to turn away, then swung back around, taking hold of her again. "Let me tell you this. I love you, Eden. I'll always love you. And whom I love I do not leave." With that, he shouted to a groom at the far end of the stable to ready the Greathouse coach.

She stood slightly openmouthed at his audacity.

"Make ready to go," he told her, turning toward the tavern. "I'll fetch the coachman. If he refuses to come, I'll drive you to Hope Rising myself."

31

Be silent and safe—silence never betrays you.

Though Silas sat beside her in the coach, shutters drawn against the encroaching cold, Eden was hardly aware of him. Wrapped in a blanket and his arms, she slept mile after mile as they lumbered west through spitting snow and bouts of hail, the coachman driving the team at a fever's pitch. They changed horses once—a formidable feat given they had no coin—and she was vaguely aware, through the haze of illness, that Silas promised payment from Hope Rising.

After that she succumbed to thirst and fever, her throat so dry she couldn't speak no matter how much water he gave her. Her head throbbed against the upholstered seat, and every jolt and jarring of the coach seemed to rattle her very bones. If it was this hard going to civilized York, what would it be like heading west over the Allegheny Mountains? But she shut her head—and her heart—to the notion, allowing no second thoughts, no second chances. Surely Silas was having them as well, realizing how unfit she was for such a trek, plagued with headaches and near-hysteria at the tavern . . . and far worse.

Yet he was tenderness itself every step of their journey. Through her feverish cocoon, she was aware of his gentleness as he laid cool hands on her hot brow, trusting in his reassurances that all would be well. When he carried her into the familiar cottage, Margaret wept with relief.

"Oh, Eden. Thee have the look of Jemma about thee, God rest her soul."

"Jemma?" Silas's low question pierced the fog of Eden's grief.

"She died the very night thee left . . . the same day as Jon." She spoke in whispers. "She suffered so at the end. 'Twas little to be done. We buried her straightaway. Pastor McCheyne came and offered prayers. I've sent word to Anne and Beatrice in Philadelphia."

As he eased Eden onto Margaret's feather bolster, she began removing Eden's shoes. Tears flowed down their faces as Silas stood at the foot of the bed, misery pulsating all around them. "You're no doubt wondering about Greathouse."

Margaret nodded. "Thee must have left him Atticus in exchange for the coach."

"Aye, something like that." He moved to the hearth, standing tall but a bit stoop-shouldered. In the fading firelight, his profile pierced Eden's heart. Weariness lined his person like a garment. He'd not eaten or slept for days other than dozing in the coach. His linen shirt was stiff with dirt and dried blood, his breeches torn. She longed to rake out the tangles in his hair with her fingertips, kiss the rough stubble that marked his jaw.

He was speaking to Margaret again, his tone grim. "I'm reluctant to leave her."

The words brought about a searing ache. Despite everything, despite every ugly thing that had happened . . . he still wanted to stay?

Margaret studied him thoughtfully. "Thee are in need of rest, Silas. A good meal. Clean clothes." Her calm practicality returned, and she moved toward a clothespress. "If thee do not want to return to the Lees', the cottage next to mine is vacant."

"I'll not trouble you further," he replied, though he did accept the clothing she pressed into his hands. Pausing at the door, he glanced toward the bed a final time. "If she worsens, promise you'll send for me, no matter the hour."

"Of course. Will thee be at the Lees', then?"

"Aye." The terse answer was weighted with resignation. Eden could hear it in his voice, though she couldn't lift a hand in goodbye.

Lord, help him escape this place, she prayed before sleep claimed her.

❧

"She *what*?" From his seat by the hearth, Liege glared at Silas with the force of a sledge hitting hot iron.

Silas's voice was weary but firm. "I said Eden lies ill at Margaret Hunter's."

Pushing himself up from his chair, Liege puffed furiously on his pipe till the smoke formed a ragged halo above his head. "For four days we've done naught but wonder where she's gone, only to find her ill and at Hope Rising! Fetch her home where she belongs—"

"Nae." Silas cut him off, done with his foolishness. "She stays."

Mrs. Lee appeared in the doorway, Thomas in her arms instead of Jon. Silas felt a twist of remorse for bearing such

304

bad news. "Jemma Greathouse is dead of a fever. Margaret Hunter fears Eden may be ill with the same." Her sharp intake of breath made him pause. "She promises to send word if Eden worsens. I rode to York for the doctor before coming here . . ."

He fell silent, wanting nothing more than to escape to his room. But for the moment he was looking at them with sudden insight, privy to secrets they weren't aware he knew. Liege's irascibility suddenly made sense. Mrs. Lee's ceaseless activity and melancholy were born of a thousand regrets. And Thomas—was he truly Liege and Louise's son? Elspeth was missing. And Jon . . . The cradle was empty. The room was empty. Without the grace of Eden's presence, everything seemed a bit hollow—off-kilter. Or mayhap it was simply the echo of his own despair.

You were never there. 'Twas always the work . . . We have no future.

Passing a hand over his eyes, he was vaguely aware of Mrs. Lee at his elbow. "Come, Silas. There's meat, bread. I'll make you something to drink."

Slowly they moved into the sanctuary of the kitchen. Of all the rooms in the house, this was Eden's favorite—and the most bereft of her.

"You look," Mrs. Lee breathed, taking him in from head to toe, "like you've been far."

"Halfway to Philadelphia and back."

"For Eden."

"Aye."

"How did she happen to get there?"

"David Greathouse took her by coach."

The silence stretched taut. She set a plate in front of him, and he noticed her hands were shaking. "Master David, you say? All that way? Did he—"

He pushed back from the table, appetite gone. "Nae . . . speak of anything but that."

Leaving by way of the arbor, he entered his room and took a chair, eyes on the cold hearth. Minutes ticked by, marked by a small clock, prodding him to take some sort of action—make a fire, lie down, return to the kitchen and still his aching, empty stomach. But the solace he sought was of a far different kind.

Eyes on the dog irons, he tried to grapple with all that had happened, a harsh wind blowing through his soul.

Provide Thou, O Lord, for my heart.

⸎

Eden heard a violin, low and sweet, coming from the parlor. Was Silas playing for Margaret? Nay, Margaret was missing. He was playing for her, the songs she especially loved—strathspeys and slow airs . . . haunting, lyrical. When Margaret returned, they sat around the fire like old friends, his music substituting for conversation. Sequestered in the bedchamber, Eden could see and hear them clearly through the open doorway.

Hers was not a virulent fever, Margaret told him in low tones. Exhaustion, perhaps. A vile headache. Some other malady, but nothing fatal. Hearing it, Eden felt a crushing disappointment. She welcomed death.

She lay still, eyes closed, and drifted like flotsam on a pond. Fragments of her time with David at the inn threatened to plunge her into the darkest despair, and then the sound of Silas's voice, his playing, brought her back. His presence, his prayers, were all that kept the shock and sorrow that wrapped round her like tentacles from crushing her completely.

"You'll be needing this, Eden." Gently he took her hand, placing a small square of linen in her palm as he knelt by the bed. "'Tis a lock of Jon's hair."

She started to open it, took one glimpse at the sunny strands within, and couldn't. Unable to speak, she simply brought the cloth to her heart with a closed fist.

"I buried him beneath the willow in the far pasture, the one you like so well."

She nodded through her tears, somewhat solaced.

"I set a stone atop it. I'm going to make a cross. When you're better I'll take you there."

He left her side, and no one else came. It hurt her that her own mother stayed away. She supposed Mama's secrets kept her at a distance—that and the fact she and Margaret hadn't spoken in years. Without Jon and Jemma, neither home nor Hope Rising felt the same. She sensed the loss even on her bed. When she was back on her feet, the grave sites were the first place she wanted to go, as if doing so would somehow ease the sting of what her heart couldn't bear.

"'Tis too soon for thee to be out of doors," Margaret cautioned one day. "The wind is harsh. I fear the winter will be ferocious."

Feeling old and unkempt, Eden made her way from the bed to the crackling hearth, hands gripping the chair back where Silas usually sat. He hadn't been here in a day . . . two? Alarm rose up and turned her breathless. 'Twas now mid-October, Margaret said. Turning a face to a window limned by twilight, Eden fought down her disappointment and wrestled with new fears. Had Silas already left for Fort Pitt? Without saying goodbye?

"There's no need for Silas to come round so often now that thee are better." Margaret began making tea, her voice matter-of-fact yet soothing. "No doubt he's busy preparing for his journey now that his apprenticeship is at an end."

Sitting in his empty chair, Eden stared into the fire without focus, grappling with his leaving. Tears blurred her vision and she looked about blindly for a handkerchief, resorting to the sleeve of her nightgown.

The tea forgotten, Margaret brought one of her own and squeezed Eden's hand. "'Tis clear thy heart is breaking—over Jon and Jemma, to be sure. Or is there more?"

More? Aye, far more. The loss of her purity. Her future. The only man she'd ever loved. How did one put such heartache into words? All the Scriptures she'd hidden in her heart now seemed to leave her. She couldn't recall them, couldn't pray. In a word, she felt forsaken.

They sat in silence and drank the tea as daylight faded and smothered the small hope in her heart that Silas would come. Despite Margaret's company, she felt an overwhelming, aching emptiness. Tomorrow she must return home. Every hour she tarried added to her angst. In the mayhem of the last few days, she'd nearly forgotten the ugly reality before her. Silas was leaving. Papa wanted her to marry another. Once repulsive, the plan was now palatable.

After what David had done, what choice did she have but to marry Giles? Any babe that she carried would be considered his. None would suspect it was David's instead. The thought of the future, once so joyous, now turned terrifying. She was disgraced, perhaps pregnant. How would she care for a baby? How could she bring trouble to her family after what Elspeth had done? The solution—if that was what it was—smacked her in the face as hard as Elspeth's hand.

Oh, Silas, you must be well away from here. If David returns, if you discern what he has done . . .

32

The music in my heart I bore,
Long after it was heard no more.

WILLIAM WORDSWORTH

Before Eden turned down the lane toward home, Sebastian bounded toward her, a mass of fur and snapping black eyes, his irrepressible enthusiasm nearly making her smile. Dropping to her knees on the cold ground, she stroked his silky ears, thinking how lonesome he would be when Silas went away.

"You should be minding sheep," she said through her tears, but he simply cocked his head and nudged her hand as if she were his sole concern.

Side by side they walked, Eden's gaze touching on every familiar place. Sheep dotted the meadow like windblown bits of cotton, and the beloved church on the hill sat empty and silent, awaiting the next Sabbath service. Everything looked the same—only she herself had changed. Her thoughts were muddied and unfocused. Her body was no longer her own. Her dreams forsaken. She could hear unrelenting hammering at the forge and wondered who it was. Papa? Silas? Giles?

Her senses seemed blunted. She could no longer discern the difference in tone. Before she stepped onto the front stoop on shaking legs, her mother, clad in mourning garb for Jon, threw open the front door in welcome.

"Eden! I hardly recognize you!"

Beneath Mama's scrutiny, she felt a tremor of self-consciousness, as if the stain on her person was just as apparent. But it was her dress Mama was looking at as she removed the cape Margaret had lent her. The gown was stunning with its dark lace, painstakingly dyed a deep blue-black. Slowly Mama's eyes rose from the quilted petticoat to her hair. Margaret had taken great pains to secure it at the back of her head, pearl-tipped pins scattered throughout. A few freshly washed strands escaped, framing her face. She looked older and sadder, or so Margaret's mirror told her. More maid than maiden.

Like Naomi.

Eden smoothed the faint wrinkles on the skirt with nervous hands. "'Twas Jemma's—worn for her father's . . ." She paused, overcome by the irony that Eben Greathouse had been her own father too. "Passing."

Mama looked away and motioned her inside. Stepping into the foyer, Eden saw Elspeth standing in the kitchen. No warmth crossed her face, nor was any expected. She simply turned on her heel and disappeared.

"You've just missed noonday dinner." Mama's voice reached out to her, a bit hesitant, leading her toward the winter parlor. "But we've some food left if you like."

Eden realized then she'd erred in not seeking Silas out first. Was he still at table? A quick look into the dining room assured her he wasn't there. His place sat empty. The parlor, then . . .

"So, Daughter, you've come home at last." Liege's voice

310

was hardly welcoming as she stepped into the room. "You have the look of Hope Rising about you."

The cloaked rebuke brought a telling stain to her face. She swept the room in a glance, trying to get her bearings. Jon's cradle was missing and there was no sign of Thomas. Silas was also absent, but Giles rose to his feet at the sight of her. He ran a hand over his high forehead in a gesture riddled with unease, and the silence turned uncomfortably thick. This man was to be her husband. She felt a mixture of revulsion and resignation.

"Sit down." Gesturing to a stool by the hearth, Liege surveyed her like an item at auction. "'Tis mid-October. Silas has won his freedom. Giles is here to take his place—and your hand in marriage. Mourning aside, I can think of no further impediment now that you're well."

Impediment? She tried to school her distress. *None but that I love one man and might be carrying another man's child!* She gave no assenting nod. Looking down at her hands folded in her lap, she bit her lip till it nearly bled.

"The coming Sabbath seems a fair wedding day. All that remains is to summon the magistrate and secure a license. For now we'll have a little toast. Mistress Lee will bring the whiskey." His voice took on feigned warmth, suffusing the parlor with strange tension. "Elspeth, call Silas in to join us. We may as well celebrate the end of his apprenticeship to boot."

From a corner, Elspeth moved toward the door, but Eden sprang to her feet, skirts swirling, hands clenched at her sides. "Nay. I'll see to Silas."

With a shrug, Liege waved her away, attention fixed on Mama and the coveted whiskey bottle. The sight made Eden sick. 'Twas spirits that had made David an animal and turned her world upside down. She still bore the bruises beneath her borrowed dress. Tears blurred her vision as she passed through the rose arbor withered with frost—straight into Silas's arms. He shut the door hard, hemming her in.

"F-Father wants you," she stuttered.

"And you, Eden?" His gaze held steady. "What d'ye want?"

She looked away as his gaze slid to her gown, her upswept hair, the tiny silver earrings Margaret had fastened to her ears. There was little doubt he found her pleasing, even in black, only she felt stained, soiled beyond repair—she whose only thought had been to save herself for him. Her attention faltered and fell to her shoes.

"Eden, look at me."

For a moment her resolve slipped as she succumbed to the warmth of his words. "You . . . you didn't come back to Margaret's."

"I wanted you to come to me."

Her heart quickened as he took her face in his hands. Tenderly. Carefully. And then she stiffened, thinking of how David had touched her amidst the noise and filth of the tavern.

"Tomorrow we leave, ye ken."

"Tomorrow?" She swallowed hard, a bit breathless. "Nay, 'tis impossible. I cannot." The ugly words seemed to poison the air between them. He drew back a bit as she rushed on, "I—I told you—at the tavern—things have changed—"

"Aye, changed." His intensity heightened. "Jon is gone, as is Jemma. You got into the Greathouse coach and ended up halfway to Philadelphia. None of that alters my love for you or the plan we have in place."

"Y-you don't understand." The room began to spin. She'd been too long on her feet. Every hurtful word seemed to exact what little strength she had left. "I cannot go west. I—I never wanted to. 'Tis better I remain. You have your freedom. You're going where you want, far from here—a new start—"

"Enough, Eden." He took her none too gently by the shoulders. "Let there be no more talk about your fears of leaving here or your own fickle affections."

"But my feelings for you—" She stumbled over each word, fighting for calm when she felt none. "I don't care for you the way a wife should. I—I thought I loved you once—"

"Once?" He gave her a sudden shake, his gaze grieved. "Say what you will, Eden, but *do not* lie to me!"

"Silas, please!" She pulled away. "You've won your freedom. You don't want a weak wife. A taint—" Lord save her, she'd nearly said the words! *A tainted wife. Another man's child.* "You deserve better—better than York. God has His hand on you—"

"Not only me, Eden. *Us.* God brought me here not simply for an apprenticeship but for you. You're to be my bride and no other."

Desperate, she tried to shield her heart from his passionate words and turn away. But he stepped around her and blocked her path. "Tell me you do not love me, Eden. Tell me that."

"I—" She choked back a sob. The lie hovered on her tongue. She nearly mentioned Giles Esh but couldn't bear to see the hurt it would bring him. "I care enough to let you go—to wish better things for you—"

"For me? What about you? Am I to believe you're to throw your life away on a place you loathe? And people like Elspeth, who despises you? Who wishes you harm? Who might well have hurt her own child? Wheest, Eden! Speak sense!"

She covered her face with her hands, tears wetting her fingers, fearful Elspeth or Papa would overhear. "I belong here—my place is at home, at Hope Rising."

"At Hope Rising?" The words were so barbed it seemed he spat them at her. "Did Greathouse sway you into staying? Is that it? And for what? His spinning operation? Or is there more?" Anguish wet his eyes. "Am I to believe you're as false as your mother and sister? You make me think 'tis Greathouse you love, that you got into that carriage with the hope of being his mistress if not his wife—"

"Nay!" The word rang out with the force of a gunshot, echoing to the far corners of the smithy. Catching up her skirts, she fled, the door banging in her wake. Down the lane she ran, seeking asylum at Margaret's, painfully aware Silas would think she was fleeing to Hope Rising, giving credence to all he'd just said.

∾

Eden awoke against her will, buried in the feathery warmth of Margaret's bolster, the bed curtains drawn against the cold. Snow lined the windowpane, and everything beyond was a glittering, blinding world of white. Today marked Silas's leaving, their hoped-for wedding day. Instead she was to marry another, not knowing for another month or more if she was to be a mother, and if so, just whose child she carried.

David's . . . or Giles's?

The thought of being with a man so soon after being used by David left her shaking and sick. She felt feverish again, a swell of misery expanding inside her with every tick of the clock. When she'd dressed, Margaret, also clad in deep black for Jemma, made her a cup of chamomile tea, but she couldn't swallow a sip.

"Eden, thee are clearly not thyself. And I confess I do not understand thy situation. A man awaits thee—one thee do not love—while the man who clearly loves thee is leaving today, never to return." Margaret looked into her eyes with heightened candor. "Once you asked what I thought of Silas Ballantyne. I'll tell thee this. One finds such a man once in a lifetime if thee are truly blessed."

The words, though weighted with warning and far more vehement than Margaret's usual utterances, failed to dent Eden's resolve. She steeled herself against the truth of them and heard herself say, "Silas is an uncommon man. I've no doubt he'll make his mark wherever he goes. He deserves far better than York." Turning her back so Margaret couldn't see her intense struggle, she began putting on her cape. "I need some air. 'Tis time I see Jemma's grave—and Jon's."

"But 'tis snowing—and growing colder." Margaret started to rise. "Let me go with thee."

"Nay—please—I'll not be long." She raised her hood over her head and pulled on her mittens. The simple act elicited a strange hurt. Did Silas have gloves? 'Twas so cold and he would go so far . . .

"Take care to return soon." Margaret was hovering now, already adding wood to the fire. "I'll keep thy tea warm."

Eden stepped outside, nearly blinded by the bright beauty. *Wash me and I shall be whiter than snow.*

She'd been cleansed of sin by believing in her Savior. Would He not, in time, cleanse her of the sins committed against her? Or must she always feel . . . defiled? Tears froze on her face as she walked, her gaze averted from Hope Rising's brick façade, fastening instead on the church atop the rise as if it were an anchor in the swirling storm.

'Twas early. The landscape yawned empty. No one was about at such an hour. All stayed huddled by their hearths, seeking warmth after a shivering night. Smoke puffed from the smithy chimney, but she veered away from it, crossing fields and fences, secure in the knowledge that she was alone. The willow in the far field beckoned, its ice-clad arms bent low over a lone grave. Her throat grew tighter the closer she came.

Oh, Jon, I loved you so.

A wooden cross poked through the new-fallen snow,

straight and solemn. Silas had taken care to fashion it, the babe's name carved in careful letters. Time and the elements would soon erase it, but the lovely if lonely image would never leave her. Kneeling, she uttered a quiet prayer.

Slowly she turned back toward Hope Rising. The snow was unbroken across field and road till she started uphill. A lone horseman had recently passed this way, the hoofprints clearly marked. *Silas.* Her heart, so ravaged and torn, seemed about to burst. Through a whirl of wind and blowing snow, she changed direction, walking westward till the tracks grew so faint she could not follow.

When she looked up again, she felt lost. All was white, windswept, radiant as a bride. Her hands and feet, benumbed by cold, no longer seemed to belong to her. Her cape was an icy white, her boots blocks of ice. Would that her heart could feel the same . . .

Yet nothing mattered but that Silas was free.

She continued on, unsure of where she was. Nothing looked familiar. In time a welcome warmth stole over her and she grew sleepy. The air beneath the pine she huddled against was sharp and sweet. She dreamed she heard a violin.

Her last thought was of him.

33

Gather ye rosebuds while ye may,
Old Time is still a-flying.

ROBERT HERRICK

PHILADELPHIA
APRIL 1793

The spring sky was a brazen banner of pink and gold, deserving attention, but Eden's gaze was fixed on the stone steps at her feet. As she stepped out the foundling hospital's front door to greet the dawn, she took a bracing breath. In the profound quiet she could detect a lingering sense of loss—an almost palpable heartache. Nearly every morning her response to the poignant sight awaiting her was the same. As she knelt among baskets, boxes, and crates, the newborns within became a crying, cooing blur. Thankfully, a handkerchief was always on hand, as was her assistant, Betsy Simms.

"God be praised, Miss Lee! Only three this morning, I see."

Only three. Eden expelled a relieved breath. Once nine had been waiting. Rarely was there but one. A small sign near the courtyard's entrance instructed mothers to attach an identifying token in the unlikely event they returned to claim their child. None did. Still, Eden was careful to pin each offering to the baby's admission billet, marveling at the variety. Lush scraps of velvet. Lumpy wool. Sheer slips of ribbon. Buttons. Tiny pieces of embroidery in multihued thread. A bit of verse in an unknown hand.

Her painstaking care was one of the qualities that had propelled her from a fledgling assistant to assistant director of the Philadelphia Foundling Hospital six years before. That, and the fact her predecessors had all married or been buried as she quietly and competently performed her duties round the clock, becoming a favorite of staff and children alike. Stephen Elliot, the board's president, once remarked, "If only we could collect and keep competent hands like Miss Lee's the way we collect foundlings each and every morning."

But such praise did not turn Eden's head, nor elevate her in the slightest degree. The hospital board's premise was plain: "He must increase, but I must decrease." Surrounded by Friends who lived out this principle from Scripture day by day, she found it easy enough to emulate. Yet deep down, Eden couldn't escape the niggling certainty that her position had more to do with her Greathouse connections than her own competence.

"Ah, this one looks a mite peaked," Betsy crooned, examining the tiny boy cocooned in a tattered blanket. "Needs a bit more nourishment, looks like, to set him right."

"A great deal more." Eden bit her lip in contemplation. "It matters not that we have the best record for saving babies from Boston to Charleston. We still lose far too many."

Though the hospital was renowned for its staff and procedures, half the infants perished within a few weeks of arrival. Those who thrived continued to be suckled by wet nurses and cared for by nursery staff till they were of age to begin their schooling. Eden had been there long enough to see a few of the babies she'd gathered off the steps apprenticed to tradesmen, the girls prepared for service in fine Philadelphia houses. But she most remembered the babies they'd lost.

"He simply needs a mother's arms," Eden said as Betsy passed the whimpering boy to her before attending to the girls in the admitting room just inside the hospital doors.

Gently Eden removed his soiled clout, murmuring soothing words all the while. Cornflower-blue eyes looked up at her—so like Jon's her throat tightened. Around his tiny neck was a faded silk ribbon, which she attached to his admission papers. A warm bath awaited, followed by a linen gown, snug cap, and clean blanket. This was her favorite part of the work.

As she made her rounds and supervised the staff, she often returned to the nursery and rocked the babies herself. After a few weeks, the infants seemed to recognize her, rewarding her with wide smiles and outstretched arms. If she couldn't have her own children, she had these, she reasoned. Sometimes that seemed enough.

"What shall we name them?" Eden mused aloud, more to herself than Betsy.

"You're fond of biblical names, and glad I am of that." Betsy placed the baby girls together in a portable crib, ready to whisk them to a feeding. "Why not call the lad Daniel? He's in need of a strong namesake."

"Daniel it is. As for the girls, the fair one shall be Ruth, and the dark-haired one Naomi." The latter name brought a little pang. Bringing the whimpering boy to her chest, she struggled to push the unwelcome memory down.

"Worthy names, all," Betsy said in a sort of benediction. "Seems like our Daniel is ready for Peggy Grimes's milk. She has enough for all three, from the look of her this morn. Here, let me take him."

Pensive, Eden watched the door swing shut in Betsy's wake

before consulting the calendar she carried in her pocket. 'Twas Monday, and every hour was taken, beginning with a board meeting and then rounds with the doctors. Next was overseeing a delivery of linens and laudanum and, she recalled with a sigh, tiny caskets. Twin girls, shockingly premature when they'd arrived at the hospital's door, had died soon after and were to be buried in the hospital's cemetery. The chaplain, Betsy had reminded her moments ago, was on his way.

Hours later, as the clock in the hospital's entrance hall struck six and the streetlamps were lit, Eden walked from the furthest reaches of Prince Street to her boardinghouse at Fourth and Walnut, spirits low and head aching. The supper smells wafting from Mistress Payne's kitchen issued an invitation she was too tired to accept, unlike the noisy boarders already at table.

Shutting the front door as quietly as she could, she collected her mail from a table at the foot of the stairs before ascending to the second floor. A quick perusal confirmed it was more the post than her throbbing head that now stole her appetite. Letters from home, though rare, resurrected a host of unwelcome memories.

Her tiny wallpapered sitting room and bedchamber were dark, the door to the balcony ajar. She backtracked to the hall and lit a taper from a sconce before shutting the door and returning to the letter. In the pale orb of candlelight, the familiar handwriting was terse if heartfelt.

> *Dear Daughter,*
> *'Tis been a while since I have written.*
> *Liege is unwell.*

Eden sighed. Unwell or inebriated?

Thomas and Elspeth man the smithy in his stead.

She stared at the paper without focus, trying to recall the little brother who'd been but three when she left and was now . . . eleven?

I am still taking eggs and cheese to Hope Rising each week. Margaret sends her warmest wishes.

This never failed to make her smile. Mayhap the Lord did redeem difficult situations. She was glad for Mama, for Margaret—she missed them both. But pondering such things opened the door to the past and everything she'd tried so valiantly to forget.

The aching cold. The heartache of it all.

Would she never make peace with Silas's leaving? When she'd gone to Jon's grave and nearly frozen to death? To this day she had no feeling in her fingertips. If not for Sebastian, she would have died that snowy afternoon. He'd led the search party to her and then disappeared.

There had been no wedding to Giles Esh. No illegitimate child. Neither had she gone home again. Mama had come to Margaret's, where Eden recuperated from frostbite and a lingering fever, and somehow, miraculously, the two had resumed their foundered friendship.

She looked again at the letter.

You may know that Master David has taken a bride. Her name is Angelica, and she's just arrived at Hope Rising . . .

The paper fluttered from Eden's hand to the floor, the feel of it like poison. She nudged it into the ashes of the hearth, where it would serve as kindling come morning, and returned her attention to the rest of the post.

A scarlet seal foretold an invitation to a May ball. Another, from Beatrice Greathouse, requested Eden be a godmother. She set them aside, thoughts adrift. Bea had borne her sixth child a fortnight before. Shortly before that, Anne had married. And now . . . David. She tried to summon some fine feeling, some spark of pleasure for their good fortune, yet all she felt was emptiness.

Happiness, she'd long since decided, was something that happened to other people.

34

An honest man's the noblest work of God.

ALEXANDER POPE

PITTSBURGH
APRIL 1793

The two rivers hemming him in, Silas decided, were akin to the currents at work within his soul. The Monongahela, deep and still, flowed past like blue silk while the Allegheny foamed and churned, ever fitful. Of late Silas had felt more like the latter.

He hung a lantern from an iron hook along the moonlit dock. The light cast a broad beam across the water, a beacon for vessels traveling at night, and illuminated a sturdy wooden shingle: Ballantyne Boatworks. In time he hoped to replace it with something more substantial.

Ballantyne Ironworks.

When he'd first come to Pittsburgh, he'd been but a blacksmith fresh from the East, a hireling of Fort Pitt. Now he paid men to work iron in his stead. With a steady stream of settlers pushing west, his time was better spent building boats. Keelboats. Flatboats. Schooners. Sloops. He pored over plans by night and oversaw a dozen men in construction by day, working alongside them amidst the ever-present distillation of freshly sawn lumber, river water, and pitch.

His gaze swung from the night watchman he'd hired as a precaution against trouble to the dog nuzzling his hand. A cold west wind was keening, and the air smelled storm-damp, heightening his disquiet. "We've a long walk, Sebastian," he said, "and the weather is about to turn ugsome."

He'd considered spending the night on a cot in his waterfront office, but the lure of the tavern atop Grant's Hill was too great. He had rooms there, and Jean Marie, the French émigré who owned it, employed the finest cook this side of the Allegheny Mountains.

"Send for the sheriff at the first sign of trouble," he told the barrel-chested Irishman who stood near the locked office door. "I'll not be long behind."

Turning his back on his livelihood, he committed it to the Lord's hands and started up the hill, a Scots saying trailing him.

Sorrow and ill weather come unsent for.

Mayhap he was about to get a bit of both.

❧

Although the dining room of Grant's Tavern was empty, a corner table held a steaming plate, a chill tankard, and the latest copy of the *Pittsburgh Gazette*. Just like every night Silas could remember for the past five years. Jean Marie had a particular talent for anticipating her patrons' needs, thus making her the most popular innkeeper in Allegheny County.

He shrugged off his greatcoat, draped it over a chair back, and took a seat, eyes drawn to the window at his elbow. From here he had an eagle's view of the valley now aglitter with candlelight far below. Night had drawn a benevolent curtain over a crude assortment of brick and timber houses, never-ending mud, prodigious wharf rats, and more. Yet Silas felt at home in every foot of it, raw as it was. He had a foretaste of what Pittsburgh, not yet a town, would someday become.

"Ah, Monsieur Ballantyne . . ."

The accented voice echoed across the room, holding a warm if weary note of welcome. Jean Marie swept through the foyer doorway, looking more mature Philadelphia belle than Pittsburgh tavern keeper. The copper silk of her gown shimmered in the low light, and her eyes shone with good humor. "I have fed the ravenous Sebastian."

"*Merci*," Silas said, eyeing the dish of apple tansy she set down. "You don't have to wait supper on us, ye ken."

"And why not? You are my best boarder, no?"

"Your most tardy," he said contritely.

"Did I ever tell you that you work too hard?"

"Aye, nearly every eve."

"Yet you pay me no attention." When he motioned to the seat opposite, she took it, work-worn hands folded atop the table. "You need a home, a family. You need to be married to something besides boats."

Silas cut a bite of steak, eyes on his plate. "D'ye have some-one in mind?"

"No, but you do, surely." Her voice fell to a whisper. "What is this I hear about a ton of bricks being hauled out the river road to your new property? Word is you're getting ready to build a house . . . for a bride."

He forked the bite of steak to his mouth, chewing thought-fully, and smiled back at her with his eyes. "A ton of bricks does not make a bride."

"Oh, you Scotsmen are so stubborn!" Exasperation lit

her features. "You've a brick head—and heart. Would that I could give you a measure of French passion, convince you of the finer aspects of life and family."

He shrugged. "I have you and Sebastian. A fine supper. Conversation. What need have I of a bride?"

Sighing, she placed bony elbows on the table and stared him down. "There should be more for you, my friend. Time is of the essence. Though today you walk tall and strong in the dark along Water Street, tomorrow . . ." She hunched her shoulders, a furrow lining her brow.

"You're uneasy about the whiskey boys," he finished for her.

"*Oui*, more than uneasy. I have heard things . . ."

Taking a sip of cider, Silas looked from her to the window, as if expecting a rock to hurl past the pristine, Philadelphia-made glass. "Such as?"

She leaned nearer, her eyes pale as agates. "Since Judge O'Hara appointed you to the Allegheny Court, there has been bad blood between you and the Turlocks, no?"

"Aye," he said quietly, "they bear me a grudge for every fine and jailing." The animosity the clan bore him was an ongoing concern, but as a jurist he took his oath seriously and insisted on order. "'Tis common knowledge they've been found guilty of each assault and battery charge against them, all involving whiskey. If the Turlocks kept to farming and distilling and no collieshangie—"

"Collieshangie?"

"Brawling and quarreling," he said without missing a beat, "then they'd not come before the court, and we'd have no reason to fear walking along Water Street or otherwise."

"Word is they saw you supping with one of the tax collectors at this very table a few nights ago. There is talk they feel you support the tax on whiskey."

"They have faulty memories, then. 'Twas I who introduced a resolution against the tax to begin with." Tired, temper rising, he swallowed some cold cider as if it could cool his ire. "The Turlocks can well afford the excise. 'Tis the poor farmers and distillers I worry about, which was the reason for that shared supper."

Jean Marie turned her troubled profile toward the window, and Silas sensed what she wouldn't say. Though the "whiskey boys," as the Turlocks and their supporters were called, had only tarred and feathered tax collectors thus far, threats of doing greater violence now swirled thick as the mud that lined Pittsburgh's streets. His gaze fell to the headline splashed across the *Gazette*'s front page: FIRE DAMAGES MERCER MERCANTILE.

He pushed it aside. "I'd rather talk bricks—and brides."

She smiled, revealing a silver-capped tooth. "Very well, then. The judge's daughter has just ridden out to see your new property, no? The future home of all those bricks?"

"Has she now?"

Jean Marie rolled her eyes. "Why is it that you always answer my questions with a question, Silas Ballantyne?"

"Do I?"

Sighing, she went to the kitchen and returned with an urn of coffee and pitcher of cream. "Lest I forget, the judge sent this round earlier." She plucked a folded paper from her pocket and passed it to him, curiosity edging her thin features.

Smoothing it out atop the scarred tabletop, Silas took a reluctant look at the fine Italianate hand.

A reminder, my friend—dinner party at eight o'clock, Saturday eve, at River Hill. Dancing to follow. Isabel is home and anxious to see you. Hugh

The note was a not-so-subtle reminder that he'd forgotten the judge's last party, buried as he'd been in sawdust and cordage. Fresh from the frenetic launching of the sloop *Western Endeavor*, he'd only wanted a quiet room and a week's sleep. This time he had no ready excuses.

He glanced at the open kitchen door, where a stoop-shouldered Indian woman was scrubbing pots at a stone sink, and gave Jean Marie a quick wink. "Thank Mamie for the fine supper. I'll not be here tomorrow eve but at River Hill."

Pushing back his chair, he tucked the newspaper and note beneath one arm, weariness and worry dogging his every step.

35

Never think that God's delays are God's denials.

COMTE DE BUFFON

Lately Eden's small office looked and felt more like a jail cell. Sparsely furnished and smelling of disinfectant, it had one saving grace—the sole window overlooking the physic garden below. During the scorching Philadelphia summers, she opened the casement wide, ignoring the buzz of insects, hoping for a welcome breeze. On a good day she was rewarded with the heady smell of herbs and gauzy memories of her York garden, not the wharf with its pungent whirl of oakum and brine.

This afternoon her gaze drifted to the wall clock, slightly askew, and the hospital rules framed and posted by the door. *No profaneness. No spitting on the floor. No running. No removing the foundlings from hospital grounds.* As the clock struck the hour, she took a seat at her desk, thumbing through a stack of paperwork till she found what could no longer be pushed aside—the latest endowment from David Greathouse. Tomorrow she'd present it at the board meeting, pasting on a pleased smile as her colleagues nodded and expressed their gratitude. Though his patronage nauseated her, the funds were always needed and put to good use.

In the past they'd been able to build a new wing and summer kitchen, a second garden and small chapel. The latter she'd quietly dedicated to Jon, the cornerstone half hidden beneath a willow tree reminiscent of the one that shaded his grave in York. Thankfully only Beatrice had set foot inside the chapel, surveying everything with the cool detachment of a queen granting her subjects a rare visit.

Looking up from the letter of endowment, Eden took a deep breath. Over the years she'd grown used to her brick-and-mortar prison. Within its walls she felt safe. Cocooned. Insulated from the past. But today the sunlight frolicking outside her window seemed to issue a subtle invitation. Pushing down the urge to leave work early and take a carriage to Bartram's Gardens or Solomon's Book Shoppe, she made note of the hour. Half past three.

Time for tea.

∞

Eden rounded a corner, sensitive to the wails of infants echoing down the corridors, eyes drawn to the painting in the tiled foyer of Christ blessing the little children. The enormous oil never failed to move her. Perhaps she simply needed a painting or two to brighten her office, remind her of her mission—or she was in need of a holiday as the board had recently suggested. Aside from a brief illness, she'd not taken time away since she'd first set foot in Philadelphia.

Knocking on the director's door, she was greeted by a woman's familiar voice and saw a tea party already in progress by a far window, Stephen Elliot presiding. Eden felt a start of surprise. The board president—at tea?

330

"Oh my," Eden said with a sheepish smile. "Am I intruding? I apologize—"

"Don't fret, Eden. 'Tis only tea, not a board meeting. Stephen has come early to discuss something with me—and thee." Constance Darby gave her a lingering glance that held a hint of warning.

Be obliging, the look seemed to say. *Don't be too surprised.*

Eden looked from the woman whose counsel she always heeded to the spritely, gray-headed man she so respected, and still felt a prickle of alarm. Stephen Elliot got to his feet, clasping Eden's hands warmly as was his custom, his smile so infectious she found herself smiling back despite her wariness.

"Miss Lee, I simply have an interesting proposal. 'Tis spring, after all, a time to look forward and be thinking of our foundlings' futures."

"Has there been a change in plans?" she asked. "Are you not going to Boston?"

"No, not Boston. The foundling hospital there is flourishing and has no need of my direction at present. I've another destination in mind." He pulled out a chair and seated her before resuming his own seat. "A fortnight ago, an old friend from my Dartmouth days sent me a letter. He's one of Pittsburgh's founders and is in need of apprentices. Since we have a great many twelve-year-old-boys at present, I feel his request serves us well. Why don't we apprentice these lads to the tradesmen of Pittsburgh? There are a few girls awaiting placement who could also be of service. There's no rule that says we're to keep them in Philadelphia. And if there was," he said with a benevolent twinkle in his eyes, "I'd overturn it."

And well he could, Eden thought, as he was the wealthiest man in the city. Though not a Quaker, Stephen Elliot was a leading philanthropist and had made extensive bequests to many charitable institutions, including their own. Rarely had he steered them wrong.

"We must get approval from Dr. Rush, of course, and the rest of the board," Constance added. "But I foresee no problems there."

"No, it's a capital plan. I wish I'd thought of it myself." He stirred a heaping spoonful of sugar into his tea, eyes returning to Eden. "So sure was I of everyone's approval, I took the liberty of writing my friend straightaway and confirming our arrival in mid-June."

Our. The tiny word sent a chill clear through her. Her fingers brushed the curved handle of her teacup, but she didn't raise it to her lips. "What have I to do with this, Mr. Elliot?"

"You, my dear Miss Lee, are to act as chaperone and accompany the girls. I'll oversee the boys. There won't be more than a dozen children total."

"But—" The word escaped her lips before she'd put thought behind it. She tried to soften her reluctance with a smile. "I—I've not traveled beyond the outskirts of Philadelphia since coming here. And Fort Pi—Pittsburgh is so far."

"Precisely," he said with a smile, "which is why your name kept coming to mind as I was pondering the trip and praying. A change of scene will be good for us all. I'll fund the excursion myself, of course. All expenses will be paid, including a suitable wardrobe for both you and the children."

No more drab Quaker gray.

She met his eyes, a bit disbelieving. Though the words lodged like splinters inside her, how could she say no? It was this man who had taken her in when she'd first arrived in Philadelphia, a mere foundling herself, lost and bewildered as she'd been. Beatrice had made the introductions after Eden refused to stay in the Greathouses' townhouse. Not once had he or his wife, Harriet, delved into her past. They'd simply welcomed her with open arms, treating her like a daughter. Never had they asked anything of her.

Till now.

Still, half a dozen empty excuses leapt to mind, none of which had held the slightest appeal till this very moment. *I must attend a reception for President Washington on behalf of the hospital. Accompany Dr. Rush and his wife to Chestnut Street Theater. Be on hand when the hot-air balloon is launched from Robert Morris's garden . . .*

"But what of Harriet?" Eden kept her voice even, masking her disquiet. "She almost always accompanies you on these trips."

"I'm afraid Harriet has promised our niece a debut and is already neck-deep in the social season, starting with the Binghams' ball. You received an invitation, no doubt?"

"Yes, but . . ." It went without saying she wouldn't attend. She shunned society whenever she could, and always had.

"Say you will, Eden." His eyes—so kind and entreating—held hers. She felt herself give way. "I can think of no one better suited for the trip. The girls adore you—you'll put them at their ease and give them a proper introduction into Pittsburgh society."

"Society?" The word nearly made her smile. "Surely there's little of that to be had on the frontier."

"On the contrary, Miss Lee. Pittsburgh just might surprise you."

Withholding a sigh, Eden took a sip of tea. Now even Constance looked a bit dubious as she passed round a plate of scones. "Aren't circumstances in the West a bit . . . tentative at present? I remember hearing about a brewing rebellion involving not tea and taxes but whiskey and taxes."

Mr. Elliot gave a decisive shake of his head. "The newspapers paint a torrid picture of Pittsburgh, depicting it as a hotbed of rebellion. Don't believe a word of it. Congress has

reduced the tax on whiskey, and my friend the judge main-
tains law and order." He took a letter from his waistcoat
and scanned it thoughtfully. "There are several thousand
inhabitants in Allegheny County and a number of tradesmen
in need of apprentices. Let's see . . . a saddler, a blacksmith,
a boatwright, a gunsmith, several merchants . . ."

"Where will thy party be staying?" Constance asked.

"We'll lodge at the Black Bear Hotel, though my old friend
has graciously opened his home to us as well." Passing the
paper to her, he took out a pocket calendar. "Travel by stage
should take three weeks. Once we arrive, we'll get the children settled and stay on to oversee a smooth transition. I
foresee spending the summer in Pittsburgh and returning to
Philadelphia by September."

Eden sat straight-backed in her chair, her mouth dry despite
the delicious tea. They were waiting for her to say something—
to accept—but the words seemed to stick in her throat.

Mr. Elliot leaned nearer. "Miss Lee, I truly believe you'll
enjoy the West—"

"I—nay—" She was on her feet but didn't remember standing, was only cognizant of the closeness of the room, her
sudden breathlessness. The past seemed to be pressing in
on her all at once from every direction. Just yesterday she'd
had a letter from Elspeth. Elspeth! Who'd informed her she
was coming to the city to visit after nary a word for years.
"Please, I—"

"Eden, are thee unwell?" Constance rose abruptly, reaching
out a hand in concern.

With a shake of her head, Eden made it to the hall, mum-
bling some excuse before fleeing to the physic garden beyond
the nearest door. The scent of sun-warmed earth and peren-
nials in their spring infancy surrounded her like old friends,
releasing their perfume beneath her feet. Soon the grounds

would burst into full bloom, only she'd not be here to see it. If she went west—nay!

Her mind raced to come up with a suitable replacement. Sinking down atop a stone bench, her skirts swirling around her, she tried to calm her tangled thoughts.

Lord, help . . . please.

When the name finally came, she expelled a relieved breath. Hannah Penn.

The Morris mansion was extravagant in the extreme, yet the Philadelphia elite and a great many Friends gathered there whenever its doors were open, stuffed into one of its marble drawing rooms like cargo in a ship's hold. Tonight was no exception. Eden breathed a prayer of thanks for the cool evening air, wanting to escape as soon as she could. Surrounded by liveried servants, she took a seat at the back of the grand room, watching the guests flow past in a parade of jewels and rich fabrics, hoping to catch sight of Hannah Penn.

With a flick of her wrist, she snapped open her sandalwood fan, praying silently as her gaze roamed the room's candlelit interior.

Please, Lord, let me find Hannah before the music starts.

Since leaving York County, not once had she attended a musical soiree. But tonight, a bit desperate, unable to rest till she'd stilled the tempest inside her, she had little choice. Her wary gaze returned to the musicians on the dais again and again, dismissing every instrument in the large ensemble till she came to the violins. The musicians were tuning their fine instruments just as Silas used to, yet it seemed they tore at her heartstrings instead.

I will not cry.

Tears lined her lashes, only to be dried by the frantic fluttering of her fan. For years she'd carefully schooled her emotions. If loosed now, what a torrent that would be! The last time she'd wept was at his leaving, when she'd discovered his tracks in the snow. An eternity past . . .

"Miss Lee."

The masculine voice loomed from behind. She pretended not to hear. She mustn't be distracted from her mission. But it came again, ever nearer. "You're looking lovely this evening."

'Twas Robert Morris's oldest son, Andrew, just returned from London and resplendent in the latest fashion—trousers, not breeches, a lily affixed to his frock coat. Eden thought of the lemon trees in the Morris greenhouse from which the fragrant flower had surely been taken. Just before he'd left for England, Andrew had sent a basket of lemons and lilies to her rooms at the boardinghouse. Their mingled fragrance—one so pungent and the other so sweet—had given her a headache despite her fondness for them.

"Very lovely," he repeated.

"Thank you," she said with a self-conscious smile, gaze falling to her lap. He meant her gown, surely. Though a bit outdated, the heavy silk was the hue of honey, the bodice and sleeves a confection of Irish lace. It had been one of Jemma's favorites.

"You seem to be looking for someone. I was hoping it might be me."

His gentlemanly phrasing tugged at her, and she stood, if only to be polite. "'Tis good to see you on American soil again, Andrew, but in truth I'm seeking Hannah Penn."

Her voice fell away as the chatter rose around them, and she rued his obvious disappointment. Extending his arm, he led her down a candlelit corridor to Hannah's side before bowing and returning to the drawing room.

"Eden Lee? What on earth?" Hannah's eyes widened. The

gentleman beside her excused himself, as if expecting their need of a private tête-à-tête.

"'Tis me, not a ghost," Eden said to make light of her surprise.

"Why, thee are pale as one. I haven't seen thee at a social function for . . . *forever*."

"I've come to ask a favor." Nay, a favor it was not. Eden groped for the right words and came up woefully short.

"If thee are wanting someone to teach the foundling girls embroidery—needlework—I'll be happy to help."

"Nay." The opening strains of the program—Haydn— threaded through the warm foyer, which had suddenly begun to empty. Eden seized the moment. "I remember some months ago you spoke of going west—to Pittsburgh—to visit a relation . . ." The rest of her request poured forth, Eden hoping she didn't sound as foolish as she felt.

Hannah's fair features clouded. "I wish I could go in thy stead, Eden, but my Pittsburgh relation has passed away, and—" She waved her fan at a distant figure, leaning in to whisper in Eden's ear, "'Tis no time to be leaving the city, my friend. I'm practically betrothed."

With a squeeze to Eden's arm, she moved away, the silken swish of her skirts a mesmerizing coral. Watching her go, Eden felt mired in a puddle of disappointment. Yet why should she be? Hannah had a full life away from her charitable work at the foundling hospital—and a wide circle of friends. The large Penn family seemed to have a hand in everything.

She continued to stand, fan dangling limply from her wrist, the impassioned trill of half a dozen violins in her ears. The exquisite sound was sheer torment. Why had she come? The folly of it filled her to the brim and overflowed as she sought the nearest exit. Nodding to the footman at the door, she hurried out into the rain-laden hush of twilight to hail a carriage home.

36

In the election of a wife, as in a
project of war, to err once is to be
undone forever.

THOMAS MIDDLETON

Frolics at River Hill were a distillation of tobacco smoke, brandy, fine food, a great deal of business, and a little dancing to pacify the women. Ever since Silas had come stumbling into Pittsburgh on that icy December day in 1785, River Hill had seemed a sort of paradise. Situated on the high, rocky banks of the Monongahela, it was grand yet unpretentious and had none of the negative associations of Hope Rising or Blair Castle.

River Hill's master, Hugh O'Hara, was a former trades-man who had come up in the world by dint of hard work. A true visionary, he'd put Pittsburgh on the map and was already reaping her fortunes, and he had the capital to back every business venture Silas brought him. Never having lost his ties to his humble beginnings as saddler turned soldier turned lawyer, he opened his vast library at River Hill to young men with a bent toward self-improvement. Silas had been one of them.

Tonight they'd been talking iron, but the conversation had taken a personal turn as the ladies cajoled the men into the ballroom—all but Isabel. Recently returned from the East, where her father had sent her to acquire some Philadelphia polish, she seemed to be waiting for Silas to seek her out. Though they'd touched elbows at the ornate mahogany dining table where they'd been seated side by side, she'd said little, leaving Silas to wonder what Philadelphia had done to her in the six months she'd been away.

He felt a bit unsettled by the sight of her in a formal gown of painted silk, jewels circling her throat and adorning her ears. She'd returned from the city with a lady's maid, Hugh said, and from all appearances she was an experienced one.

Standing beside an open French door that led to a wide terrace overlooking the river, Isabel looked his way. The candlelight gilding her fair hair and the way she fluttered her fan was invitation enough. Silas extricated himself from the cluster of politicians and industrialists and took her by the elbow onto the empty terrace.

"Welcome back, Isabel." His words were almost lost over the swell of the cotillion beginning inside. "How was Philadelphia?"

She smiled up at him over the fan's lace edging. "Crowded. Smelly."

"That I remember." He half chuckled at her forthrightness. Some things never changed, he guessed. "Did you see Bartram's Gardens? Solomon's Book Shoppe?"

Her powdered nose wrinkled in distaste. "You forget I'm not interested in fussy flowers and boring books. Rickett's Circus was much more to my liking. Besides, Aunt Bess kept me plenty busy. Between the theater and tea shops and visits

339

to the dressmaker, I hardly had time to breathe." She fluttered her fan as if trying to master it. "But I was often homesick. For Papa . . . River Hill . . ."

And you, she didn't say, though Silas suspected. Her feelings were plain—had been for some time. He looked down at her, struck by how tiny she was. He'd met her soon after coming to Pittsburgh, when she was but twelve. Now nineteen, she'd always seemed more child to him. But tonight, with her grown-up gown and her expression rapt, he saw something more.

"And you?" She touched his coat sleeve with her fan. "What new business ventures have you dreamed up in my absence?"

His mind stretched back over the frenzied fall and winter, eyes on the water. "Ironmaking. A glassworks. Soon there'll be a mercantile and warehouse by the boatyard."

"Papa said you'd acquired more lots in town, made some shrewd investments."

He nearly smiled at her phrasing. That she was her father's daughter there could be no doubt. "Aye, some land sold by the sheriff in execution of legal judgments. Insolvent debts and bankruptcies and the like." He'd spread himself too thin in the process. But life on the cusp of the frontier, he'd learned, was an ongoing gamble, and if he didn't rise to the challenge, a great many other men would.

"I only want to hear about the four hundred acres further downriver." In the moonlight her amber eyes were beguiling. "Tell me everything."

He leaned into the railing. "You tell me, Isabel. Word is you've ridden out to see for yourself." At her surprise, he smiled. "Pittsburgh spies, ye ken."

"Jean Marie, you mean." She sighed and folded her fan. "I simply wanted to see where all those bricks were headed. Fort Pitt's fall is like losing an old friend. I was born within its walls, remember, when Papa was an officer there. I rather enjoy the thought of a new beginning with all those bricks."

Though he hadn't succumbed to the same sentiment, he liked the idea of preserving the past. But the old garrison's dismantling meant little to him except as a sign that east had met west and the Indian question was now forever settled in Pennsylvania. He could finally begin building a home of his own.

She moved nearer, and he was enveloped in a floral scent he couldn't name. "What will you call the place?"

"I've given it little thought," he said, looking from her expectant, upturned face to the French door, now shut. Who . . . ? Her father, no doubt. He was trying to give them some privacy, foster a tender reunion after long months apart. Whatever Hugh's motives, Silas *was* glad to see her. She offered him something beyond the unceasing busyness of the wharf and the worrisome distraction of the whiskey rebellion. Jean Marie might well have been right. Mayhap he needed to be married to something besides boats.

Bolstered by a bit of brandy, he reached out a hand and brushed a stray curl behind the curve of her ear. Against his calloused fingers the strand was whisper soft. He'd never touched her except in the most casual way, never touched any woman since . . .

Eden.

The memory bore the brunt of newly forged nails. He leaned closer, desperate to block it, to replace it with another, fresher memory. Isabel offered no resistance. Their mouths met, tasted, returned for more. Pleasure shot through him in a way it hadn't in years, along with a latent realization. Beneath his hands was a woman who wanted him. Who'd never been courted by anyone but was admired by many. Whose dowry, Hugh had just told him, contained half of Pittsburgh.

Who bore no taint of the past.

37

Thou art mine, thou hast given thy word.

EDMUND C. STEDMAN

Eden looked up from her open trunk to the small spinning balcony adjoining her room. Her Saxony wheel rested there, still and silent at dusk. The little terrace overlooked a narrow alley crooked as a dog's hind leg, and offered a small if stingy window of the city. Tonight the horizon was a lush lavender-gold, a sort of benediction on her momentous day. How, she wondered, would it look without the spire of Christ Church or the crush of buildings along Market Street in the way? Soon she would find out.

In warmer weather she would sit outside and spin, trying not to think of home or the fact that the spinning jenny and rotary steam engines in the city's textile mills made her task quaint and nearly obsolete. There was a beauty and simplicity in the old ways, in the gentle whirr of the wheel and the feel of the thread against her practiced hand. She'd let go of so much of her old life, of the past; this was one comfort she wanted to keep. That it would sit idle for a summer hurt her somehow. If only it could be heaved atop a lumbering coach!

Had it only been a fortnight before that she'd agreed to accompany the children to Pittsburgh? Thinking back on her conversation with Stephen Elliot, she wished she could begin again, say far less with half the emotion. In the comfortable familiarity of Constance Darby's office, the story had spilled out of her, so unrehearsed and rusty the memories seemed to belong to someone else.

"I want the children to have a fresh start in Pittsburgh," she'd told them. "'Twas selfish of me to almost refuse you. I've pondered it and prayed about it, and I'll gladly go." Yet even as she spoke the words, she felt duplicitous. Her agreement had more to do with avoiding Elspeth's visit than being a help to the hospital, truly. Yet even without Elspeth's coming, she felt inexplicably led to accompany him.

Stephen looked relieved, though his wrinkled features held a touching concern. "I must say, Miss Lee, I'm glad you've come round. We'll be taking the Forbes Road west, of course. I remember you have family in York County. We'll be passing by there, should you want to see them."

The mere suggestion, kind as it was, gave rise to second thoughts. How could she explain the cold reception they'd likely receive? After so long a time, Mama might be willing, but . . . "I wouldn't want to delay us," she said quietly, wondering how much to reveal. "There are things you don't know about my past. Years ago I left home under a . . . a cloud."

After finding out I was the illegitimate daughter of one of the founders of this very hospital, upon being ill used by his heir . . .

She could well imagine their consternation if she was to speak of that. 'Twas far safer to speak of Pittsburgh. "I—I was once betrothed to a man—a blacksmith's apprentice.

We'd planned to go to Fort Pitt, but circumstances conspired against us." There was a catch in her voice, but she forged on. "Our betrothal was broken. I came here instead."

"Oh, Eden, I had no idea," Constance said. "What became of thy betrothed?"

Eden fingered a crystal inkwell, her damp eyes on the plumed quill. "I don't know. He was a good man—a godly man. I only wanted what was best for him. I try not to look back. God has been so good to me, and I try to dwell on that."

"Wise words," Stephen murmured, more serious than she'd ever seen him.

She folded her hands in her lap and tried to smile in expectation. "No doubt a trip west will be good for us all, like you said. Lately I've felt a bit . . . unsettled. I'll miss Philadelphia, of course, and you, Constance—the babies especially."

Constance dotted her eyes with a handkerchief. "Oh yes, and don't forget the sweltering summer heat, flies and mosquitoes big as bats, and those everlasting board meetings."

Their shared laughter lifted the heavy mood and lingered, lightening Eden's spirits hours later in the confines of her rented rooms.

They'd be leaving around the middle of May. She'd made arrangements with Mrs. Payne to let Elspeth lodge in her stead while she was away, hoping she'd have gone back to York by the time Eden returned. She wondered what Elspeth's motives were for coming and how long she'd stay. The mere thought of their reunion left her shaky and sick. She had no wish to see her half sister again, not after the fire or Jon's death, for she was certain Elspeth had had a hand in both.

In need of a distraction, she returned to packing, taking stock of the new dresses befitting her age and station. Though still girl-slim despite her eight and twenty years, she could no longer wear the pure whites and pastels of younger women.

Those had been replaced by more matronly mosses, plums, nutmegs, and navies. 'Twas hardly the trousseau of her youthful dreams, but the Elliots had been more than generous, so much so that she had need of another trunk for all the hats, gloves, fans, and shoes.

Kneeling beside her bed, she reached for another, smaller chest, then nearly let go of the leather handle as misgivings crowded in. More memories. In the near darkness her fingers fumbled with lock and key, and then it opened, the scent of dried lavender and rose petals filling her senses. Shut away for years, the contents still held a bittersweet familiarity. A candle was needed, but she shied away from the light. It was better to feel her way through the dusty remains of her former life.

Here were her old journal and a few of Jemma's favorite books. Garden seeds, mostly everlastings. The blue dress she'd worn to Sabbath services on the hill. Her fingers stilled at the feel of soft linen. Within its folds was a lock of Jon's hair. It had been so fair. Sunlight itself. That he was now in heaven she believed with all her heart.

Biting her lip, she sat back on her heels as a hundred questions assailed her. What if . . . what if he hadn't died? What if she'd never gotten into the Greathouse coach that day? What if she'd told Silas the truth of what had happened at the Black Swan Inn? What if she'd trusted that his love was enough to overcome her hurt? That God could heal her over time?

Her fingertips brushed a scrap of paper. Some fragment of poetry, perhaps, or a note. Rising, she went in search of a candle, kindling it from the hearth's fading embers. The room rebounded with yellow light. She was on her knees again, reaching for the last treasure. The ink was faded and time had turned the paper yellow, but the handwriting was all too familiar. Her eyes fell on a telling line, her heart about to burst.

I will betroth thee unto me forever.

"Silas, we simply *must* have a summer kitchen."

We. He made note of her words but merely said, "A summer kitchen." He hadn't asked Isabel's opinion, but she was, with her usual exuberance, informing him anyway. With the dimple dotting her left cheek, her hands framing her shapely hips, he could almost forgive her for it.

She shifted her open parasol to rest against her other shoulder, the May heat spackling her high forehead with sweat. Dew, she called it. She'd been reading one too many copies of *Lady's Magazine*, he suspected, and was getting high notions. Her father imported all the latest periodicals from London, plying him with the same, but he had no time to give them more than a glance.

"Papa says it's better to build big from the first than add on later. Once the children come, there'll be a need for more room. You don't want to be tripping over servants and babies in a too-small house."

"I've no servants or bairns to speak of," he told her, stubbornness in his tone. "And only so many bricks."

Twirling her parasol's ebony handle, she sighed. "Then order more bricks or build in stone. Goodness knows there are rocks enough on this property to outfit all of Pittsburgh!"

"I'm putting the rock to good use," he said. "I'm having a chapel built first."

"A chapel? Whatever for?"

He didn't answer. He simply felt compelled to do so, something he hadn't sensed in regards to his marital prospects.

Sebastian wagged his tail and barked, interrupting his musings, then turned and bounded toward an open carriage turning off the main road. Shielding his eyes against the sun's glare, Silas watched the new contraption bounce over rocks and navigate sinkholes in its quest to reach them, Hugh at the reins.

The warmth of Isabel's gaze reached out to him. "Papa has promised to send some servants over when you're ready to begin building."

He finished driving in the last stake to mark off the house's west corner and straightened, mallet in hand. *I'll not use slave labor,* he nearly said, but sensed that the rising heat—and his reticence to go along with her plans—might put her in a high temper. "We'll speak of that another day."

She simply shrugged as Hugh climbed down from the carriage and cast an appreciative eye over the stump-littered clearing. A lush wall of trees—enormous oaks and elms and hickories—hedged them on three sides, but it was the rocky southern slope he lingered on, as it gave way to the Allegheny River, offering a tremendous view. Silas never tired of taking it in, though the pride and pleasure it wrought was bittersweet. 'Twas a fine land on which to raise sons. Daughters. He'd hoped to have both long before now.

"Magnificent." Hugh squinted beneath the sun's brilliance despite his wide-brimmed hat. "I believe I like this tract of land even more than River Hill. The only drawback, I'm sorry to say, is your neighbors."

Silas felt a twist of regret. He'd almost passed on the land because of that, but at three dollars an acre, how could he have refused? "The Camerons are to the east. They're good, God-fearing folk. As for the Turlocks, mayhap they'll come round."

Hugh looked dubious, pushing back the brim of his hat with a gloved finger. "I admire your optimism—and I'm glad your home is to be made of brick. The whiskey boys seem to have a fondness for wood." He thrust the latest copy of the *Pittsburgh Gazette* toward Silas before helping Isabel into the carriage. "You've missed all the excitement, occupied as you've been out here the last day or so."

Silas took the paper reluctantly, eyes falling on another boldfaced headline: TEAGUE'S TAVERN BURNS. His jaw tensed. "Was anyone hurt?"

"No, but there's plenty of damage. I've sent the sheriff to bring the Turlocks in for questioning. The general consensus is they're the ringleaders of this rebellion, being the foremost whiskey distillers." Stepping up into the upholstered carriage, he took a seat beside Isabel and reached for the reins. "On a lighter note, I've received word the Elliot party is on their way. They left Philadelphia a few days ago. Hopefully the Black Bear will still be standing once they arrive. If the hotel burns, I'll have to lodge them all at River Hill."

"*That* should be interesting," Isabel said. "I imagine those foundlings are a wild bunch. They might well burn our place down before the whiskey boys." Rumbling away in the carriage, she looked back at Silas briefly. "Don't stay overlong, mind you! And watch your back!"

With a nod, he wiped the sweat beading his brow, the mallet heavy in his hand, and surveyed his land. A wind was rising, laying the waist-high grass low all around him. In the far meadow, white wildflowers grew so thick it looked like a late snow had fallen. Everywhere else, clover pushed up thigh-high. He needed a few head of cattle to keep the growth down, but first he'd finish fencing. Weathered chestnut rails lay in a line as far as he could see. If only there were two of him . . .

He picked up a few more stakes and marked the boundaries of the dependencies he had in mind—smokehouse, spring-house, stable. But his enthusiasm was soon spent. Tossing the mallet into the grass, he ruffled Sebastian's burr-flecked coat, evidence he'd been neglecting him.

"You should still be tending sheep at Hope Rising," he muttered, "instead of keeping company with a conflummixt Scot."

How the dog had followed him west in the midst of a howling snowstorm years before was still a mystery, but he thanked God every day for such a faithful companion. "Come along now," he called, unhobbling his horse. "We'll arrive on time for supper just this once and give Mamie and Jean Marie something to talk about."

Besides bricks and brides.

⚬⚭⚬

The ride into Pittsburgh was but five miles, and Silas made it before sundown. His gaze traveled to the point of land that had once sustained Fort Pitt, that vast tract looking like an arrowhead trained west. There the three rivers intertwined in a silvery knot before slipping toward the horizon. Sometimes the sunsets were so spectacular, the view from Grant's Hill so mesmerizing, he was able to forget for a few minutes all that weighed on his heart and mind. But tonight the clouds stole away any beauty and he dismissed the familiar scene, bent on supper instead.

After stabling his horse, he entered through the back door of the boardinghouse to a noisy dining room and took his usual place, thankful when Mamie served him promptly. Talk of the latest fire and the Turlocks' culpability commandeered the conversation as forks clanked against pewter plates and mugs were raised. Silas said little but listened hard, drawing his own conclusions. The Turlocks were trouble, whiskey-laden or no. He doubted the county jail would hold them. Leaning back in his chair at meal's end, he found Jean Marie at his elbow.

"You've not touched Mamie's fine tart. Are you feeling dwiny?" The Scots word on her French tongue nearly made him smile. "Perhaps you simply need more coffee, no?"

"Nae. Sleep." Excusing himself, he started for the stairs, but she followed him into the foyer, silk skirts rustling.

"Don't forget these." She passed him what looked to be the post.

Taking the letters, he felt the familiar tug of hope, only to have it extinguished by a strand of sadness. Tonight, tired as he was, it seemed keener—and lingered longer. He simply held an announcement for the opening of the new Presbyterian Church. Two dinner invitations. A letter from a business acquaintance in Boston. Once, years before, he'd written to Eden but had received no answer.

"On second thought, I'm going to the boatyard." He looked at Jean Marie, and understanding passed between them. "If I'm not back in an hour . . ."

"Take Sebastian," she cautioned, eyes dark with worry.

He returned in half the time after going to both jail and wharf and speaking with the warden and night watch. Standing in the doorway to the parlor, Jean Marie drew a relieved breath when he reappeared.

"You can rest easy now, as can I. Most of the Turlocks are in custody." With that, he took the stairs to his room and removed his boots, barely parting with his shirt and breeches before sleep claimed him.

⁓

Fire!

The heat singed his hands, the smoke his senses. With a cry he shot upright. He was in Scotland—nae, York. In the stairwell. With Eden. Over the years she'd become no more substantial than river mist, but there she lingered, the light of affection in her eyes. Mercifully, the vision vanished as fast as it had come.

He came awake to a still, smokeless room, moonlight edging the windowpane. Still, his heartbeat pulsed in his ears and sent a tremor through his body. 'Twas the burning of Teague's

Tavern that plagued him, surely. Leaning back against the bed's knobby headboard, he drew an uneasy breath.

Only at night, when his head and hands were idle, did he look back. Unwillingly. Often. He hated the night. Everything was so clear then, his missteps plain. 'Twas as fresh as yesterday, their parting. Hundreds of miles and too many years had done nothing to erase it. Though, God help him, he'd tried.

Eden's face still haunted him as it had been at the last. She'd been so distraught that day, and he'd gone over the edge with his anger. Over time, once his temper had cooled and he'd reviewed the events with a more dispassionate eye, her frantic rejection still made no sense. Why hadn't he simply stayed on a bit longer and tried to win her again? Because his pride had been wounded by her refusal? Because he sensed it was David Greathouse she wanted instead?

He dragged himself to the window, looking down the long hill toward the boatyard. Fear baited him to keep watch lest flames erupt and take down all he'd worked to build since coming here. Arson and whiskey would be the ruination of Pittsburgh if the trouble didn't end. He didn't want to be caught sleeping if it turned to char and stubble. Though the Turlocks were in custody, save one, other troublemakers abounded.

He began to dress, thrusting his knife into his boot at the last and securing a pistol to his belt. The chiming of the foyer clock proclaimed it four in the morning. Stepping quietly, he descended the staircase and found Sebastian waiting on the wide front porch, just like countless other mornings. Ignoring the aroma of coffee from Mamie's kitchen, he started down the hill to the waterfront.

He'd gone no further than Chancery Street when the hair on the back of his neck tingled in warning. Sebastian gave a low whine, brushing his leg in the darkness. Before he'd taken another step, someone emerged from an alley, blocking his path. Moonlight limned his fair hair a queer white-gold, turning the scar that trailed his jawline more grotesque. Though he was as young as Silas himself, Henry Turlock's face was like a well-worn map, defined by countless lines and markings, all bespeaking vice.

"Ye take such risks, Ballantyne." He came nearer, his lilt thick, slurred with the whiskey he distilled, the gleam of silver calling attention to the pistol in his hand.

Silas stood his ground, stung by a near-blinding, white-hot fury. This was the man who was at the bitter heart of the rebellion, whose genius for trouble made him feared clear to the ports of Louisville and New Orleans.

"For a Scot to wander in the dark when trouble abounds leaves this Irishman no other choice but to—"

With a savage growl, Sebastian lunged at the threatening figure, eliciting a string of oaths even as the pistol discharged. Nerves taut, unable to see which way the bullet had traveled, Silas wrestled the gun away in a heart-pounding rush. Stepping toward the river, he flung it into the rushing Monongahela.

Dazed, senses stinging from gunpowder, he let Sebastian have his way with the writhing man on the ground, only numbingly aware when the sheriff hastened to his side, asking him to call off his dog. He did so reluctantly, knowing Turlock meant more than mischief.

Henry Turlock wanted him dead.

38

One meets his destiny often in the road he takes to avoid it.

SAMUEL JOHNSON

Clara. Helen. Ruth. Annie. Abigail. Molly. It seemed Eden prayed for them every bump and jolt of the journey, through coach sickness and broken axles, girlish spats and tears. Secretly, her heart ached for her charges. *Please, Lord, in Your goodness and mercy, protect them and place them well. Help their masters and mistresses to be good and kind and fair. Godly.* It was a large petition, but these girls, left on the hospital steps as infants, needed so very much.

"How much longer, Miss Lee?" 'Twas Clara this time, her chunky blonde braids and spattering of freckles making her look far younger than twelve years.

Eden nearly smiled. The question was asked a dozen or more times each day, and she always tried to give a patient answer. "Nearer than yesterday. We've traveled a fortnight so far. One hundred miles more." But she herself was growing weary. They'd run out of hand games to play with yarn,

353

and reading aloud to them while they lumbered along left her queasy. As the weather grew hotter, thick clouds of dust prevented them from looking out the coach windows to the hilly, green country beyond.

She wondered how Stephen Elliot was faring with his six charges in a separate coach just ahead. They were making good time despite the primitive roads, but at dusk, after long, pent-up days, the boys came alive and required a firm hand. Eden had never seen such appetites. Thankfully, the taverns they stayed in were respectable, the food plentiful, and their benefactor generous, tipping the merest stable boy handsomely.

"Are all these children yours?" one astonished innkeeper asked them.

"How I wish," Eden said, much to the amusement of the childless Stephen Elliot.

He fixed her with a droll stare. "Really, Miss Lee—all twelve?"

She smiled back at him a bit wistfully, having long ago discarded that dream. "Twelve seems rather small, given I once knew a family in York blessed with one and twenty." A happy family they'd been too, the children like stair steps. She couldn't help but remember it now with a little twinge.

They stopped at a rushing creek to let the children play in the heat of the day, the coach drivers stretching their legs and puffing on their pipes while Eden sat on a blanket beneath a shade tree, trying to stay awake but dozing. Beside her, Stephen read the *Pittsburgh Gazette*, his deep baritone rousing her.

"Listen to this, Miss Lee. 'There is not a more delightful spot under heaven to spend any of the summer months than in Pittsburgh. It may be observed that at the junction of the rivers, until eight o'clock of summer mornings, a light mist of aromatic quality and salutary nature is ever present.'"

Eden opened one eye. "So even the fog is finer in Pittsburgh."

He chuckled and passed her the paper. "Better that than what an acquaintance of mine said years ago after visiting: 'An excellent place to do penance in.'"

Smiling, she placed the copy in her lap, the happy laughter and splashing of the children like music to her ears. Stifling a yawn, she scanned the front page before moving inside to the advertisements. For a frontier town, Pittsburgh was full of surprises. A day school for young ladies offered French, reading, and knitting. A dozen competing stores boasted European and West Indian merchandise. Multiple listings of taverns crowded the page. The Green Tree. The Sword and Crown. Eagle's Rest.

When she came to the business section, she went completely still.

Six horses bought at auction by Brackenridge and Ballantyne.

A coincidence, surely. She shifted uncomfortably and read further, lingering on the notices of property sold in execution of legal judgments.

Six lots between Market and Water Streets acquired by S. Ballantyne.

She blinked. She had to remember to breathe. A docket from the Allegheny County Criminal Court was listed on the next page.

Judge Hugh O'Hara presided. Jurists: J. Wilkins, D. Duncan, P. Addison, S. Ballantyne.

"Miss Lee, are you all right?" Stephen's shadow fell over her.

Her mouth turned to cotton. She put a hand to her brow. "I . . ."

"It must be this heat," he said. He withdrew a handkerchief from his waistcoat pocket, went to the water's edge, and wet it in the rushing current. When he returned, he regarded her with fatherly concern.

"I thought I recognized a name—in the paper," she mumbled.

"A name?" His tone turned searching, as if waiting for her to say more.

She kept quiet, taking the handkerchief and cooling her flushed face while he returned to the creek and called for the children to ready themselves so they could be under way. Sighing, she stood and smoothed her skirt, folding the paper into a small, soon-to-be-forgotten square—or so she hoped.

'Twas a coincidence, surely. Pittsburgh was known to be a Scots stronghold. Ballantyne, though not common, was Scottish to the core. There might be any number of men by that name. As for the *S* before it . . .

Disbelief and dread stirred like a whirlwind inside her. She could deny it all she wanted, but deep in her spirit she knew.

It could be no other.

∞

If trading one strange bed for another in countless taverns had left her a tad sleepless, perusing the *Pittsburgh Gazette* left Eden wide-eyed all night. They were two days away from their destination. The realization left her bewildered and slightly sick. But she couldn't turn back. Once she reached their lodging, perhaps she could keep to her room and plead exhaustion, hardly an exaggeration. Her fervent hope was that the place was big enough that they'd not cross paths.

Still, her imagination ran wild. Silas was now older—three

and thirty. Surely in that span of time he'd taken a wife, fathered a family. The thought, hardly new, was still shattering. That she might witness such a thing—his bride and children—was more hurtful to her than anything that had passed before.

Father, please. Shut my eyes, my heart, to his happiness. Keep us apart. I don't begrudge him a full life. I'm simply haunted by what might have been.

The pillow slip was cold against her damp cheek. All around her in the humid June night, the girls slept, some fitful, some soundly. At last she dozed, but when she did her dreams were full of old fears and blighted hopes, and she awakened wearier than before.

∞

As she alighted from the coach in Pittsburgh, Eden realized she needn't have worried about being recognized. Grime covered her from head to toe, and her traveling suit was no longer blue but a dusty, gritty gray. The Black Bear Hotel rose up in three-storied splendor, as much as a log structure could, its wide piazza so reminiscent of Philadelphia architecture she almost felt at home. To her surprise, a small welcoming committee awaited, but for a few frantic minutes she and Stephen were preoccupied, counting ten children instead of twelve, as two boys had snuck off to the waterfront.

"Elliot, my old friend! Is it really you?" The booming voice belonged to a lanky man in a fine top hat descending the hotel steps. Clapping Stephen on the back, he gave an appraising glance at the children and winked. "A fine group of Philadelphians you've brought me. We'll turn them into Pittsburghers yet."

"I certainly hope so," Stephen replied with his usual gusto. "Miss Lee, this is Hugh O'Hara, my old friend from college."

He took Eden's elbow and made introductions, then looked toward the feminine figure in back of the judge. "This can't be your daughter Isabel, surely?"

The young woman nodded from her position beneath the hotel's shady eve, obviously reluctant to step into the noon sun. Though her features were partially obscured by a wide-brimmed bonnet, Eden could see she was exquisitely dressed and very pretty.

"The apple of my eye," the judge responded with a smile, motioning them toward the porch.

"So this is Pittsburgh." Stephen guided Eden up some steps, where they turned and took in the view. "I daresay it bears no resemblance to the Fort Pitt I remember."

"The old fort has been dismantled, all but one bastion, and we've nearly the numbers to become incorporated as a town." The pride in Judge O'Hara's features bespoke years of personal toil and planning. "If you'll look down Market Street toward the Monongahela, you'll see a few public buildings and signs of industry. New structures are springing up by the day. We've a courthouse and jail, some fine homes . . ."

But Eden was barely listening. La Belle Riviere stretched before her like molten silver, toward western lands she'd only dreamed of. She hadn't expected Pittsburgh to be so breathtaking, nor so mountainous or treed. So unlike Philadelphia.

As the children crowded round, the judge looked them over soberly. "I'm sure you're all tired and in need of a good meal. Tomorrow, once you're rested, we'll welcome you with a dinner party at River Hill. Until then, the Black Bear is the finest Pittsburgh offers in accommodations."

"I'm sure we'll be very comfortable," Eden reassured him with a smile.

Though they'd only just arrived, she was already becoming more at ease with her predicament. In a place this size, it was unlikely she would encounter any people from her past. Nor would a tradesman like Silas keep company with the leading citizens of Pittsburgh, surely. For now, other more pleasant matters awaited. She and the girls were in urgent need of baths.

39

*To what happy accident is it that
we owe so unexpected a visit?*

OLIVER GOLDSMITH

A floating walnut staircase. French wallpaper and mirrors. Creamy Wedgwood china and silver-handled cutlery. River Hill, Eden decided, was a charming blend of rusticity and gentility. The men and women filling the large parlor were wigless, unlike their Philadelphia counterparts, though their clothing was nearly as fine. Not one Quaker was in sight, nor were the foundlings, who, in their Sabbath best, had been whisked away by a housekeeper and two maids upon their arrival. They were to have a children's party out of doors, and from their excited chatter, they seemed not to mind the separation one whit.

"Miss Lee, I've never seen you looking so lovely," Stephen said as she entered the foyer on his arm. "I think the West agrees with you."

She smiled and smoothed a fold of her gown a bit self-consciously. "If so, I have you and Harriet to thank for that."

Still, she wondered what her Quaker friends would think to see her in countless yards of Spitalfields silk, a double strand of pearls about her throat. A gift from Harriet before they'd departed.

To their left, three sets of French doors were open to the riverside, and the setting sun gilded the water so beguilingly she stood transfixed. The parlor's furnishings and window dressings were a pleasing mix of diamonds and stripes in worsted damask, and an immense case clock chimed eight along a paneled wall. The large room was filling fast, and the temperature was rising accordingly.

Eden held her breath, then released it in relief. She didn't know a soul. They were making the rounds with Judge O'Hara now, meeting Pittsburgh's leading lights, and Eden was vaguely aware of Isabel standing near the parlor door, a vexed expression on her face. It brought back the past with a vengeance, reminding her of Elspeth's moods and whims. Was the judge's daughter a trifle spoiled?

"Yes, we'll begin apprenticeship negotiations in a few days," Stephen was saying to an elderly, treble-chinned gentleman. "Miss Lee will be overseeing the girls and I'll assign the boys. Our goal is to make sure the children are well placed and all parties satisfied."

A difficult task, Eden reflected, one to be handled carefully—and prayerfully. She'd grown so fond of the children the past three weeks and would be sorry to see them go, Clara especially. The girl was terrified of being bound to strangers and clung to Eden like a burr.

"Miss Lee, is it?" A tall, bejeweled woman clasped Eden's gloved hand. "And how do your Philadelphia sensibilities find the wilds of Pittsburgh?"

Eden smiled. "You may well convert me. The air is fresher, the view unsurpassed. I shall be sad to leave at summer's end."

"Well said. Not everyone is so kind, I'm afraid. You and Mr. Elliot must come for supper soon at our home on Cherry Street. My husband and I have long had an interest in the education and welfare of orphans."

"In that case, we're at your beck and call," Stephen told her warmly. "There's nothing I like better than discussing—"

A momentary hush in the large room made them turn. Another arrival?

"Ah, at last." Judge O'Hara's resonant voice overrode the conversations swirling around them as he glanced toward the parlor door. Isabel was threading her way toward them through the press of guests, a man following. "Stephen, Miss Lee, allow me to introduce my good friend and business partner."

Isabel stepped into their circle, transformed, beaming. The tall figure at her side became clear, and Eden's composure collapsed. She went completely still. The fan she held fluttered to a stop.

Silas.

"My apologies for arriving late. Business, ye ken." His rustic Scots speech had mellowed to a more refined lilt, smooth and self-effacing. He was looking at Stephen Elliot, extending a hand. He hadn't yet seen her, and Eden felt an overwhelming urge to pull back—disappear. Stephen shook his hand heartily, inquiring after some business matter, to which Silas answered thoughtfully.

Dumbstruck, Eden drank in every freshly shaven, tailored inch of him. Clad in rich, charcoal broadcloth, he looked the equal of any man she'd seen in Philadelphia. His ivory cravat set off his deeply tanned face and turned his eyes a keen, unforgettable green.

Her heart was pounding beneath her stays, as loud as the clock chiming nine across the room. When Silas turned from Stephen to her, she met his eyes reluctantly. His handsome, composed features went slack. He looked . . . stricken. Speechless, he shot a questioning glance at Stephen before returning to her. Did he think Stephen was her husband?

"Mr. Ballantyne, permit me to introduce Miss Eden Lee, assistant director of the Philadelphia Foundling Hospital." Stephen's warm voice reached out to her, jarring her into coherency.

Her voice came out a whisper. "Good evening, Mr. Ballantyne."

"Miss Lee."

She recovered first, opening her fan and forcing a practiced if tremulous smile.

"Ballantyne Boatworks, isn't it?" Stephen asked. "Soon to be Ballantyne Ironworks?"

"Aye, in time," Silas answered.

"In record time," Judge O'Hara echoed with a knowing smile. "Since Silas arrived in '85, Pittsburgh's had a hard time keeping up with him. You've no doubt heard of the brigantine he's building, the *Lady Liberty*. One hundred thirty-eight feet on the keel with a twenty-foot beam. He's even begun to traffic with New Orleans despite the trade restrictions . . ."

No longer listening, Eden tried to anchor herself. But the pain sweeping through her heart was so intense she felt a childish desire to burst into tears. Though she didn't dare look at him, she felt his eyes return to her as she fluttered her fan, as if he doubted it was she.

Mercifully, they soon went in to dinner in pairs, her partner a young lawyer whose name she couldn't remember. At least her frantic prayers had been answered, for she and Silas were seated at opposite ends of the table. In the minutes that followed, she had no recollection of what she ate. If she looked up, she would have a sidelong view of Silas over the wealth of roses that graced the table's center. Mostly she kept her eyes on her plate, glad when a berry sorbet was set before her, half-melted in the heat, its mint garnish wilted.

Bursts of children's laughter erupted beyond the open French doors, merry and familiar. Eden tried to concentrate on this, not the beloved Scots voice wooing her at table's end with quiet talk of cargo and transport fees and New Orleans. She took a sip of champagne, something she usually shunned, and felt its bracing bubbles clear to her toes. What had the judge said earlier? Business partner . . . good friend?

Oh, Silas, you've done so very well. I never doubted you would.

Seated beside him, Isabel was clearly pleased, peppering the conversation with business matters she obviously knew much about. It seemed Eden had only imagined her vexed expression. They made a striking couple—he so tall and she so tiny.

"Do you like to dance, Miss Lee?"

Numb with dismay, she'd scarcely spoken to the gentleman beside her and felt a twinge of guilt. "Oh yes, I love music . . . dancing . . . though I've kept company with Friends— Quakers—for so long I fear I've forgotten how."

"Allow me the pleasure of reacquainting you with the allemande, then."

People were rising from the table, and there was little to be done except join in. Eden half expected to find Silas among the musicians in the adjoining ballroom, cradling his violin, but he partnered with Isabel instead. By midnight Eden had danced with nearly every man in the room save him. He'd not asked, and if he had, she doubted her trembling legs would have held her. One touch of his hand at her waist . . .

His presence was bringing it all back, unearthing the past she'd long buried. Her practiced smile was slipping as images crowded her head and heart. Hazy stairwell meetings. Scraps of penned Scriptures. Every stolen kiss.

I will betroth thee unto me forever.

And Silas—he seemed to be doing his level best not to look at her. When she brushed past him on the ballroom floor, he averted his eyes as she did, or tried to, yet she detected a fierce tension in his face.

At last it was over. Stephen was helping her into the coach amidst six giggling, exhausted girls to return to the hotel and sleep till breakfast and Sabbath service. As they pulled away from the lights of River Hill, Eden felt the black anguish of old take hold. Sleep—such a sweet, sought-after refuge—would not visit her this night.

40

No disguise can long conceal love
where it exists, or long feign it where
it is lacking.

François de La Rochefoucauld

Silas sought the familiar, hard-backed pew numbered twenty-seven, relieved Isabel would be too exhausted to attend services after the frolic at River Hill, thankful Hugh was indulgent enough to break the fourth commandment as he so often did. Silas had been tempted to do the same this sultry morning, but his church attendance of late had been less than stellar, given he was oft at the boatyard. *God, forgive me*, had become his frequent Sabbath prayer. This morning it had changed to something more desperate.

Lord, deliver me.

Numb, still stunned, he replayed the previous evening in his mind, painful as it all was. He'd arrived at River Hill in high spirits, if only because the whiskey boys were in custody, and he and the rest of the county could enjoy one evening in peace without brooding over the next bout of trouble. Dinner parties were a good venue to mix business with pleasure, and he'd wanted to broach the subject of another public enterprise, a lottery-backed levee to protect the riverbanks against flooding. He'd hoped to find support for the project among the guests at River Hill.

He leaned back in the pew as the clanging of the kirk bell yanked him out of his reverie. All around him congregants were entering and finding seats, preparing for worship. Despite the distraction, he couldn't dislodge the shock he'd felt seeing Eden again and prayed the tangle in his soul didn't show on his face. Seeing her had proved far more jarring than his encounter with Henry Turlock.

Fickle, unfaithful Eden.

When she'd raised those soulful eyes to his last night, he'd nearly fallen headlong into their blue depths, just as he had years before. Only she wasn't a timid blacksmith's daughter clad in simple homespun any longer, her fiery hair hanging down in girlish abandon and tied with a simple ribbon. The Eden who now haunted him was a woman wearing the richest silk he'd ever seen, the silver threads of her dress reflecting the light of a hundred candles, her body graceful and erect, her creamy neck and shoulders framed with a cascade of curls. He'd breathed in her rose-carnation scent from where he stood and watched her languidly swish her fan against the rising heat. If she was as shaken by their meeting as he, she gave no indication, save the slight tightening of her jaw as they'd stumbled through introductions.

He'd heard the Elliot party had arrived but had given it little thought. The philanthropist was known to him, if only through the *Pennsylvania Gazette*. Stephen Elliot made good press, and Silas admired his charitable bent. With that in mind, he'd gone to River Hill hoping to arrange for apprentices at the boatyard. The task of taking two unknown, half-grown boys and trying to steer them right was sobering. He'd have to lodge them, though he knew Jean Marie had an extra room. He'd have to clothe them, act as a sort of father to them. Yet he felt the Lord leading him to take on the responsibility, come what may.

The evening at O'Hara's had promised to settle a great many things. Instead it unleashed a Pandora's box of complications. For a few agonizing seconds he'd thought Eden married to the much older Elliot. The wrench of it still lingered.

He leaned back in the pew, wanting the service to begin, wishing the room would still. But a sudden commotion from behind was causing a stir, turning every head in the church. He gave a discreet tug to his overly tight cravat before looking over his shoulder. The Philadelphians were entering, Stephen Elliot herding the rambunctious boys and Eden shepherding the sleepy-eyed, yawning girls.

Across the humming, hallowed room, her eyes locked with his. Flummoxed to the core, Silas rose and went out.

⸎

Eden lowered her head as Silas exited, the pain she'd felt upon seeing him last night pummeling her afresh. She should have realized he'd be at the First Presbyterian Church, the very one within walking distance of their hotel. In Philadelphia, Pine Street Presbyterian had been her Sabbath home, as it was the Elliots'. She'd not thought to attend anywhere else this morning, though Pittsburgh boasted several denominations.

She glanced at Stephen, half expecting him to comment on Silas's abrupt departure, but thankfully there were so many people coming and going it seemed to have escaped his notice. Still, she felt an overwhelming longing to be back in Philadelphia, amidst the safety and sameness of life there. When troubled, she would escape to her spinning balcony or sit and rock the foundling babies in the hospital nursery, savoring their exquisite newness. Here there was no such respite, only an aching, unrelieved emptiness, and the nagging certainty she'd encroached upon Silas's life and he was begrudging of her presence. Biting her lip, she bent her head.

Lord, please help redeem this difficult situation. You're the only one who can.

∞

The June Sabbath promised a fine day for a walking tour of Pittsburgh. With the sun tucked behind high clouds in a lapis sky, the weather had turned slightly cooler, coaxing them outside. Below, the three rivers glinted gray then blue as the clouds shifted in leisurely fashion. Carrying a lace parasol, Eden followed Stephen down dusty streets devoid of the lamps that lined Philadelphia thoroughfares, a dozen children in their wake. Walking toward the point where Fort Pitt once reigned, they took note of a great many brick and timber buildings along a grid of streets in dire need of curbstone walks.

A post office, a printer, a glass-front mercantile, a jail, and a courthouse were but a few of the newest buildings. Eden grew dizzy looking at so many shingles. Clock makers. Tanners. Hatters. Weavers. Saddlers. Tinners. Wheelwrights. Sail makers. A ferry cut through the glittering water on the Monongahela side to an enormous sandbar where buckwheat was grown.

"'Tis bigger than I expected," Eden admitted, looking back to the eastern swell of hills and wondering where Silas lived.

"I'll wager it will become the Birmingham of America," Stephen replied. "One day the coal coming out of these hills will turn the air black with soot."

They spent the afternoon along the point. There the children explored the remains of Fort Pitt and the King's Garden, and Eden distributed the picnic lunch packed for them by hotel staff. She tried to savor the beauty of the day but kept returning to the crush of events the last four and twenty hours. Would she never forget the shock of last night or Silas striding out of church this morning?

Stephen, thankfully, kept up a steady discourse. "I've arranged a boat trip for the children," he told her. "Silas Ballantyne has a small sloop perfect for a day trip and a bit of fishing upriver on the morrow. I don't suppose you care to go along."

"No!" she burst out before amending, "Only if you need me." Fingering a pleat on her dress, she wondered if she should tell him about her overriding desire to leave Pittsburgh as soon as possible, upsetting his carefully made plans. "I'd rather spend the time doing paperwork, preparing for the apprenticeship meetings."

Nodding, he pulled the brim of his hat lower. "I think one or two of the girls may want to remain behind as well. No doubt we'll have plenty of boatmen to keep anyone from falling overboard." He frowned and reached into his coat pocket. "I had a letter from Harriet waiting when we arrived."

"Oh?" Eden brightened.

"I'm afraid it brings some unsettling news." He opened it slowly, as if weighing the wisdom of sharing the contents. "It's early yet, but Dr. Rush has confirmed a yellow fever outbreak along the waterfront. It appears Haitian immigrants brought it ashore."

"Yellow fever?" The news was more than unsettling, though the city had its share of disease, especially in summer. "Is Harriet all right?"

"At this posting, yes. But she fears an epidemic and has advised us to stay in Pittsburgh till the danger passes. I pray the trouble will be short-lived, but one never knows."

Lord, no. She could imagine the quarantine now in place. Yet she held on to the hope they could place the children quickly and return east earlier than planned. Why, she'd wanted to pack her trunk this very morning. The thought of being here through the summer, perhaps beyond . . .

"The papers will soon carry word of it, and we'll keep up with the outbreak that way." The heaviness edging his voice led to darker thoughts.

Eden knew how helpless the foundling babies were against disease. And there was Constance Darby, Betsy Simms—and Elspeth. Elspeth would have arrived by now, and she'd be walking into . . . death.

"I'll write to Harriet tonight and assure her we'll stay on here. In the meantime, we'll pray for Philadelphia and our friends and interests there."

The chicken and biscuit she'd just eaten sat uneasily in her stomach, aggravated by the dull ache behind her eyes that was now building in light of the letter and her dashed hopes. "Would you mind if I take the girls and return to the hotel a bit earlier than planned?"

"Of course not," he said benignly. "But can you find your way back?"

She stood and brushed crumbs from her skirt, glancing at the congested hill. "Up Penn Street to Fifth, if I remember."

"Very well, then. We'll meet you for supper later."

They trooped up the hill as far as Fourth Street, winded and perspiring, when a great, shaggy object bounded toward them, scattering the squealing girls. Slowing her steps, Eden shifted her parasol and squinted against the sun's glare as a dog came into focus. For a few disorienting moments, she was cast back to the past, to a lonesome meadow overhung with clouds and dotted with sheep, hazy as a dream.

Sebastian?

It could be no other, the telltale cropped tail and ears shattering her uncertainty. He seemed to know her, truly. Stunned, she dropped to one knee alongside the quiet street and sank a hand into his lush fur. The pronounced gray about his nose and whiskers turned her a bit melancholy.

"You're older, aye, but still just as handsome." *As is your master.*

He nuzzled her quivering chin, sniffing at her skirts as if to make sure it was she. The girls gathered round and took turns petting him, laughing when he thumped his tail and barked in glee. Amazement trickled through her when she remembered the last time she'd seen him. Had Sebastian followed Silas that snowy day? All the way here?

With a sudden bark, he turned and ran away, disappearing down a narrow alley toward the waterfront. Eden longed to follow—but didn't.

∞

Eden's gloved hand had just touched the stair banister when a clerk stopped her. "Miss Lee? I have a note for you."

She hid her surprise, waiting till the girls traipsed up the carpeted stairs to their rooms before crossing to the front desk, where a sealed paper waited. The indigo wax bore a bold *B*, and she ran a finger over it, awash with trepidation. Silas? There could be no mistaking the sender. This was best read in the privacy of her room.

Once there, she splashed cool water on her flushed face, taking a deep breath and trying to untie the knot in her stomach. The note lay unopened on a desk by the window, the Allegheny gliding idly by the glass. Her fingers shook as she broke the seal and drank in the familiar slant of each letter.

Eden, we must talk. Silas

She felt a swell of disappointment. All that fine foolscap and wax for five terse words? Her heart picked up in rhythm. She wasn't sure what she'd expected. A meeting place? A time and date? Perhaps he was simply letting her adjust to the idea first. Or was trying to do so himself.

In the warm confines of Grant's Tavern, the aroma of game pies and beeswax candles lingered. Though the dining room had emptied half an hour before, Silas continued to sit at a corner table by an open window, the lights of Pittsburgh spread before him in the river valley below. Would that Eden had come in winter when the hills wore a silvery-white coat and the stench of the waterfront was subdued. As it was, dust and insects clouded the summer air, dissipating just a bit as night moved in and spread a mist over the water, long and white as a bridal veil.

"Care for a dram of whiskey?"

He glanced up to find Jean Marie holding a glass and bottle. "Aye," he said, though he usually shunned the stuff, relegating it to weddings and wakes. Lately it reminded him of the whiskey boys, which lessened the guilty pleasure.

She perched in the chair opposite and pushed the offering toward him. He took a drink, glad for the bracing brunt of it after so long a day. Though it burned his throat, it spread languorous warmth to all the rest of him, easing his turmoil.

"You look tired tonight—and no wonder." Her appraising gaze raked him with unusual vigor. "First you frolic at River Hill, and then you stride out of church before the service even begins." Leaning nearer, she whispered, "Your unorthodox courtship habits are the talk of Pittsburgh."

"Wheest!" The glass came down with a clatter, sloshing amber liquid onto the tabletop.

Her mouth bowed in a knowing smile. "How many hearts must you break? Mary Duncan, the banker's daughter . . . Jenny Jones, sister to the doctor . . . Kesiah Jenkins, Reverend Cosby's niece—"

He shot her a warning look. "Who looks to have been baptized in a pickle barrel, I remember you saying."

Undaunted, she continued. "Frances Epperson, Bess Aldrich, Isabel O'Hara. In all this time not one of them so much as turns your handsome head. And then a lady from Philadelphia comes to town . . ."

His jaw tightened.

"And it is love at first look."

"Or so the gossips say." His gaze returned to the window, where a sudden gust of wind wafted over him and nearly snuffed the candle flame.

She sat back and crossed her arms, dark brows nearly touching in contemplation. "Something happened at River Hill to set their tongues wagging."

He shifted uncomfortably in his chair. Was his shock at seeing Eden so apparent, then? Granted, she'd recovered faster than he . . .

"You are the most eligible bachelor in Pittsburgh, no? People are watching." She refilled his glass. "I hear the newly arrived Miss Lee is lovely in both appearance and manner."

"Aye," he admitted grudgingly, ignoring the whiskey.

"If you were to ask my opinion—which you won't, stubborn Scot that you are—I would tell you that I admire your discernment. Choosing a Philadelphia bride is not only wise but considerate and will lead to less discord among your brokenhearted admirers here."

Silas nearly rolled his eyes. "I've no wish to wed the lass. I've only just met her." The half-truth stung, as did the intricacies of their predicament. How was he to explain such

374

a relationship? Not once had he spoken of his time in York County. He had no wish to break the silence now.

"I would proceed cautiously if I were you. Isabel is not so pretty when she is angry, and her dear, widowed papa dotes on her a trifle much. Things could become . . . ugly."

I've not encouraged her, he thought. No more than the others. But indeed he had. That night at River Hill he'd kissed her, spurred on by the need of the moment and Jean Marie's heartfelt words. *You need to be married to something besides boats.* But there had been no talk of marriage since, nor any further intimacies. He'd made sure of that.

Though Isabel and other lasses had flirted and cajoled and tempted him, he'd come up against a wall, a promise made and kept. Having given his heart long ago, there was nothing left to give. Though he'd tried to move past it, some invisible cord seemed to bind him to Eden Lee, no matter the distance or passage of time.

Jean Marie motioned to the glass. "You look in need of some spirits, Silas Ballantyne."

"Nae," he told her, pushing away from the table. "I simply want a conversation. Some honest answers. Nothing more."

41

Hopes, what are they? Beads of morning strung on slender blades of grass.

WILLIAM WORDSWORTH

The next week slipped past, the heat ravishing the hotel's rose garden and turning the entwined rivers into a shimmer of blue. Eden spent the time meeting with prospective employers and masters, trying to match each girl's interests and temperament with the proper people before binding all parties in writing. After much forethought and prayer, final arrangements were made, to everyone's relief.

Annie and Ruth were to be housemaids in town. Abigail was assigned to a dressmaker on Market Street, and Molly to Grant's Tavern as a maid. Helen was to work for a hatter, Clara a chandler. Stephen placed the boys with his usual panache, confident of a good outcome. Two of the lads, Jacob and Luke, had been apprenticed to Ballantyne Boatworks, the rest to other tradesmen.

Tonight was the culmination of their efforts. A small reception was to be held in the hotel's parlor, after which the new employers would take their apprentices home to new trades and new lives. Excitement—hope—seemed so palpable it lessened the angst of separation.

"'Twill be lonesome without them," Eden remarked, though in truth she was tired and in need of some quiet.

"We'll see them oft enough in the weeks to come," Stephen assured her. "I look forward to visiting each situation and monitoring their progress."

She nodded, thinking how conscientious he was in all the little details that mattered. "You were right to bring them here. Pittsburgh is growing, and they'll grow along with it."

He extended his arm. "Shall we? 'Tis almost seven o'clock."

They passed from the foyer to the parlor, where several open doors invited a breeze. The sunburnt lawn just beyond was crowded with their high-spirited charges. Turning toward the crystal punch bowl where she would play hostess, Eden caught a glimpse of herself in a gilt-edged mirror. Startled, she put a hand to her carefully coiffed hair. Why did it suddenly matter how she looked when it hadn't before? The glass reflected smudges of sleeplessness beneath her eyes, and the summer heat had turned her cheeks primrose. She looked, she lamented, anything but cool, prim, composed.

When the clock struck seven, Silas was the first to arrive, and what little courage Eden had fled. He was freshly shaven, his hair riotously curling along his collar, just as it had been long ago by the forge's fire. Tonight was nearly as hot.

Stephen thrust out a welcoming hand. "Silas, you surprise me. Last I looked you were knee-deep in cordage at the pier, and now you're here ahead of schedule. The boys are still talking about that boat trip earlier this week."

"No doubt we'll be eating catfish for a fortnight or better," he said with a wry grin, looking Eden's way. "Miss Lee."

She nodded in acknowledgment from behind the table, glad to be occupied, eyes on the cups she was to fill. Silver étagères of sweetmeats stood on both sides of the punch bowl, an enticing offering of sugared almonds, macaroons, candied flowers, and muscovado-sprinkled cakes. Stephen's doing, surely, she thought, groping for a distraction. He'd spoken of a confectioner on Market Street. She snuck a candied violet, more from nerves than hunger, her eyes on the children as Stephen went outside to speak with them.

When a sudden shadow fell over her, she couldn't look up, couldn't meet Silas's eyes. "Would you like some punch, Mr. Ballantyne?"

"Aye . . . if you please."

She ladled the liquid into a cup, hands atremble. Would she slosh it onto the linen tablecloth? His finely tailored suit? Nay, it was her own dress she spoiled, staining the lace overlay of her skirt a brilliant berry red. Her face, she knew, was the same hue.

Lord, help. She'd forgotten her handkerchief.

Silas reached into his waistcoat pocket, withdrew his own handkerchief, and passed it to her. She took it gratefully, eyes down as disbelief crowded in. 'Twas her own cloth, spun on her beloved wheel, his initials embroidered in a frayed corner. Emotion flooded her.

His voice was low, hesitant. "Did you get my note?"

"Y-yes." Her voice was as unsteady as her hand. She dabbed at the stain on her skirt, afraid to look at him.

"I thought—I hoped—we might talk. I can send a carriage round—"

"Nay . . . please." She clutched the hankie harder, sensing his own disquiet, unsure if it was her refusal or Isabel's sudden entrance that most upended him.

"Silas, there you are! I thought you'd be waiting in the foyer."

The censure in her tone raised the fire in Eden's cheeks, and she looked past Silas's broad shoulder to find Isabel looking directly at her, brown eyes smoldering. Abandoning her father's arm, she drew nearer, plucking a macaroon from a tray with a gloved hand, her voice equally cloying. "No doubt the sweets are a trifle tempting tonight. Come, Silas, and introduce me to your hirelings."

Hirelings? Jacob and Luke? Silas said little in return, made no move to do as she bid. Judge O'Hara filled the gap, stepping between them and smiling at Eden. "Miss Lee, a bit of punch would do me well in this heat."

"Of course," she said, trying to smile under the weight of Isabel's gaze. At least her hand had ceased its shaking. She passed him his cup, spilling nary a drop.

He surveyed her with thoughtful eyes. "Stephen tells me you're like a daughter to him, devoted to the foundling hospital as you've been. I was surprised, given your graces, to find you're not fresh from the Young Ladies' Academy of Philadelphia but rural York County." He took a sip and continued. "I believe, if I'm not mistaken, that Silas once apprenticed there."

"'Tis no secret," Silas said. "'Twas long ago."

The judge drained his cup. "Might you know friends of mine there, Miss Lee? The Greathouses?"

Eden groped for words as full-fledged panic struck. She looked toward Silas entreatingly, wishing Stephen was near and could steer the conversation in a safer direction.

"The Greathouses are known by many," Silas said evenly. He turned toward a woman in dark blue silk, slim and straight-backed, who was looking at Eden as intently as Isabel. "Miss Lee, I believe you've met Jean Marie, proprietress of Grant's Tavern. I have rooms there."

Eden felt a tug of surprise. "You . . . and Sebastian?"

He smiled in affirmation, and Jean Marie took the cup of punch Eden offered. Eden had spent the afternoon atop Grant's Hill with Molly two days past, meeting the staff and trying to put the girl at ease in the busy tavern. She was unaware Silas boarded there.

"You must wander up the hill and visit us again soon, mademoiselle," Jean Marie told her as Isabel laid a hand on Silas's sleeve.

"Come, Silas," Isabel urged, her displeasure plain. "I must meet your apprentices."

They moved toward the French doors, the judge following, leaving Jean Marie alone with Eden at the table. Eden invited her to partake, eyes on the cut of Silas's coat as he walked away. "Please, have some refreshments. Once the children come in, I'm afraid you'll be left to nibble on crumbs."

As Jean Marie surveyed the offerings, Sebastian gave a shrill bark from a side door and made straight for the table. The children spilled in after him, trying to catch his wagging tail as he rushed Eden and licked her hand, sniffing the table-cloth and eyeing the étagères greedily. A ripple of amusement passed over the room before Silas intervened and herded the lot of them outside again.

Leaning nearer, Jean Marie reached for a cake and whispered, "Which confection do you fancy, Miss Lee? Besides the handsome Scotsman, I mean."

Eden lowered her eyes, unable to resist a slight smile. "Macaroons . . . though they don't hold a candle to him."

With a knowing chuckle, Jean Marie joined Stephen across the room as other guests came for punch and the children reappeared. Perspiration beaded Eden's brow, and she dabbed it away with Silas's now-stained handkerchief, amazed that he'd kept it, or wanted to. After her outright rejection of him years before—and again moments ago when he'd asked to talk—she doubted he'd want it back. Yet he'd offered to send a carriage round . . .

Oh, Silas, I care not to revisit that night.

The Black Swan Inn loomed dark in her thoughts like the blackest scourge. She'd told no one about what had happened there. How could she? How did one speak of the shock and shame? 'Twas a wounding she had no words for. Though she couldn't know, she sensed Silas's mind was awash with the same memories. It seemed only yesterday that they'd stood in the inn's darkened stairwell and he'd asked, "Eden, what has happened here?" She'd been unable to tell him. She'd simply wanted to protect him. And her silence, or so she'd thought, had set him free.

Her gaze fastened on his handsome profile as he stood near a window, deep in conversation with Stephen. His two young apprentices stood at his side, their eager faces tipped up as if hanging on his every word, full of promise and hope. Her heart gave another lurch.

Lord, please let them have the happy ending I cannot.

42

*Love and scandal are the best
sweeteners of tea.*

HENRY FIELDING

At dawn Eden awakened, expecting girlish chatter and giggling, but all that met her ears was a bird's sweet song. The
girls were gone, and the day stretched before her to do as she
pleased. Jean Marie had spoken of the beautiful vistas to
be had out the Greensburg Road along the Allegheny River.
She remembered it now, perhaps providentially. Craving a bit
of quiet, she decided to go to the nearest livery stable and
procure a carriage. But first she'd join Stephen in the dining
room below. Breakfast was one meal she couldn't miss, not
with the Black Bear's flaky biscuits, orange marmalade, and
oversized cups of congou tea.

The foyer was gloriously empty, the tap of her heels the
only sound in it. Had Stephen overslept without his charges
to wake him? She took their usual table by a window and
settled in to enjoy the view, looking up when an Oriental
woman brought tea. For all its rusticity, Pittsburgh boasted

a surprisingly diverse population. Smiling her thanks, Eden looked past panes of glass toward twin waterfronts that were already bustling. Masts and rigging jutted upright, their stark canvas reflecting the rising sun.

Where, she wondered for the hundredth time, was Ballantyne Boatworks?

In a few minutes Stephen took his usual place across the table, easing his hat off his head, eyes questioning. "And how is the belle of Pittsburgh this morning?"

"I'm hardly that," she protested with a smile, stirring sugar into her cup.

"Oh? At least one of its citizens seems to think so."

"Sebastian, surely."

He cocked an eyebrow. "Who?"

"Mr. Ballantyne's dog."

He chuckled. "I see you haven't lost your sense of humor in this heat, though I have detected a certain tension about you."

Avoiding his eyes, she took a sip of tea. "I'm just a bit homesick and keep wondering if we shouldn't leave now that the children are placed, given the situation in Philadelphia."

He gave her an apologetic glance. "I'd like nothing better than to go east myself. But President Washington himself has just left the city, and others are evacuating as well."

The unwelcome words marred the beauty of the morning, and she felt disbelief take hold. "But I'd thought—hoped—it was a false alarm."

"The papers are now saying it's an epidemic."

A chill spilled over her. "And the hospital? Harriet?"

His eyes were grieved. "I've written to Harriet asking her to join us here. And I've just received word from Dr. Rush." He took a letter from his waistcoat and unfolded it slowly, putting on his spectacles. "The news doesn't sound encouraging. You know Rush, he's not one to make rash judgments. Yet he writes, 'Shafts of death fly closer and closer every day. All is thick and melancholy gloom.' Even if we were to return, we couldn't be of help. The hospital has been locked to protect the foundlings and staff against infection. Philadelphia is a closed door, my dear. We'd best return to matters at hand, like—"

A plate of biscuits appeared. Eden hardly noticed as the Oriental woman padded away.

"Like Silas Ballantyne," he finished.

She nearly flinched, though he lowered his tone as a couple came into the room. "Last night at the reception I overheard Judge O'Hara say that Silas apprenticed in York County. And I couldn't help but wonder if by any chance . . ."

"Yes," she breathed, still overwhelmed by it all.

His eyes mirrored surprise. "He was the apprentice in your household? The man you were betrothed to?"

She simply nodded, eyes on her tea. There was a stilted pause in which all the angst of the past returned to her tenfold.

"Miss Lee, unless I'm gravely mistaken about the man's character, why on earth did you part with such a prize?"

She paused, trying to stem her rising emotion. "I didn't— willingly. Someone else intervened and came between us."

"Well, there's no one intervening now," he said quietly.

Oh, but there is, she thought as she reached for her handkerchief.

Isabel O'Hara—and her father.

⤬

Tobacco. Beeswax. Leather. It was the essence of River Hill, the unforgettable scent that had greeted Silas when he'd first come to Pittsburgh and Hugh O'Hara had opened his library to him. A fine book had the power to improve a man's mind, especially a tradesman's, the judge said, and Silas was but one who made a regular trek out Braddock's Road to borrow a tome or two and revel in the comfortable, unpretentious grandeur that was River Hill.

This morning the housekeeper met him at the door and led him down a familiar hall to the judge's book-lined study. Silas hoped to talk to Hugh alone first, then Isabel, and had prayed accordingly. Still, trepidation ticked inside him with every step. He'd rather face the whiskey boys than the man who'd been a friend and financier to him for so long. But since Eden's arrival, it had all come clear. He'd deal honestly about matters from the outset. His faith required nothing less.

"Silas, come in!" The warmth of Hugh's greeting cut him afresh. Rising from behind a massive desk, Hugh gestured to a wing chair. "I thought you'd be at the boatyard with those two new apprentices of yours."

"They're in good hands, and I'll soon be back," he said. "I apologize for arriving unannounced."

"Coffee? Brandy?"

Silas took a chair. "Nae. Just conversation."

Hugh's gaze clouded. "Not about the Turlocks, I hope. They've been a bit too quiet since their release from jail. It bodes ill, I fear. Or have you a business matter in mind?" His tone lightened. "The mercantile, perhaps, or the ironworks? Something to do with Isabel?"

Silas took a measured breath. "I'm here to talk about Eden Lee."

"Miss Lee?" All the expectancy left Hugh's face. "Word is she's anxious to leave here and return to Philadelphia."

Was she? Even with the fever spreading? The knot of turmoil in Silas's chest tightened. "I've asked to speak with her."

"Speak with her?" Hugh's eyes narrowed. "Surely you're jesting. You've only just met her."

Silas looked down at his branded thumbs, voice low. "There's much you don't know, much I've not spoken of regarding the past. Miss Lee and I were once betrothed."

"Once? In York County?" Hugh gave a derisive snort. "That has little bearing on the present, surely."

The ensuing pause was rife with tension. Clearly the judge was in a defensive posture usually reserved for the courtroom bench. Silas decided to meet it head on. "As a lawman, you well know the legalities involved. Until a pre-engagement is fairly and mutually dissolved, no future marriage is lawful. As far as I'm concerned, the betrothal still stands."

Hugh set his jaw. "Why did the two of you not wed?"

"She refused me—"

"And what if she refuses you again?"

"She well may." The thought was razor-sharp. "But it will not keep me from asking."

Hugh leaned forward in his chair, incredulity hardening his features. "My daughter is willing, yet you dally with another."

Silas's voice held firm, his gaze level. "I plan to speak with Isabel, to explain."

Hugh gave a vehement shake of his head. "Nay, I won't have you break her heart unnecessarily. When Miss Lee refuses you a second time and you come to your senses, Isabel will be waiting—and none the wiser."

Silas regarded him in surprise. Did Hugh still want him as a son-in-law? Even on such shallow terms? He could give Isabel his name, a home, mayhap children. But not his heart. "I cannot marry a woman I do not love."

Hugh batted the air as if dismissing the thought, then belied his distress by reaching for a decanter and pouring himself some brandy. "Men wed for all kinds of reasons, understand, the least of which is love. I married Isabel's mother for her dowry and expect no less of you. My daughter is quite well situated, as you know. Half of Pittsburgh is yours for the taking. I doubt the reluctant Miss Lee has a shilling to her name."

Nae, perhaps not a shilling, but a gentle and quiet spirit, worth more than any coin. Or so Silas believed. Sadly, it was a quality Isabel lacked. But he stayed silent, letting the judge expend his anger.

"Silas, I'm surprised by you, I must say." Hugh took a swallow of brandy and set the glass down a bit forcefully. "You seem to forget our business dealings, which will come to an abrupt end if you should wed anyone but Isabel." The words, quietly spoken, carried an ultimatum nevertheless.

Silas stood, knowing there was little left to discuss. "I regret it has come to this, but my convictions stand."

"You'll soon be back," Hugh said, downing the last of the brandy. "Remember, not a word to Isabel—"

"Come, Papa. Not a word?" The study door pushed open. "I've heard more than enough, truly." Isabel stepped into the room, face flushed, hands twisting a handkerchief into an ivory knot. "Leave us, Papa, please."

For one disorienting moment, Silas was cast back to York County, mired in the spitefulness now mirrored on Isabel's face. It was Elspeth he saw, poisonous in her malice, her lovely features contorted with rage.

The door shut behind Hugh, returning Silas to the present. Isabel was coming straight at him, steady as a sloop at full sail.

"How dare you come here and humiliate me in such a fashion, Silas Ballantyne—you, a former tradesman!" She smacked him hard on the cheek, then brought her other hand up when he stayed stoic.

He caught her wrist, his voice low. "Isabel, listen to reason."

"Reason? All I know is that you lied to me, led me to believe—"

"I never lied to you. Misled you, mayhap, with a single embrace." *Which I heartily regret.* He released her wrist. "There was no mention of marriage, ever."

"Your kiss was promise enough." She was crying now, though still furious, brown eyes hard as agates. "Yet all the while you were betrothed to another, a woman who wouldn't have you, thus breaking your bond—"

"The bond, as you call it, was never broken, not on my part. 'Tis why I've remained unwed till now. No other woman has had my heart—" He left off, overcome by the futility of the moment. He should be saying such heartfelt things to Eden, not Isabel. Isabel wouldn't accept his words till they turned in her favor. "I simply want to be honest with you and your father and state my intentions."

Her chin jutted in a stubborn, unforgiving line, so like Hugh's. "If you expect me to wish you well or be waiting when Miss Lee rejects you once again, you're sorely mistaken. I hope she laughs at your so-called intentions and all your future business prospects turn to ashes."

He said nothing more, relieved when she passed through the door Hugh had taken moments before. Left to see himself out, Silas trod the darkened hall to the foyer and then outside where his horse was tied to a hitch rail. He mounted and turned toward the main road, weary but resolute.

Every fiber of his being pulled him to town. He merely had to head to the Black Bear Hotel and settle matters once and for all, come what may. Turning onto the main road, the Monongahela a wash of blue alongside him, he breathed another prayer, a Scripture flashing to mind.

Many waters cannot quench love, neither can the floods

drown it: if a man would give all the substance of his house for love, it would utterly be condemned.

So, Lord, what should I do? he prayed.

In the silence of his heart he heard the answer.

Let her come to you.

43

*Absence diminishes little passions
and increases great ones, as wind
extinguishes candles and fans a fire.*

FRANÇOIS DE LA ROCHEFOUCAULD

Eden clutched Silas's handkerchief in one damp palm, the only visible sign of her disquiet, or so she hoped. All morning she'd taken pains with her appearance, the hotel bed weighted with one cast-off garment after another. The looking glass finally reflected a woman bent on a midsummer's walk. She'd settled on an ivory linen dress with lace fichu, clocked stockings, and leather slippers, an organdy cap imprisoning her curls. The midsummer sun begged for a wide-brimmed straw hat, so she chose one trimmed in rosettes and navy ribbon, anchoring it with two large hat pins.

Fortunately, at Judge O'Hara's invitation, Stephen had gone to River Hill after breakfast and was unaware of her slow walk down Penn Avenue to the Monongahela waterfront. Though she was becoming more familiar with the maze of Pittsburgh streets, she'd not ventured this far. The maid who tidied her room had given her directions, smiling slyly as if she was privy to the latest gossip.

As soon as Eden saw the quay, she regretted asking for help. Such a place could hardly be missed.

Ballantyne Boatworks took up a good quarter mile of waterfront, every inch teeming with shipwrights and carpenters and crew busy outfitting the vessels built there. She stood for a long time in an adjoining alley and tried to gather her courage. She'd last seen Silas at the hotel reception a fortnight before, when she'd refused his offer to send a carriage round. Ever since, she'd been haunted by the certainty her denial mattered little when any number of Pittsburgh belles would leap at the chance to be with him, including the lovely Isabel. Still, she was a knot of nerves, her prayer a pathetic plea.

Be Thou not far from me, O Lord my strength.

Despite her qualms regarding what she was about to do, she felt an overwhelming impulse to settle matters between them and part on good terms. She would honor his request to talk, given their history, if she could manage to skirt the issue of David Greathouse. It seemed to be what the Lord wanted of her as well. Yet more than anything, her desire to see Silas, to be alone with him—if only for a few final moments—was irresistible, if terrifying. She was in love with him, had never stopped loving him . . . though she'd tried.

A brisk wind tugged at the ribbons of her hat, and the smells of the waterfront washed over her. She breathed in the invigorating tang of freshly sawn timber, oakum, and pitch while wanting to cover her nose at the smell of mud and silt. Cargo crowded the loading docks—saltpeter, iron, sugar, hempen yarn, and more—stamped and bound for New Orleans.

Nowhere did she see Silas—or Sebastian. Her gaze swept the pier, finally finding Jacob and Luke, both straddling barrels, rope in their hands. Silas stood over them, sleeves rolled up, the pensive contours of his face twisting her heart even at a distance. By the time she reached them, he'd disappeared, leaving her to second-guess her coming. Might he not want to see her after all?

"Miss Lee, is that you?" Jacob jumped down from his perch and rushed toward her, Luke on his heels. "Mr. Ballantyne is teaching us to tie knots. See this?" He held up a tangle of rope, face beaming, hands spotted with pitch.

"Well done." She smiled back at him. "What sort of knot is it?"

"A midshipman's hitch," Jacob said. He elbowed Luke, his eyes widening in alarm. "Best get back to work. Mr. Ballantyne's a fine master, but Wallace, his head shipwright, is hard as iron."

They scampered away, leaving her alone on the sun-scorched dock as a thick-chested, half-scowling workman made his way toward her. Wallace? Suddenly she felt at sea, but the twinkle in his eyes when he faced her and his pleasing Scottish lilt soon set her at ease.

"Yer no doubt here to see the master, Miss Lee."

Surprise peppered her, though she tried to keep it from telling on her face. First the maid, and now this? Stephen had told her she was the talk of Pittsburgh, but she'd thought him joking. "Yes, please, Mr. . . . ?"

"Michael Wallace, at your service." He whisked a faded cap off his head and pointed toward a timbered building set back from the dock, the door ajar. "A lady like yerself needn't be too long in the sun—or in the presence of so many tradesmen."

A lull seemed to have seized the boatyard as one too many eyes turned her way. 'Twas a bold move to be seen in such a place, lady or no. She guessed she'd earned their scrutiny.

392

Lowering her head, she followed him past scaffolding and spars and massive coils of cordage to that open door. Rather than announce her, Mr. Wallace simply gave a nod and disappeared, leaving her alone on the threshold.

The office was small, well lit, and redolent of aromatic hemp. Wide windows afforded a view in all directions, surely a necessity for managing so busy a place. Unaware of her, Silas sat behind a large desk, head bent, penning something in a ledger. He looked tired, she thought, worry tugging at her. Even at the forge he'd done the work of two men. Here he wasn't simply a shipwright but a master, a juror, a landowner, and more. She'd heard about the ongoing trouble between the tax collectors and whiskey distillers, and it needled her now, deepening her concern.

"I'd rather wear out than rust out," he'd once said years before, echoing the words of the evangelist George Whitefield. She guessed he hadn't changed in that respect.

She took a silent, unsteady step, then another. The knot in her throat rivaled that of Jacob's rope. The bench to her left begged her to sit, but somehow she managed to cross to the desk, placing the freshly laundered handkerchief in front of him.

⤫

Silas looked up at Eden, blinked, and glanced at the neatly folded linen. Was she here to return the handkerchief . . . tell him she was leaving? Misery overrode the surprise that churned inside him. Forgetting to stand, he simply braced himself and leaned back in his chair, wary.

She glanced round the office. "So this is your domain."

A far cry from the forge. Or so her tone seemed to say. Silas looked around at the swirls of dust and less-than-spotless panes of glass and wished they were elsewhere. Somewhere pristine and private. Like his land downriver . . .

Pulling himself to his feet, he met her eyes and found them a lovely if red-rimmed blue. His awkwardness soared. He no longer knew what to say, to call her. Miss Lee? Eden?

Beloved.

"I met your master shipwright, a fellow Scotsman." She turned back to him with a tentative smile. "Mr. Elliot told me you paid passage to America for some of your workmen in exchange for their services."

He nodded, throat tight. "Most are indentured from five to seven years. Time enough to establish the boatyard, build a better life for themselves." He picked up a watch resting on a ledger, then returned it to his pocket, aware of his wrinkled shirt and rolled-up sleeves. He was, he thought ruefully, as unkempt as his office.

"'Tis an ambitious venture." She was studying him now as if trying to reconcile the man she'd once known with the one standing before her. "How—" She broke off and looked away, a splash of color pinking her cheeks.

"How do I afford such an arrangement?" he finished for her, wanting to reach out and tip her chin up with his hand so she'd look at him again. Did she think Hugh O'Hara . . . ?

"I—I'm sorry, I don't mean to pry. You've done so very well. You should be proud." Turning her back to him, she crossed to the largest window and looked out, clearly awed.

He found himself a bit weak-kneed, more at a loss for words than ever. The delicate contours of her profile, the alluring tilt of her hat, the fetching way she had her hands clasped behind her back . . . She wasn't the girl he'd once known. Time and experience had only deepened her appeal. She was so incredibly lovely his heart ached.

"Eden . . ." He came to stand beside her at the glass, wishing he'd not said her name, wondering if she minded. "When I first came here, I worked as a blacksmith at Fort Pitt. It didn't take long to realize I'd not get very far on such wages. I arrived with the coin I'd earned in York and was awarded a tract of land per the terms of my contract. It did not suit me, so I sold it. The land I wanted was too costly, so I took my father's violin . . ."

Her eyes went wide with anguish.

"To a collector in Philadelphia." He swallowed, struggling to frame what seemed reprehensible in hindsight. "I couldn't keep it, understand. It reminded me too much of the past . . . my father . . . you. The fiddle was appraised and fetched a handsome price. I was able to buy waterfront land and build the boatyard."

A tear spotted her cheek. He stepped back to retrieve the handkerchief she'd brought him and pressed it into her palm. He didn't dare dry her tears himself, though he wanted to. Badly.

She grew quiet, and regret riddled him afresh. Till now he hadn't let the weight of what he'd done take hold. In a sense he'd sold his birthright, his history, his Scots heritage. Or so her silence seemed to say. Or was she remembering all the music, their shared barn dance long ago? The many nights he'd played at taverns and frolics, for her? For their future?

His voice was low yet laden with emotion. "I may have given up the instrument, but not the memories. Nor thoughts of us." His voice fell away as an unwelcome presence filled the doorway. A sudden knocking was as jarring as a thunderclap.

She looked startled, confused. "I must go . . ."

He felt a sinking to his boots. Was this goodbye, then? She passed him back the handkerchief, but he shook his head. *I do not want it back*, he longed to say. *I only want . . . you.*

The knock came again. He answered it and sent a carpenter scurrying, then shut the door.

Her eyes held his all too briefly. "Please—send a carriage round, if you like."

He hesitated, surprised. A thread of hope, however tenuous, strengthened. "Later today—five o'clock?"

Her face held regret. "Mr. Elliot and I are having supper with the Brackenridges tonight. Tomorrow, perhaps?"

"Aye," he answered, tamping down his disappointment. Tomorrow was far better than the refusal he'd been handed a fortnight before.

44

For my heart is true as steel.
WILLIAM SHAKESPEARE

'Twas a carriage, Silas mused, fit for a bride. The Boston-made chaise was handsomely gilded and lined with crimson cloth, its leather top new and unweathered. The two horses harnessed to its genteel frame were a bit shabby, but the livery stable was busy today and he'd not complain. His only concern was that Eden be waiting. He seemed to traverse the short distance to the Black Bear Hotel in a sort of haze, half believing she'd change her mind at the last, just as she'd done years ago. He steeled himself against a fresh onslaught of pain and prayed.

Since she'd left the boatyard the day before, he'd felt a strange calm he couldn't explain. He'd lain awake in the heat of his room half the night, unaware of the whine of insects or the growl of thunder that threatened to mar the coming day. His only thought was of her. He'd told her he wanted to talk. She'd graciously agreed. And now he felt as dry as a well for words. Nigh speechless. Once he had her alone, what would he say?

Lord, please give me the words.

She was waiting not in the foyer but on the porch, slightly pale beneath her straw hat, her vibrant hair spiraling down, reminding him of the girl she'd once been. When he helped her into the carriage, he sensed her uneasiness—mayhap her reluctance—and dread sank like lead in his belly. He snapped the reins and the team shot forward in a swirl of dust, obscuring them from the stares of onlookers who tarried in the street or gawked out windows.

"Where are we going?" she asked, breaking the silence.

"Home," he replied.

∽

Home.

When he said it—firmly yet gently—Eden's fingers unclenched from her fan. He didn't mean Jean Marie's boardinghouse, surely. He was well beyond the outskirts of Pittsburgh now, going the opposite direction. Palms damp with anxiety beneath her snug gloves, she turned her eyes to the low clouds riding the horizon, gray with rain. Wooed by his nearness and the beauty unfolding all around them, she wished their destination was as far away as Philadelphia.

The Allegheny glided by on their left for several silent miles, faithful as a chaperone, its blue eye unblinking. When they turned away from it, the carriage slowed, flattening waist-high grasses and wildflowers before rolling to a gentle stop. From her perch on the edge of her seat, Eden spied a vast clearing and then a mountain of bricks. Several enormous shade trees were standing among a great many stumps, and she took in the timbered beginnings of a sizeable house.

She tore her gaze away as Silas's hands spanned her waist and lowered her to the ground, lingering. Trying to get her bearings, she put a hand to her hat as the wind threatened to tear it free. Silas was looking down at her the way he once had, returning her to a spring day in a wet woods when he'd untied her bonnet strings and first kissed her.

Oh, Lord, to go back and regain what was lost . . .

His voice was low and sure, easing her. "I've had the land but six months. The bricks are from Fort Pitt, enough to build a house, dependencies." They walked around the framework, and she looked up at two-story timbers backed by blue sky. "I've a fine carpenter and bricklayer who've agreed to build in exchange for a boat."

"'Tis beautiful—all of it. The river view . . ." She left off, overcome.

"I've decided to call it New Hope."

The name struck a chord deep inside her. *New Hope.* Not Ballantyne Hall or some Scottish title. It had special significance for him . . . for her, if only for a moment. Her hopes rose, then tumbled. There was no going back. As much as she'd like to turn the tide of years, too much had changed.

His hand was on her elbow now, leading her across a plank that spanned a trickle of creek and a tangle of water lilies. Shade soon enveloped them, and the rustle of a thousand leaves distracted her before she set eyes on the treasure half hidden in the trees.

A small chapel?

Made of stone set in clay, it was framed by oaks and elms, so new it was missing a door and windows. A squirrel stood sentinel on a sill, scampering away at their footfalls. She wanted to sigh with delight. She wanted to cry. 'Twas a perfect place to pray . . . or wed . . . or christen a baby. She let herself imagine ivy hugging the outer walls and flowers sprinkled along its foundation in glorious, heavenly hues.

When he took her inside, she found it cool, the stone and shade holding the July heat at bay. An old bench invited her to sit, so she did, eyes roaming the empty interior as he took a seat beside her. Shoulder to shoulder, they faced forward, and she realized with a little start she'd left her fan in the carriage. Without it she felt at loose ends, as if it were an anchor in her internal storm. Entwining her fingers in her lap, she groped for something to say and came up woefully short.

"Eden, I want to know what happened after I left York."

Her breathing thinned. Oh, why had she agreed to come? "I . . ." Tears stung her eyes. The silence turned excruciating. Nothing, she realized, was as burdensome as a secret.

"What is said here stays here, ye ken." His voice was calm, even gentle. Yet she sensed an undercurrent of tension in his tone.

Lord, where to begin?

She swallowed past the frightful ache in her throat. He deserved some answer, at least. "After you left for Fort Pitt, I took ill again. Margaret Hunter nursed me back to health." Her voice was flat, as unemotional as she could make it. She wouldn't tell him about the snow, the frostbite, how she'd nearly lost her life. It no longer seemed to matter. "When I was well, the Greathouse girls—Anne and Beatrice—returned to Hope Rising to mourn Jemma." David, thankfully, had stayed in Philadelphia. She'd not seen him again. "Before you came to York as an apprentice, there had been a plan in place for me to work at the foundling hospital. Bea and Anne urged me to return to the city with them, so I did."

He looked down at the stone floor. "What of Giles Esh?"

Giles. She'd nearly forgotten all about him. "That came to naught. I told Papa—" Nay, she'd not call him that ever again, for he was not. "I told Liege that he hadn't the authority to make me marry, as he wasn't my father."

She sensed Silas's surprise. How she'd summoned the courage to confront Liege was a mystery, but by then she'd known she wasn't carrying David's child and Philadelphia seemed the only option. In an eruption of volcanic proportions, he'd all but thrown her out of the smithy, calling her—and Mama— names she'd never before heard. 'Twas a memory time would not erase. Even now her skin warmed at the humiliation.

After a lengthy pause, Silas said, "So you went to Philadelphia . . ."

"Yes. I—I couldn't stay with the Greathouses, so arrangements were made for me with the Elliots."

She could sense Silas's mind churning along with his emotions and braced herself for the inevitable question. *Why didn't you stay with the Greathouses?* Fearing it, she plunged ahead. "I took a position at the hospital working with the infants there. Mr. Elliot is on the board—he's the hospital's most generous benefactor. My lodgings are on Fourth and Walnut Street now, near enough to walk to work . . ."

She was rambling, trying to skirt the heart—and dire hurt—of the matter, hoping he'd be satisfied and she could return to the hotel. But he reached over and took her hand, tethering her, shocking her. The feel of his fingers, roughened by years of toil yet still warm and familiar, sent a shiver clear through her.

"I sent you a letter."

Her head came up. A letter?

Every angle of his face was thoughtful, as if he was trying to put together the missing pieces of the past. "After I came to Fort Pitt, I wanted to write, make sure you were settled. The post was addressed to Margaret Hunter, though I didn't expect a reply."

"I received no letter." Disappointment coursed through her. Had it been lost? Misplaced? Forgotten? Margaret was not one to be careless. "If I had, I would've written."

"Would you have?" The doubt in his tone tore at her heart.

Their eyes met. His were tender but clouded with confusion. Anguish flooded her from head to toe. She'd loved him then—she loved him still. Yet he didn't believe her. Why should he? She'd given him no reason to think she was anything but fickle, unfaithful . . .

She glanced at a tiny bird sitting on the windowsill, daring to sing. Her eyes glazed with tears.

"Eden, you're not a woman of half measures. When you love, you love with your whole heart." His voice fell a notch. "Something happened to make you turn from me at the last. I would know what it is."

The chapel was too quiet. The bird had stopped its song. She could only hear the frantic rhythm of her pain-bound heart. "After Jon died, I—I didn't know my own mind. Nothing made sense—I was frightened, confused. When you found me at the inn—" Her voice broke.

"At the Traveler's Rest?"

She nodded and nearly flinched. Glimmers of that terrible time began pelting her like hailstones. David's rum-laden scent. His rough hands. How he'd laughed when she cried afterward. She couldn't chase the shame of it away, though she'd spent years trying. Nor could she speak of it now.

Lord, nay!

Tearing her hand from his, she darted across the tiny chapel on trembling legs, intent on the carriage. Rain spattered down, surprising her as she cleared the doorway. She was running, heedless, tripping over rocks and roots, the rising wind keening through the trees like a dirge. Behind her came a steady footfall, loud as thunder to her ears. Silas caught up with her and spun her around.

His hands framed her shaking shoulders. "Eden, nothing you say will make me love you any less." The passion in his face begged her to believe him. "*Nothing.*"

She looked up at him through a haze of rain as disbelief swept through her. "I—I was not fit to be your wife then. I'm not now." The words were more sob than speech. "That night—at the tavern—David—"

His jaw clenched. "Did he—"

"Yes." It was a grieved whisper, no more.

Eyes dark with pain, he pulled her against him, enfolding her so tightly in his arms it seemed he'd never let go. Nestled against his chest, she wept as she'd not done since his leaving.

"I—I feared I might be with child. Like Naomi." She tried to frame the hated words, praying he would understand. "Marrying Giles Esh seemed the only way. When I found I wouldn't be a mother, I went to Philadelphia instead." Her voice broke anew. "All I wanted was for you to be happy, safe—to have a future like you planned. Far beyond York."

His fingers stroked her hair. "You didn't tell me what happened because you knew I would have killed him and suffered the consequences. So you stayed silent . . ."

The words rippled over her like the rain, soft and warm. He continued to hold her, and she grew so lost in him she hardly noticed when a ferocious gust of wind stole her hat and sent it scurrying across the clearing. She felt nearly weightless when he picked her up and returned her to the chapel. There he set her down on the threshold as thunder cracked like a rifle above their heads.

Spent, she stood under the stony eave and faced him. "I know about Judge O'Hara and Isabel, Silas." Fresh sorrow welled in her heart as she prepared to give him up a second time. "I didn't come here today to make a way for us. You're truly free—of our betrothal, the taint of York—"

"Nae, Eden." The tanned contours of his face grew more grieved. "I have no tie to the O'Haras. My place is with you, no matter the past. I love you as much now as I did then, though you might not believe it. I am yours. All I have is yours. My only concern"—his eyes glittered with a telling wetness—"is if you love me still."

Did she? Had she not thought of him night and day these eight years past, longing for such a time as this? Wedding him in her most secret thoughts? Imagining holding his wee son or daughter? The vulnerability in his expression tore at her.

"I never stopped loving you, Silas." She reached into her bodice and withdrew the Scripture he'd penned long ago. "Nor did I blame God for our parting. He's proved Himself faithful in countless ways, but perhaps never so sweetly as returning me to you."

He took the scrap of paper but made no move toward her. "D'ye forgive me, Eden? For leaving like I did? For being so angry that last day?"

"You're not angry now," she said softly. "And there's been no talk of leaving."

He simply stood silent as if locked in the wonder she herself felt. Was he hesitant to touch her again? Afraid doing so might bring back a bad memory? Nay, she was done with the past, beginning now.

Her fingertips brushed his coat sleeve, and she smiled through her tears. "I won't break, Silas Ballantyne."

"Nae . . . you Philadelphia belles are made of sterner stuff." His arms went round her, his voice turning husky. "Eden Lee, you're more beautiful to me now than you've ever been."

She went weak inside, his tender words redeeming all they'd lost. Standing on tiptoe, she pressed her mouth to his. His answering kiss wasn't like the Silas she remembered but the man he'd become—bold and successful and certain yet riddled with unmistakable yearning. A river of pleasure, healing and heartfelt, seemed to spill over her at their closeness.

"Tomorrow we will wed," he said, the joy in his face chasing away every shadow. "Here in the chapel . . . home." He kissed her again, turning her a bit breathless. "Where will the next few years find us?"

"Only heaven knows," she whispered, awed and humbled by the thought. "We'll be here at New Hope, with our children, Lord willing."

"Amen," he said in a sort of benediction, kissing her again.

Epilogue

*Beauty and folly are old
companions.*
BENJAMIN FRANKLIN

As the coach rumbled into Pittsburgh, Elspeth pulled on her
gloves and peered intently out the window, not wanting to
miss the opportunity of finding Eden walking down some side
street or shopping in the market district. 'Twas October, and
the surrounding hills were aflame with vibrant color. Several
weeks of travel had not dimmed her desire to come here,
especially in light of all she'd learned while in Philadelphia.
When she'd arrived in the city, expecting to see her sister,
she'd succumbed to yellow fever instead. Gravely ill at the
boardinghouse, she'd sent word to Dr. Rush. He came round
quickly enough after she told him she was Eden's kin. And
he brought tidings she never expected to hear . . .

Eden had at last wed Silas Ballantyne.

The announcement had stunned her and impelled her to
action within a heartbeat. The least she could do was come
west and offer congratulations to the happy couple.

Couldn't she?

Acknowledgments

Heartfelt thanks to The Providence Forum and Dr. Peter Lillback, renowned author, historian, and seminary president, for an unforgettable five-day walking tour of historic Philadelphia. I've never lived or breathed history so well—even in the heat of July! Hats off to Cheryl, Chris, Lori, and Steve for making *every* moment unforgettable.

Also, a million thanks to my college roommate, Heather, for being both tour guide and taxi during my stay in Pittsburgh, and for putting up with all my puttering around Fort Pitt. You are such a treasured friend!

My deepest gratitude to the staff at Revell, especially sales and marketing, for going above and beyond on my books, always. And to Cheryl Van Andel and the art team, including designer Brandon Hill, for providing the cover of my heart.

I'm so blessed to have my gifted agent, Janet Grant, and the like-minded folks at Chi Libris, from whom I learn so much.

To faithful readers everywhere who've embraced the stories of Lael, Morrow, Roxanna, and now Eden. You bless me more than I can say.

And lastly, I'm forever thankful to the Shepherd of my stories, who provides green pastures and still waters and the passion behind every book I write.

Take a sneak peek
at the next installment!

The Ballantyne Legacy, book 2, by Laura Frantz

Available Fall 2013

Prologue

Beauty and folly are old companions.

BENJAMIN FRANKLIN

PITTSBURGH, PENNSYLVANIA
OCTOBER 1793

"You've a visitor, sir. Just wanted to warn ye." The young apprentice at the office door stood in the glare of autumn sunlight, the brilliant blue Monongahela waterfront behind him.

Silas Ballantyne thanked him and looked out the door he'd left open to see a woman stepping carefully around cordage . . . and seeming to court the stares of every boatman in her wake. What was it about Elspeth Lee that made even a lad of twelve take notice and feel a bite of warning? Silas could hardly believe it was she. He'd not seen her in years. And now the shadows of the past came rushing back with a vengeance, stirring up unwelcome emotions.

She stepped into his office without invitation and looked about with appraising blue eyes, her beauty undimmed by the passage of time. He gave no greeting. The tension swirled as thick as the sawdust in the boatyard beyond the open door.

"Well, Silas," she finally said, lifting her chin and meeting his grudging gaze. "I've come to see my sister and wish her well."

Wish her well?

He felt a sweeping relief that he'd not wed this woman. The sweetness he'd had with Eden couldn't be measured. Those sultry days following their July wedding had been the happiest he'd ever known. He'd not even gone to the boatyard at first. They'd kept to the bridal suite at the Black Bear Hotel as if to make up for all the time they'd been apart, emerging only for meals or to ride out to New Hope. Their house was half-finished now and would be done by the time Eden delivered their first child in April. But he wouldn't tell Elspeth that.

"Eden is indisposed." The words were clipped, curtailing conversation.

Her eyes flared. "Indisposed?"

He didn't mean ill, he meant unwilling—yet she seized on the former. "My, Silas, you're hard on a wife. 'Tis glad I am I didn't become Mistress Ballantyne." She looked about as if getting her bearings. "I suppose I shall bide my time here in Pittsburgh till she recovers and can have visitors—"

"Nae. You'll be on your way."

She assumed a surprised petulance, eyes sliding back to him. "That's hardly the welcome I expected from my new brother-in-law."

"You'll get no greeting from me now or in future. But I'll gladly pay your return passage back to York." He took a slow breath. "And if there's any harm done to Eden between now and then, any loss to my property or business, I won't bother bringing you before the Allegheny Court. You'll answer to me."

The words held a telling edge, sharp as the dirk that lined his boot. He had enemies aplenty in Pittsburgh, namely the Turlock clan. He wouldn't be adding to their numbers with this woman. But his most pressing concern was Eden, already aglow with the babe inside her, the harm done her in York a fading memory.

He continued with a calm he was far from feeling. "I'll have my head shipwright escort you off the premises, and I'll make sure I'm present to see you leave Pittsburgh on the first stage tomorrow. Now if you'll excuse me, I have work to do."

Back stiff, she stood on his threshold, malice hardening her fair features. "I'll be back, Silas Ballantyne. You can't keep me away from Eden—or Pittsburgh—perpetually."

Their eyes locked, but hers were the first to falter when he said, "Say what you will. I'll not welcome you. Ever."

1

The city of Philadelphia is perhaps one of the wonders of the world.

LORD ADAM GORDON

ALLEGHENY COUNTY, PENNSYLVANIA
APRIL 1822

Elinor Louise Ballantyne is an agreeable young lady with a fortune upwards of twenty thousand pounds . . .

Nearly wincing at the words, Ellie fisted the latest bulletin from the Matrimonial Society of Philadelphia and hid the paper beneath the generous folds of her spencer. The gray kerseymere fabric was too warm for an April day that had begun in an overstuffed coach and was now stalled on the Pennsylvania Turnpike to Pittsburgh, but she'd chosen the nondescript garment for a purpose.

She *was* an agreeable young lady.

She *was* traveling alone.

And she *was* indeed worth a fortune.

These three things were a tempting combination on any

day, but here in the wilds of western Pennsylvania, they were potentially lethal. Hadn't she just seen a handbill warning of highwaymen at the last stage stop?

Emerging from the coach, she stood in a patch of sunlight slightly apart from the other passengers and tried to ignore the oaths emanating from beneath the vehicle as the driver dealt with a broken axle. The other passengers looked on in consternation, some muttering epithets of their own.

"Miss . . . ?" The inquiry came from a robust, heavily rouged woman to her left, her hazel eyes appraising.

"Elinor," she replied with a hint of a smile, clutching her purse a bit tighter.

"Care to walk with us? We might well make it to Pitt ahead of the driver. It ain't but a dozen miles away, so the marker right there says."

Relieved, Ellie glanced at a stone pillar along the roadside that confirmed the words before falling into step with the others, eyes shifting to an unshaven man bearing a silver-plated pistol. A little walk would hardly hurt, given she'd been cooped up in a coach for days on end. Her travel mates had boarded just twenty miles prior and were far fresher than she but just as anxious to see the smoky valley that was Pittsburgh, the three rivers entwining there in a silvery knot.

She'd been away far too long. The surrounding woods now seemed more stranger than friend. How different Pittsburgh must have looked to her father when he first came all those years before. Raw wilderness then, not the industrial city it was rapidly becoming. Their home, New Hope, had been merely a poor blacksmith's dream in 1785, not the jewel crowning the Allegheny bluff that now stopped river traffic midstream.

A furious honking of geese and bleating of sheep disrupted her reverie. She and her companions hurried to the side of the road as several drovers came toward them in a whirl of dust, driving their herds eastward to market.

Sighing, she shook the dust off her skirts. The thought of sleeping atop her own feather bolster, twelve inches thick, and slaking her thirst with orange ice on the veranda made her walk a bit faster. Could anyone blame her for leaving finishing school in Philadelphia earlier than planned? If she'd written home and told them of her coming, they'd have tried to stop her—or arranged for a chaperone. As it was, she'd saved them the work and the worry. She simply wanted to surprise Papa on his birthday, an event she'd missed four years in a row, given she'd been east.

No more Madame Moreau. No tedious lessons in French or embroidery. No performing harp solos in stifling assemblies or declining dances at society balls. And most importantly . . .

No more being hounded by the Matrimonial Society of Philadelphia.

∽

They'd walked but a mile or so when the sky cast off its blueness like a discarded dress and clad itself in shades of Quaker gray. As if conspiring, the wind began to race through the newly leafed timber on both sides of them with a fickle ferocity that slowed their progress and left them clutching their caps and bonnets.

Any moment the repaired coach would overtake them and they'd come to Widow Meyer's Tavern just ahead. Or so Ellie hoped. At the first stinging drops of rain, she quickened her steps, the thin soles of her London-made slippers padding along in dusty protest. The rising wind was making sport of her full skirts, blowing them up in an embarrassing display so that anyone who wanted could see the pantalets beneath.

"Egads!" a burly man uttered to her left, lifting his hands in alarm.

Hail, big as goose eggs, was raining down, giving rise to grunts and cries as all made for the cover of the woods. Thankful for the broad brim of her bonnet, Ellie huddled beneath a sycamore as the wind keened higher. All around, branches snapped a staccato tune, followed by eerie stillness that foretold further trouble.

Fixing her eye on the western rim of the horizon, she felt like uttering an oath herself. A funnel cloud was whirling, black as pitch, and the wind was tugging her chin ribbons and unseating her bonnet. Backing further into the forest out of the funnel's path, she slipped and nearly fell on the hail-littered ground.

Like a brightly plumed bird, her feather bonnet took wing, and for a few teeth-chattering moments she feared she might follow. The purse string snapped about her wrist and was flung away into the whirlwind, all her coin with it.

Oh, if only Rose were here!

Never in all her twenty years had she witnessed anything like this! Grabbing hold of another sycamore's shaggy trunk, she anchored herself and squeezed her eyes shut against the swirling debris, cowering at the tremendous roar of the wind. Terror clawed at her as she bent her head. She couldn't think, couldn't breathe. The scent of damp spring earth and wind-whipped leaves was nigh on suffocating. Shaking, she hugged the rough bark and prayed the tree would hold fast like the iron anchors of her father's ships. She felt fragile as a butterfly about to be shorn of its wings, certain the tumult would tear her to pieces.

Twice the storm nearly upended her, prying her fingers free from their fierce hold. Then somehow, miraculously, the funnel cloud departed and sheets of cold rain took its place, soaking the mass of her waist-length hair now matted with leaves and twigs. Nary a hairpin remained. But that was the least of her worries.

The road was now oozing with coffee-colored mud, hail, and downed trees. Through the haze of rain she could make out a few of her traveling companions ahead, scrambling for a light in the distance. It beckoned like a star, golden and beguiling, promising shelter and peace.

The Widow Meyer's? The last stage stop just shy of Pittsburgh?

When she stumbled toward its broad wood steps, she found the tavern yard was as littered as the road, full of stranded coaches and damaged wagons and hysterical horses, its cavernous public room just as chaotic. Night was falling fast, and she was terribly homesick and near tears.

Her purse was gone—all her coin—pickpocketed by the wind, just like her bonnet. The realization edged her nearer the hysteria rising all around her. Looking up, she noticed the western portion of the tavern roof was missing, shingles agape. Rain was pouring in like water through a sieve, drenching a far corner and sending people scurrying.

"The storm of the century!" someone shouted amid the din, raising the sodden hair on the back of her neck.

Hot and cold by turns, she unfastened the braid trim along her collar, shrugged off her spencer, and draped it over one arm, mindful that one too many men were watching. Unbidden, a memory crawled through her benumbed conscience and turned her more wary. Something had happened to her mother in a tavern long ago, the murky details never broached. What she most remembered was her father's aversion to such places and his insistence she stay clear of them.

Oh, Papa, if you could see me now . . .

Toward dawn, Jack Turlock and a collection of the most able-bodied men finished clearing a three-mile path from the tavern toward Pittsburgh. The storm had touched down slightly west of Widow Meyer's before blazing a new trail east and inflicting more damage. By lantern light they worked, thankful the rain and wind had abated as quickly as they had come, all relieved to see the sun creep over the far horizon in reassurance that the world had not ended after all.

"Now what?" asked a squat young Irishman with a thick lilt when the men had returned to the tavern yard. He and his companions looked to Jack, who simply stared back at them through sleep-deprived eyes.

Somehow during the long night, Jack had assumed a leadership position he'd not wanted. Clutching an ax, he turned toward the tavern yard. "We'd do well to examine the coaches and wagons and bring the injured out first. The women and children will follow."

He moved slowly, the heavy canvas of his trousers mud-mired to his thigh, his boots soiled beyond repair. He'd misplaced his coat in the melee, and his dirty shirt had snuck past his waistband and now ended at his knee. Rubbing the crick in his neck, he remembered his cravat was adorning someone's broken arm as a sling. It had been a very long night.

A gentle wind was stirring all around him after a dead calm, reminding him of his near escape the night before. In the thick of the storm, a falling oak, broad as three men, had missed him by mere inches. The crashing thud of it echoed long in his thoughts, and on its heels was the voice of his former schoolmaster.

Pulvis et umbra sumus. We are dust and shadows.

He tried to shake off the memory, but the tempest inside him lingered, of greater fury than the storm now bearing east. Ducking beneath the low lintel of the tavern's main entrance, he sensed a hush fall over the public room at his appearance. At the mud-spattered sight of him? Or his family's reputation? Likely the latter. In the keeping room of this very tavern was cask after cask of Turlock whiskey. He could smell its distinctive tang and felt a shiver of disgust, though he needed a drink himself.

Stepping up onto the raised hearth, he faced the waiting crowd. "We've cleared the road west well enough to get a few of you through. The injured will go first, followed by the women and children—"

"Injured, aye." A gentleman in a top hat got to his feet, a frown marring his features. "Then those of us who are well bred and have business to attend to are next, surely—"

"Nay. The plan is in place." Jack's voice resounded to the room's damp corners. "I'll wager there's little business being transacted this day short of saws and ox trains. For now, we're ready to escort the wounded into Pittsburgh. All else can wait."

A few children began crying, making him second-guess his decision, if only briefly. Returning outside, he helped load the hurt onto what wagons hadn't been damaged, trying not to linger on bleeding limbs and gashed faces. Some contraptions were in dire need of repair. Given there were a good hundred people left to transport, it could take far longer than planned.

Toward noon he returned to the public room, the stench of spirits and unwashed bodies colliding in a sickening rush. A bit light-headed from hunger, he began assembling women and children, keeping families intact for travel. A few genteel ladies murmured in complaint at being made to wait, but he gave them no notice other than a cursory reassurance they'd not linger long. The room had emptied by half now, and he could better assess the situation.

"Mr. Turlock, sir, what d'ye want me to do with Cicero?" The stable boy at his elbow shifted from one bare foot to the other, looking befuddled beneath his many freckles. "Ain't like ye to stay on."

"See that Cicero gets an extra nose bag of oats." He pulled a coin from his pocket and flipped it into the air, and the boy caught it with a grin. "I hope to leave come morning."

Truly, he rarely lingered long, his restless nature never settling. He only needed a tankard of ale. A meal. Mayhap a bath. Aye, that was a necessity. His mother tolerated no mess at Broad Oak, nor did her housekeeper. Glad he was that he had a change of clothes in his saddlebags.

It was twilight when the last of the wagons and coaches pulled away and he arranged for a room. There were now mostly men and a handful of women left, eating and making low conversation at the surrounding tables. As he stood by the counter, sipping from his tankard, his attention was drawn repeatedly to a corner cast in shadows. Had he overlooked someone?

A young woman sat alone, back to the wall, her gray cape reducing her to shadows. He'd noticed her earlier helping with the children and assumed she was part of a family. He drew closer, breathing past the tightness crowding his chest.

Aye, he'd overlooked someone. But he couldn't believe it was she.

❧

Although Ellie had kept her eye on Jack Turlock, if only to stay clear of him since he'd first set foot in the tavern, she now looked away. Toward the gaping kitchen door, where the smell of roast goose and apple tansy and bread she had no coin for mingled with the smell of pipe smoke and spirits. Folding her hands in her lap, she sat as erectly as she could despite spending the previous night in the chair, her backside as stiff as the splintered wood.

Mercy, it couldn't get any worse, she thought, as her sister Andra was wont to say.

But yes it could, and he was coming straight for her.

She'd not seen Jack Turlock in years. Last she heard he was touring Europe, taking inventory of distilleries in Scotland, Ireland, and France, or so the papers said. In that time she'd nearly forgotten all about him. Clad in mourning garb due to his grandfather's passing, he'd cut a sober if striking figure when she'd seen him on the streets of Pittsburgh. As the younger son and not the heir, he wasn't nearly as interesting as his brother Wade, at least not to meddling society matrons. Jack shunned social functions, preferring the gin rooms along the waterfront to genteel ballrooms. Little wonder he'd not noticed her till now. His taste ran to tavern wenches.

As he walked her way, their many childhood encounters came rushing over her like the rivers at flood stage. She felt like a little girl again, about to be struck with a stone or at least belittled by his terse tongue. They'd often faced off at the creek dividing Turlock and Ballantyne land back then, her brothers Ansel and Peyton the same age as Jack and Wade. Sometimes Andra had been there—and Daniel Cameron. As the youngest, Ellie had escaped most of their wrangling. The look on his face assured her she'd not escape now.

He stared down at her, his low voice skipping any pleasantries. "Why didn't you tell me you were here?" She stiffened at the censure in his tone, then softened when he said, "I'd have put you on the first wagon out of here."

"There was no need. I'm not injured." Her gaze fell to her lap.

I'm simply a bedraggled mess, without coin or comb.

As badly as she wanted to be home, she did not want to be singled out. This preferential treatment was what she was running from. Rose, her former maid, usually handled all the details of travel. Without her capable, plucky presence, Ellie hardly knew what to do.

She raised wary eyes to Jack's, finding him more mud than man, his clothes in tatters. He managed to look bemused . . . and apologetic. Odd for a Turlock. He broke her gaze and leaned into the table, motioning to a serving girl in a checkered cap and kerchief.

"Tea," he said quietly. "Some bread."

With a smile she disappeared as if taking orders from the inn's owner. But the owner, Ellie realized, was busy pouring Turlock whiskey behind a long, scarred counter hedged with a cage. Business, from the looks of all the thirsty gathering there, was brisk.

"You're in want of a room," he told her. "Then we'll leave in the morning."

"We?" Her mouth formed a perfect O as she said it.

His sharp gaze pinned her so there would be no mistaking his meaning. "You're in need of an escort to take you home—a chaperone."

"I'm in need of a chaperone?" she echoed in disbelief.

To keep me safe from the likes of you.

Humor lit his gray eyes and warmed them the color of molten silver, as if he well knew what she was thinking. "I'll return you to New Hope myself, out of respect for your father."

My father? The man who jailed you countless times?

Speechless, she felt a swell of gratitude override her surprise as the requested tea and bread arrived, the latter slathered with butter and honey. Her stomach gave a little lurch of anticipation, but she pushed the plate his way. He'd not said they were hers, so she'd make no assumptions.

With a long, grubby finger, he pushed the plate back toward her, along with the steaming tea. Famished, she bent her head and breathed a quick prayer before biting off a cor-

426

ner of stale bread, a cascade of crumbs spilling down her wrinkled bodice.

"I can do little about how you look, but I can certainly feed you," he said drily.

She stopped chewing, heat creeping into her cheeks, and remembered her trunk. Had the coachman ever repaired the axle and gotten this far? Or was he still stuck, hemmed in by countless fallen trees—or worse? Concerned for his safety, she nevertheless rued the loss of her belongings. Perhaps she could beg a comb. Some hairpins. Taking a sip of tea, she felt immediately better. Tea was comfort. Tranquility. Civility.

"I can walk home," she said, setting her cup aside and brushing the crumbs from her dress. "'Tis but a few miles more. I don't need an escort."

Quirking an eyebrow, he looked beneath the table at her feet. Ever-practical Jack. Quickly she drew her sodden shoes beneath the muddy hem of her skirt.

"Five miles and you'd be barefoot. Ten and you'd end up begging a ride. There's a sidesaddle in the stable—or a coach."

Those were her choices then. Since her riding clothes were in her trunk, she'd have to take a coach. Only she had no coin . . . "My belongings were atop the stage that broke down a few miles east of here. The driver—I trust he's all right—"

"There's been no loss of life that we know of, just injuries. But I'll send someone back that way to be sure."

Relieved, she confessed, "My purse is missing—lost in the storm."

His gaze was like granite. "Why aren't you in Philadelphia?"

She nearly winced at his bold question. Her father would soon ask her the same, only his tone would be more gracious, surely. "I—I'm done with finishing school. 'Tis time I return home."

"You picked a poor time to do it," he murmured.

She took another sip of tea, unable to refute this fact, glancing toward the kitchen but snagging on his profile instead. He was looking up at the men repairing the roof, the feeble light framing him as it spilled through. His coloring shocked her, so deeply tanned one would think he was a common laborer and spent all his time outdoors. His features had always been sharply handsome, almost hawkish, his hair the color of summer straw, not whiskey-dark like Wade's. That he was a worldly man there could be no doubt. He even moved with an ease and agility far removed from the stiff formality of society's drawing rooms. He was, in a word, different. And dangerous.

Papa would not approve.

Laura Frantz is the author of *The Frontiersman's Daughter*, *Courting Morrow Little*, and *The Colonel's Lady*. A two-time Carol Award finalist, she is a Kentuckian living in the misty woods of Washington with her husband and two sons. Along with knitting, cooking, gardening, and long walks, she enjoys connecting with readers at www.LauraFrantz.net.

MEET LAURA FRANTZ AT
WWW.LAURAFRANTZ.NET
Learn more about her books,
read her blog, and learn fun facts!

CONNECT WITH LAURA ON
Laura Feagan Frantz
LauraLFrantz

To mail Laura a note, please send your letter to:

Revell, a division of Baker Publishing Group
6030 E. Fulton
Ada, MI 49301

"You'll disappear into another place and time and be both encouraged and enriched for having taken the journey."
—JANE KIRKPATRICK, bestselling author

Find yourself immersed in this powerful story of love, faith, and forgiveness.

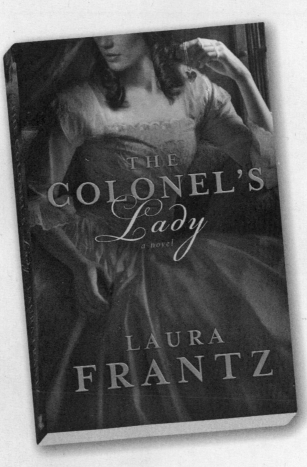

In 1779, a search for her father brings Roxanna to the Kentucky frontier—but instead she discovers a young colonel, a dark secret . . . and a compelling reason to stay.

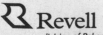

Revell
a division of Baker Publishing Group
www.RevellBooks.com

Available Wherever Books Are Sold